# THESE THORN KISSES

## ST. MARY'S REBELS
## BOOK 3

### SAFFRON A. KENT

This is a work of fiction. Names, characters, places, and incidents are either the product of the author's imagination or are used fictitiously, and any resemblance to actual persons living or dead, business establishments, events, or locales, is entirely coincidental.

These Thorn Kisses © 2021 by Saffron A. Kent
All rights reserved. No part of this book may be used or reproduced in any manner whatsoever without written permission of the author except in the case of brief quotations embodied in critical articles or reviews.

Cover Art by Najla Qamber Designs
Cover Model: Jeff Kasser
Editing by Olivia Kalb & Leanne Rabesa
Proofreading by Virginia Tesi Carey

December 2021 Edition

Published in the United States of America

# OTHER BOOKS BY SAFFRON A. KENT

The Unrequited

Gods & Monsters

Medicine Man (Heartstone Series Book 1)

Dreams of 18 (Heartstone Series Book 2)

California Dreamin' (Heartstone Series Book 3)

## ST. MARY'S REBELS

Bad Boy Blues (SMR book 0.5)

My Darling Arrow (SMR book 1)

The Wild Mustang & The Dancing Fairy (SMR book 1.5)

A Gorgeous Villain (SMR book 2)

These Thorn Kisses (SMR book 3)

Hey, Mister Marshall (SMR book 4)

The Hatesick Diaries (SMR book 5)

# BLURB

Eighteen-year-old, Bronwyn Littleton is in love with a stranger she met on a summer night a year ago.

A stranger who was tall and broad in a way that made her feel safe. He had dark blue eyes that she can't stop drawing in her sketch book. And he had a deep, soothing voice that she can't stop hearing in her dreams.

That's all she knows about him though.

Until she runs into him again. At St. Mary's School for Troubled Teenagers – an all girls reform school – where she's trapped because of a little crime she committed in the name of her art.

Now she knows that her dream man has a name: Conrad Thorne.

She knows that his eyes are way bluer and way more beautiful than she thought. And that his face is an artist's wonderland.

But she also knows that Conrad is her best friend's older brother. Which means he's completely off-limits. Not to mention, he's the new soccer coach, which makes him off-limits times two.

What makes him off-limits times three however, and this whole scenario an epic tragedy, is that, Conrad, Wyn's dream man, has a dream girl of his own.

And he's as much in love with his dream girl as Wyn is in love with him…

**NOTE: This is a STANDALONE set in the world of St. Mary's.**

*To all the dreamers and artists who stay awake at night and create, so we can see the beauty in this world.*

*And my husband, who encouraged me to pursue my dream and aim to live an extraordinary life. I love you with all my dreamer heart.*

# READER'S EXTRAS

Official Spotify playlist

**Pinterest Boards**
Conrad & Bronwyn
St. Mary's School for Troubled Teenagers

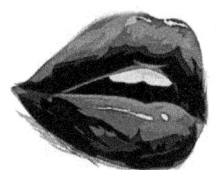

# ST. MARY'S GUIDE
## to Lip Lovin' for One and All:

**FOR GIRLS DOOMED IN LOVE**

Teenage Decay
Dream Broken Darling
I Jinx U
Drip Drip Gasoline
Good Bad Girl
Sweet Little Sweetheart
Golden Eyed Queen

**FOR GIRLS BETRAYED IN LOVE**

Heartbreak Juju
Crazy-Hearted Loner
Moon-Eyed Wasteland
Queen of the Bards
Sex and Candy
Train Wreck Princess

**FOR GIRLS WHO DREAM**

Red Addict
Pink and Shameless
Cherry Picker
Lollipop Lover
Pinky Winky Promises

**FOR GIRLS WHO LOVE TROUBLE**

Troubled Sweetheart
Handmade Heaven
Cute Corruption
Young and on Fire
God of a Girl
Purple Witchcraft
Wild Child Bad Child

**FOR GIRLS WHO FALL FOR THE BAD**

Desert Rose
She-Desperado
Watermelon Sugar
Dangerous Woman
Pink Lemonade
Glitter Glitter Baby

*Dream (n.):*

A mosaic of thoughts, ideas and images that run through your mind while asleep.
Also, a goal or an ambition

*Broken Dream (n.):*

No such thing. Because dreams don't break. They evolve and morph and grow as you grow. Dreams are what you make them.

# PART 1

# CHAPTER ONE

Eighteen Months Ago

There's a man I'm staring at.

Let's call him Mystery Man.

He's tall. And broad.

In fact, he's so tall and so broad that he's bursting out of his clothes. He is.

The black suit that he's wearing can barely contain him. It looks like his shoulders, muscular and so totally sculpted, will bust out of his suit jacket. And that chest which appears rock hard and cut will tear out of his white dress shirt.

That's the first indication that he's not from here.

Not the fact that he's quite possibly the most built and athletic man I've ever seen in my short sixteen and a half years of life. But the fact that his suit is clearly ill-fitted and outdated.

Making me think that he doesn't wear it often, or even if he does wear it, he doesn't care about keeping up with the latest styles and fashions or the fact that his body is too large for it.

How *fascinating*.

To not care about such silly, superficial things.

Actually no. That's not the most fascinating thing about him.

The most fascinating thing about this Mystery Man is his hair.

It's long.

Well, long-ish.

It not only curls at the ends, brushing and grazing the collar of that outdated suit jacket, but it also falls over his forehead. Some strands are even hanging down to his brows. And then there are strands that flutter over the side of his face.

By this town's standards, he totally needs a haircut and hair gel. A comb too, maybe.

And I so very much don't want him to get any of those things because God, I've never seen hair like that. I might have seen a physique like his — although I doubt that; no one's as tall or large as him where I come from — but not the hair.

I wish I could tell the exact color of his hair but he's standing in such a dark, lonely corner of this spacious yet crowded ballroom that I can't. I can't even see his face very clearly. All I can see are lines that ride high in his cheekbones and angles that slant so beautifully in his jaw.

But whatever I *can* see has me utterly convinced that he is definitely, *definitely* not from Wuthering Garden, the town I live in. The town that I don't really venture out of.

Because the towns surrounding our town are "beneath us."

At least that's what my mom says.

She says that those towns are full of poor, desperate, middle-class people who know nothing about our rich and fabulous ways. In fact, those people would do anything to learn our ways and be like us.

So we need to protect ourselves from them.

We need to stick to our town, to our people and to our posh society where people get regular haircuts and never ever wear anything last season.

So maybe I should just stand here, in my *own* dark and lonely corner which is very graciously doubling as a hiding spot, and not walk up to him.

I should probably not think about asking him his name or where he came from. Or what he's doing here at this party.

Not to mention, why does it look like he's not breathing?

I could be wrong about that though. About the not breathing part.

Because as I said I'm all the way over here, hidden between two potted plants, and he's all the way over there, at almost the opposite end of the ballroom. But

I swear to God, I haven't seen him move once in the past ten minutes that I've been watching him.

I haven't seen him reach for a drink when the waiter passed by or nod at any of the people who have walked by him and actually paused to throw him a second look. I have a feeling that it wasn't because he looks like he doesn't belong here but because of how rugged and interesting he is.

Because mostly who did pause and give him a second look were women. Mothers of some of my classmates even.

But anyway, it's none of my business why he appears so deathly still or what exactly is the color of his hair. I should just stick to my hiding spot and stop watching him.

I should worry about my own self.

I should; tonight is a big night for me. Sort of.

It looks like I'm not going to though, worry about myself that is. It looks like I'm going to come out of my hiding spot and walk up to him. I even take a few steps in his direction, and of course that's my first mistake.

Because *of course* I get caught.

By my mother.

"Bronwyn." Her angry voice behind me halts me in my tracks. "What are you doing?"

I clench my eyes shut and hang my head.

Shit.

And I was doing so well.

For someone who doesn't get to hide much at these parties, I was doing phenomenally well. I'd managed to find this lovely spot on my second try. And I'd even managed to calm myself halfway down about the whole big night thing until I got distracted by my Mystery Man.

And now I've lost my chance.

Damn it. Damn it. Damn it.

"Bronwyn!"

When my mother's voice reaches screeching level, I open my eyes, sigh and turn around, pasting a casual, cheery smile on my face. "Hey, Mom."

While my mother's face is serene and so beautiful, her eyes — brown and pretty — are furious. "What are you doing? Where have you been?"

"I was just, uh, trying to find water," I fib, keeping the smile in place. "Remember?"

That's what I said to my mother as soon as we arrived at the party. That I was going to find water. She told me to come right back and I told her that I would.

Only instead of water, I wanted to simply... breathe. So I took cover and hid.

But I was going to go back. I was.

I wouldn't ever do that to my mom or my dad.

"For the last half hour?" she asks, raising a suspicious brow.

Yikes.

"I also went to the bathroom," I say, lying again, trying to keep her anger at bay. "There was a long line. And then I ran into Christine from school and we got to talking. She was telling me about her trip to Europe this summer with her parents. She said that it was amazing. Rome was magical. She wants to go there again next year and..."

I trail off because Mom has stopped listening. Which is just as well because I'm not sure if Christine did find Rome magical or if she's really planning on going back.

I asked her about it a few days ago, when I ran into her at yet another party like this, but she didn't respond. I'm sure she heard me; we were the only two people in the bathroom at the time and she was standing two sinks down, retouching her lipstick.

But the thing is that Christine doesn't talk to me very much; she thinks I'm weird. And strange.

She told me so. A couple of years ago.

I've tried to dispel that notion, hence the casual chit chat I was trying to start the other day, but so far I haven't been very successful.

But that's not the point here.

The point is that my mother has stopped listening and has started watching me.

In the same way that Christine and all the girls in my class do.

In the way that tells me that they're checking to see if I've improved since the last time they saw me. If my ghostly pale skin has bloomed with color. Or if my brown hair, as dull as dirt, has developed an overnight sheen. Oh, and if my eyes, gray and, again, as pale as a ghost, so that they appear silver, look... less ghostly.

Which is fine.

I'm used to it.

I'm more worried about what and if my mother has found something on me. She shouldn't. I mean, I'm impeccable right now. As impeccable as I can be with my strange looks, but still.

"Have you been chewing on your lips?"

Oh shit.

I completely forgot about that. That I've been doing it because I've been so nervous and that I wasn't supposed to do it. Because it would ruin my lipstick.

"I'm sorry. I..."

I trail off because I realize that I've made the second mistake tonight: putting my hand on my lips and in turn, exposing my hands to my mother.

If I thought she was mad before, I was wrong. She is mad now. So freaking mad that she reaches out and snatches my hand in a tight grip. She stares down at them, at my fingers, dirty and smudged with ink. And before she can say anything, I burst out, "Mom, I just —"

"Why don't you ever listen to me?" she hisses. "Why is everything so difficult with you? I told you, didn't I? That tonight is important. You need to behave. You need to look perfect. But no, of course you didn't listen, and now you have dirty hands because you can't keep away from your useless habits. Martha has better hands than you."

Martha is our housekeeper — and my friend — and she *does* have better hands than me. They're always clean and her nails are somehow never broken even though she scrubs every inch of our house from top to bottom every week. And she's always giving me tips to keep my fingers and my nails clean. But I always forget.

I struggle in her tight grip. "Mom, I'm sorry. I'm going to wash my hands now. I —"

"What's going on here?"

This time it's my dad who cuts me off.

He arrives with a glass of red wine and a huge frown between his brows, which I know is only going to get more huge when Mom answers his question.

Which she is going to. My mother never disobeys my father. Ever.

"She's been doing it again," Mom says with an annoyed sigh, letting my hands go.

I was right; Dad's frown does get huge. His lips purse as well as he looks down at me. "Is what your mom's saying true?"

Bringing my hands back and hiding them from my father, I swallow.

"Is it true, Bronwyn?"

I jerk out a nod. "Yes. But I —"

He grinds his teeth. "How many times have I let you get away with it?"

"Dad, I —"

"How many times, Bronwyn?"

"For years." I give him the expected answer.

"Yes. For *years*. And why?"

"B-because you're my father and you love me. But I need to grow out of it now."

"And why is that?"

My heart squeezes in my chest and I swallow to keep my emotions at bay. "Because I'm not a child anymore. I'm a grown-up and I need to... I need to be a good daughter."

"And whose daughter are you?"

I swallow again. "Jack Littleton's. The DA."

He is.

An extremely well known DA and well liked; mostly because he comes from a wealthy family but has chosen to serve the public. He's always on the news, always giving interviews, being invited to events and parties. He's also very popular in DC, is friends with congressmen and senators.

So basically everyone knows my dad.

Which means everyone knows my mom, Jack Littleton's wife, and me, Jack Littleton's daughter.

"Exactly," he says, his eyes pinning me in my place. "Which means you have responsibilities. You have duties you need to fulfill. An image you need to portray. Which means you can't waste your time on things that are useless and inconsequential. Is that understood?"

I know the answer that's expected of me.

I've given it to him multiple times before when I've gotten caught wasting my time.

But for some reason tonight, I want to argue with him. I want to say that it's not useless, what I did — what I want to do. It's not inconsequential.

It's my... passion.

It's something I love.

And I know that it makes me strange because of who I am and what's expected of me. Not to mention, no one in our circle or town, which is made up of rich, influential, political people, has this passion. But can't they try to accept it or at least see it, just once, through my eyes?

I won't say it though.

I can't.

Because it's not their fault that I'm strange. That I like the things I like. They didn't ask for a daughter like me. And he is right. I do have responsibilities.

So I jerk out a nod like I always do. "Yes."

My father watches me for a beat before sighing and stepping back. "Good. Now your mom has already told you how important tonight is. The Rutherfords are waiting. They're eager to see you. Robbie is eager as well. So I expect you to meet us out on the balcony in ten minutes."

With that he turns around and walks away, leaving me alone with my mother.

Who focuses on me and says in a much calmer voice, "You heard your father. I want you to go touch up your lipstick and wash your hands, all right?" She looks me up and down critically. "Although I don't know what I was thinking with the yellow. It doesn't do you any favors. Especially under these lights. But it'll have to do. Good thing Robbie is already interested in you."

He is.

Robin Rutherford, or Robbie, is very interested in me.

He's the son of my dad's friend.

Who could potentially turn into an important campaign donor.

My father is up for re-election this year, which means he needs all the donations and all the money – in addition to our family money – for a successful campaign. And since Robbie has recently shown an interest in me, my father is trying to use that to his advantage.

That's the whole reason why tonight is important.

The Rutherfords are here and Robbie has specifically asked for me.

Actually, my mom told me that he's specifically attending this party for me.

"Which makes me think that this dress might not be such a bad choice after all," she murmurs, looking at my chest. "It's at least showcasing your assets."

Right.

My assets. Meaning my breasts.

That's the only thing about me my mother approves of: my C cups that appear like D cups if I wear a padded bra.

Robbie approves of them as well.

Given that that's all he stares at whenever we talk.

She fiddles with the diamond necklace that she gave me to wear for tonight, continuing, "Look, I know you think we're being harsh with you, but as your dad said, you have responsibilities. Things are expected of you. Believe it or not, we want what's best for you. We want you to be happy. And I know you're not a fan of Robbie. I completely understand that. But you need to trust us, okay? Remember what I said?"

"Yes, I remember," I say.

She nods. "Despite how he seems, he's a good guy. He knows his responsibilities. He knows what's expected of him. So it's going to be okay."

Robbie is the reason why I was hiding in the first place.

He gives me the creeps with the way he keeps staring at my boobs, and I know he'll do it again tonight.

But my mom is right. He is a good guy. He comes from a good family and I should give him a chance.

Like her, I nod too. "Okay."

Finally my mother smiles, satisfied. "Good. Now go, okay? And you know what?" She reaches out and viciously pinches both my cheeks, making me flinch. "Do your cheeks a little bit too. You're too pale and it's clashing with the yellow. And come right back, okay? Don't make your father wait for too long."

I rub my sweaty hands on my thighs. "I won't."

My mother leaves then and I go to the bathroom and touch up my lipstick and do everything she tells me to. I really psych myself up to face Robbie and the Rutherfords and do what's expected of me.

I psych and psych and psych myself up before coming out of the bathroom. I even start walking in the direction of the balcony, where everyone's waiting for me.

But then I stop.

For some reason, I look over to the same spot that I saw that man.

My Mystery Man.

He's not there anymore. That dark and lonely corner is empty.

I'm not sure why but I start to search for him in the crowd. I sweep my gaze around and start to look for the man I'd never seen before tonight.

Maybe because I'm still convinced that he's not from Wuthering Garden. That he's from out there.

From somewhere I'm not allowed to go. From a place I'm not allowed to think about.

Because this is my life.

My responsibilities, my duties.

And for some reason when I can't find him, my Mystery Man, I start to panic. I start to hyperventilate. I start to feel suffocated. Hopeless.

It's silly. I know that.

Even so I can't stop myself from feeling faint and afraid.

I can't stop this urge to flee, to escape.

So despite promising my mom and myself that I'll be a good daughter, the daughter that my parents deserve, I run away.

I turn around and walk out of the ballroom and into the night.

---

I've made a huge mistake.

I know that.

I shouldn't have done it. I shouldn't have run out of the party like I did. My parents must be so embarrassed. Angry. My dad must be seething right now and my mom must be trying to calm him down despite her own anger at me.

But I couldn't do it.

I couldn't see Robbie. I couldn't stay there and smile and mingle.

So here I am.

Sitting on the side of the road by a lamppost.

Because first, judging by my current location — a dark road flanked on both sides by the posh golf course that my dad and the rest of the town loves — I think I've walked close to two miles from the party, and in my heels no less. So I'm tired now.

I'm also tired from crying, but I don't want to think about that.

And second, I need the light from the lamppost.

Because I want to see.

And that's because I want to indulge in what my parents, Christine, my classmates and the rest of the town thinks is useless and inconsequential. The thing that makes me strange: painting.

Drawing, sketching.

Art.

I'm sitting here because I want to draw. Because when I'm nervous and agitated, that's what I do.

I also do it when I'm happy and excited and bored and inspired. I do it all the time, actually. I have a whole secret sort of studio set up in my attic, hidden from everyone's sight; my parents don't like it when they catch me sketching so I've found a safe place for myself.

I root around in my clutch. I go past the lipstick and the powder case that my mother always makes me carry at such events and find the magic thing that I'm looking for: a pen.

It's pink and has a thin sharp nib.

Then I pull the hem of my dress all the way up to my upper thighs and expose the patch of skin I want.

So I can make it my canvas and draw things on it.

On my skin.

Because I draw on anything and everything that I can find. And because the lack of paper will never stop me.

I start with a rose.

Because where there are roses, there are thorns. And for some reason, thorns have always been my favorite things to draw. Maybe because they're protectors.

They protect the roses from the world, and I like that.

So when I make thorns, I make them extra sharp and pointy.

Dangerous.

I make them things to be reckoned with. And that's what I'm doing, making them all stabby and piercing, when I hear something.

Footsteps.

They're sharp and sure. Authoritative, at least from the sound of them, and they seem to be getting closer.

Much closer.

Fuck.

Is it Robbie? My dad?

*Holy fuck.*

Have they found me?

Yikes.

I snatch the hem of my dress and pull it over my half-finished sketch, covering it up, hiding it from them, and throw my pen aside. Then I snap my eyes up, my heart in my throat, all ready with a heartfelt apology, but I shouldn't have bothered.

To practice an apology in my head.

Because I can't form any words. I've forgotten them all.

It's not my dad. Or Robbie.

It's *him*.

My Mystery Man

# CHAPTER TWO

"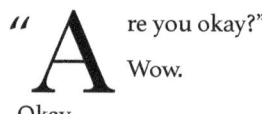re you okay?"

Wow.

Okay.

His voice. Low and scratchy. Deep.

I wasn't expecting it to be this deep. So deep that I could take a plunge in it. So deep that it sounds powerful.

As powerful as his tall frame.

And God, he *is* tall. I was right about that.

He's so tall, in fact, that craning my neck up to see him isn't enough. I have to actually lean back slightly to look up at him, at his face.

Which to my utter dismay I still can't see clearly.

I mean, I can see him some. Like I can see that he's got a broad forehead. Not so broad as to make it unseemly, but broad enough that it makes me think of stubborn frown lines.

I was right about his cheekbones too. They're high. So high that I think under certain lights they might cast shadows on his jaw. Which I was right about also: sharp and slanting.

But it's not enough.

I want to see more and I want him to step into the yellow pool of light instead of standing outside of it. And I want it so much that I open my mouth to tell him that.

But he speaks again, his voice deep and cozy. "Do you need help?"

Again I go to answer him but in the wake of his words, a light summer breeze wafts past us and I get distracted.

By his hair.

His long-ish, fascinating hair that flutters on his forehead and on the side of his stunningly lined face. The curls at the end brush against the collar of his suit jacket, which still seems too small to contain his bulk.

A second later it looks like his suit is really going to come apart at the seams because somehow his shoulders and his chest bulge out and expand and he says, his voice taking on an impatient sort of edge, probably because I haven't spoken for so long, "Look, are you lost? Do you want me to call someone for you?"

"I'm not lost," I blurt out thankfully.

I also blink.

Which makes me realize that I hadn't. Blinked I mean. Ever since he got here.

I've been staring up at him without talking, without *blinking,* like a creep.

"You're not," he says in a flat voice, his face dipped toward me, his strong chin almost touching that muscular chest.

"No." I shake my head.

"Are you sure?"

"Yes," I reply.

Then he looks up.

He glances around, sighing.

I'm not sure what he's looking for but I don't have the time to wonder because his perusal is over in a split second, after which he comes back to me.

"So this is usual for you. Sitting on the side of an empty road, in the middle of the night like this," he says, shifting on his feet.

"It's not the middle of the night," I tell him, looking back up at him, at his darkened features. "It's probably just eleven."

"Eleven fifteen," he corrects me.

Actually, he accompanies his words with actions.

Up until now, his hands have been in his pockets. But now he takes one out, shifts his eyes away from me and dips them toward a gleaming silver watch that's strapped around his wrist.

It's the largest watch I've ever seen, with the biggest dial and the shiniest metal strap.

I bet you could tell the time on it from a mile away.

He looks at it for a second before lifting his eyes and focusing on me, his eyebrows raised as if making a point. And when that point has been made, he puts his hand back into his pocket, still watching me. "Probably way past your curfew."

I want to smile.

No, actually I think I want to laugh. Which is such a change after all the crying I've done.

Not because of what he said but because how he said it.

How he looks right now: so... *responsible*. So authoritative and mature. Like this is his job. Telling people that it's way past their curfew so they should go home now.

And something about my Mystery Man's authority makes me say, "I don't have a curfew. And eleven fifteen is still not the middle of the night."

He frowns at my flippant tone and it makes me want to smile some more.

This urge only grows when his voice takes on a severe tone as he says, "Eleven fifteen is also not the time to be sitting on the side of a deserted, potentially dangerous road all by yourself. So again, is there someone I can call for you?"

I duck my head then.

And bite my lip. So I don't smile.

Who *is* he?

I can't believe he's trying to help me. That's what he's doing, isn't it?

He's trying to make sure that I'm okay. That I'm not lost.

I don't think anyone has ever done that before.

So maybe I should tell him what I'm doing here and that this part of town is extremely safe. And that I came from the same party he was at.

But I don't. Not yet.

Instead I spring to my feet and say in the same flippant tone as before, trying to ruffle his responsible feathers some more, "And now I'm not sitting on the side of a deserted, potentially dangerous road either. Oh, and I'm definitely not by myself now. You're here. See?"

This time along with his brows bunching, his chest moves as well as he sighs. "Yeah. Which clearly is a mistake that I need to rectify. So I think I'm going to l—"

I take a step toward him. "Where are you from?"

He takes a step back. "What?"

I know that was abrupt but I've been dying to ask him that question ever since I saw him tonight. So I ask as I take another step close. "You're not from here, are you? You can't be."

Automatically he takes another step back. "And what gave me away?"

Everything.

From his clothes to his hair. To the fact that he stopped to check on me.

Not to mention, I've just realized that he keeps moving away from me.

Every step I take toward him, he takes one back. As if determined to keep a distance between us. Respectable, *responsible* distance.

Again, so fucking fascinating after my run-ins with Robbie.

"Because first, you stopped to check on me," I tell him. "Make sure that I was okay."

I feel him studying me for a second or two, quite possibly baffled. "So?"

"So that's a very nice gesture," I reply. "People in this town aren't that nice."

I feel bad about saying that.

It's my town; I grew up here. And even though I'm not the most well-liked or regarded, this is still my town. I'm probably going to live here for the rest of my life. But it is what it is and I'm not going to *not* give him a compliment when he deserves one.

This time his scrutiny lasts longer than two seconds before he asks, "And what's the second thing?"

"Second thing?"

"First I stopped to check on you," he explains. "What's the second thing I did that gave me away?"

"Your hair."

He draws back slightly. "What?"

Okay *that*, I wasn't expecting to say.

I mean I was thinking it but I wasn't planning on saying it. Out loud.

I'm weird. I'm not crazy.

But.

Taking it back now would seem even crazier. Besides, he does have good hair. Just look at it: the strands fluttering in the summer breeze, grazing the collar of his shirt. Some have even fallen over that beautifully broad forehead of his, hanging in his eyes.

I wish I could tell the color of both.

His eyes and his hair.

Just so I could mix up the exact shades and paint my body with them.

"Well, you have... interesting hair," I say.

He's squinting as if in thought. "Interesting hair."

"Yes." I nod. "People in this town have boring hair. All polished and cut close to the scalp. All gelled up, you know? I guess they're all trying to look sophisticated and civilized and whatever. But you, your hair's gorgeous. It's long and free and I bet you could actually feel the wind in your hair. Which I would love to feel too, but if I take down my hair right now, it's going to take me forever to get it back up, looking like that. So anyway, I like your hair. It's super interesting. Unlike anything that I've ever seen."

I'm blushing, really hard, when I finish my word vomit, again feeling slightly bad about dissing the hair of my town's people.

And he probably can see it all, my blush I mean.

Since I'm standing under the yellow pool of light, all exposed while he enjoys the cover of darkness. He can probably see my fisted hands too, and I know for a fact that he just swept his eyes of unknown color over my hair.

But when his scrutiny goes on for too long, all silent and heavy, I say, "It's a compliment."

To which he responds in a very dry, sardonic voice, "Ah. A compliment. I'm still hung up on the fact that there's such a thing as interesting hair."

At this I forget my embarrassment and smile. "There totally is. And you should probably thank me now."

"Because it's a compliment."

"Yes. And I was nice enough to give you one."

Still watching me, he murmurs, "So then by your estimation, you're not from this town either. Because apparently people here aren't that nice."

"I'm allowed to be nice though," I tell him.

"Why?"

"Because I'm special."

And not in a good way, but he doesn't need to know that.

Something moves on his face at my words.

I can't tell what, but it washes over his features, making those tight high lines loose and slightly pliable. "And what's so special about you?"

"The fact that I'm an enigma." I shrug, chuckling at my own self-deprecating humor. "A total mystery. I'm super weird and super different from everyone else in this town. People call me strange. Bronwyn Littleton, the strange one." I put a hand on my chest. "That's my name by the way. Bronwyn." Then, "But you should totally call me Wyn."

Because no one ever does.

Everyone always calls me by my full name: Bronwyn. And honestly, she sounds like a total disappointment.

Not Wyn though.

I think Wyn is cute and pretty and an ideal daughter and all the things Bronwyn isn't. So I want him to call me that.

I also want him to tell me *his* name now.

I mean it's only polite, right?

But all he does is take a sharp breath, his forehead bunching up in a frown. "Is that why you're out here?"

"What?"

"Someone say something to you?" he asks in a low voice. "Did someone call you weird or some crap like that?"

I blink at him.

Then I blink again because for a moment, I don't understand his tone. I don't understand the tightness that has come over his frame and the fact that his frown has become even thicker if possible.

But then I get it.

I get what's happening and why and... and I'm just so floored right now.

That I can't help but take another step, two steps in fact, toward him. Which he by default responds to by taking a large step back.

And this time instead of making me smile, it makes me swallow a large lump of emotions.

Because he's just so... *good*.

And responsible.

For not only keeping an appropriate distance between us but also for getting angry on my behalf.

That's what it is, isn't it?

His change in tone and demeanor is because he's upset over what I so carelessly said. I was just making a joke.

Shaking my head, I say, "It's nothing. No one said anything. I just... I came here to get away from stuff for a little bit. And this place is extremely safe. Very low crime rate. And I'd know that because my dad, Jack Littleton, is the DA. You see this? This golf course?" I wave my hand around. "My dad comes here every Saturday to play with his buddies. So I know this area. Trust me. Everything is fine. Even if it's eleven fifteen at night and way past my curfew, which I don't have. So I am fine. Thanks though." I swallow again because that lump of emotion has only grown bigger. "I really appreciate it."

My last words are thin and fragile.

They barely come out of my mouth and make a dent in the world. Because I have this large weight sitting in my chest. This *crushing* weight, which comes from the knowledge that I should probably get back now.

I should probably be brave and go back to face my parents.

To face Robbie.

And this meeting — that has been so wonderful and enchanting so far — is going to be over.

"So what is it?"

I look up at his voice. "What?"

He's watching me with a dipped chin and grave eyes. "The stuff that you're trying to get away from."

Again I blink at him because again, I'm unable to understand what he's saying. Until I do understand it and my eyes widen. "Are you... You want to know the stuff I'm trying to get away from?"

"And I'm guessing that's another thing that people in your town don't do," he concludes.

"No, they don't," I say in a high, surprised voice. "I mean they do go, 'hey, how are you' or 'how was your weekend' or 'are you okay?' But I don't think they really mean it. Maybe it's just the thing that rich and polite people do. Ask things they don't mean."

Maybe.

I'm not really sure.

All I know is that no one has ever asked me if I'm okay and wanted an honest answer to that.

He shrugs then, a lazy roll of his massive shoulders. "Well, good for you then. That I'm not rich or polite *or* from this town."

"I knew it." I jump up in my spot. "I *knew* it. I knew you weren't from this town. I was right."

He, my Mystery Man, watches me with what I can only assume is a cool, bored expression, his eyes going down to my bare feet — the first thing I did when I sat down was to take off my heels and push them aside — for a second before coming back up to my beaming face.

How he manages to keep his features blank in the face of my utter happiness at being right is something I'll never understand. But he does. "Now that we've established *and* celebrated the fact that I'm not from here, are you going to talk about it?"

I am, I realize. I am going to talk about it.

I *so* am.

It might be foolish to tell him everything, this stranger I know nothing about. Whose name I don't even know. Or where he comes from, except that he's not from here. And that I'd only seen him for the first time probably an hour ago at the party.

But he's also the very first man to ask me things.

So I have to tell him.

I have no other choice.

"It's a long story," I warn him with raised eyebrows.

He watches me. "Yeah, in my experience, it usually is."

I frown. "What?"

He shifts on his feet, his chest moving on another sigh. "I've got a sister your age," he tells me. "She has a habit of telling long stories too, so…"

Trailing off, he looks away from me again and peruses the area. And when he finds what he's looking for, he begins to walk.

To the other side of the empty road we're standing on.

Not only that, when he reaches it, he lowers his large body onto the curb.

His long, muscular legs fold at the knees, his arms settling on them and his hands steepling together in the middle, his big silver watch gleaming in the dark.

"Uh, what are you doing?" I ask him.

He's watching me from his spot on the curb and God, he doesn't even have to tilt his neck up to look at me. It's as if it doesn't matter if he's standing or sitting down, he'll always be taller and larger than me.

"Sitting down," he replies.

"Why?"

"Because it's a long story and as I said, I've got experience in listening to them."

"Because you've got a sister my age," I repeat his earlier words and realize that it's the first personal thing he's divulged to me.

"Yes."

And then I have to ask him, "Is that why you stopped to check on me? Because I sort of remind you of your little sister?"

The thought is unpalatable to me.

Extremely.

In fact, it's so unpalatable that I almost grimace. I don't want him to think of me as his little sister or something. I'm not sure why but I don't.

Not at all.

"If she were in trouble," he says, "I'd hate to think of someone not checking on her if they could." Then, "Although she knows better than to break her curfew. So no."

"No what?"

He lets a beat pass where he keeps his eyes of still indeterminate color on me before he replies, "No, you don't remind me of my little sister."

I smile.

No, I beam and I can't help but tease him a little. "Why, is she scared of you? Because you're such a scary big brother."

His answer is immediate. "Yes."

Chuckling, I reply, "Well then, you're right. I can't *possibly* remind you of your little sister because I'm not scared of you at all."

His eyes turn dark, which is a feat. Because his eyes were already super dark looking in the night. But now they have turned darker than earlier and before he comes back with a response, I interrupt him. "Do you have any more siblings? I'm an only child so I don't really know how it feels to have siblings. It must be so great to have like, by default, lifelong friends. I'm…"

I trail off when he throws me a flat look with his dark-going-darker eyes. I tuck the loosened strands of my hair behind my ear. "Right. My story."

"Yeah. Your story." He jerks his chin up. "Before I change my mind."

My eyes go wide and I hasten to take a seat myself, directly opposite him. Because I'm not letting him change his mind now. He asked me for my story and he's getting it.

I fold my legs and thread my fingers in my lap. I try to think about where to begin or even how.

But then I decide that I'll begin with the most natural thing about me: "So the first thing you need to know about my story is that I'm an artist."

"You're an artist," he says in a calm, non-disgusted tone.

Something that's a very rare reaction to what I've said.

And his calmness, his utter lack of objection, is what gives me the strength to go on.

"Yes. I'm an artist." I grin because I always feel happy and elated when I think about my art. "I love to draw. I *live* to draw actually. I'm not sure where my love for the arts comes from. Because as you know my dad's a lawyer and my mom organizes all the charity events and whatnot. But I think I get my love for painting from my great-grandmother on my dad's side, Bertha. She was an artist. I've heard so many stories about her, you know? How she would shut herself in her room and spend her entire day drawing and painting. How nothing held her interest except her urge to draw. Everyone hated her though. They all thought she was wasting her life and that she was crazy. My mom compares me to Bertha a lot. At least when my dad isn't around. She'd never say anything against my dad's family in front of him though. But anyway, *I* think Bertha was extremely cool. I even look like her. Sometimes I think we might even be soulmates."

It's true.

I have her eyes and her hair and her artistry. And I really would've liked to meet her. And I think, I *think*, that Bertha would've liked me. Or at least I really hope that she would. She would've taught me things too. I've seen her work, only in photographs but still. She was extremely talented.

"So what's the problem?" he asks.

My shoulders sag at his question and my lightness vanishes.

I duck my head and, staring at my hands, I continue. "Well, as you might have guessed from Bertha's story, my parents hate that. My art. They think it's useless and inconsequential and it gets my hands and my clothes dirty. They want me to give it up because it doesn't look good in the media. Or really goes with who they are, and... And I always thought that I would. I truly did. Because I do want to be a good daughter to them, you know? I do want to obey them, do all the things they want me to do. Go to the college that they like, pick the major that they want me to. And knowing my dad and because that's all he talks about, it's going to be law school. Which is fine. I can be a lawyer if they want me to be. I can marry the guy that they choose for me too. I can."

"But you don't want to."

I shake my head, feeling like such a traitor. Such an epic fucking traitor.

"No." Sighing, I look up. "We have this ritual in our town where in your junior year, your parents send you to this boarding school in Connecticut. It's this super posh prep school where all the rich kids go. And I'm going there in two months. And I always knew that. I knew that I was going to go. I knew that the day I was supposed to give up my hobby was coming but..."

Yeah, the boarding school.

It's something that's inevitable. It's coming, and yes, I've always known that.

"But," he prods when I don't pick up my thread.

I shake my head again. "But a few weeks ago I found out something."

"Found out what?"

I swallow, looking into his dark eyes. "That I'm an artist."

He frowns, confused. "What?"

Which I totally get so I explain, "See, there's this new art teacher at our school, Mr. Pierre. He's so amazing. Like so freaking amazing, you don't even know. He's French and he's got an accent and he's just a genius when it comes to art. He's been to the Louvre. He's actually seen the Mona Lisa and he said that it's just as inspiring as I thought it would be. And he's taught me so much. He's taught me so many things that were beyond my reach until him. And he was the one who *offered* to teach me. He actually offered to give me private lessons, and of course I said yes. *Of course*. And I thought that getting private lessons from someone who's been to the Louvre was the best thing that ever happened to me. But I was wrong."

"Wrong," he repeats. "How?"

"Because the best thing that happened to me was when he called me into his office on the last day of school."

"What?"

His voice is all clipped and tight and I don't understand why that would be. Because it's a good thing and I tell him that. "No, it's a good thing. He actually called me in to say all these wonderful things about me."

"Yeah, like what?"

I frown at his continued irritation. "Like the fact that he was sorry that the year was over. That I was his best student ever and it was such a privilege to teach me. And *he* was the one who told me that I was an artist. See, I always suspected that but I never knew for sure. I mean, I'm like Bertha and I do love art yes, but am I *really* an artist? An *artist*, you know. Someone… *special* like that. I never knew. Until *he* told me.

"He told me that my art isn't just a hobby like I thought it was. I could do something with it. He said I could go to art school even. How crazy is that? Me, going to art school. He even offered to help me with my applications. He said he would love to continue our private lessons next year because he wants to nurture me, my art. But I'm leaving next year and —"

"He wants to *nurture* you. Is that what he said?" he almost lashes out, speaking over me.

It takes me a second to get my bearings after he cuts me off mid-speech. "Yeah. So?"

"So," he says, his jaw clenching, the muscle in his cheek beating, "your Mr. Pierre is clearly a pervert."

I draw back. "What?"

"You need to stay away from him."

"Excuse me?"

He leans forward slightly. "He called you into his office. To tell you that he wants to nurture you. And that he wants to continue giving you private lessons. Lessons that I'm sure your parents know nothing about, do they?"

"Of course not. These are private lessons. *Private*," I explain to him slowly. "Of course they don't know. And haven't you been paying attention? They hate my art."

He scoffs. "I think it's you who needs to start paying attention because as I said, your *teacher* is a fucking pervert. He knows your situation at home. He knows you're lonely. He knows your parents are shitheads and he's trying to take advantage of you. That's what men like him do. You ever see him again, you need to run the other way. In fact, you need to run to the principal's office and fucking report this son of a bitch."

I open my mouth to say something but then close it.

Because this is insane.

He's insane.

I can't believe that my Mystery Man who I've been so fascinated with is actually a crazy person. "You haven't even met the guy. How do you know that he's a pervert? How do you know he's taking advantage of me?"

His jaw pulses again. "Because I've got a sister your age. It's my job to know these things."

"That's…" I shake my head, flabbergasted. "Mr. Pierre isn't even the problem right now. He's the good guy here. He's the one who told me that my art is worth pursuing. That I'm an artist. But I can't do it because I'm leaving for boarding school in two months. Where there's no art whatsoever. Instead, what I get is Robbie."

His frown is blacker than the night. "Now who the fuck is Robbie?"

"Robbie is the guy who I'm pretty sure I'm going to have to marry one day and who'll get to grope my breasts for the rest of his life," I tell him with a raised chin. "And he's none of your *fucking* business."

"Language."

"Excuse me?" I say again but this time it's higher pitched than ever.

"Watch it."

I can't believe he said that. I can't believe he thinks he can get all high-handed over me like this.

I was right.

My Mystery Man *is* insane.

"Yeah? Why, because you've got a sister my age and so you think I should be bowing down to you like she does?" I ask, raising my chin.

He watches my defiant gesture with an intense, heavy look. "Bowing down is a bit much but don't let me stop you."

I watch him back. "How old are you?"

"Older."

"How *much* older?"

"Much."

I exhale sharply. "You know what, I'm glad I'm an only child. Because I would've murdered my big brother if he was anything like you." Then, I spring up to my feet. "I'm taking a walk."

To my dismay and also anger, he comes up to his feet too.

All fluidly and gracefully for someone with such a large and tall body.

"What are you doing?" I ask, ignoring his sheer display of athleticism.

He approaches me. "Taking a walk *with* you."

"Absolutely not," I protest. "I have no desire to walk with you."

Sliding his hands inside his pockets, he drawls, "Noted." Then, "May I suggest we walk to your house? Where hopefully your parents are."

My parents aren't at the house. They're at the party.

Where I should be as well.

In fact, I never should've left the party in the first place. I never should've abandoned them. I realize that, but then...

But then I never would've met him and yes, he is crazy — I know that now — but he's also the first person to talk to me about my stuff. To stop to check on me.

"I told you this area is extremely safe. So you don't have to walk with me." Studying his dark, mysterious face because he's somehow still out of the yellow light, I continue, "But I'm guessing it won't stop you from escorting me to my house anyway."

He studies my lit-up face in response. "No."

I raise my eyebrows. "Because you've got a sister my age and it's your job. To protect all naive and innocent teenage girls. From dark roads and pervy teachers."

"If I can."

I lose my ire then.

I don't think I can stay mad at someone so good. And responsible.

The best big brother a sister can have.

Sighing for probably the hundredth time, I bend down to pick up my heels. I also reach up and untie my hair, letting it fall down my back in a long, messy waterfall.

Because it looks like I'm going home.

I don't think I can face anyone tonight. I'll apologize to everyone tomorrow.

And because if he wants to escort me somewhere, my commanding and confusing protector, he should take me to my safe place, my house where my attic is.

Slinging my heels over my shoulders, I swat my wayward strands away. "You don't mind if I walk barefoot, do you? I don't think I can wear my heels again tonight."

For a moment I think he's frozen.

His frame, his eyes. That seem to be on my newly freed hair that flutters around my face and my shoulders. Around the small of my back too.

But then he moves and I think I was imagining it.

Nodding in response to my question, he clips, "After you."

And I tell my heart to stop going crazy at the prospect of being escorted by him as I begin walking.

My heart doesn't listen though.

It races and pounds with every step I take — *we* take. Because he's walking beside me as he said. He's keeping his steps small in order to match my naturally short ones.

And I don't know what to do with that.

I don't know what to do with him.

Who is he?

What's his name? Where's he from?

How does he know the Halseys? Because that's the party we both came from. Why did he look so still back there? So frozen, so breathless.

Lifeless.

Suddenly that's all I can think about.

Him appearing devoid of life.

And I want to ask him about it. I mean, he asked me for my story even though it ended so abruptly like that. Shouldn't I at least ask his?

I'm all ready to do that but I realize that we've stopped moving.

Or rather, I have.

Because we've reached our destination, and I don't even remember walking or turning the corners and crossing the streets.

"This is my house," I tell him, looking at the huge mansion we're standing in front of.

It has tall, thick pillars and a lavish garden along with sprawling marble stairs that lead up to the large polished brown doors. A Lamborghini — my dad's recent purchase — is parked in the circular driveway.

And even though my safe attic is waiting for me in there, I don't want to go in.

"Would you…Would you like to come inside?"

It's a last-minute invitation and I know he's going to refuse it. I already know that but still I had to issue it. Because strangely, I don't want him to leave.

I don't want this night to end.

When he remains silent, I abandon the sight of my house and face him.

And it's my turn to freeze.

Blue.

His eyes are blue. Finally I can see them; the driveway is lit up and even though we're standing at a distance from it, the glow still reaches him and lights him up.

Dark, gleaming denim blue.

With which he's taking in the house behind me before he focuses on my face. "You're an artist."

My tongue is thick in my mouth because I can see his hair too, somewhat at least and I think, it's dirty blond. And so all I can do is nod.

He bores those eyes into my light silver ones. "You're an artist because you *are* one. Because you draw. You paint, you sketch. Because that's what you do and that's what you love. Not because some asshole teacher *told* you that you are. He didn't make you an artist. You were one long before you met him and you're going to *be* one long after him. You will be one even if you give it up. Because that's who you are. It doesn't matter what the world wants or says. What your parents think. All that matters is what *you* want. All that matters is what you love, what makes *you* feel alive. Because this is your life. You're the one who's going to live it. So you should be the one to make all the choices. You should be the one who should do the things you want to do and dream all the things you want to dream."

He pauses here because I think he has to.

Because I think something passes through his eyes, making them bright and fraught with mysterious emotions.

"Because sometimes you don't. You don't get to do what you want. You don't get to dream. You don't get to choose. Sometimes you don't get to *make* your life because your life's made for you. And it's… hard. To live like that. It's difficult." His gaze flicks back and forth between mine. "So if you're an artist, you should stay one."

"H-how do you know the Halseys?" I ask.

Even though I can't hear my own voice over the drumbeats of my heart, I still know I've asked him that.

I still know that I want to ask him so many things, so I just blurt them out. "I saw you at the party. The wedding party? I was there too. Before I ran out of it. I saw you in a corner, all alone and so... still. I thought you weren't even breathing. I don't... I don't understand that. Why did you look like that? Why... Are you friends with the groom? The bride? What's... Who are you?"

My words are disjointed. I know.

I might not even be making any sense right now. At least that's why I think he hasn't said anything.

That's why I think his jaw is all tight and clenched as he watches me with intense eyes.

And maybe that's why he takes a step back from me.

From my crazily breathing and shivering body. My body that's buzzing with curiosity. With his words that he just said. With panic that I'm never going to see him again.

That he's going to leave any second and I know I won't forget him.

Even though I know nothing about him.

Not one thing.

And he does do that. He does leave.

Only before turning around and leaving into the night, he says, in that same deep rough voice of his, "Good luck, Bronwyn."

## CHAPTER THREE

The Original Thorn

Dreams and choices.

These are the two things I never think about.

Because I don't have them.

And so it doesn't make sense to waste my time longing for the things that I no longer have. Things that are meaningless. Things that only drag me down and make me angry.

Make me feel hollow and heavy at the same time.

But tonight is different.

Tonight is the night I can't keep my useless thoughts at bay. Tonight I can't help but feel angry.

Furious.

Left behind.

Like a fucking child on a playground.

I can't help but feel that the world moves on while I stand here, unmoving.

Still.

*Why were you so still?*

Her voice echoes in my brain as I walk away from her after dropping her off at her mansion. And even though I've been trying really fucking hard tonight to shut down my foolish thoughts, I can't help but answer her in my head.

I looked still probably because I was.

Probably because that's what my life is: still. And because I'd just witnessed someone move on.

Her.

I was so still at that party tonight because I watched my dream walk down the aisle in a white dress with a man who wasn't me.

Who would never be me.

# PART 2

# CHAPTER FOUR

Present

There's a girl I'm staring at.

She has messy black hair, thick bangs hanging in her eyes. And she's glaring at me.

Possibly because I just woke her up from sleep.

By throwing a glass of water in her face.

In my defense, I tried everything before this. I tried waking her up gently, talking to her, reasoning with her. But you can't really reason if a person is snoring in their pillow. So I had to get creative.

"Hey," I greet her, putting the glass back down on the nightstand by her bed. "Good morning."

"I'm going to kill you," she seethes, pushing her wet black hair off her face. "I swear to God, *Bronwyn*. I will end you."

"No, you won't, Poe Austen Blyton. Because you love me," I tell her, smiling because she does that when she's trying to annoy me, use my full name. So I use *her* full name, complete with her middle name, back. "Now, time to get ready. We're going to be late for class."

She flops down on her bed again. "Ugh. Stop using my full name. And don't try to be nice to me right now. I'm mad at you."

"You're not allowed to be mad at me. I'm trying to save your ass."

Her only response is throwing both arms on her face and growling.

I sigh. "Poe, you can't be late to any more classes, okay? School's only been open for like a couple of months and you've lost almost all your privileges. You can't afford to lose any more."

"I don't care. I hate this place," she declares from behind her arms. "Let them take all my privileges away. I'll start a revolution, you'll see. I'll burn down this whole school, trust me."

I do.

I do trust her.

If anyone can start a revolution and destroy this place, it's Poe. One of my very best friends and the resident troublemaker of this place.

By this place, I mean St. Mary's School for Troubled Teenagers.

"Well, I have complete faith in you. You will start a revolution, Poe. One day. But before that happens, you still need to go to class. Besides, do you remember what day it is?"

That gets her attention.

She lowers her arms from her face and blinks up at me. "What?"

"It's Monday after Thanksgiving."

It takes her a second to make sense of what I'm telling her and when she catches on, it happens. And I realize that I should've probably led with that. I'm an idiot.

Poe jerks up to a sitting position, finally looking alert. "Oh my God, it is."

"Yup."

"So today's the day."

"Today's the day, yes," I agree.

Then she jumps off the bed and starts scrambling. "Oh my fucking God, Wyn. I need to prepare. I need to get extra ready. Why didn't you wake me up sooner? You know I haven't seen him in months. *Months*, Wyn. I need to look my best. I need..."

And I know my job is done. She's awake and I know she's going to get ready on time. So I leave Poe to her devices and tackle my next project: waking up my second best friend, Salem Salinger.

Who doesn't need to be woken up at all, apparently.

Because unlike Poe, she remembers *exactly* what day it is. So she's all awake and ready to go, and as excited — if her huge grin and shining eyes are any indication — as Poe.

And I have to say it's a rare sight, seeing my friends excited about a day at school.

Because St. Mary's is slightly different than a regular high school.

It's definitely *a lot* different from the boarding school my parents wanted to send me to last year.

For one, this school is located in the middle of the woods in the town of St. Mary's and not in Connecticut. And secondly, St. Mary's is an all-girls school that people send their daughters to because of a very specific reason.

To be reformed.

Rehabilitated. Restored. Remade even.

Meaning, people send their delinquent, troublemaking daughters to St. Mary's School for Troubled Teenagers — a reform school — to become good.

Like if you steal something, say money, and try to run away with it. And you think your getaway plan is foolproof but it's not and you get caught. And the person who catches you — let's say your guardian — wants to teach you a lesson? This is the place they'll send you to do that.

Or instead of money, you could steal a car and drown it in a lake for revenge on your ex-boyfriend. That will land you here as well. Or maybe you've always been a troublemaker and people around you are tired of your wild ways. In that case too, this is where you'll find yourself.

So it's safe to assume that in order to rehabilitate us bad girls, this school has many rules.

Stringent and iron-clad rules.

Rules about showing up to classes on time, about turning in your homework on time. Eating on time, sleeping on time, waking up on time. Then there are rules about when to go off campus and for how long, when to use electronics and again for how long, and so on.

And when you follow these rules, you get rewarded. In privileges.

For example, you get to watch TV for more than an hour every night, which is the allotted time. Or you could use the school computer for an extra hour. Or you could go off campus more than once in a week, things like that.

That's basically the gist of how things work around here.

So as I said, it's a very rare thing that my friends are happy to begin the day.

The only person who's not happy about what day it is today is my third best friend, Calliope Thorne, or Callie.

Actually she was my very first friend in this place.

I got here a year ago, for my junior year, and Callie was the one who befriended me. In fact, she was the one who befriended all of us when we first got here: Poe in her sophomore year, and Salem, just a couple of months ago for our senior year.

Basically, Callie is the glue of our group. She's the reason all four of us had a chance to meet each other and become very best friends.

We see her as soon as we enter the cafeteria for breakfast and rush over to give her a big hug. She already has trays loaded with bagels and yogurt and cut-up fruits for us. And she's brought us cupcakes; Callie loves baking. But none of us really care about the food right now.

We're more concerned about our friend, who these days looks perpetually tired and pale.

"Hey, how are you doing today?" I ask, taking a seat beside her.

She grimaces, doing the same. "Bad. I threw up *twice* before getting here."

"Yikes." Poe echoes the grimace, taking the seat on the opposite side of the table. "But maybe this will cheer you up." She roots around her bag and produces a jar of peanut butter. "Ta-da."

Callie's eyes grow wide and in a display of strength — a rare one these days — she lunges for it. "Oh my God. Where'd you get this?"

Poe shrugs and answers proudly, "I stole it from the kitchen."

"What?" That's Salem, who's sitting beside Poe. "And you never told me?! I could've gone with you. I'm the thief here."

She totally is.

A very good one at that. Only the one time that *really* counted, she got caught.

She's the girl who stole money from her guardian and was running away with it but got caught. And the rest is history.

But Poe's no slouch either. Along with potentially starting a revolution and destroying this place, she can steal things too. She's the girl who's always been a troublemaker and the bane of her guardian's existence. So he sent her here not only to punish her but also — we all think — to get away from her.

While Callie gets busy with the peanut butter and soothing Salem, offering to let her steal a book from the library, I root around in my bag because I have something for her as well.

A sketch.

All my girls gather around and take turns admiring the image I've created.

It's a testament to how deep my friendship is with them that I'm able to show off my work without a hitch in my breath or my palms getting sweaty. Before St. Mary's, I'd hidden my passion and my work for so long — only showing it to my art teachers — that putting my sketches on the table like this for someone else to admire would've been unthinkable for me.

Not anymore though.

Especially when Callie looks up at me, tears shining in her eyes. "This is beautiful. *She* is beautiful."

I smile too. "Well, duh. She's yours. Of course she's beautiful."

A happy tear streams down her cheek and she swats it off, giving me a hug. "Thank you. Ugh. I'm so emotional all the time. Being pregnant is freaking draining."

It is.

We can all see it on her exhausted but beautiful face.

So we only just found out that our best friend is pregnant. And as she said, being pregnant is freaking draining. But when you're pregnant while you're a senior in high school, it's more than that.

It's scary and complicated.

Especially when the high school you go to is a reform school known to rehabilitate girls and getting pregnant is a sure-shot way to get expelled.

Which up until a few days ago we all thought was going to happen.

Only it didn't. Because someone came to her rescue: the guy whose baby she's pregnant with.

Her ex-boyfriend.

So remember the girl who stole her ex-boyfriend's car and drowned it in the lake for revenge? That's Callie. She did it because Reed Jackson, her sort of ex-boyfriend — long story there — broke her heart two years ago and she wanted to hurt him back. But now she's pregnant with his baby — another long story about how it all came about and how it doesn't mean that they're back together.

But anyway, because of him — and his influential last name — Callie not only gets to stay here, she's also the very first girl in the entire history of St. Mary's who gets to live off campus. Reed pulled all the strings and managed to get her that exception as well.

"And today's the worst," Callie continues, sticking her finger in the peanut butter and licking it off. "I'm so nervous."

Ah, yes.

Today.

Monday after Thanksgiving.

I knew today would be amazing for some of my friends — Poe and Salem — and not so amazing for others — Callie.

Salem's the first one to console Callie, squeezing her hand on the table. "It's going to be fine. You're worrying for no reason. Trust me. In fact, I think it's going to be epic. We're getting a new soccer coach. I honestly can't wait. I'm so excited to see him."

Callie bites her lip. "Yeah, but you don't know how girls are here. You only got here this year. Girls here always, *always* give new teachers a hard time." She waves a hand at her stomach even though she's not showing yet. "Plus I'm pregnant. I'm a laughingstock. Girls are bound to give him a hard time because of this. Because of *me*."

Okay so, Callie is right about one thing: girls here *do* give new teachers a hard time.

Because girls hate this place. They hate the rules and the fact that their freedom has been taken away.

And of course the teachers.

So whenever we get a new one, tensions are always high.

Fights break out in the hallways or in the cafeteria. There's always bound to be a girl or two who starts an argument with the new teacher, just to test their limits. There are more instances of girls getting their privileges revoked in one day when a new teacher starts than in a normal week.

Our group hasn't really cared about that before, but today things are different.

Because the new teacher, new soccer coach, who's starting at St. Mary's is Callie's big brother. Or one of her big brothers, anyway; she's got four.

Conrad Thorne.

But I also get Salem's excitement because she's a big soccer fiend. She actually has a very deep connection with the game. Not only does she play the sport herself, and very beautifully I might add, she's also in love with a soccer player, Arrow Carlisle.

Yup.

Callie isn't the only one in our group of friends with a complicated love story, Salem has one as well. In fact, her now-boyfriend, Arrow, was our soccer coach — a temporary one — until he had to leave for California. Where he plays for a pro soccer team, the LA Galaxy.

I'm not going to go into the whole thing about Salem and Arrow but I will definitely say that they had a bumpy and a complicated road, given that Arrow is our principal's son, Principal Carlisle. Almost as complicated as what Callie is going through right now, and I'm so happy that Salem found her happy ending.

I'm crossing my fingers for Callie and Reed as well.

"I think they're more likely to give him an *easy* time rather than a hard one," Poe says nonchalantly, going for the cupcake. "I mean, have you seen your brother? He's a fucking god. He has BDE."

Right.

Now Poe is excited because she has a teeny-tiny crush on Callie's big brother. As evidenced by not only her words but also by how quickly she jumped out of bed this morning when I reminded her of what day it was.

"What's BDE?" asks Salem.

Poe takes a bite of her cupcake. "Big dick energy."

"Ew. Gross." Salem shakes her head, swatting Poe's shoulder. "You're gross, Poe."

She only shrugs. "It's the truth, my friends."

"Salem's right. You're gross," Callie says, a grimace lining her features. "He's my big brother." Then wringing her hands in her lap, "I just want everything to go okay today. I don't want anyone to make trouble for him. I mean, I know he can take care of himself. But still. He's my brother and —"

"Hey, listen. Everything is going to be fine," I tell Callie, trying to soothe her. "You'll see. Your brother wouldn't want you to worry about him like this. Especially now. So just relax. Besides, we're all here. We'll look out for him and make sure things go smoothly."

"Exactly," Salem says. "Poe even laid down the rules yesterday after dinner."

"Yup, I made sure to let them know that he's not to be messed with," Poe says proudly.

After dinner last night, Poe did make an announcement in the TV room, warning everyone who would listen to stay away from Callie's brother. Or else they would face her retribution. And as the resident troublemaker, Poe's retribution has proved to be super inconvenient in the past — loose rats in teachers' offices, frogs in beds and drawers, itching powder in school uniforms and whatnot.

"See? I'm sure girls know better to mess with him now," I say.

"Of course they know better." Smiling slowly, Poe winks. "I told them that I'm the only one who can hit on him so everyone better watch out."

Finally Callie's nervousness abates and, rolling her eyes, she laughs.

Good.

Because honestly today *is* a good day. And like Poe and Salem, I am excited too.

Not because I'm interested in soccer or because I have a crush on Callie's brother — I know Poe jokes around about it but none of us would ever do that; Callie's our best friend and there are certain lines you don't cross — but because today's the day I get to meet Conrad for the first time.

Salem and Poe have both met him because he's usually the one to visit her on visiting weekends or the one to come pick her up before holidays.

But so far I've missed all the opportunities to meet him or her other brothers.

Because whenever he comes around, I'm already gone.

A car, sent by my father, comes around to pick me up first thing on such holidays or visitation mornings and take me back to where I came from. My town, Wuthering Garden.

So today's the first time that I'll get to meet him and I'll finally be able to put a face to the name of the person I've heard so much about.

The day goes by in a flash. Classes, classes, lunch; Callie rushing out of biology to throw up; Poe is given extra homework because she didn't turn in the original one on time; Salem nodding off in trigonometry and getting caught by the teacher; more classes and then finally, the moment we all have been waiting for arrives.

Soccer practice.

We all get changed into our school-issued soccer uniforms — white t-shirts with mustard-colored shorts; mustard is basically our school color, which means our uniform consists of a mustard-colored skirt along with a white blouse, white knee high socks and black Mary Janes — in the locker room before heading out to the soccer field.

Even though Callie is getting a pass on soccer because of her condition, she still accompanies us to the field to see her brother before she'll leave for the day.

All our footsteps are fast and eager and there's a sense of anticipation in the air.

So it's unexpected, *shocking* even, that I slow my pace down as I grow closer to the soccer field.

The girls don't notice it because they're already a few steps ahead of me, their eyes glued to the crowd on the field.

And to this very tall figure in the midst of them.

My eyes are glued to that tall figure too, of course.

A figure who up until now was facing away from us.

But then he turned around and that's when my pace slowed down. That's when my limbs got heavy.

My heart got heavy too, slow and lethargic, beating way too slowly. Dangerously slowly. And my eyes, they got narrow and squinty.

They still are that way actually. As I stare at him.

And I want to blame the sun for it.

I want to blame too much heat for my body acting so strangely. But the thing is that it's December and the winter sun is hardly visible through the gray clouds.

So it's not the elements of nature.

No.

It's something else. *Someone* else.

Him.

It's *him*.

That tall figure in the middle of the crowd on the soccer field.

*He's* making my body go haywire for some reason.

His hair, to be specific.

It's golden brown. Rich and thick, luscious. But the most important part is that it's cut close to the scalp. And so the golden brown strands stand up in places, looking all spiky, with absolutely *none of them* even touching the collar of his t-shirt.

Which is fine.

Why should they?

Only my crazy brain — and my squinty eyes and my stupid slow heart — can't stop imagining those strands grown out. They can't stop imagining those strands curling at the ends, hanging over that smooth forehead and grazing the side of that face.

But that's not all.

I can't stop imagining those shoulders, which are wide and muscular, draped in a suit jacket instead of in the light blue t-shirt that this man is wearing. And not only that, I can't help but imagine that suit jacket being a little too small to contain all that tall muscular bulk.

What's wrong with me?

Why am I imagining these things?

Especially when I've never seen this man in my life before.

Right?

*Right?*

So then how is it possible that I know exactly and to what extent I would have to crane up my neck and stretch my toes if I stood beside him, to be able to look into his eyes.

Eyes which I haven't seen yet because he's looking down at something but again, I imagine them to be blue.

Dark, *dark* blue.

Denim blue.

And then he does look up.

He *does,* and I find out that I was right. His eyes are blue. Navy blue.

Exactly as I remember them, and I remember them quite vividly.

So vividly as if I'd seen them yesterday. Last night. Only a few hours ago instead of when I actually saw them: eighteen months ago, on a random summer night when he ran into me and escorted me back home.

Not only did I see him that night, I drew him too.

I drew him on my dad's car.

I drew that face, those eyes, and got sent here to St. Mary's for it.

## CHAPTER FIVE

Everyone has done something to land at St. Mary's.
Which means I've done something too.
Something bad.

Something that has made my parents hate me.

Before, I merely disappointed them with my strangeness and useless hobbies. But after what I did the summer of last year, they can't stand the sight of me.

My mother told me that she wished I'd never been born. That she had a different daughter, a normal daughter. A daughter who wouldn't be so ungrateful and selfish. After all, they've done everything in their power to give me a good life. A life of money and prestige.

But in return, I rejected everything, and in the process humiliated them in front of everyone. Not only that, I did it all in an election year. In a year when our family was already under so much scrutiny. When my dad was already under so much pressure.

And if I'd had my way, I would've ruined everything and lost him the re-election.

Thankfully though, he — along with his aides and of course my mother — came up with the last-minute idea of sending me to this reform school. They thought that it would resurrect his image in the eyes of the people. My actions were raising questions about our family, about how my father could be the keeper of the justice system when he'd failed to control his own daughter. So if he punished me for my crimes, he'd do what was necessary to bring justice to them as well.

It totally worked and he won the election.

Which I'm really happy for.

Because it wasn't my intention to ruin things for him.

The reason I did what I did was because of my art.

Because I'm an artist.

Because I love to draw. I *live* to draw. And so I drew graffiti on my dad's car, his brand new Lamborghini to be specific.

Maybe I should've thought it through though. Maybe I should've gone with a different, subtler approach than to vandalize my dad's car that night. Something that didn't embarrass my parents later and put my dad's career in jeopardy.

But I wasn't thinking about those things in that moment.

I was simply inspired.

By him.

The man whose face I drew on my dad's Lamborghini.

Who had said that I was an artist not because someone had told me so but because I just was. I would be one even if I gave it up. And so maybe I shouldn't.

Maybe I should just live my life.

So I did.

I lived my life that night and I drew him.

His face. His eyes. His long-ish hair.

That clenched jaw.

I drew his shoulders, his gleaming silver watch, his suit.

And then I decorated him.

I made fluffy clouds around his gorgeous face, rainbows around his shoulders. I wrapped his tall body in a chain of roses and thorns. I sat butterflies on his fingers and dropped stars on his shoes.

By the end, it was a mess of colors and shapes behind which his beautiful face was hidden like a secret code.

My Mystery Man.

The one I never thought I'd see again.

But I am.

I *am* seeing him.

He's standing on the soccer field, in front of me.

Somehow, on my heavy limbs, I've managed to walk to the edge of the field where the crowd has gathered, and somehow my heart, which had slowed down like my legs, has also picked up speed.

My heart is beating and pounding as I stand here, staring at him.

But how is he... What is...

My racing thoughts vanish when a second later my best friend, Callie walks up to him.

I see her smiling up at him, happily and brightly.

At my Mystery Man.

I even see her touch him on his arm as she says something to him. And he listens.

And then I hear something, his deep soothing voice, in my head: *I've got a sister your age.*

His words are followed by another set of words, spoken by Callie: *What if they make trouble for him? Because he's my brother...*

Holy...

Holy shit.

*He's* the brother.

Him.

Holy fucking shit. And Callie is the sister.

Callie's the reason why he wouldn't let me walk home all alone that night, why he stopped to check on me in the first place. Because he's a big brother.

He's *Callie's* big brother.

He's...

"Conrad," I whisper to myself, my eyes wide as I watch them together. "His name is Conrad."

Something twists in my chest then.

At finally finding out his name.

At finally, *finally* finding out who he is.

Conrad. Conrad Thorne.

Con. Rad.

Con.

That's what Callie calls him, doesn't she?

*My brother, Con. Con this, Con that.*

*Conrad* is my Mystery Man.

How is that possible? How is...

A shrill noise breaks through the air, making me wince and stealing my thoughts. It alerts us to the beginning of practice, and so not only does Callie leave, but I also have to gather myself and pay attention.

I'm not sure how I do it but I manage to tear my eyes off him and focus on the moment. On Coach TJ. On Salem and Poe, who find me in the crowd and come to stand next to me. On forming a line when Coach TJ asks us to and putting one foot after another until I find my place in it.

And then the entire group settles down and I have nothing else to distract myself with.

I have nothing else to focus on.

Except him.

I take a deep, shaky breath and wipe my sweaty palms down my soccer shorts before daring to look up at him again.

It's a punch to the gut, my chest. A sharp sting to my heart and my lungs.

The sight of him.

And my eyes can't stop staring at him. My eyes can't stop feasting, *gorging* on his face. Even when Coach TJ begins talking, introducing him as our new coach. Before telling us to come forward in turn and introduce ourselves and what position we play one by one.

I can't take my eyes off his hair. Dirty blond, thick and rich and short. Much shorter than it was that night, making me wonder what happened to it. Not that it takes away from the beauty of his face, but I find that I miss his long strands. I miss them grazing over his brows, fluttering over the fine bones of his cheeks.

His cheeks.

That's another thing I can't take my eyes off of. The height of them, the arch. The hollows. The shadows that they do cast — as I thought they would — on his jaw. Which is clean-shaven and square.

So unapologetically beautiful and masculine.

And then there's his body.

The suit that he was wearing that night was too small for him. Too constraining.

Of course it hid his size, his power.

Which is fucking breathtaking in his light blue t-shirt and black track pants.

His clothes not only mold to fit his muscles, they showcase them.

The breadth of his shoulders, the globes. The bumps of his biceps, which are even more enhanced because he has his arms crossed over his chest. Those lean hips that then flow into powerful thighs.

He stands on the soccer field, watching girls coming forward one by one as they introduce themselves.

And I realize I'm going to have to do the same.

I'm going to have to introduce myself. Or re-introduce, rather.

Because we've met before, haven't we?

And then there's no controlling the beats of my heart or the buzz on my skin. No controlling my breaths and my anticipation until it's my turn.

And when it comes, I step forward on trembling legs.

Looking into those electric blue eyes, I tell him, "Bronwyn." I swallow. "My name is Bronwyn Littleton. But you could call me Wyn."

I repeat the words I said to him that night.

And so I wait for it.

I wait for it to happen.

Even though it's killing me and I can barely contain my breaths, I wait for him to recognize me.

"And."

This is the first word he's spoken ever since practice started, and somehow at the sound of it, the air becomes silent. I can feel every girl on this field inching closer and hanging on to it.

His very first word.

Spoken in his deep, deep voice, the deepest voice I've ever heard.

The voice that I now know I have remembered correctly.

"And?" I ask with my heart in my mouth.

His eyes flash at my question, making them look sparkly. "And are you going to tell us?"

"Tell you what?" I ask confused.

His flashing eyes narrow slightly. "What *position*. Do you play. On the team," he explains slowly, very slowly, before inquiring, "Is that clear enough for you?"

Oh.

*Oh*. Okay.

Right. I completely forgot that I was supposed to answer that as well. Like all the other girls.

But then... shouldn't we be talking about the other thing?

The thing where I know him and he knows me.

Isn't that more important and surprising and crazily coincidental than soccer?

I smile uncertainly. "Are you... Are you asking me what position I play on the team?"

My question makes him shift on his feet. It also makes that temporary narrowing of his eyes permanent as he stares at me for a beat or two in silence.

Then, "You understand English, don't you?"

I shake my head. "I don't —"

"Do you understand English?" he cuts me off, his deep voice going deeper, more authoritative. "Yes or no."

I'm so fucking confused right now but his tone can't be denied, so I reply, "Of course I do."

"And you understand what's been asked of you."

"Yes."

He throws a short nod. "So then why don't you answer the question and stop wasting everyone's time?"

I study his face then.

Not that I wasn't doing it already, but this time I see it in a different light. In a light where I don't focus on the fact that I've seen that face before but on the fact that his brows are bunched and his mouth is tight. That his eyes have something in them akin to irritation.

I focus on the fact that nothing on his face or in his body language, which is still as authoritative as ever, suggests that he knows me.

There is *no* indication, not even a teeny tiny bit of it, that he's seen me somewhere. Or that he even vaguely remembers me.

My eyes go wide then.

My mouth pops open as well and before I can stop myself, I breathe out, "You don't know who I am."

As soon as I say it, I flinch.

I know it was the wrong thing to say. Very wrong. I realize it when his arms unfold and come down to his sides. When that silver watch glares at me from where his fingers are fisted and when he dips his chin toward me as if now I have his full attention.

*Now* I have his full focus.

"And who are you, Bronwyn Littleton?"

My own hands fist at my sides when he says my name.

Bronwyn.

Because it sounds exactly the same as it did that night. Beautiful and delicate. Unique. Instead of how it always sounds when people from my town say it: uncouth, disappointing, a mouthful.

And yet he doesn't remember that he's said it before.

I need time to process that.

I need to absorb the blow, the wound that he's dealt me just now. So the logical course of action is to get my shit together and answer his original question before falling back into line and licking the bruises he gave me.

Only I don't.

I stand my ground, my hands still fisted as I reply, "Well if you must know, I'm an artist."

I don't flinch this time.

Even though his eyes have narrowed some more and my unexpected words have shocked everyone else on the field. This is the very first time that they have heard this tone from me, I think.

This sort of bored and *rebellious* tone.

I'm one of the good girls at St. Mary's.

I never behave badly.

So this is new.

"You're an artist," he repeats in a tone that I'm sure is sending chills down everyone's spine.

Not mine though for some reason.

For some reason, his tone is only making me bolder. Maybe because there's still no sign of recognition in it.

"Yes. I love to draw. I *live* to draw, actually." I raise my chin. "I always carry a sketchpad with me and a pen. I draw first thing in the morning, during breakfast. During lunch, during dinner. I draw up until they put the lights out at 9:30 every night. And then sometimes I draw under the moonlight." Probably shouldn't have said that but let's go with it. "In fact, I'd be drawing right now if I wasn't here."

It's true.

I do draw.

Mostly I draw him – yup, I've been drawing him for eighteen months now – like my little fingers are his slaves and my obsessed mind is his wonderland.

But even so I have absolutely no idea where I'm going with this. Why I'm saying the things I'm saying. But keeping quiet and falling back into line like everyone else isn't an option right now for some reason.

"If you weren't here wasting my time with your life story, you mean," he concludes.

And I commend myself for again not flinching at his '*life story.*'

Wasn't he the one who said he had experience with long stories? That's why I told him mine. That and because he was the very first person to ask.

But of course he doesn't remember that, does he?

He remembers nothing.

And God, it's making me angry.

So irrationally angry right now.

"Actually I would be drawing right now, if I wasn't wasting *my* time on soccer," I tell him.

Damn it. Damn it. Damn it.

I've lost my mind.

What am I doing? What is wrong with me?

This is not how I behave.

"Is that so?" he murmurs silkily, condescendingly.

But somehow I can't stop. His tone provokes me, dares me to keep going, to be a rebel. "Yes. I have no interest in soccer. I think soccer is boring." I swear I hear Salem gasp beside me, also Poe. "I think it's the most boring sport in the world. And forcing me and all of us, actually, to play just in the name of team building is completely useless and bordering on cruel."

I can't believe I said that.

Not that any of what I've said is a lie.

Soccer practice *is* boring. It's not so much about the sport but about an exercise in team building, or maybe just getting some physical activity. Most of the girls here aren't even players. Well, except for a few, like Salem and a couple others. So it's a constant source of frustration for most of us that they make us do this.

And this isn't the first time someone has said something about canceling soccer and the other couple of sports they make us choose from.

It's just that this is the first time *I'm* the one doing it.

He speaks. "Well, that's the one thing I don't want to be."

His tone is as soft and as silky as ever. Like melted dark chocolate, both sweet and bitter.

And addicting.

I hate that mine in turn is high and stumbling. "What?"

It feels like his lips barely move when he replies, "Cruel."

"So then —"

He tilts his face to the side slightly, as if in thought, as he interrupts me. "How about I make an exception for you?"

"An exception?"

"Yeah." He nods, still appearing as if in thought. "Because I'm getting the impression that you're special."

That gives me a pause. That gives me all the pauses actually.

Special.

"What?"

"Aren't you? Your classmates don't care about soccer either, but no one has had the audacity to say a word." He jerks his chin at me. "Except you. An artist. Different from everyone else. *Special*."

I'm aware that things are heading in a bad direction for me. I can feel it. Even though he hasn't changed his soft tone or his thoughtful expression.

But it's hard for me to care about that right now because my heart's throbbing inside my body.

With hope.

Because every word that he's said is the exact replica of what *I* said to him that night.

*Because I'm special. I'm an artist. I'm different from everyone else in this town...*

God.

*God.*

Does that mean that he remembers after all? He *remembers* me?

"Do you remem —"

He cuts me off again. "So it's only fair that I return the favor by making an exception for you."

I look into his eyes. I study them. They're navy blue, the color of my favorite jeans. But except for a sharp shine, they hold nothing else.

They hold no remembrance.

So maybe not then.

Maybe I'm simply making connections because I want to. I so desperately want to.

"How?" I ask.

He's quick to respond, as if he's been waiting for me to ask the question. "By writing you a note."

"What kind of note?"

"Actually, it's going to be a letter. I don't think a simple note will do you justice," he replies, flicking his gaze up and down my body in a quick, dismissive way, but still it makes things move inside me, in my belly. "I'll start by describing how utterly brave you are. How courageous to stand up to me like that. People usually keep their mouth shut and eyes lowered when I'm around. Then I'll say how original it was to see someone — a slip of a girl no less — do the exact opposite of what I asked her to do. Mostly the people I come in contact with — players and the rest of the general population really

— just do what I tell them to do. They walk when I tell them to walk. They run when I tell them to run, and they stop wasting my time the second I mention it. Because I don't really care for disobedience. Or people, especially teenagers, using their little *teenage* brains when I've ordered them to do something. But not you, no. How…" Another flick of his glance. "Unique. Which makes me think that when I'm done describing all your *singular* qualities in detail, I'm going to put in a further request for you."

I don't think anyone has ever insulted me by using such glowing adjectives. And I don't think I've ever been *so not afraid* in a situation where it feels like my doom is impending.

And near.

In fact, I feel exhilarated and thrilled and such a rebel.

"Is it going to be as special as your letter?" I ask, raising my eyebrows in defiance. "This request of yours. Because I think I want something special."

And I think he wasn't expecting that, me standing up to him again, because his jaw pulses. Only once, but it's enough for me to notice it and revel in it.

That I'm getting to him.

Even if it's just a little bit.

Because maybe this time, he'll remember me.

Remember the girl who's picking an argument with him on his first day.

"I understand that you're graduating at the end of this year," he says finally, his tone still as soft.

I frown even though I don't want to. I don't want to show him that he's getting to *me,* but I can't imagine why he'd ask me that. "I am."

He hums. "I was afraid of that." He shifts on his feet. "Since students like you are so rare and since you've made such an impression on me, I'm thinking that maybe you shouldn't."

"What?"

My voice is loud and high, the loudest and highest it's been so far. But *holy shit* he didn't say what I think he said.

He wouldn't.

It's crazy. It's… cruel.

Something similar to satisfaction passes over his features then. Like he's finally managed to scare me. Like he's finally managed to put me in my place, which is with my mouth shut and eyes lowered, as he said.

"Students like you are so hard to come by. Especially those who make your day, your first day no less, so memorable. I mean, I don't think I'm going to forget this day. I don't think I'm going to forget you." He pauses here, his eyes boring into mine, stealing and strangling my breaths. "So I'm going to put in a request, a very special one as you wanted, to make you stay. After graduation."

Things explode in my chest then.

Just like the air explodes with murmurs. Everyone is hissing and whispering and gasping. Even Coach TJ is shocked. She has her mouth open as she moves closer to him and tries to get his attention.

He's not giving it to her though.

Because his attention is on me.

On my frozen form.

That somehow is still throbbing. This time not from hope that he remembers me but from what he just implied.

Well, he did more than imply.

He said it.

He said The Unspeakable.

We call it that. We call it The Unspeakable.

The thing no one ever talks about. Not at St. Mary's. Not at a *reform* school where everyone is sent to be punished. Where rules are ironclad and prison-like.

No one, not even a teacher, ever jokes about it or mentions it in passing. About stopping someone's graduation.

Because it's like extending someone's prison sentence.

In fact there have only been eight cases ever since the school was established in 1939 of girls having to repeat their senior year. The teachers, no matter how stern they are or how unpopular with the students because of their strictness, always work *with* you to get your grades and your performance and your behavior up to scratch so you can graduate.

So for him to say that, to mention The Unspeakable is... unprecedented.

It, as I said, is crazy and cruel.

And flabbergasting.

"Are you..." I begin and this time the field goes silent because of me. "Are you saying you'll stop my graduation?"

His satisfied glint only increases at my question. "Just so I could keep you here." Then, "With me."

"Are you…" I begin with the same words because I don't know what to say. "Are you insane? You're insane. You are, aren't you? You're talking about stopping my graduation because I talked back a little. That's insane. You're fucking *insane*. You're —"

"Language."

His growl — a break from his so far soft and silky voice — cuts me off. It also punches me in the gut. Just as big and drastic of a punch as I felt at the sight of him.

Maybe even more.

Because he looks exactly the same as he looked that night when he asked me to watch my language. The only difference is that I can see the tightness of his features clearly now.

So clearly that I know, I *know*, I'm going to draw them.

I'm going to draw him exactly as he is, bunched up brows and tight lines, later. When I get out of here.

*If* I get out of here.

"What about it?" I ask, dooming myself further.

"Watch it."

I swallow. "Why?"

A muscle starts up on his cheek. "Because I said so."

"And because…" I open my fists, letting go of the last bits of my self-preservation as I look into his furious eyes and figuratively jump off the cliff. "Because you're older than me. And because you've got a sister my age and so you think you can tell me what to do. Don't you? You think I'll bow down at your feet."

What. Have. I. *Done*?

Seriously?

That muscle on his cheek stops at my words. That last throbbing piece freezes over as if to prepare for his anger, hot and explosive, to go off.

And it does.

"No," he says. "You will bow down at my feet because I'm your new soccer coach. And because if you don't, I'll teach you such a lesson in obedience that my threat of stopping your graduation will feel like a Christmas gift. It will feel like the best thing anyone's ever done to you and you'll thank me for it."

While keeping his eyes on me, he raises his voice slightly and addresses the rest of the girls. "Is that clear to all of you as well or do I need to repeat myself?"

Initially no one says a word.

Not until he swivels his gaze away from me and onto them.

Then a burst of *no*s sounds all around me.

And he speaks again. "I'm not sure how things were done before I got here and I don't really care. What I care about is how things will be done from now on. I've got one rule and one rule only: obedience. This isn't a democracy. What you want doesn't matter. I'm not here to listen to your opinions or your life story. From now on, you will do as I say. If I ask a question, you will answer it. If I want you to form a line, you will form a line. If I want you to run a lap around the field, you will run a lap around the field. And if I want you to be here on time, you will be here five minutes early. Is that understood? This might only be a team building exercise for you. But if you want to pass this class, you're going to have to put in the work. You're going to have to play soccer."

He grinds his jaw once before continuing, "And you," he says, his eyes traveling back to me, "I'll see you in my office. Tomorrow after school."

---

Conrad.

His name is Conrad.

I finally know.

It's been elusive to me for the past year, his name. Even though I heard it a million times from Callie's mouth.

But I know now.

And so when my roommate goes to sleep, I crawl over to the barred window and under the moonlight, I draw his name.

Up on my thighs.

*Really* high up, with thorns and roses snaking through it.

It seems both silly and appropriate at the same time.

Because his name sounds like thorn.

Sharp and protective.

Conrad Thorne.

# CHAPTER SIX

The Original Thorn

People think I'm predictable.

They think that I have a routine. A schedule that I follow strictly. A schedule I don't like to deviate from.

They are not wrong.

I *am* predictable. I *do* have a schedule that I follow stringently.

For example, for at least the last decade, I've gone for a six-mile run at the same time every morning. For years I've shopped at the same grocery store, eaten at the same pizza place, worked out at the same gym. I've bought the same brand of milk, the same brand of detergent and the same brand of cereal. I've driven the same kind of truck, gotten gas from the same gas station and slowed down at every yellow light on the way back home instead of flooring it through them.

I also never text and drive.

And everyone who knows me knows that.

So when I took this job at St. Mary's, people were surprised.

They weren't expecting me to quit my old job — coaching soccer at my town's high school, Bardstown High — and take a job at a different high school, in another town. Without any prior indication.

First because I'd had my old job for at least the last decade. And second, along with my predictability, people who know me also know about my hatred for this place.

For St. Mary's School for Troubled Teenagers, an all-girls reform school.

To be fair, I didn't have any opinion of it up until two years ago. It was just a school, a different, more extreme kind of school, located one town over from mine and nothing more.

I'd never given it any thought whatsoever.

But then I was forced to send my sister, Callie, here.

I was *forced* to watch her leave the safety of her home — where she belonged; where she *still* belongs — and walk through those black metal gates to go live with a bunch of delinquents.

That changed things a little bit.

That changed my apathy to hatred. To anger.

That she was trapped here.

Still is, until she graduates, and I can't do anything about it.

I *couldn't* do anything to protect her. To stop her from going, and I regret that.

I've regretted it every single day for the past two years.

So then it's not such a surprise, is it? It's not so unexpected that given the opportunity, I would take a job here. Because I'm predictable, yes, but I'm also one other thing.

The thing that defines me: I'm a brother.

A big brother.

And my siblings are my everything. My life. My purpose.

Everything that I do, I do for them.

For Stellan, Shepard, Ledger and Calliope.

Born three minutes apart, Stellan and Shepard are identical twins and are eight years younger than me. Then comes Ledger, who's twelve years younger, followed by Calliope, or Callie as we call her, who was born when I was fourteen.

Even though I was a kid myself when they were all born, it somehow happened that the responsibility for them fell on me. I'm the one who looked out for them, took care of them. Who fed them on time, helped them with their tests and homework, took them to soccer practice and recitals. And when they grew up, I'm the one who put curfews in place, made sure their rooms were clean, their chores were done.

I'm the oldest Thorne. The head of the family. Their protector.

Especially for Callie, our baby sister.

I've raised her. Actually all of us brothers have raised her together. She's never known any other authority or parent figure than us.

But when the time came, I failed her.

I couldn't stop the chain of events that led her to St. Mary's.

It's *my* responsibility to make sure that no harm ever befalls them. It's my job to sniff out potential danger and eliminate it before it can touch my family.

So of course when I heard about an opening at St. Mary's, I quit my old job and took this one.

Even though this job is pretty much bullshit and can be done by anyone who knows what a soccer ball looks like. Someone like me — someone who has led his teams to state championships, who has trained players that have gone on to become pros and some of the best athletes in the country — is way overqualified for a job that's more about team building than anything else.

But it doesn't matter because I'm here for my sister.

Besides, it's not as if I like coaching.

I'm good at it. I'm famous for it, even. In this state and many others. But no, it's not something I like or something that I choose to do out of passion.

But that's neither here nor there.

The point is that it's just a job. So it doesn't really matter to me if I'm doing it at my old school or here as long as I can take care of my sister.

Who right now is insisting that I go say hi or something to her friends.

"Come on, Con. It will only take two seconds," she says, all excited and hopping on her feet as she looks at me with her big eyes like she used to do when she was little and wanted me to buy her ice cream before dinner or watch Disney movies with her.

I could never refuse her back then. None of my brothers could.

And it's even harder to refuse her now because those big eyes of hers look tired this morning and my anger at failing her mounts.

This time though, it's not only directed at me.

It's also directed at that motherfucker because of whom I was forced to send my sister here.

Reed *fucking* Jackson.

The guy who broke her heart two years ago and almost ruined her life in the process.

"Should you be running around like this in your..." I search for a word. "Condition?"

She frowns. "I'm absolutely fine, Con."

I study her tired face, her sunken eyes. "You don't look fine."

That makes her smile. "Con, I love you for worrying about me so much. But trust me, I'm fine. It's just a little morning sickness. Now come on, I want you to meet one of my best friends. You haven't met her yet."

Morning sickness. Right.

Because my sister is pregnant.

Because that *fucking* motherfucker got my eighteen-year-old baby sister *pregnant*. Because apparently he's *still* not done ruining her life.

I should've killed him two years ago. I should've ended him the moment he looked at my sister.

"Come on, Con. Let's go," she insists again.

Taking a deep breath, I rub the back of my neck, massaging the tired muscles even though it's only morning of my second day at St. Mary's, and school hasn't even started yet. "Shouldn't you be heading to class though?"

She rolls her eyes. "We still have like ten minutes before the first bell." Grabbing my hand, she smiles sweetly up at me. "Please? You will love her."

I'm in no mood to meet a teenage girl when I know I'm going to have to spend the next eight hours dealing with a school full of them. But the thought of refusing Callie anything is even worse so I give my neck a last squeeze and nod. "All right."

Callie beams and her happiness takes away some of the pain throbbing in my neck and shoulders.

We're in the depressing main hallway of the school building and I follow her out the entrance, down the stairs that lead into the courtyard. The grounds are filled with students, trying to get to class or getting some breakfast before the bell rings. Some are occupying the concrete benches, their books sprawled open in front of them, presumably trying to catch up on homework.

Callie stops at one such bench but the book that's cracked open in front of the girl sitting there isn't a book at all.

It's a sketchpad.

And a pink pen is poised over it, making, from what I can see, the petals of a rose. Which is weirdly flanked by two eyes. Two very familiar looking eyes.

"Wyn!" Callie calls out and the pen stops scratching as she looks up.

Bronwyn Littleton.

The girl from the soccer field yesterday. The artist.

She's been sitting bent over her sketchpad, her long braid slung over her shoulder and her brows furrowed. But at my sister's voice, she looks up and a smile breaks out on her face.

She opens her mouth to say something but that's when her gaze falls on something else and her smile vanishes.

Me.

Her eyes, light gray, silver actually, widen and she hastens to snap her sketchpad shut.

She also rushes to stand up, which not only bumps her knee against the concrete table but also sends her pen flying out of her hand to the ground.

"Oh my God, are you okay?" Callie rushes over to her and she looks away from me.

I bend down to pick up her pen.

Pink and sparkly.

I flick it between my fingers, looking down at it for a second before pocketing it, then glancing up.

And back at her.

"Yeah, no. I'm fine," she says hastily, tucking a strand of her hair behind her ear. "I'm just stupid."

Callie frowns. "Are you sure? It looked like you hit your knee really hard."

Grimacing, she shakes her head and sets that recently tucked strand free and flying around her reddened face. "Yeah. Uh, no. It's okay. Really. I think I just got startled. But it's all good." She throws Callie another smile and tucks that piece of hair behind her ear for a second time. "So what's up?"

Callie beams at her enthusiastically before saying, "Well, I want you to meet someone." She turns to me then. "This is my brother, Conrad." Shaking her head, Callie turns back to her. "I mean, I know you met him yesterday at soccer practice. But I wanted to officially introduce you to him, my big brother. My *oldest* big brother, because, you know, I've got four big brothers. But Con's the nicest and the most amazing of all. And Con," she looks back at me, "this is one of my very best friends, Bronwyn Littleton. But you can call her Wyn."

Bronwyn but-you-can-call-her-Wyn Littleton looks at me hesitantly, her cheeks flaming and her silver eyes apprehensive.

I wonder if it's because of what happened on the field yesterday.

"Hi," she says in a soft voice. "It's nice to finally meet you. O-off the soccer field I mean."

I take her in, her long braid, hanging down to her hips; her school uniform, the mustard-colored cardigan over her white blouse; and her neatly pleated skirt.

And her hands, small and fragile looking, not to mention smudged with ink, tightly clasped in front of her.

When I come back up to her face, her cheeks are as pink as her pen in my pocket. "Best friend, huh."

My sister continues, giving her friend a side hug. "Yes. Roommate actually. Or ex-roommate since I moved out. But anyway, Wyn is amazing. She's like the calmest person you'll ever meet. She's so good, Con. Such a rule follower. Ask any teacher here at St. Mary's. They'll tell you how much they love her."

"Rule follower," I murmur, watching her cheeks burn even brighter due to Callie's praise.

She didn't look like one yesterday.

And she's probably thinking the same thing because her tiny nose wrinkles and she goes to say something but my sister speaks first and proudly. "Yup. In fact, she's got the highest privileges around here. Even more than me."

"I'm not," she blurts out finally, averting her eyes away from me, and my lips twitch. "Such a good girl, I mean. Callie's exaggerating."

Callie's *not* exaggerating, in fact.

Since we're meeting at the end of the day today and I like to be prepared, I grabbed her file from the office yesterday.

Bronwyn Bailey Littleton.

The good girl of St. Mary's School for Troubled Teenagers.

Goes to classes on time; turns in her homework on time; never gets involved in an argument or a fight; keeps her head down and does the work. And yes, teachers do love her.

Which makes me wonder what she's doing here in the first place.

When Callie goes to protest at her friend's comments, I get there first. "I disagree."

She snaps her eyes back up at me. "What?"

"I don't think she's exaggerating at all. I think she may be spot on." Looking at the slight frown between her brows, I add, "About how special you are."

Those silver eyes of hers, which were fraught with embarrassment until now, narrow.

Somehow I knew they would.

Not to mention, defiance flashes through them like it did yesterday and for some reason, my lips twitch again. Maybe because people have a hard time looking me in the eyes, let alone letting their feelings show.

But not her.

Not Bronwyn Littleton, the artist.

"Callie's just being kind, but thank you," she says then, her voice soft as before but more confident. "She's talked a lot about you too. About how amazing you are. The best big brother a girl could ask for. But she forgot to mention one thing."

"And what would that be?"

She raises her chin at that. "The fact that you're such an *excellent* soccer coach. I don't think I've ever had a coach this good."

She's brave, isn't she?

Or foolish.

There's a very thin line between the two.

Especially when she's provoking me. A teacher. At a reform school.

I've read their bullshit manual and from the looks of it I can make her life miserable if I want to. I can stop her graduation even, which I did threaten her with yesterday and which I have to admit was just an exaggeration.

I wanted to see what she'd do.

But anyway, I don't need a manual to tell me how to make a student's life hell. I'm quite good at that anyway. A coach usually is, but still.

Very brave and very foolish.

For now, all I do is throw her a short nod of acknowledgement. "Maybe if you did, you wouldn't find soccer so boring. And maybe your skills wouldn't suck so much."

Because they do.

I don't think I've ever seen a worse player in my life before, and that's saying something because there were some *really* bad players on the team. Not to mention, my own sister knows nothing about soccer and I've seen her kick a ball around in our backyard numerous times.

Both their mouths fall open at my comment and my sister says, "Oh my God, Con. That's such a rude thing to say."

"I wouldn't be such an excellent coach if I didn't point out my player's flaws now, would I?" I respond to my sister while keeping my eyes on her best friend.

Whose eyes narrow further at my jab.

"I can't believe this. And I just said you were the nicest of all our brothers." Callie turns to her friend. "I'm so sorry, Wyn. Con's —"

"He's right," she cuts my sister off, keeping her fiery eyes on me. "He wouldn't be. Such an excellent coach. And I wouldn't be such a good student or player if I didn't tell him — again — that I have no interest in soccer whatsoever. I'm an artist."

I stare at her a beat before pushing my hand into my pocket and fishing out that pen of hers.

I offer it back to her and she glances down at it. "Here."

She looks up at me before taking it from my hand. "Thank you." Clutching it tightly in her fingers, she says, her voice soft, "It's my favorite pen."

I push my hand into my pocket again. "And you probably have it on you twenty-four seven."

Her silver eyes slightly light up at my comment, reminiscent of what she told me yesterday. "Yes. Just like my sketchpad."

"Just like your sketchpad." When she nods, I glance down at it, her sketchpad, before looking up and saying, "Well then, you should get back to it."

With that, I step back, ready to turn around and leave, but my feet become frozen when I catch sight of something.

Of someone. Her.

They shouldn't though. My feet shouldn't freeze. As if I'm surprised, or worse, entranced.

Because I'm neither.

I'm not surprised to see her here. At St. Mary's. I knew she worked here when I took this job. I also knew that I'd have to see her every day. Five days a week for as long as I worked here as well.

In fact, I saw her yesterday too.

Just like this.

Walking down the concrete path before the first bell, a handbag slung over her shoulder. Yesterday too, she had a bunch of files in her arms that she was juggling, her blonde hair fluttering around her face.

And even though I'm not entranced either, I can't help but look at her.

Just like I did yesterday.

I can't help but look at her blonde hair, sleek and short.

As sleek and short as it was back when I knew her. Years and years ago.

It was also soft.

A thick, silky mass you could run your fingers through.

Not to mention, her smooth skin. That frown between her brows as she carries everything in her arms. I can't help but look at all of that.

And as I look at her, I realize that I'd forgotten about it all.

I'd forgotten her over the years.

I actually told myself to forget. Because I didn't have the time to remember. I haven't had the time to remember or feel anything or think about anything other than my siblings.

Again, for at least the last decade.

But here she is now.

All real and looking like she did before. When I knew her intimately.

I fist my hands in my pockets at the sudden tightness in my chest. At the sudden onslaught of pain in my shoulders. The pain that I surprisingly hadn't felt in the past few minutes when it always stays with me.

When she finally gets all the things she's carrying in order, she looks up and her eyes clash with mine.

The pain in my chest increases and I clench my jaw as I see a pleasant surprise color her features at the sight of me. When her lips stretch up in a small, familiar smile, I look away from her.

I shouldn't have looked at her in the first place.

She's my past and I don't have the time or any inclination to look at my past. Besides, she's not mine to look at anyway. She belongs to someone else.

So I should leave and get on with my day.

But this time when I go to turn around and leave, my eyes land on *her*, Bronwyn Littleton, the artist.

My sister's best friend.

Who's looking up at me with a frown, as if trying to figure me out.

I clench my jaw in irritation — I don't need a teenager to figure me out — before finally turning around and leaving.

For my sister or not, I'm beginning to think that taking this job was the worst fucking idea of my life.

## CHAPTER SEVEN

I'm standing in front of his office.

Ten minutes earlier than when he'd asked to see me today.

Just to make a good impression on him.

Because apparently, I have not.

Not earlier this morning when Callie introduced us in the courtyard, and definitely not yesterday on the soccer field. God, I don't know what I was thinking yesterday.

I don't think I *was* thinking anything other than how shocked I was to see him. To see the man I've been obsessed with for over a year, *here*, at St. Mary's, as our soccer coach no less.

Also how... heartbroken.

Which is weird. Probably an overly emotional reaction on my part.

But I was that. I was heartbroken to realize that he didn't remember me.

I still am a little bit.

To be fair though, from *his* perspective, nothing really did happen that night. I mean, yes he met a girl whom he walked home because he thought it wasn't safe. And yes, he talked to that girl out of the goodness of his heart and listened to her story before giving her some great advice.

But maybe he does that to everyone.

Maybe he helps every girl he meets on the side of the road.

And why wouldn't he?

He's a big brother, a natural protector. He's got three younger brothers. Not to mention a *sister*.

Whom he loves to pieces.

And who also happens to be my very, very best friend.

That's the second reason I need to make a good impression and put what happened yesterday behind us. Actually, I need to put this *whole* Mystery Man thing behind me.

Because something occurred to me last night that I'd completely forgotten about: Callie *knows*.

She knows everything there is to know about that summer night.

I told her a couple of months after I'd come to St. Mary's. We'd always stay up late into the night, talking and whispering to each other, and on one such night, I told her the story of how I came to be here. She knows that I met a man who changed my life. She knows that I've been thinking about him, wondering about him. In fact she's been an active participant in all those wonderings. She's spent hours talking about him with me.

Although she calls him my Dream Man.

I'm not sure how she's going to react if I tell her that *hey, I finally know who he is and funny thing, you know him too*.

I mean, she'll be surprised. That's a given.

But I'm not sure if it will be a good surprise or not. Maybe she'll be unsettled by this revelation. Maybe she'll hate the fact that the man I've been so obsessed with — the man that *she's* been obsessed with too, for me — is her older brother.

Or maybe it won't matter to her at all.

I'm not willing to find out though.

I'm not willing to risk losing her friendship or making her upset when she already has so many other things to worry about. Like her pregnancy and morning sickness, and her relationship with Reed.

Especially when her brother doesn't even remember me.

So yes, I'm going to put this behind me and get back to being a good girl who never argues with teachers or students alike.

Only he's not here.

His office is empty and the door is ajar. I think he's still on the field, finishing up practice, and so I'm waiting outside.

I'm also staring at that door and thinking...

Of doing something silly and inappropriate. Like I did last night when I wrote his name on my thighs.

I'm thinking of going inside his office and taking a look around. A really quick look around.

Just because the hallway is deserted and he's not here and I just...

Maybe this is my goodbye. To my obsession.

Maybe this is my way of cutting all ties with him.

From the man that I've only known as a mystery or as a big brother to my best friend. Although I didn't know about the latter up until yesterday, but still.

This is my last chance to see his space, to *be* in his space, even for a few minutes.

So without wasting any further time, I walk to the door, push it open and step inside.

Into his space.

And then I take everything in, slowly, bit by bit. Although there's not much to see.

The desk that sits in the center of his room doesn't hold anything except for a clipboard with the sophomore year's roster and a St. Mary's mustard-colored brochure. And the bookcase by the wall is more or less empty, filled up with old files and books and all that. It's also very dusty, meaning no one has touched it recently, not even the cleaning crew that comes in after the school building has emptied out.

And the walls, as beige-y and dull as the door, are bare.

So bare that my artistic heart and restless fingers want to fill them.

They want to fill his bare walls with colors.

With pretty things, quirky things, things that he can look at while he sits in that boring chair of his.

But of course I can't, so I turn away from it with a sigh, disappointed.

There's nothing here, not a single clue about him.

About who he might be as a man.

I run my finger over his bookcase, drawing a wavy line and a little flower in the dust. I touch his chair, his desk, even open his drawer really quickly and...

Completely and utterly come to a halt.

Because there's something in it.

A piece of paper that I know right away is not a receipt or some forgotten trash. It can't be.

Because look at how neatly it's been folded. There's just one sharp crease in the middle and even the edges of it are so crisp and cared for.

Whatever it is, it's personal.

Extremely personal.

*Out of bounds* personal. Even more out of bounds than checking out his office.

But it doesn't seem to matter right now.

I'm so desperate for any connection with him, so *pathetically* desperate, that I don't even take a breath before I reach out and grab it like a shameless, reckless thief. And my criminal eyes eat up the words on the page.

*Thanks for seeing me. I know it was hard for you, Con. I know that. You're a good man and maybe that's why I can't stay away - H*

As soon as I finish, a strong shiver overcomes my body and I drop the note.

Like it has burned me.

Or pricked my skin like a thorn.

But I don't have the time to think about that. I have to pick up the note, which has thankfully only floated down to the bed of the drawer, and put it back.

So I do that, my mind deliberately blank.

*I can't stay away...*

No, no, no. I'm not thinking about that. I don't want to think about that.

I *refuse* to think about who's written it — even though it's clear from the delicate handwriting that it can only be a woman — and what it means. I just want to get out of here, go back to standing in the hallway like I should've been doing in the first place.

*You're a good man...*

*Damn it, Wyn. Stop thinking about it.*

I dash to the door, grab the handle to pull it open, but as soon as my trembling fingers touch the cold metal, the door opens on its own. And then I don't think that I'm going anywhere.

Because there's a man standing at the threshold.

A man I met eighteen months ago on a random summer night. Whose name is written high up on my thighs.

And whose personal space I've just invaded.

Conrad.

He thinks so too, actually. That I've invaded his personal space.

Because I can see he's upset. Angry even.

It's in the way his chest expands on a breath, filling, *spanning* the doorway, as if blocking out all escape, and in the way his muscular arms go taut and immobile, one of them in the midst of pushing the door open. Not to mention, his jaw that's already so sharply sculpted has clasped so tightly that I think he's grinding his teeth to dust as he stares down at my own startled self.

Thankfully I come out of my stupor. "I was just leaving."

It's his turn to come out of his stupor then. At my words.

His expression clears of any shock or anger and goes all smooth as he lets go of the handle. Then, keeping his eyes firmly planted on me, he puts his hand on the door itself and splays his fingers wide before pushing on it, his biceps flexing from the force, and opening it completely.

He steps over the threshold then, finally entering the room.

I automatically take a step back to make space for him, for his large, looming body. And I automatically wince as well when, still without taking his eyes off me, he brings his arm back and shuts the door behind him.

Although with a soft click instead of the loud bang that I was expecting.

Which somehow makes everything seem even worse.

"Were you?" he asks, murmurs almost, his voice soft as well.

Just like it was yesterday on the field, all silky and smooth and dangerous.

Shiver-inducing.

I clear my throat. "Yes."

At this, he folds his arms across his chest and leans against the door, as if *telling* me through his actions that I'm not going anywhere. "Why?"

"What?"

"Why were you leaving?" he asks as if he doesn't know and is really curious to hear my answer.

As if it isn't obvious.

"Because I…" I fist my skirt. "This is your office and I — I shouldn't have been in here like this and —"

"So you're aware of it then," he cuts me off as he asks. "That you shouldn't have been in here. In my office."

I blush. "Yes. Yes, I'm aware. I just —"

"So if you're aware that you shouldn't have been in here in the first place," he interrupts me yet again with a mocking, thoughtful tone, "then what were you doing? In *my* office."

Swallowing, I wince again even though he still hasn't raised his voice. "I know this looks bad. I know that. But I just came in here to look for you and —"

"To look for me," he speaks over me yet again, for the third time. "In an empty room." I open my mouth to say something but this time, he doesn't even let me get to the speaking part as he continues, "So where were you looking? Behind that bookcase? Or under the desk, perhaps."

"I —" I try again and *again*, he cuts me off.

Oh God, why won't he let me talk?

"Or maybe you thought I was hiding in that storage closet. Just by my desk. Maybe *that's why*," he continues, his voice finally catching up to his ire, "you were taking a leisurely stroll through a *teacher's* office like it's your personal fucking amusement park. Is that it?"

"Oh my *God*, I was doing it because of *you*," I blurt out then.

The truth.

Why would I do that?

Why?

*Why, Wyn?*

"Me," he repeats in a flat tone.

Damn it.

Why do I have to be so pathetic?

*So* pathetic that I now need to salvage this situation after I've so carelessly blurted out the truth.

"Yes," I nod. "Because you traumatized me yesterday."

He did.

He did traumatize me, by bringing up The Unspeakable.

Everyone was talking about it at the dorms after dinner. About how I — Bronwyn Littleton, the good and quiet girl of St. Mary's — talked back to a teacher for the first time ever. And how that teacher threatened to stop my graduation. Poe looked extremely proud of me while Salem looked worried that I was coming down with something.

I'm just glad that Callie doesn't live in the dorms anymore or she would've heard about my absurd behavior and definitely gotten suspicious. As it is, I've asked Poe and Salem not to breathe a word about it to her.

His chest moves as he takes a breath and repeats my words again. "I traumatized you."

I swallow, shifting on my feet and trying to sound more confident. "Yes. You did. When you crazily threatened to stop my graduation."

Something flickers in his eyes then.

Something bright.

But before I can read it or understand it, he moves them. His denim blue eyes.

He brings them down to my body.

To my braid first, which is lying limp and messy over my shoulder. It starts out pretty neat though, in the mornings. But then over the course of the day, it starts to unravel. Maybe because I stick things in it, pens and pencils and paintbrushes.

My cardigan and my skirt share the same fate as my braid. Ironed and neat in the mornings but wrinkled and ink-stained by the end of the day. Even my knee-high socks somehow have pink ink stains, and my Mary Janes are dirty as if I've been kicking a ball around on the soccer field when all I've done today is go to classes and sketch.

He's probably coming to the same conclusion.

That I look like a disaster as compared to how I looked a few hours ago in the morning when Callie innocently brought him over for introductions.

"You don't look traumatized to me," he says, bringing his eyes up. That bright thing is still alive in his gaze, only it has become brighter and ever so mysterious.

I blush for some reason.

Even more than before.

I ignore it though. I ignore his scratchy sounding words as I insist, "I am. Extremely. Because it's not something that you just *say* to a student. It's unspeakable. That's what we call it here at St. Mary's: The Unspeakable. You *never* talk about The Unspeakable. You don't threaten a student's graduation.

That's like the first rule of being a teacher at St. Mary's. This is a reform school. It's like a prison. You can't talk about extending someone's *prison sentence* just for the heck of it. And then you made that big bad speech about making everyone's life miserable if they didn't do what you say. 'You need to show up like ten minutes early to practice or I'll make your world come crashing down around you.' Or something. Of course I was traumatized. Of course I came here early and wanted to check if you were really here or not. I didn't want to be unnecessarily punished even though I did everything right."

His face is unreadable as I finish my rambling explanation.

It's not false, what I've said. But it's also not the whole truth. And since I'm *never* going to tell him the whole truth, I just hope he buys it and we can put this stupid, ill-thought-out incident behind us.

"What's the second rule?"

I frown. "Second rule?"

His features are arranged in a cool mask so I don't know what he's thinking, as usual. But his eyes are still bright and they are still watching me in the way that makes me clasp my hands in front of me.

"If the first rule is to never talk about The Unspeakable," he explains, "what's the second rule?"

My heart thuds in my chest.

At his innocuous question. Because he asked me something similar on the night we met. Maybe that's why I say, "The second rule is to be careful."

"Of what?"

"Of the girls here."

"And why's that?"

"Because they can be… dangerous."

"Dangerous," he murmurs, dipping his head slightly.

I nod, my voice dipping as well. "They like to prank new teachers, make trouble for them. Start fights and arguments, trying to get them to quit. Things like that."

At this, he dips his chin even further as he says something that makes me feel like I'm floating. "So maybe I should really start hiding in the closets then, huh. Just to be safe." He looks me up and down really quickly. "From all the danger."

And just because I'm so light that I'm floating, my dusty Mary Janes in the air, I say, "Actually, scratch that. I don't think you have to worry about girls trying to get you to quit. I think you should worry about other things. Because your problems are going to be different."

Yeah, definitely.

I mean, just look at him.

He's still leaning against the door and his arms are still folded.

But somewhere in the middle of our tumultuous conversation so far, he's bent his knees some. His shoulders are a little less rigid than they were when he entered the room and his mouth is slightly tipped up in what I can only assume is a very tiny dose of amusement. The smallest dose of amusement that anyone has ever felt maybe.

But it's enough, you see.

It's enough to transform him.

It's enough to make him look relaxed and casual. A picture of arrogance and masculinity.

And if I wasn't so obsessed with him already, I would be now.

Like all the other girls at St. Mary's.

Poe was right yesterday. Callie shouldn't worry about girls giving her brother a hard time. Because they're already halfway in love with him. That was the other topic of conversation at the dorms last night.

How hot our new coach is.

"What should I worry about then?" he asks, bringing me out of my thoughts.

And before I can stop myself, I reply, "About the things they might do to get you to stay." Looking into his eyes, I continue, "You should worry about all the things they might do to get you to notice them."

He watches me back. "Yeah, like what?"

"Like..." I pause here for a second because it feels like my heart will burst out of my chest. "Girls stopping you in the hallway to talk to you for no reason. Or hanging around your office or on the soccer field, pretending to like soccer just so you'll talk back."

"What else?" he murmurs in a voice made of velvet.

I'm running out of breath right now but I don't care. I don't even care about what I'm saying as long as I get to keep going. "They might pretend to get in trouble just to get you to save them. They might drop their books when you're around just so you'd help pick them up. Or they might pretend to stumble on their feet just so you'd catch them."

Then, "Or they might... they might sneak out of their rooms and walk the midnight streets, hoping that they'd run into you. Hoping that you'd help them find their way back home. Like it's a Disney movie and they're damsels in distress and you're their knight in shining armor."

I did that.

Several times.

After that night, I did walk the midnight streets, looking for him. That summer before I was sent to St. Mary's, I'd sneak out of my house and go to the same spot, sometimes wearing that same dress, buttercup yellow.

It was silly, I know.

Going to that same street, wearing that same dress.

But I wanted to do all the right things. I wanted to appease the Fates, line up the stars just right.

Just so I'd run into my Mystery Man again.

"Because I think..."

"You think what?"

"I think every girl here is obsessed with you," I say while his eyes bore into mine.

And as soon as I do, his silver watch — the biggest and the brightest that I've ever seen — glares at me.

Reminding me that even though he looks all lazy and casual right now, approachable with his bright eyes and deep voice, he's still a teacher here.

This is still his office and I'm still a student.

And then he reminds me with his words. "Well then, you should tell those girls that they're wasting their time. I'm not interested in damsels and their teenage distress. Something about having a little sister who wouldn't watch anything but Disney movies growing up. Thereby torturing the ever-loving shit out of me. So now I prefer to stay away from situations that would force me to swoop in and save the day."

With that he straightens up from the door, losing his relaxed and approachable demeanor and going back to his aloof self.

Silently mourning the loss of it all, I watch him walk to his desk and pull out his chair. He takes a seat, spanning the back of it like he did the door. In fact, he even partially blocks the window, throwing his office into shadow.

Then in the most professional, coach-ly voice that I've ever heard from him, he says, "I read your file."

"M-my file."

He stares at me from his perch as he continues, "As I said this morning, my sister was correct. About your stellar record. It's all in your file. Top of your class, great privileges, never causes trouble, never gets involved in a fight."

I don't know where he's going with this so all I do is simply nod. "Yeah. That's correct."

Resting his elbows on the arms of his chair and rubbing his lips with his thumb, he asks, "So what is a good, quiet, artistic girl like you doing at St. Mary's?"

I swallow.

I also press my thighs together. Because his name on my skin has started to buzz.

The thorns on my thighs that I've made in his honor have come alive and they now prick my pale skin.

They sting.

Because he's the reason.

*He* is why I'm at St. Mary's. Because he inspired me. He told me to live my life as I wanted to and I did. And that in turn, led me to my wonderful freedom.

I know other girls hate this place but I don't.

How can I when I get to be myself here? When I get to draw all day long. When I have such great friends here as well.

But I can't tell him how wonderful he is, can I?

Because he doesn't remember.

"Because I drew graffiti on my dad's car," I say, telling him the basics like I tell everyone.

"Why?"

I grab the back of the chair in front of me and press my thighs together even harder. "Because my parents hated my art. They always have. They wanted me to give it up. But I didn't."

"And now?"

"I still don't want to give it up," I tell him. "Actually I want to… I want to go to art school."

I do.

Even though I know my parents will hate the idea of it.

That's why I haven't told them yet.

According to them, that graffiti incident was a one-time thing. They think that it was me pulling a stunt, throwing a tantrum. And now that I'm at St. Mary's, I have been reformed. Meaning I'm not thinking about art anymore.

But that's not true of course.

I *am* thinking about it. More than that, I want to go to art school. So much so that I've even been applying to them. Well, in addition to all the schools my parents want me to apply to. Or rather, *school*.

My dad has a preference, of course – his alma mater. And since I'm his daughter, I'm sort of already in, so.

"And they know that?" he asks.

"Uh…" I press my lips together. "Not exactly."

That gets his attention and a frown emerges between his eyebrows. "Not exactly *how*?"

I'm not sure how we got here but I don't know how to refuse him.

How not to tell my story to him.

I didn't know eighteen months ago and I don't know now.

In fact, I want to tell him, and so I do. "Well, after the graffiti incident, my parents got really distressed. Which is to be expected. I mean, I vandalized my dad's car. When I'd never so much as raised my voice in front of them. They were angry and baffled and stressed. They thought that it was a one-time thing and so I let them think that." I shrug, feeling slightly embarrassed. "I didn't tell them my future plans."

He studies my face then for a beat or two, and when it looks like he's going to say something, I speak. "Which is totally fine. It doesn't even matter right now. Because I'm still applying for colleges and scholarships. Which means I'm not in yet. And so I don't have to tell them right this second. I can tell them when I get in. At the right time."

Which is what my plan is.

I don't want to stir the pot just yet. When I don't even know if I've gotten in. When they're still reeling from my previous insurrection.

I want to give them time to cope with it before I drop another bomb on them.

A beat passes before he asks, "What kind of a car was it?"

"Uh, Lamborghini."

"Lamborghini."

"Yes." I nod. "It was my dad's dream car. He'd only just bought it like a couple of weeks ago. And I also drew on the siding of my house and on the front door. Which was sort of my mom's dream door. She had it specifically imported from Italy."

And my mom was furious about it. Even more so than about what I did with Dad's brand-new car.

"Was any of that salvageable?"

I slowly shake my head. "My mom had to replace the door. And my dad just shelved the car after that. He said it still smelled like spray paint."

I'm not sure but something like... satisfaction passes through his features. Pride even.

"Good."

"What?"

His jaw clenches slightly before he says, "Now that you've spray painted and ruined their so-called rich-ass dreams, they'll think twice about ruining yours. So you should tell them. Now." Then he adds, "About art school."

The sting in my thighs ratchets up then.

Delicious, glorious sting.

Because I was right.

He *is* satisfied. He *is* proud about what I did for my art. And no one has ever done that. I mean, yes my girls here at St. Mary's are proud of me and they accept me for who I am.

But the very man who inspired me is the one who's proud and I love that.

"I'm sorry," I blurt out then. "About what I did yesterday. I was such a jerk to you. And on your first day no less. I'm not like that. All the things in my file and all the things that Callie said, they are true. I'm a good girl. I don't make trouble. And I especially don't want to make trouble for you."

"For me."

"Yes," I say, digging my fingers into the chair. "Because you're my best friend's brother." *And the man who set me free.* "You're my best friend's *best* brother and I... I've heard so many things about you. So many wonderful things. About how much you love your family. How you have kept them together. How you've brought them up, taken care of them. How you've given up so much to be there for them."

He has.

Callie has told me all about it. All about how their dad was never much in the picture when they were growing up and so everything fell on their mom. And Conrad, being the oldest son, shared her burden.

And when their mom died, he was the one who was there to pick up all the pieces. He was eighteen at the time — Callie was four and her other siblings were all kids too — and in college on a soccer scholarship. But he gave all that up and came right back.

Not to mention, what he's doing right now.

He's here because of his sister.

"And now, you're here," I continue, feeling such a rush of warmth for him. "You took the job for Callie, to look after her and that's just... amazing."

I've never met anyone like him. So strong and so devoted to his family. So protective.

So good.

*You're a good man...*

She wrote that, didn't she? H.

Whoever she is, she was right.

"Look after her, yeah," he mutters, narrowing his eyes slightly as if in thought. "But as it turns out, I'm a little too late for that."

I frown.

Is he talking about Callie's pregnancy?

Because I know Conrad and the rest of her brothers haven't dealt with it very well. They were all angry and upset in the beginning, mostly at Reed. And even though they've decided to work together now to help Callie get through this, there's still some tension between her brothers, especially Conrad, and Reed.

"But that's not true," I say. "You're not too late. I know you think that but you'll see. I think Reed isn't as bad as everyone thinks he is."

A few moments pass as he studies me before completely ignoring what I just said and going, "The reason I called you in here is to tell you that I'm revoking your privileges."

"What?"

"Just because everyone else including you thinks you're not trouble, doesn't mean that you aren't. So starting from this weekend, I've asked that your outing privileges be revoked for the next four weeks."

My eyes are wide. "Four weeks?"

"Yes." He nods curtly. "Maybe this will be a further incentive for you. To be a good girl. As you think you are."

My heart skips a beat at his *good girl* and I part my lips.

Then, "Okay. All right. I deserve it."

He studies my straightened posture before saying, "You can leave now."

With that he slides that roster lying on his desk toward him, dismissing me.

From his office. From his mind.

So very easily.

So very, *very* easily. How glorious it must be, how convenient that he can forget me just like that.

While I stand here on buzzing legs, watching him for a few seconds more.

Mourning the end of our meeting.

Sighing, I turn around and walk to the door. My trembling hands turn the handle and open it. But my legs that are prickling with his name on them won't move and I turn back around.

And my mouth blurts out a question that I wasn't expecting to.

"Can I draw you?"

In the two seconds that it has taken me to walk from the chair to the door, he's picked up his pen and he's already on the second page of the roster, completely and utterly absorbed in it.

Not anymore though.

The paper crinkles as if his fingers have tightened around it. And the pen clutched in his hand stops moving.

Good.

I've stolen his focus then. I've won back that little space in his mind that he so easily just thrust me out of.

He lifts his eyes, his gaze electric. "What?"

"Can I... would you let me draw you?"

I'm not sure what I'm saying.

This was so completely not the plan.

But still I go on. "I mean, I'm an artist, as you know. And artists draw. And I'd love to, uh, draw you if you'd —"

"Leave."

"But I —"

He abandons his pen then, straightening up and away from the desk. "Out."

"But maybe you should —"

This time I stop talking because he stands up.

His eyes flash and pin me in my place as he rounds the desk and approaches me with long, purposeful strides. As if that's needed. As if he *needs* to pin me in my spot. As if I'd move.

I won't.

I'm not going anywhere. I don't even want to.

Even though he looks so dangerous, so... predatory while walking up to me. And then he reaches me and he still doesn't stop destroying the distance between us.

He leans down and down and I go up and up.

Until he does something beyond my imagination – he touches me.

He grips my bicep over my cardigan, his fingers firm and strong.

Warm.

And he uses them to sort of push me back — not harshly but not gently either — making me take a step back, and it's the step that takes me out of the room. And while I'm letting that sink in, that I'm not in his office anymore, he takes his hand off me and grits, "We're done here."

With that, he slams the office door in my face.

## CHAPTER EIGHT

I've fallen from grace.

At least that's what Poe happily calls it.

In the last week, I've argued with a teacher, been called into his office, and gotten my outing privileges revoked.

For *four* weeks.

The last no one knows except for Poe and Salem. And again I've asked them to keep it to themselves and not tell Callie. Getting called into a teacher's office is one thing, but getting your privileges revoked is something else. Especially for me, because this has never happened to me before. If Callie knew, she would no doubt force the truth out of me.

So as much as I *hate* to keep a secret from my very best friend, I'm doing it.

I'm also sticking to my original plan: move the fuck on.

From my obsession, fascination, preoccupation with him.

My Mystery Man.

Because not only could my friendship with Callie be at stake, I could potentially lose everything that I've been working toward.

Something my guidance counselor brought to my attention.

Needless to say, she's extremely upset over my recent behavior. Which I also hate, because I really don't like to upset her. Something not a lot of students at St. Mary's can say.

At St. Mary's, guidance counselors are the keepers of our privileges. We meet with them every week to evaluate our performance, our behavior, our future plans. They are the ones who keep tabs on all your good and bad deeds and hence what privileges we're afforded or not.

So of course they aren't very popular with the students here. And for good reason, because guidance counselors can be mean and intimidating. They can be unfairly strict depending on who you are assigned.

But my guidance counselor is genuinely nice.

She only started mid-year last year but she's helped me a lot ever since. She's encouraged me to apply for art schools and she diligently works with me on my applications. And she said that if I continued down this current path, I might screw up my grades and recommendation letters, thereby screwing up my chances of fulfilling my dream.

So I need to be careful.

I agree with her. I need to focus on my college applications and my goals and forget about this madness.

The only problem is that the man I'm trying to move on from is everywhere.

*Every. Where.*

Since he's the new soccer coach — Coach Thorne — the first place I have to see him at is practice.

The next two practices are much like the first one.

Where Coach TJ is the one who talks, and the new coach — *him* — simply stands there either with his arms folded across his chest or behind his back and watches everything critically.

He only deigns to speak when one of the girls screws up massively. And even then in grunting monosyllables.

It actually has become a game for us, the girls. Who will screw up the most and collect the most grunting one-words. So far Poe and a couple of other girls are in the lead. While I'm at zero. And I'm sure it's not because my soccer skills have magically improved.

He just doesn't say anything to me.

I don't even think he looks at me.

I mean, after what I did in his office — you know, the thing at the end — why would he?

*Can I draw you?*

These are my words. I can't believe they came out of my mouth though.

I don't know what I was thinking. Again.

All I know is that in that moment it was a compulsion. A deep, gutting *need* of my artistic heart and my desperate soul.

But anyway.

He said no, obviously.

Well, he kicked me out of his office and slammed the door in my face but I got the message.

And now just like him, I try not to look at him either.

Especially when he also stops by the cafeteria every day.

Every day at lunch, he shows up at our table to see Callie. To check up on her, see how she's doing. He also brings her all the things she's been craving lately, or at least been able to keep down. Which are mostly greens – kale, lettuce, arugula.

During such times, I try to keep my head down.

I try to focus on my lunch, my ink-stained hands in my lap, on my wrinkled mustard-colored skirt.

I even ignore how Poe always flirts with him. Or is the first to engage him in conversation. Which he responds to politely but with his usual aloofness. Then comes Salem with all her soccer questions. These, he answers with a little more interest than his responses to Poe.

"You're wasting your time," Callie sing-songs one day when her brother leaves. "He's not interested in you."

"And how do you know that?" Poe asks.

"Because I know my brother," Callie says proudly. "He is good. He's moral. He has principles. He will never ever look at a girl who's a student in a way that's less than appropriate. In fact," she says and looks around the cafeteria, "I should probably tell everyone this. Like, stop giggling and blushing when he comes around. He's never going to be like, 'oh my God, you're really pretty. Let me have you. I don't care that you're a teenager and my student.' Especially if that student is my friend. He's super particular about that. The rest of my brothers are animals. They don't care about the code or whatever. But not Con. My oldest and sweetest and also scariest brother is too morally responsible to do any of that."

Callie is right.

Her oldest brother would never look at any of the St. Mary's students in a way that's less than appropriate. Not that I want him to look at me in a way that's inappropriate — I *do not*.

But whatever.

It doesn't matter.

I have other things to worry about.

Because he not only is everywhere *during* school hours, but he's also here *before* them.

Just like he shows up at our lunch table every day, he also shows up at the soccer field. Way before classes start and the campus is buzzing with students.

And on that soccer field, he goes for a run.

*Every* day.

The only reason I know this is because I'm the first girl to wake up at St. Mary's. I wake before everyone else, usually an hour or two before, and go outside with my sketchpad. I have a spot that I usually sit at, under this tree on the soccer field, and sketch in peace before the day begins.

Anyway, the first time I saw him was the very next day after our office meeting.

I was under my favorite tree, bundled up in my favorite sweater and a knitted cap — both Christmas gifts from Callie, she's hardcore into knitting — my sketchpad in my lap as the winter sun slowly, very slowly rose up in the sky.

I was busy working on my sketch.

Of him.

So when I looked up and saw a flash of someone up ahead on the field, I was taken aback.

I was more taken aback when I figured who that flash was.

Him.

There was no question that it was his tall broad form.

He was close to the brick wall, running along the length of it. I'm not sure when he got there because I was busy with my work, but from the looks of it, he'd been there for a while.

He was sweaty from his ongoing workout and tanned even under the winter sun, and I could see... things.

I could see that his t-shirt was sticking to his body.

The fabric was clinging to his broad chest and shoulders like a needy little thing. It also clung to his ridged and muscled torso, that then tapers into his hips.

And don't get me started on his thighs.

His thighs were bulging under his workout pants as he ran and kept running even as he drew near me.

And then he stopped by the net on the field, directly in my line of vision, bent down and picked up a water bottle that I hadn't noticed before.

He gulped down half of it before letting the other half pour down on his face.

My fingers tightened around my pencil and my lips parted, my breaths erratic and unrhythmic as I watched that water rain down on him.

As I watched it drenching his face, drenching that hair of his, pouring down his moving, gulping, veined throat to his t-shirt, turning the already darkened fabric to almost translucent.

When he was done, he ran his fingers through his wet hair, scrubbed a hand over his face, picked up something else from the ground — his discarded hoodie, apparently — and left without a backward glance.

So that was the first day.

Since then I've seen him run laps — ten of them, I've counted — around the soccer field every single day.

I sit under my tree and sketch, him of course, while he exercises.

He never once looks at me or talks to me, and neither do I. We both pretend that the other is not there. Or rather, *he* pretends. I don't think I can with all the watching that I do.

So it's a surprise — big, epic, breath-stealing — when one day he stops.

Pretending that I'm not there.

It's been two weeks since that meeting in his office and it's a typical morning before school starts. I'm in my usual spot under the tree with my sketchpad. I got here a minute or two ago, just like him. But instead of doing what he does every day, taking off his hoodie, leaving it on the ground by the net and starting to run, he's walking over to me.

At first I can't believe it, and then my heart can't stop racing with every step that he takes.

My thighs can't stop buzzing.

Where his name is.

I still write it every night like a ritual. And decorate it with thorns and little roses.

I know I have to stop. I know that.

But it's my guilty pleasure. A secret *stinging* pleasure.

Just like watching him run every morning.

When he gets about ten feet from me, I shut my sketchpad, set it aside and spring up onto my feet.

"Hi," I say, when he stops in front of me.

Instead of greeting me back, he almost clips, "What the fuck are you doing?"

*Watching you.*

It's on the tip of my tongue.

Probably because this is the first thing he's said to me in two weeks. This is the first time he's even looked at me and I'm... jarred.

And breathless.

But I still have the good sense to leave those words there, at the tip, and not let them fall out.

"Uh, sketching," I reply, swatting a strand of hair off my face. My answer only makes him frown even more, which in turn makes me point to where I was sitting. "I sketch here every day. In this spot. This is my spot." When all he does is grit his jaw in response, I'm compelled to go further. "I'm Bronwyn." I point to my chest. "Littleton? Remember? People call me Wyn but you call me Bronwyn. I'm one of your students. Or players. Whatever. You called me into your office the other day. And took away my outing privileges for four weeks. Does any of that ring a bell?"

His nostrils flare and he finally speaks. "Is that supposed to be funny?"

I chuckle slightly. "Sort of." When his jaw clenches again, I hastily add in, "But given that you're not amused, I'm thinking no."

"What are you doing out here," he asks with clenched teeth, "in the *snow*?"

Oh right. The snow.

It's snowing this morning.

Little drops of white sugar falling on the ground, but it's nothing to worry about.

I look up at the gently falling snow. "Oh, the snow doesn't bother me. It's super light anyway. It's kinda pretty, don't you think?"

His jaw moves again, along with his chest. Probably with a sharp breath. "No. I think it's cold. The snow. And so you should go back inside."

I stare at his tightened up but beautiful features. "I'm not cold. I'm fine. Really."

I'm telling the truth.

This winter has been super mild so far. Except for one heavy snowfall back in mid-November, we've had no snow days or even chilly days whatsoever. And I should know because I'm out here every morning in just a sweater and sit on the ground that's barely chilly.

"Besides, I draw here every day," I continue. "It's my routine. And I read in a book once that discipline is very important if you want to be successful at something. *Especially* if you want to be successful as an artist. It's a unique passion, see. It's super self-driven, so I need to stick to a schedule." *And also watch you.* "But I don't have to tell you that, right? I mean, you're here every day too. Right on time." Then, without even taking a breath, I ask, "Do you know you do that a lot?"

"Do what?" he clips again.

"Stare people down like that." I tip my chin up at him. "Like you want to crush them under your boots. Like they're a bug or something." I point to his watch then. "Your watch does that too."

He continues to stare at me like I've just described, before sighing. Sharply. "Go back to the dorm."

"But I just said —"

"Just go to your room. Now."

"But you're out here too. In the *snow*."

"We're not talking about me right now."

And I really can't help it then.

A burst of laughter escapes me and he frowns. "Again. Is that supposed to be funny?"

I get my mirth under control as I reply, "Don't kill me, but for a second there, you sounded just like my dad. 'Go to your room. We're not talking about me right now.'" I chuckle despite his ire. "Like, how old *are* you?"

His eyes sweep over my face for a beat.

I do think they lingered on my smiling lips for a second but I may be imagining it. I may be imagining that dark glitter in them, the intense look.

I may be licking my lips too, just because I want him to keep looking.

He doesn't though.

He flicks his eyes up when he's done studying me, murmuring, "Your dad."

I lick my lips once again. "Yes."

"Whose car you drew graffiti on."

My heart races at his lowered tone. "I did."

Those eyes of his that I thought were on my lips darken even more. His jaw clenches as well. But only for a second or two. Then he sighs — not as sharply as before but still — and shifts on his feet.

Followed by doing something else. Something spectacular.

Incredible.

He goes up to the zip of his hoodie and yanks it lower. Then he grabs the front of it and opens it wider, rolling his shoulders and taking it off.

Leaving himself in only a t-shirt, light gray and fitted.

"Here," he offers it to me.

My eyes are wide. "What? I don't —"

"I don't need it for running."

"But I can't —"

"If you insist on sitting out here in the snow, then at least bundle up for it." He looks at his black hoodie. "It's not a lot but layers should be better than your..." He thinks about it, "Little sweater."

My lips tremble and my thighs prick with the imaginary thorns I've decorated his name with.

"I don't know," I swallow, "what to say."

I really don't.

Like that night when he stopped to check on me by the side of the road, he's offering me warmth now.

Something no one had ever done before him.

"Just take it before you die from the cold," he says. Then, "And deprive me of the chance to crush you under my boots like a bug myself."

I smile.

It's impossible not to. At this grumpiness. At the way he plays the reluctant hero.

*My* reluctant hero.

I also take his hoodie, which makes him take a step back, probably ready to leave. "A flower."

He halts in his tracks then. "What?"

"I'm a flower." I hug his hoodie, so soft and cozy but most of all warm. "Not a bug. A wallflower."

"What's a wallflower?"

"A type of flower that grows on walls and loves it," I explain, rubbing my chin in the cozy fabric as his eyes focus on my actions. "I'm a wallflower. And you're a thorn." He looks back up, his eyes dark and slightly narrowed. "Get it? Because your last name is Thorne."

He lets a second pass in silence before he asks, "What color is it? A wallflower."

"Oh. Uh, blue. And purple and pink and red. Orange." Then, "Oh, and yellow."

The color I wore the night I met him.

"Yellow," he murmurs, staring into my eyes.

"Yes," I whisper, staring back, *willing* him to remember.

For a second it looks like he does, when things flicker across his gaze, but then he breaks the connection, takes another step back before commanding, "Just wear the fucking hoodie."

I do.

I wear his hoodie that drowns me, that goes even more against my plans of moving on, but I don't care.

I don't care at all, because I smell him.

For the first time ever.

He's always been at a distance from me, at arm's length, and so this is the first time I get to discover his scent.

He smells of spices. Warm and wintery. And of something sweet.

Something like roses.

I realize then that this is what thorns must smell like: edgy and biting but with a hint of sweet flowers.

Despite my resolve and good judgement, I think about this all day and all night.

I think about this the next day too while I'm in the library during my free period. I'm trying to get a book on French Impressionism and I almost have it.

It's high up on the shelf and I've stretched myself enough that my fingers are almost touching it.

*Almost.*

Until someone else reaches up and snatches the book off the shelf.

I drop back down to the floor and spin around.

And there he is.

My thorn. Just something I've gotten to call him now that I know what his name is.

The color of his t-shirt today is unusual, the darkest color of all, black, and somehow it makes everything on him even more vivid — his tanned skin, the navy blue of his eyes, even the dirty blond of his hair — and with the winter sun streaming through the large windows behind me, he looks like a painting.

He's got my book in his hand and he glances down at it for a second before looking up at me. And like yesterday when he surprised me on the soccer field, I say, "Hi."

And again like yesterday, he doesn't greet me back.

Although his words don't carry the same venom as he murmurs, "Another book."

"Yes." I smooth my hands down my skirt. "It's on French Impressionism. The origin, the early years." Then, "It's a nineteenth-century art movement. The name Impressionism is derived from Claude Monet's painting, *Impression, Soleil Levant*. It means sunrise. In French. It was super radical at the time. Started by a handful of artists in Paris. And obviously people didn't like that. They didn't like that a group of people were violating the typical rules of art at the time and coming up with something new. So yeah." I nod. "Anyway, it's very interesting. You know, for a little light reading."

He glances down at the book again — a black hardcover with the title written in gold — before coming back up. "Light reading."

"Before bed."

Something passes through his features, making them look even more beautiful and slightly... soft. Especially with the light playing over them as he asks, "What about a ladder?"

"What?"

"Is there something about that, in *this*?" He offers me the book then. "The thing that you should use while grabbing a book from high up on the bookshelf. Because you can't reach it. Because you're short as fuck."

I grab the book from his hand and, like the hoodie from yesterday, I hug it to my chest. "I'm not short as fuck." Danger flashes through his eyes at my *fuck* because for some reason he's obsessed with correcting my language. I narrow mine in response as I continue, "I'm five foot four."

He flicks his eyes up and down my body.

I'm afraid to say that I look the same as I always do: messy clothes and messier braid. But I don't feel as self-conscious about it as I did the first time in his office.

Maybe because when he finishes and looks into my eyes, his are even darker and prettier. "If you say so."

I raise my chin. "I'm also eighteen." He frowns and I explain, "Years old."

"Random," he murmurs. "But okay."

"Now it's your turn," I say, waving a hand at him.

"My turn for what?"

"To tell me things. Your height for example. And how old are you?"

I'm not sure why I asked him these things, especially his age.

When I really know now. I know that he's thirty-three. I know that he's the tallest of all his brothers at six foot four.

But I think this is our thing.

Even if he doesn't know it. Or remember it.

"Older," he replies.

"*How much* older?"

I expect him to come back with something evasive or distracting because that's *his* thing. For some reason.

But this time he bores his eyes into mine and replies, "I'm much closer to your dad in age than I am to you." Then, "Have a good day, Bronwyn."

He's ready to leave but I'm not ready to let him go. So I blurt out the first thing that comes to mind just as he's about to turn around. "Uh, have you thought about growing out your hair?"

And like yesterday, he halts in his tracks and throws me a look.

A baffled one because I've asked him such a stupid, abrupt question.

But at least he stopped and that's all I wanted.

Actually that's not true.

That's not all I want.

I want something else. Something that I've decided, right now, right *this second* as the afternoon light hits him and makes him glow, that it's a good thing — the *right* thing — despite everything.

Despite my plans.

In fact it should *help* my plans.

"What?" he asks, his tone baffled as well.

I swallow, hugging the book, almost losing my nerve. "I-I mean, don't get me wrong. Your short hair looks great." I wave a hand at his cheeks. "It brings out your cheekbones and your jawline and everything. But I'm thinking — from an artist's perspective — that *maybe* you should think about growing out your hair a little. You might like it. How free it is and how you can feel the wind in your hair. It might look good on you." I shake my head at myself because I'm beating around the bush right now, and then just go for it. "But that's not important. The important thing is that I need your help."

He keeps staring at me, the baffled look still in place before he cocks his head to the side, his eyes narrowed. "Have I thought about growing out my hair because it might look good on me. And you need my help. Is that the gist of it?"

I clear my throat. "Just the second part. The first part about the hair was..."

"Useless," he supplies the word.

My cheeks warm and I mumble, "Not really but okay."

He then goes ahead and folds his arms across his chest and widens his feet, as if planting himself in front of me. "So what do you need my help with?"

Okay, good.

He took the bait.

I clear my throat again. "With, uh, my college applications."

"What about your college applications?" he asks, blank-faced.

"So as you know, I'm applying to art schools," I begin. "And since it's an *art* school, they require art. Like a portfolio. With sketches and stuff. And I have them. I do. But they're not like, where I want them to be. Quality wise. And I realize it's because I'm sort of blocked."

"Blocked."

I nod. "Yes. Like creatively. And so I was thinking..." I lick my lips, which are drying out under his heavy scrutiny. "I know that you were opposed to the idea before. When I asked you, back in your office. I mean, you shut the door in my face so I'd say you *hated* it. The idea. But I was wondering if you'd reconsider."

With his jaw set in a firm line, he watches me a beat before asking in a flat tone, "Reconsider what."

I press the book to my chest and clamp my thighs together where his name is. "The idea. That I proposed, of drawing you. Can I?"

It's a dangerous question.

On many levels.

One of which is that on the surface, it looks like me going against the original plan of moving on from him. But it's really not. It's going to *help me* move on from him.

Because I've realized something this very second.

I've realized that he really *is* everywhere.

I mean, I *knew* that, but what I'm saying is that since he's going to be around at St. Mary's, I'm going to run into him. I'm going to watch him being all silent and commanding at practice, or run laps early in the morning. I'm going to watch him get hit on by other girls. I'm going to watch him take care of Callie.

I'm going to watch him... take care of me as well.

By giving me his hoodie even though I didn't need it yesterday. Or by grabbing a book for me from the shelf. Even though I *almost* had it.

And this obsession of mine, this curiosity would just never end.

So this is the way to end it.

This is the way to kill my curiosity about him.

If I get to spend some time with him, talk to him, draw him to my heart's content, I wouldn't need to think about him late at night. I wouldn't need to draw his name on my thighs.

I wouldn't need to dream about him, if I spend my waking hours with him.

So this is it.

This is how I will move on.

So I keep going, for the sake of my friendship with his sister and for the sake of my own sanity. "It's just that your face really inspires me. It gets my creative juices flowing, so to speak. So this would really help me out. Because again as I told you, I'm trying for a scholarship and I need to bring my A game for that. And you're a teacher, right? It's practically your duty to help a student, so yeah. Would you let me draw you?"

Nothing changes on his face when I finish.

And somehow his blank face and his continued silence have started to make me blush even harder.

Then he speaks, and I feel like someone has just started to unravel me. "But from what I understand," he says, his head tilted to the side in a thoughtful look, "you already do."

"What?"

He unfolds his arms and he bridges the gap between us.

Like he did back in his office and like that day, I stand rooted to my spot. I watch his shoes cross the carpeted floor of the library as he draws near me, all slowly and dangerously.

And when he gets there, where I am, I'm flooded by his spicy thorn scent as he murmurs, "Every morning." His eyes move over my face and I can't help but tip it toward him. "When you sit under that tree of yours with your sketchpad. Wearing that little pink sweater and that knitted white cap. And you follow me around the soccer field with your big silver eyes. You draw me then, don't you?"

Silver eyes.

He knows my eyes are silver.

I mean, of course he knows. He's seen them. He's looking into my eyes right now, but people have a hard time pinning down their color.

But he didn't.

He's figured it out. The color of my eyes, and also me.

That I watch him. That when I sit there every day I draw him.

"I don't follow you around with my big silver eyes," I say in a tone that sounds more breathless than confident. "And I told you I sit under that tree every day. It's my spot. I sketch early in the morning every day too. Because I —"

"Because you read it in a book. Yeah, I know," he states, his gaze still roving over my face. "I know what you told me."

"So there," I reply this time with more confidence. "I told you that. You *know* that."

"But I also know," he rasps as he gets closer to me, stealing whatever little breaths I have left, "what I'll find if I open that sketchbook of yours. The thing you carry around twenty-four seven. Along with your favorite pen. Pink, isn't it? Because you're an artist."

My heart is leaping out of my chest.

It's trying to fly out of my mouth but I swallow it down and say, "You won't find anything. I don't know why you think —"

"I'll find myself," he says, plowing right through the middle of my sentence. "My eyes. Surrounded by roses. That's what you were drawing that day, weren't you? Out in the courtyard." Then after a pause, "Bronwyn."

Oh... fuck.

He saw that.

He fucking *saw* what I was drawing the day Callie brought him to introduce us. But I thought... I thought I'd shut the sketchpad before he had a chance to see anything. I thought...

"No you didn't," he tells me as if reading my mind. "Not in time."

And the way he says it, with the slow shake of his head, with this bright arrogant glint in his eyes, takes my breath away.

It makes me think that this is glorious.

He is glorious.

So fucking glorious.

Still I protest.

I have to. For more reasons than one.

"That may be so. But I'm an *artist*. And assuming that you're my only muse is ridiculous."

"Is it?"

"Yes." I nod. "So I think that you've lost your mind."

"My mind."

"Uh-huh," I go on, for the sake of my plan, for the sake of my friendship with Callie. "I think that your *mind* is going away. Since, you know, you're closer to my dad's age and all. Because *I* think that I've told you a million times that my name is Bronwyn but people call me Wyn. And so I'd appreciate it if you did too."

I won't.

I won't appreciate it at all.

I want him to call me by my full name. I want him to call me Bronwyn.

But of course I can't. So I try to look all innocent and outraged.

"Not a million times, no," he says. "Just two." Before I can figure out the math on that, on how many times have I actually told him to call me Wyn, he rasps, "And I think you like that."

"L-like what?"

"That I'm older," he explains. "Than you."

I hug the book tighter, using it as a defense against the war he's waging on me, on my senses. "Why would I like that?"

But his response to my question makes me realize that there is none.

There is no defense against him.

Against my thorn.

"Because you, *Bronwyn* Littleton," he says, his eyes penetrating, "have daddy issues."

"What?"

He usually takes his time responding to me, as if carefully choosing his words. But not this time.

This time he has his answer ready and he delivers it to me in low, rough words.

"Your dad's an asshole," he says. "He's a fucking piece of shit who deserved everything you dished out to him. In fact if I could get my hands on him myself, I'd break so many bones in his body and rearrange his face in a way that he wouldn't recognize himself in the mirror. For sending you here. For making your life miserable. For making you cry."

Pausing, he drops his gaze to my lips for a second. He studies my trembling mouth.

He studies my red cheeks too, my partially unraveled braid, my ink-stained hands before looking up at me, his eyes more serious than ever.

"But what I won't do," he continues, "is let this bullshit continue."

"I-I'm sorry?"

"You weren't your daddy's princess, so you want to be mine," he rasps, dipping his face toward me. "Don't you? You're a textbook case. That's why you watch me every morning. That's why you blush and duck your head and pretend to not notice me. That's why you talk and talk and never stop when I'm around, correct? That's why you provoked me that first day. That's why you snuck into my office. Did you think I wouldn't notice? That I'm the object of your teenage obsession? That my little sister's best friend is fascinated with me. I did. I *noticed.* And so let me make this very clear to you because I don't think slamming the door in your face got the message across.

"I'm not interested in you. I will never be interested in you. In fact, I'm fucking allergic," he says, his jaw clenched. "To you. I'm allergic to your big silver eyes and your pouty pink lips. To your blushing cheeks and your breathy voice. I'm *allergic* to the way you can't stop watching me. I told you I'm not interested in Disney movies, didn't I? I *meant* it. So I suggest you find someone else to play damsel in distress with. Someone else to solve your teenage problems. Someone your age, someone who's probably still going through a fucking growth spurt or someone who spends his weekends playing video games and jerking off. From now on, if I catch you looking at me across the hallway or if I find you within ten feet of my office or me *without reason*, my sister's best friend or not, I'll personally make sure you never see the outside of that brick wall and those black metal gates for the rest of the year."

And then before he straightens up, he adds, "And I might be closer to your dad's age than yours, but I do remember what people call you. And I also know what your name is, Bronwyn."

# CHAPTER NINE

There's a row of cottage-like houses on one side of campus.

Away from the school and cafeteria buildings, away from the dorm and the library and the soccer field.

They're backed up against the brick wall surrounding the school and are supposed to be partially private and for the faculty.

In the olden days — in 1939, specifically — when the school was newly opened, the school was all there was.

Meaning the town of St. Mary's was built after the school came into existence.

So a lot of faculty members lived on campus, in these cottages. But as time went on, the town grew and teachers started to live off campus. Now no one lives here. These cottages are abandoned and in disarray, with peeling paint and overgrown ivy. There was some talk of tearing them down and building a new hall, but the funding has always been a problem.

I don't mind though. I actually like these cottages.

I like that they're shabby and old. And isolated and lonely, because for the most part, girls at school keep their distance. So when I'm not in the mood to talk to anyone or to draw like a possessed girl, I can come here for a little bit and hide out.

That's where I'm headed.

To get away from everyone. From the loud chatter and from my girls' concerned eyes.

I've told them numerous times since the day in the library, which was two days ago, that I'm fine. There's nothing to worry about at all. Maybe I'm really coming down with something. And maybe that's why my eyes are swollen and my nose is red all the time.

It has nothing to do with a man.

A man who so thoroughly broke my heart two days ago.

The man who walks around campus unconcerned. Unaffected by what happened, by what he did.

By how he *really* crushed me under his boots.

But anyway, I don't want to think about that.

I'm tired of thinking about it and I just want to get away for a bit, away from everyone else.

But it looks like that's not in the cards, because when I get to the far end of campus and round the corner to make my way to the dogwood tree that's located behind the cottages and where I usually sit and draw, I see that there's already someone there.

Someone so unexpected that for a second I can't believe what I'm actually seeing.

My guidance counselor, Miss Halsey.

She's standing under the tree, her head bent and her hands wringing in front of her.

What the hell is she doing here?

For a weird second I think that she's here to see me.

But how did she even *know* that I was going to be here?

I know that she knows about this place, because I told her in one of our sessions that I love to go here when I want to get away from things. And Miss Halsey must be the only guidance counselor at St. Mary's who didn't even bat an eye at this information; she thinks self-care is as important as reformation.

Even though I can't think of a single reason as to why she's here, I feel like it must be something important that brought her to these cottages, to this hiding place.

I should go ask her, see if I can do something to help.

And I do take a step toward her.

But then I stop, because she's not alone anymore. We're not the only two people in this part of St. Mary's. There's someone else here.

Someone else who's emerged halfway down the strip from between two cottages.

A man.

He's not only emerged from out of nowhere, he's also over taken my entire focus now. He's hijacked my line of vision to the point where everything else disappears.

Except him.

His broad shoulders and rippling back are covered in a navy blue hoodie, his powerful legs in a pair of track pants as he strides toward her, where she stands. And when he reaches his destination, the dogwood tree, my breaths halt.

Because he turns, revealing his profile, revealing that strong line of his jaw that always stays smooth and clean-shaven somehow.

Not today though.

Today, there's a five o'clock shadow.

A dark scruff.

Even his hair, that short cropped mass, looks ruffled. Like he's been plowing his fingers through it.

He looks how I feel.

All ruined and agitated.

And for a second I let myself foolishly think that maybe it's because of what happened between us. That it's cutting him to be so cruel to me as it's cutting me to take his cruelty. That walking around campus unaffected was just for show.

But that can't be it.

Right?

If it was then he wouldn't have been so mean that day.

Even so, I can't help but wonder. I can't help but take a step toward him like a pathetic idiot. But I stop again, because in addition to be able to see him, his profile, I'm able to see other things as well.

Things like her, my guidance counselor.

Who turns toward him and cranes her neck up. As if she's a flower and he's the sun. And she needs him to bloom.

Which she does – she smiles.

A small, sad sort of smile that I notice swells up her pretty cheeks.

He doesn't though.

He doesn't smile. Instead that sharp jaw of his tics. It throbs like my heart is throbbing.

But then it stops.

Both my heart and his ticking jaw, because she touches him.

She reaches out and takes his hand, his fist really, by his side and brings it up. Not only that, she brings it up to the point where *he's* touching *her*, her cheek.

I watch that hand, big and strong, dusky, on her delicate, soft-looking cheek, and something painful happens in my chest. Because those fingers latch onto her cheek. They hold on, the tips of them, digging, and she goes up on her tiptoes and whispers something to him. And whatever she says makes him swallow.

Thickly. Harshly.

And then after that, after that swallow from him, she reaches up and puts her lips on him.

On his scruffy jaw, her light peck leaves a red lipstick mark, faint but unmistakable. Before throwing herself at him and hugging him.

And then it's like a blast from the past.

From eighteen months ago.

When I saw him at the party, standing in a dark corner, looking all still and frozen.

Lifeless.

That's what he looks like right now, and a broken laugh escapes me then. Because I've always wondered why.

Why did he look like that?

I even asked him that night but he never answered.

Now I know why though.

It's because of *her*.

Whose red lipstick mark sits so proudly and conspicuously on his stubbled jaw. Although if it were me, I would leave my lipstick stains on his heart, on his soul. So he can never erase them.

Her.

It's her.

And *this*... this is love, isn't it?

It has to be.

Painful and intense and blazing. Stinging.

So much so that I can feel it in my own chest. I can feel it in my own body. Especially when those eyes of his somehow, *Jesus Christ* some way, travel across the space and land on me.

## CHAPTER TEN

Helen Halsey.

That's her full name. Miss Halsey's, I mean. Helen. Or H.

She's the one who thinks he's a good man and that's why she can't stay away from him. That's why she wrote him that note.

Didn't she?

The note I've been trying to forget but haven't been able to.

The note that he so dearly holds on to.

Like he held on to *her* yesterday.

I bet he looks at that note every day, several times a day in fact. I bet if I snuck into his office again and got into his drawer, I'd find that note exactly where it was the other day.

But I'm not going to.

I'm *never* going to.

I'm done with him.

I'm done with my crazy, unhealthy obsession that has the power to ruin everything that I value. My friendship with my best friend, my privileges at this school, my college applications.

My own self.

Actually, I was done with him three days ago, after the library where he crushed me so thoroughly. So much so that when I came back to my dorm, I spent thirty minutes in the shower, trying to erase his name off my thighs. And then the following day I didn't go to my spot under the tree.

I haven't been there in three days.

I haven't even drawn him in three days.

Because I refuse to spend another second thinking about him.

That asshole.

I can't believe I'm saying this about him, my Mystery Man. My thorn.

But the mystery has been solved now: he's like every other man I've known in my life. He's cruel and mean and a fucking douchebag.

So instead of wasting my time on him, I'm *going* to stop wallowing in this stupid misery. I'm an artist, damn it. And I need to stick to my schedule. And since I didn't go to my spot in the morning, I'm going to it now, after school.

Not the one on the soccer field; it's crowded there now. But the one where I was going to yesterday, before that plan was ruined.

I'm going back to the dogwood tree behind the cottages and this time I'm going to sit there and draw. And destroy the memory of what I saw there, and so when I round the corner and find the spot blissfully empty, I'm happy.

Reaching my tree, I throw my backpack down and sit on the ground. Propping myself against the bark, I snap open my sketchbook. But before I even have the chance to press the nib of my pencil onto the page, the last thing — the last man — I want to see right now appears.

Like yesterday, he emerges from between the two cottages, tall and broad, and blocks everything in my view.

He *becomes* my view as he starts to walk toward me, his lunging steps athletic and strong and beating in my chest like a drum.

They beat between my thighs, thrum on my skin like a pulse even though his name is no longer there. And I hate that so much that I shove aside my sketchpad and snap up to my feet.

Just to put a stop to this throbbing in my body.

Which only gets worse when I get a look at his face.

Because his face looks exactly like it did yesterday, with his scruffy, unshaven jaw and his messy hair. A slight strain around his eyes, his mouth.

Even his shoulders.

And like yesterday, something twists in my chest. Something compels me to take a step toward him.

But I don't.

I *won't*.

In fact I take a step back. I take *two* steps back and bump into the tree behind me.

"Don't come any closer," I say to him and he stops. "I've recently been given a ten-foot rule. And I don't want to accidentally break it and spend the rest of my days *trapped* in here. Through no fault of my own."

At my reminder of what he said to me that day, something ripples through his harsh features and I dig my nails into my palms.

"You haven't come to your spot," he says, watching me. "In the mornings."

I swallow, steeling myself against his velvety voice. "Oh, is that another rule that I'm breaking now? You're going to have to write this all down for me. It's getting harder and harder to keep up with them."

His eyes flash and his hands, fisted and shoved inside his pockets, tighten. "It's your spot. Your daily routine."

"So?"

"So you should stick to it. It belongs to you."

I fold my arms across my chest. "Actually I've just realized that I don't like the view anymore. From my spot. So I think I shall be picking a new spot for myself. Thank you though, Coach Thorne. I didn't know you were so worried about my routine."

His nostrils flare. "You're upset."

"Upset? *Moi*?" I point to my chest. "What, pray tell, do I have to be upset about?"

He stares at me a beat. I bet I look furious.

Good.

He should know that he can't talk to me that way and get away with it.

"I was harsh," he states, "with you. I was..." His eyes bore into mine. "Cruel. You shared things with me and I used them against you."

He did.

I shared my entire life story with him. Not once but twice. The first time was eighteen months ago, but of course he doesn't remember. But the second time was in his office. I told him about my parents, and he used it to crush me.

To cut me into pieces.

"You did."

His features tighten up, become brittle and harsh, cut in marble. "I crossed a line. You trusted me with something and I…" He grits his jaw. "And I broke it. Your trust. And I did that knowingly."

I know I shouldn't care.

I know I shouldn't even give him a chance to explain. What he said was shitty and yet, I find myself asking him in a strangled voice, "Why? Why did you do it when you knew it would hurt me?"

At this, he draws in a sharp breath. "Because I wanted to. I *wanted* to hurt you."

My eyes sting. "You wanted to h-hurt me."

Another sharp breath, and this time, he also shifts on his feet as if restless. "Yes. Because I wanted you to get over it. I wanted to end your teenage fascination with me or whatever the fuck is going through your brain. I wanted to take that and crush it. Because it's only going to hurt you later. Hurt you *worse*."

I unfurl my fingers and grab hold of the tree behind me as I ask, "Why? Why would it hurt me worse?"

At this, he takes his hand out of his pocket, his silver watch gleaming, and he rakes it through his hair, making it even messier.

More unkempt and somehow even more beautiful and carefree.

"Because you're young," he says with clenched teeth. "Because you're *much too* young to know what you're doing. Because I've got a sister your age. Because you're best friends with that sister. Because I'm your fucking coach. There are a million reasons. Take your *goddamn* pick, write it down in your notebook, and look at it every day until you memorize it and get the fuck over your obsession."

His voice is loud.

Louder than I've ever heard it before.

Which makes me realize that he never raises his voice. Not even when he caught me in his office. His voice was tight and angry, yes, but never loud like this. And the fact that he's raising his voice right now for some reason, that his control has been slightly chipped, makes me say, "And because you're in love with someone else."

A shutter drops through his features, closing him off completely.

I can't even make out the strain on his face now. It's all blank. And cool.

Cold.

"Aren't you?" I prod him, digging my nails in the bark of the tree. "You're in love with Miss Halsey."

As soon as I say it, I scrape my nails down the bark.

Because that's how it feels in my heart.

That a thousand thorns are pricking it, dragging through the muscles of my soft organ. Making it bleed.

Making it hurt.

"She's my guidance counselor," I continue, my voice wobbling slightly but I won't stop. "I'm sure you know that. I mean, you looked at my file. You took away my privileges. Of course you know she's my guidance counselor. But did you know that I knew her before St. Mary's?"

I wait for some reaction from him at this. Some sign of shock or surprise.

But nothing.

"Yeah, she's from my town. From Wuthering Garden. I've known her all my life. And generally, people in my town hate me. But not her. Not Helen."

Helen is different.

She's always been different. She always liked me, talked to me whenever we crossed paths. In fact, she even babysat me when I was little. And when she came here — she works here part time both as a guidance counselor and a history teacher as part of her parents' charity foundation — I got lucky and she was assigned to me as my guidance counselor.

We're friends, even. Or at least I consider her one.

"Helen was nice," I tell him. "In fact, our bond has only grown ever since she started teaching here. I was the one who told her about this spot. I gave her the tip that it's a great spot. For hiding. That's what you two were doing, weren't you? Hiding, meeting in secret. Because we both know you can't do it out in the open. Because we both *know* that Halsey is her maiden name."

It is.

Her *married* name is Turner.

Helen Turner.

She never took her husband, Seth's, name after marriage. But that doesn't mean that she *isn't*.

Married, I mean.

She is. Very much so.

In fact she and Seth, along with the whole Halsey family, came over to our house for dinner on Thanksgiving last month. And back then, everything looked fine between Seth and Helen. They looked very much in love, very much the happy couple.

Not that things have gone bad since then.

Last week in our session, Helen was telling me about this skiing holiday Seth was planning to take in Vail. For Christmas.

"You know that, don't you?" I ask him then, even though I know the answer. "You know that she's *married*."

"Yes," he replies, at last breaking his silence.

His stillness though. That doesn't go anywhere.

He's as still as he was when I first broached this conversation.

As still as he was yesterday, and even before that.

At that wedding party where I saw him for the first time.

Again I dig my nails into the bark. Again I scrape through the harsh, biting surface.

Because this time I'm imagining a thousand thorns pricking *his* heart. I'm imagining those thorns dragging through his bruised organ.

How painful it must have been for him. How *killing*.

To watch that.

To watch the woman you love being married to someone else.

And yet... *yet* he stopped to help me. He sat on the curb and listened to my petty, silly, teenage story.

Because he *couldn't* not.

Because he's a good man.

And I want to do the same right now. I want to ask him everything.

Ask him where he met her; how long has he known her? Why did she marry someone else? Why did he let it happen?

Why aren't they together when from what I saw yesterday they both clearly love each other?

I don't get it. I don't understand...

"Are you having an affair with her?" I speak out, confusion clear in my voice.

God.

I feel dirty. My mouth feels dirty.

Affair.

Such a damaging word.

I've seen the damage it does first hand. It's rampant in Wuthering Garden. Husbands having mistresses. Wives either ignoring it or swallowing down pills to battle the toxicity of it. And other times they have affairs of their own.

My mom has chosen the path of ignorance.

So I know.

I'm aware of how destructive an affair could be.

And I can't imagine, *can't fucking imagine*, that a man like him who would stop to help a strange girl on the street, who gave up everything to be there for his family, would do something like this.

He's too good for it.

Too moral to do something so wrong.

"What I'm doing," he says, "is none of your business. I want —"

"Are you serious?" I blurt out, interrupting him. "I saw you almost make out with another teacher and you're saying it's none of my business? It is my business. She is *married*. She has a husband. I know him. I know her. I know her entire family. And I know you. I *know* you can't do this. I know that. There's no way. So you have to tell me. You have to tell me that what I saw, what I'm thinking isn't real. You have to tell me that the note in your drawer doesn't mean anything. You have to tell me that —"

"The note."

That lone word from him puts a stop to my agitated ramblings. And puts something else into perspective.

The fact that I told him something I never wanted to.

I spilled a secret.

Fuck. *Fuck.*

And he knows it. He absolutely knows what I did accidentally.

"That day in my office," he concludes, his mouth so tight that it barely moves.

Swallowing, I press my back against the tree as I jerk out a nod. "Y-yes. I saw it in your drawer. I didn't mean to. I'm sorry. I know it was personal and I —"

He cuts me off.

Not by his words, no. Not even by a motion of his hand or a shake of his head.

He does it by grinding his jaw so hard that I feel the ache in my own teeth. He does it by breathing so sharply that I feel my own lungs hurting.

And he does it by taking a step — *half* a step — toward me. Before coming to an abrupt halt.

Before letting his chest expand with a large breath and letting his eyes fall shut for a second.

He kills all my words by very visibly controlling himself and his anger. Right in front of my eyes.

I bite my lip then.

At his legendary control, the effort it has taken him to gain back his patience. At the fact that I want to go to him and just... hug him. Apologize for invading his privacy.

And when he reaches up and massages the back of his neck, I want to do that for him too.

Finally he opens his eyes, blue and glittering, and says in a resigned tone, "Are you going to tell?"

"What?"

"About what you saw," he explains. "Yesterday."

"Tell..." I shake my head. "Tell who?"

He moves his jaw back and forth. "Your friends. My sister. Other girls in the school. Are you planning to tell them what you saw?"

I open my mouth to answer him but nothing comes out.

Not one word.

I wasn't expecting him to ask this question, let alone have to answer it. Because it never occurred to me. To tell.

I've been so distraught at what I saw yesterday, what it all could mean, that it didn't even occur to me to go tell someone. I've been so *distraught* over the pain that he must have gone through at that wedding party that telling someone was the last thing on my mind and...

"You think I'm going to tell someone?" I ask, disbelieving.

He watches me for a few seconds before replying, "You're a teenager, aren't you? Teenagers gossip. They tend to open their mouths and say things they don't mean to." Then, "They also tend to walk into rooms they shouldn't and touch things that don't belong to them."

I see the shadows of that anger he'd just controlled in his eyes, and guilt stabs me in the chest.

Despite everything, despite his doubts in me, it makes me almost blurt out another apology.

But I don't.

Because something else occurs to me.

Something that stabs me even harder than his anger just did.

"Is that why you came here?" I ask, frowning. "Is that why you... Is that why you *apologized* just now? For hurting me. For saying all those mean things to me. Because you think I'm going to tell someone about your secret? So you think you have to keep me happy, make nice with me. I can't believe this. I —"

This time he cuts me off by letting himself go.

By taking that step he'd stopped himself from before.

In fact, he takes all the steps. To get to me.

And he does it so fast, so lightning quick, that I don't even realize it or get the chance to back away from him.

"I *apologized*," he says, bent over me, the pulse on the side of his neck throbbing. "Because I was wrong. Because I hurt you. Deliberately. Knowingly. I hurt you so much that your spot under that tree has been empty. For three fucking days. For *three fucking days*, you haven't shown up wearing your little sweater and your little knit cap. You haven't sat on the ground, bent over your sketchpad and focused on it until a little smile tips up your lips. Probably because you finally got it right, your art, your sketch, whatever." My mouth parts as he draws even closer, his eyes all blue and angry. "I apologized because you were letting what happened between us get in the way of your dreams. Being an artist is your dream, isn't it?" I jerk out a nod and his nostrils flare. "And you were very stupidly letting something inconsequential get in the way of that. And so I *fucking apologized* and made nice with you because I'd be *motherfucking* damned if I let you do that. If I let you potentially ruin your dreams for me. Does that clear things up for you?"

It does.

It so does.

It clears everything up. That he regrets it. What he said. The way he hurt me. That his apology was sincere. That once again he's the only man who somehow cares about my dream.

Quite possibly as much as I do.

And so it's painful, a thorn in my heart, to utter, "But you still think that I'll tell."

Something grave washes over his features, mysterious but seemingly business-like, and he steps back as he says, "You're still a student here, at St. Mary's. You're still the girl who argued with me on the first day and then trespassed through my office. And whose privileges I took. So yes, I need to know if in your impulsiveness or in the throes of your teenage hormones, you're going to tell someone or not."

Teenage hormones.

Right.

Because I'm a teenager. And so I've got a teenage mouth and a teenage brain and a *teenage* fucking desire to tell him that yes, I will tell.

I will fucking plaster it all over St. Mary's.

I will draw it on every wall of *every* classroom that Coach Thorne is having an affair with Miss Halsey.

God. *God*.

I hate that he thinks I could do something like that. All because of my age.

All because I'm a student here, just another girl at St. Mary's. And I know I shouldn't take it so personally, because it's not as if he remembers me from that night.

He doesn't know that we've already met. And so he doesn't feel the same connection that I feel with him. So it's only natural for him to ask me this question.

But.

I *am* taking this personally. Because I *do* feel the connection.

I do.

So I steel my spine and take yet another deep, painful breath. "What will I get if I do? Keep it to myself."

His eyes narrow.

And I shrug. "There has to be a price, right? For keeping your secret. What is it?"

He studies me, my defiant face, for a few moments before he almost bites out, "What do you want?"

I look him up and down at his question.

Only because my heart is twisting in my chest and if I don't, my eyes will start to sting. So I focus on him, his body. Tall and proud. Beautiful. Every line, every muscle such a work of art.

"I seem to recall asking you for help," I say, glancing up. "The other day. With my college applications."

His eyes have a dangerous glint in them, a dark glint. "Is that what you want?"

"What if I do?"

He takes a second to answer. "Fine. You can draw me."

I want to laugh.

I want to throw my head back and scream. With pain.

He'd do that, wouldn't he? He'd let me draw him — something he's been so opposed to — all because he thinks I might spill his secret.

I clench my teeth and widen my stance, which doesn't escape his notice.

Good.

I want him to know that I'm prepared for battle. I tilt my head to the side and twirl a lock of hair as I pretend to ponder over his acquiescence that sounded more arrogant than anything. "Actually, I've changed my mind. I don't think I want to draw you anymore. I think that's too easy. For you. I want something else."

I can clearly see anger on his features. Clearly.

I can see how it darkens them, sharpens them as well. Chisels them into sharp, thorn-y points as he asks, "And what do you want instead?"

Looking into his eyes, I say, "I want you to kiss me."

I'm not going to lie and say that I didn't know I was going to say that.

I knew.

I knew I was going to say something outrageous, something crazy and irrational, to provoke him.

To *test* him. To see how far he would go with this.

To see how *low* his opinion is of me and my teenage years.

"You want me to kiss you," he repeats.

"Yes." I nod confidently even if my heart is thudding in my chest, my knees are trembling and my thighs are stinging. "You were right the other day. I do follow you around with my big silver eyes. I do draw you in my sketchpad. If you opened it right now, you'd find yourself. Your eyes. Your hair. That silver watch you wear. That frown you always have on your forehead. Your jaw, all tight and square. Made of marble. Your cheekbones. God, your cheekbones. They are sharp as shards of glass. Like thorns. And your body.

"Your body is... *magnificent*. So large and tall and broad. Muscular. Every single muscle is so beautifully made and I haven't even seen them bare. All I've seen is shadows and ridges through your t-shirt when you run and still I know. Still you make me feel small and dainty. And I'm not. You make me feel like I could climb you like a mountain. That I could sit on your lap, on your thighs and you wouldn't even feel it. And I..."

"You what?"

*Yeah, he what, Wyn?*

*What are you saying?*

I don't know what I'm saying and how during my rambles, I got here. But I'm staring at his hands and they become fists under my scrutiny, his knuckles jutting out, and I can't stop myself from continuing, "I see them. Your hands. In my dreams. I see *you* in my dreams. I've been seeing you ever since you arrived at St. Mary's. Ever since I picked that stupid fight with you on the field. And you got so angry. You're always angry. In my dreams. You're always agitated and frowning and clenching your sexy jaw. And you're always taking my privileges away because you want to punish me for being bad. It makes me wonder what would happen if I pushed you too far. Would you do something drastic, something crazy? Would you put those hands on me? Your big, strong hands that could turn my pale skin all pink with one smack. All pink and pretty and painful. Because you're a thorn. And I'm a flower and... So yeah, you were right. My teenage brain is obsessed with you and that's my condition: you have to kiss me."

Everything that I've just said is the truth.

Every *little* thing.

Except one thing: I haven't only been dreaming about him since he arrived at St. Mary's. I've been doing it for eighteen months now.

And every time I dream about him, I wake up squirming and hot, my thighs buzzing with his name and my belly pulsing with an ache.

Even now I'm squirming.

My thighs are pressed so tightly together. My fists are sweating and my lips have parted to let the air into my lungs.

Which, in the very next moment, feel even more starved than before.

Because whatever distance he'd created between us, it's gone.

He destroys it.

He bulldozes through it with that big body of his and looms over me.

Not only that — God, *not only that* — but he reaches out and puts a hand on the dogwood tree, up above my head, and the other he settles by the side of my waist.

His gorgeous, dreamy hands.

"W-what are you doing?" I ask, my neck already craned up to look at him.

His eyes drop to my lips before glancing up. "Giving you what you want."

"What does that —"

"Where do I put them?" he rasps, speaking over me.

"What?"

"Where do I put my hands?" He licks his lips, flicking his eyes over my arched body. "On your body."

It jerks, my body. At his unexpected question.

At his crazy, *crazy* question.

"You're asking me about..." My breaths hitch and scatter. "About my d-dreams?"

"Tell me."

Oh God.

*God.*

He really is.

He really *is* asking me and I don't know what to do.

I wasn't expecting this.

Even though I was the one pushing him and provoking him, I wasn't expecting him to play along. I wasn't expecting him to actually put his hands on me.

Or rather around me.

His hands are on the dogwood but still it feels like he's touching me instead of the tree I'm stuck to.

It still feels like his hand up above my head is actually in my hair, fisting the strands, and the one by my side is really gripping my waist. My tiny, fragile waist.

And I think that's why everything seems hazy.

The very air seems drugged and my mouth opens on its own and spills out things I never imagined saying. "Uh, the other day I... I dreamed about you in your office. When you... When I asked if I could draw you and you came up to me and you put your hand here. On my arm."

I tilt my head and hitch my right shoulder to show him. To show which arm and he dutifully takes notice of it. He shifts his gaze away from my face and glances over to where I've pointed him before asking, "And then what?"

I swallow and clutch my skirt. "You tell me to stop talking and try to push me out of the door. But I..."

"But you don't go," he rasps.

"No."

"And you don't stop talking either."

"I don't. So you get fed up and you put your hand on my... n-neck," I whisper.

His eyes darken — I see it happen — before he lowers them and glances at my throat. "But my hand is too big. For your neck."

I swallow again. "It is."

Looking up, he says, "So I span it then. Your throat. I grab hold of it and I wrap my large fingers around your little swan neck, don't I?"

I jerk out a nod. "Yes."

"And then, I probably squeeze it too, yeah?" he says roughly, his jaw ticking. "I probably tighten my fingers around that little swan neck of yours until I feel your pulse leaping under my palm. Skittering. *Throbbing*."

"Why would you do that?"

He comes closer then.

Or rather, he hangs closer.

From the corner of my eye, I see his biceps bulging as he pushes against the tree and inches forward, toward me. "To warn you."

"About what?"

"About the fact that you're pushing it now," he almost bites out. "You're *really* fucking pushing it. You're right at the edge and so you should listen to me. You should heed my fucking fingers grabbing your fragile neck and you should shut the fuck up, Bronwyn."

"But I..." I shake my head slightly. "I don't think I listen even then."

His cheekbones have a flush on them now and I don't think it's the weather. I think it's me.

I'm doing that to him.

I'm coloring his skin like the artist I am and God, it's amazing.

He nods slowly. "Yeah, I was afraid of that. I was afraid that you wouldn't listen. Despite what's written in your file. Despite what you told me. That you're a good girl. That you keep your head down and you listen. But you don't, do you? You're trouble."

"Yes," I whisper. "I am. I'm trouble. I'm bad. But only for you."

"Only for me."

I crane my neck up even more at his voice then.

I arch my body in a tighter bow.

As if I'm seeking his guidance. As if I'm asking him to show me the way. "So what now?"

He takes in my tight-as-a-bowstring posture for a second before he says, "So now I've got no choice but to take drastic measures."

"Like what?"

The bulge of his biceps expands even more as he rasps, "I'll have to put my hands somewhere else now, won't I?"

"Where?"

His cheeks flush even more and his eyes now hold a deeper shade of blue. "I'm going to have to put my hands where my fingers can not only grab you but they can *really* fucking dig in and make you shake. Where my hand can make you jiggle and bounce and fucking dance. Tell me where that place is, Bronwyn. On your body."

I know.

I know where that place is.

I'm rubbing that place against the tree right now. I'm arching it up, almost bouncing it for him.

"My a-ass."

Satisfaction washes over his features, approval, and I bloom under it like a flower.

A sick, obsessed flower.

"Yeah," he rasps. "Your ass. And of course my hands are too big for your tight little ass too. So big that I can grab each globe in one hand and worry and grope that perky, bratty thing until it turns all pink. Can't I?"

"Yes."

His lips stretch up on one side, then in a mocking smirk, a first I've seen from him and so fucking amazing and sexy.

"And when I do all that, when I get my hands on your bouncy teenage ass and color it pink, it's going to hurt, isn't it?"

"Yes," I whisper, my ass dragging up and down the tree in a rhythm.

A rhythm that is so obvious to him.

So noticeable and visible.

"You know why that is, Bronwyn? Why it's going to fucking burn and sting when I touch you?"

"Why?"

He inches ever so closer then, his eyes boring into mine, his scent drugging my brain even more. "Because you're a flower. A wallflower. And every inch of you is soft. Every inch of you is fragile and velvet. And I'm a thorn. Every inch of me is sharp and hard. And fucking angry. Because you make it so. You *make* me angry. You make me so fucking angry, Bronwyn, you push me so fucking much that I'll spin you around, grab the back of your pretty little neck and pin you to that tree so you can't get away. And then I'll flip your pleated skirt up and smack that tight *fucking* ass so hard and so many times that your skin really will turn pink like in your goddamn dreams. As pink as your favorite pen. As pink as the roses you keep drawing on your thighs.

"As *pink*," he says with clenched teeth, "as your plump teenage mouth. That will ask me to stop. *You* will ask me to stop. You'll kick up a fuss, Bronwyn. You'll throw a tantrum, squirm under my hands and try to get away, trust me. You'll whine that I'm hurting you, that I'm being mean to you. And that you'll tell all your friends. You'll tell the principal even. About how Coach Thorne put his hands on you. About how cruel he is and how he made you cry. But I won't stop, will I? Because you need it. Because I bet no one has spanked that ass before. Your ass is a virgin, yeah? No one has taught you a fucking lesson and so now it's up to me. Now it's up to me to smack that tight ass and make it hurt and teach you the ways of the world. Teach you what happens when instead of keeping your fucking mouth shut, you push and you push and you make a man motherfucking lose it."

And I can't help but touch him then.

I can't help but put *my* hands on him, on his stomach that feels rock hard and ridged. Heated.

As heated as his eyes, as his sharp breaths.

"I'd never tell. I'd never ever tell anyone *anything*." I fist his hoodie. "I'd never ever say a word about what you do to me and how you punish me because I'm sorry, okay? I'm sorry. For making you mad. For pushing you and making you angry. But you make me angry too. You make me so mad. And you *do* hurt me. You do. By thinking that I'd ever tell. That I'd ever open my mouth and gossip about what I saw just because I'm a teenager. Just because I'm a student here, you think I'd ruin your reputation. And you're so sure of that that you're ready to let me draw you. You're ready to kiss me even. Even if you don't want to. You're —"

"You don't know what I want."

"What?"

He studies my agitated face for a second before replying, "You don't know me. You've got no clue what I want or don't want."

"But you want her, don't you?" I say, my breaths heaving, my fingers clutching his hoodie even more tightly as something sharp and hot pricks my heart.

Sharp as a thorn and hot as jealousy.

I am jealous.

So, so jealous. That he's in love with someone else. Another woman. An older, sophisticated, beautiful woman, while I'm an eighteen-year-old wanna-be artist with ink-stained clothes and dirty fingers.

"I saw you," I tell him, looking into his denim blue eyes. "A year ago. At the wedding party. At Helen's wedding party. I was there too. I know you don't remember any of that but y-you ran into me later that night and you..." I swallow. "You changed my life. You inspired me to go after my dreams. You're the reason I took a stand. I drew that graffiti on my dad's car but... that's not important. What's important is that I saw you. I *saw* how you looked at that party. So still and lifeless. So heartbroken. And God, I can't imagine the pain you must've gone through. The pain you must still feel at watching Helen be married to someone else. And neither do I know your story. I don't know what happened between you two. But what I saw yesterday and that note and... it's not right.

"There has to be another way. *Has* to be. Because if you do this, if you're *doing* this, if you're having an affair, then I *know* that no matter what, you won't be happy. Because you're not like that. Because it doesn't sit right with you. It can't. You're a good man. You're not like all the other men that I've known. You're different. You're special. You're a man who stops to help a strange girl on the side of the road. You're a man who listens to her life story. Who walks that girl back home and then changes her life. You're…"

"I'm what?"

I twist and twist his hoodie between my fingers and reply, "Someone's dream man."

My dream man.

## CHAPTER ELEVEN

The Original Thorn

"Did you talk to her?"

That's the first question she asks as soon as she arrives.

Helen.

She's late.

I've been waiting for her for the past fifteen minutes. And given that I was reluctant to come here, to this hotel bar, in the first place, I want to point it out to her.

I actually want to stand up and leave because I can imagine *why* she was late.

The only reason I don't though is because as soon as she takes a seat beside me, she grabs my hand. She turns her worried brown eyes up to me and asks about *her*. "Did it go all right? What did she say? Did she already tell someone?"

Bronwyn Littleton, my sister's best friend. The artist.

I free my hand from hers, wrap it around the tumbler of whiskey I'd ordered while waiting and take a large swallow. I'm not a big drinker by any means; being blessed with an alcoholic father has always curbed my urges, but I do indulge on occasion.

And this is one such occasion.

"No, she didn't," I reply.

"Are you sure?"

Turning away from her, I stare at the rows of colorful liquor bottles in front of me. "Yes."

"Okay. But is she going to?"

I clench my teeth. "No."

At last, Helen sighs beside me. "Thank God." She shakes her head, resting her elbows on the bar. "Jesus, I've been so worried."

My hand tightens around the glass. "I know."

I know she's been worried.

She's always been this way. Worried about her reputation, worried if someone saw us. If they know something.

If they're going to tell.

I guess being rich comes with a fuck-ton of paranoia.

Putting her delicate hand on my bicep, she says what she has said numerous times to me since yesterday. "I know you didn't think it was a big deal, Con. But it was. She's a student. A student under *me*. I'm her guidance counselor. But more than that, she's from my town. I used to *babysit* her. We know each other. Our families know each other."

Babysit.

Jesus Christ.

That's how young she is, isn't she?

So young that Helen used to *babysit* her.

My ex-*fucking*-girlfriend used to babysit the girl who saw us together yesterday.

I take another swallow — this one bigger than earlier —of the whiskey before saying, "Then you should've known. You should've known that she'd never say anything."

"But she's still a student. She's still young. And she could've easily drawn the wrong conclusion about what she saw and —"

"Wrong," I cut her off, glancing at her.

Her face warms at my interruption. "You know what I mean."

I sweep my eyes over that face, smooth skin and sleek cheekbones, before turning away. "She's different."

I'm not sure why I said that.

Where the compulsion came from to defend her. To defend a girl who has done nothing but provoke me, *aggravate* me, ever since I arrived at St. Mary's.

And it's not as if Helen is wrong: Bronwyn Littleton is a teenager.

She's still young and impulsive.

Far too impulsive for her own good.

*I want you to kiss me...*

"Even so, I'm glad she didn't say anything," Helen says, breaking my dark, agitated thoughts. "Although I'm still worried about tomorrow's session. It's going to be awkward and —"

"You're not going to say a word to her." I shut her down quickly, my hand on the tumbler tightening further.

"But —"

"Not one word," I command. "I told you I'd take care of it and I have. So just..." I sigh. "Let it the fuck go."

"And I thank you for that. Although I still don't understand why you were the one who wanted to talk to her. I could've just as easily done it myself. But anyway, thanks for taking care of it for me." She squeezes my bicep, smiling slightly. "For us."

"I didn't do it for you," I clip.

I didn't.

I didn't do it for her reputation and neither did I do it for mine.

I did it because if I hadn't, then Helen was going to.

In fact, she was ready to.

As soon as she realized that we'd been 'caught' by a student and who that student was, Helen wanted to run after her. She wanted to make absolutely sure that Bronwyn kept her mouth shut. That she never ever breathed a word of it to another human being. Especially to anyone at the school or back in their hometown.

Because if word were to get out that Miss Halsey, or rather *Mrs. Turner,* is meeting a colleague in secret, her reputation would be ruined. Her parents would likely disown her like they wanted to.

Back when we were dating.

But I couldn't allow that, Helen talking to her.

For some very strange reason, if anyone was going to talk to that *student*, it was going to be me. And no one else.

*I* would talk to her. *I* would handle it.

Perhaps because I knew that she'd already been upset because of what happened at the library. So upset that for the last three days, she hadn't come to her spot to draw. She hadn't sat under her tree and done the thing that most likely is the reason for her to get up in the morning in the first place: draw. And every time I caught sight of her around campus, she looked... devastated.

Because of me.

Despite being hardened against students' tantrums and excuses over the years, I have to admit that something has been feeling tight in my chest for the past three days. What I did was wrong. Things I said to her were mean and harsh and deliberately cruel. Designed to crush her and make her forget her infatuation with me.

And I wasn't going to add to her stress — or have her get more upset — by letting someone else handle this situation.

"Well, whatever reason you did it for," Helen says, "I'm glad you did it. Although I'm not sure if you've noticed, but I think she has a crush on you."

Her chuckle grates on my nerves and I signal the bartender for another tumbler of whiskey. "No, I haven't."

Her chuckle turns into a laugh, making me tighten my abdomen. "Before you go flying off the handle and taking more of her privileges because you're crazy that way, I want to say that it's only a schoolgirl crush and it will die down after a while. But it's cute."

The bartender places the drink in front of me and I'm saved from making a response as I gulp the whole thing down in one go.

Which is just as well.

What the fuck am I supposed to say here?

I know she's got a crush on me. That's the reason I was so harsh with her the other day. And I know — I *fucking know* — that it will die down after a while.

Only I'm not sure — for the hundredth fucking time — why the thought is making me want to break the glass in my hand and signal for another drink.

And that's the thing, isn't it?

That's the thing about Bronwyn Bailey Littleton.

For some reason, when it comes to her, I never know why I do the things that I do. Why I react the way I react.

And it pisses me off.

It makes me angry.

Like it did today, only an hour ago, under that goddamn tree. Where I crossed another line with her. The way I talked to her. The way I almost...

Put my hands on her.

What the fuck was I *thinking*?

She's a student. She's my sister's age. She's my sister's fucking best friend.

Something I still haven't been able to wrap my head around.

That the girl I met eighteen months ago is not only at St. Mary's, but also she's my little sister's best friend.

I know she thinks I don't remember her. But I do.

I *remember* her.

I remember her, sitting on the side of the road, all alone. I remember her wearing that yellow ball gown, bent over something, looking like a fucking mermaid.

Well, a flower.

A *wallflower*, apparently.

Which yes, I fucking Googled the other day. Along with French Impressionism.

Anyway, the point is that I remember her.

I remember her passion. How the mention of her art lit up her silver eyes and how in turn, those silver eyes lit up the entire dark street. I remember her drive, her desire, her dream.

It was rare.

Even though she was a teenager, still is, I couldn't help but admire it. I couldn't help but admire that she knew what she wanted even though she didn't know how to get it. And when I found out that she stood up for it, for her dream, I was... glad.

No, actually I was proud.

So fucking proud. Strangely.

And then I was furious. Because instead of cherishing that, her fight, instead of nurturing her drive and encouraging her, her parents — her goddamn, good-for-nothing parents — sent her here.

Rich people aren't really good for anything, are they?

But then it's not all their fault.

It's mine too apparently.

Because I was the one who *inspired* her. I was the one who tipped the scales, led her to insurrection against her dad, and so I'm responsible for her being here.

Me.

"You're going to break that glass," Helen yet again interrupts my furious thoughts. "What are you thinking so hard about?"

I loosen my fingers around the glass and put it aside. "I'm leaving."

At this, she grabs my arm. "But I just got here, Con. And I…"

"And you what?"

Her brown eyes turn pleading. "And we never got to finish our conversation. From yesterday."

Right.

The conversation.

"Well then, you better get to it," I say, keeping my voice casual. "Because you were already fifteen minutes late."

"I'm not —"

"Or maybe not. Because I think you got to the gist of it yesterday anyway."

Helen studies me. "Why are you being this way? Why are you making this so difficult? Why can't we be friends? All I want is to be friends with you, Con."

I clench my jaw. "We both know that you don't."

"Con, please."

"We both know that every time you text me, call me, ask me to meet you somewhere, you're not looking for a friend to go on coffee dates with." Leaning closer to her, I look down at her, her slim attractive body clad in a tight red dress. "If you were, you wouldn't be wearing that. It's for me, isn't it? Tell me what Seth said about you going out wearing this dress. Is that why you were fifteen minutes late? Because he wouldn't let you go?"

Her lips purse and her fist tightens on my arm. "If you must know, Seth wasn't home. He's working late tonight. And I was fifteen minutes late, Con, because I *was* trying out dresses for you. I was trying to look nice for you."

"Well, I'm flattered." I look her up and down again. "You went to a great deal of trouble for me. And you do look nice."

She does.

Helen has always looked nice.

Fucking phenomenal actually.

That was the first thing that attracted me to her. Back when I was seventeen and a horny teenager. And I'd seen her at the restaurant where I worked. She was there with her friends and I was the guy bussing tables.

I never thought that I could touch her.

She was far too shiny for the likes of me.

She was a rich princess from Wuthering Garden and I was a lowly commoner from Bardstown who did odd jobs to help out his mom with the bills and had a perfect striking record on the high school soccer team.

But I did.

I did touch her because for some reason, the princess wanted me to.

She wanted the commoner.

And like an idiot I thought I could have that. I could have the one shiny thing in my life.

"So why don't you stay for a while?" she asks. "We can have a nice dinner, talk about things. I miss you. I've missed you all these years. You were my first thought when I came back. You know that."

I do.

Because she contacted me when she came back. She called me up a year ago, out of the blue, to tell me that she was back from New York and that she was getting married. She was kind enough to invite me to her wedding as well.

I refused.

I had no plans of going to her wedding. I had no plans of seeing her at all.

She was my past — an intense but very short-lived relationship — and up until her call, I'd buried her. I'd put her in a cage somewhere deep down in my body, where I keep all my broken dreams.

Although I did end up going to that goddamn party. I did end up seeing her and she saw me too. But before she could come talk to me — and from the looks of it, she was going to — I left.

And I'm going to leave now as well.

"I don't think we have anything to talk about," I say, standing up from the bar stool. "Because you can pretend as much as you want, Helen, but we both know what you want from me, from *this*. Why you keep calling me and texting me and inviting me over to restaurants and your house when Seth's not home. We both know that if *anyone* had seen us together yesterday, a student, a teacher, or whoever the fuck, they would've drawn the right conclusion. They would've *concluded* that we're seeing each other behind your husband's back. Because that's what you want. You want me to fuck you behind your husband's back. And I've already told you I'm not going to."

With that, I go to leave. But she doesn't let me go.

In fact, she tightens her hold on the sleeve of my sweater. "If you want to be crass, Con, then fine. *Fine*. I do want you to fuck me. I do want that. And why is that so wrong? We have a history together, you and me. We were going to get married. You *promised* that you'd marry me. You promised that when we got to college, when we got to New York, we could be together. You were going to be this big soccer star and I was going to be your wife. But you left me. Like always. You *left* me. You broke your promise to me and ran back to your family at the first opportunity."

The pain in my neck, my shoulders, that's never far away, expands now.

I did do that.

I was the one to leave her.

I was the one to break up with her in the end and come back to Bardstown. When I promised her that I wouldn't.

I promised her that things would be different when we got to college. I told her that I would have more time for her.

Time.

That was always the point of contention between us.

I never had enough of it back then. With school, soccer practice, holding two jobs, taking care of my family. Helen somehow always took a back seat.

But when we both got into the same college in New York, I promised her that we would start our own life. That she'd be my priority. I'd have all the time in the world for her.

And she promised that we wouldn't have to hide. Which was *my* condition.

Because back then we had to. From her parents. From the people in her town. Because as I said, she was the princess and I was the commoner. But once I got on the path to becoming a pro soccer player, things were going to be different. Her parents, her posh society would accept me.

While I didn't care about being accepted, I did care about not having to hide.

But then my world went to pieces. My mother died. My siblings needed me and I had to come back.

I had to break my promise to her.

"I have made sacrifices for you, Con," she continues, her fingers tightening on my sweater. "I've waited for you. Because you promised me that things would be different when we got to college. You promised me that our life would start. But again, *yet* again, you chose your family over me. So you owe me this. You owe it to me to give me what I want now. You *owe* it to me to give me this relationship however I want it. On my terms."

"On your terms," I repeat, my jaw clenching.

"Yes." She nods. "You don't want to fuck me because I'm married, isn't it? That's your whole problem, correct? Because you have some kind of a moral code that you won't break. Because you're too good to do what other men do just like that. And it's not as if you don't want to. I know you want to. I know you want me. I *know* that. Why else would you still be single and alone?"

"Get to the fucking point."

"The point is, Con, that you expect me to always give things up for you. You've always expected me to wait for you, do things on *your* terms. But not anymore." She stands up too. "I'm not upending my life or putting it on hold for you like I did before. So if you want to come to me, you're doing it on *my* terms."

I hum. "Ultimatums, huh? You sure you want to do that. What if I call your bluff? Because I think you're the one who's doing all the wanting here. Why else would you be begging so pathetically and desperately?" Then I lean closer to her and whisper in her ear because she's right, "We do have a history together. And even though I'm not a fan of looking back, I have to say that I'm tempted. But not until you lose the husband."

At last, I get to leave.

And for some reason I hear her sweet, soft voice again.

*You're someone's dream man...*

# CHAPTER TWELVE

I stand at the door and wait.

I tell myself that it's okay. I've rehearsed what I'm going to say. *If* the topic comes up.

I'm going to say that it's none of my business.

Because it isn't.

It's not my business to know what they are doing. Or what happened between them in the past. Why they aren't together and why she married Seth.

Even though I've been able to think of nothing else but that ever since I saw them under the tree.

But it's their story and they don't have to tell me.

So yeah, that's exactly what I'm going to say if she brings it up at the meeting and that I'm never going to tell anyone. Like I told *him* yesterday.

With that thought, I raise my hand and knock at the door to alert her that I'm here and then wait for her customary, "Come in."

Instead of a *come in,* however, the door is snatched open and Helen stands there with a small smile.

A small *uncertain* smile.

And all I can think about as I look at her standing there is what I witnessed under that tree, and I have a feeling that all *she* can think about as she looks back at me is that I know.

I know her secret.

"Hi, come on in," she says, her voice soft, when we've stood there for what seems like an age.

I finally remember that I can speak *and* smile as well. "Hi. Thanks."

When I step inside, Helen closes the door behind me and walks back to her desk. "Have a seat."

I swallow and do as she says.

But instead of waiting for her to bring it up like I'd decided before this meeting, I bring it up myself. "I just want to say..." I swallow and Helen's eyes turn wary. "I'm not... I'm not going to say anything. So you don't have anything to worry about. I didn't know you were going to be there, at the spot, or I would've never —"

"I know." She speaks over me. "I know that, Bronwyn. Of course, I know that you didn't know. It's not your fault that... you stumbled upon us. I'm so sorry you were put in that position. And he told me. Con said that you wouldn't."

Con.

How amazing it is that she gets to say his name with little to no thought. And how unfair that when I hear it, my body buzzes in secret.

My decorated body.

After he apologized to me about what happened in the library, like a sick fool, I wrote his name again. But not just on my thighs, I wrote his name on every hidden part of my body: my lower belly, my ribs, the valley between my breasts, around my ankles.

I wrote and wrote and *wrote* his name like a girl possessed. Maybe because I hadn't in three days and so I was making up for all that lost time.

And I dreamed about him too.

Like I do almost every night, and I woke up all hot and throbbing between my legs.

But I can't dwell on it right now. Not here.

Not in front of *her*.

Taking a deep breath, I nod. "I would never."

Helen puts her hands on the desk and leans forward. "Thank you. For saying that. I really appreciate it. It's just that... too much is at stake here. For me. And I'm not willing to risk it. And so I..." She sighs and looks me in the eyes. "Even though Con has assured me that the matter's settled, I really want you to understand that you can't say anything, Bronwyn. You can't breathe a word of this to anyone. Not to your friends, or someone from back home. Promise me, please."

I read the urgency in her tone, on her face, and lean forward myself. "I promise. Of course I promise. I would never do that to you."

She studies my face for a few beats. "Good. That's good. Because I could lose everything, Bronwyn. Everything. My marriage. My family. My reputation, and I... I consider you a friend. Even though you're young, a lot younger than me, you're one of my very best friends here at St. Mary's. Other teachers don't like me very much because I'm from Wuthering Garden. My family's rich. But you understand these things. You're my best student. So I just hope you understand how devastating it would be for me if you were to ever say something."

My heart twists for her.

I've always felt that, back in Wuthering Garden. That I was an outsider.

When my classmates wouldn't include me in things. When they would look at me like I was different just because I liked art. So I get her.

I totally get her and I vehemently say, "I won't. Not in a million years. It's not my place."

She smiles with relief. "Thank you, Bronwyn. Truly. You have no idea how happy it makes me."

And that's when I make the decision.

To help her.

Them.

Somehow.

It's laughable really. That I could do anything to help them, but maybe, just *maybe* I can and so they won't have to hide like this. So they won't have to sneak around.

*He* won't have to.

Because I meant what I said to him yesterday: that if he's doing this, if he's having an affair, he won't be happy. He can't be. He's not that kind of man.

"May I..." I begin hesitantly. "May I ask what happened? Between you two." Her features turn wary again and I hasten to explain, "I don't mean to pry. I just... I want to understand. I want to... I could see that you guys have a history. I could see that. You guys had something intense and heart-wrenching and if there's a way I can help, I don't know. I just... would like to."

At the end of my broken explanation, she smiles almost indulgently, and my cheeks feel warm. She settles back in her chair and says, "I can see why you'd like to know. What you saw most likely confused you. I'm married and I was meeting this strange man who's not my husband in secret. So you're curious. I understand that." She nods. "If I'm asking you to keep a secret, it's only fair that I tell you all about it. So yes, I will."

I fist my hands in my skirt and nod.

"I met him when I was seventeen," she begins. "I was in my senior year of high school. We didn't go to the same school, of course. I went to that horrible boarding school that your parents wanted to send you to. But I met him when I was on vacation. I was at this restaurant with some of my girlfriends and he was this very handsome bus boy. We kept watching him, you know? He was tall, muscular and he had the bluest eyes that we'd ever seen and... he was just magnificent. And well, he was watching us too. Or rather me. I didn't know that until I went back to the restaurant a few more times just to catch a glimpse of him." She chuckles self-consciously. "I was so obsessed with him. Even though I knew that my parents would never approve. They wanted me to get together with this other guy that they liked. I hated him though. But yeah, I just... I was crazy for Con."

She takes a pause here, her eyes glued to something over my shoulders, as if looking into the past.

The past that is my present.

Because I feel the same way.

I feel crazy too. I feel obsessed, possessed. Hypnotized by him.

"Anyway," she begins again. "We started dating. Although I don't think you could even call it that really. We were long distance because of my boarding school and so most of the time all we did was just... talk on the phone and stuff. And when I did visit, even then it would be super hard for us to get some time together. And it always had to do with his schedule. His schedule was crazy. His school, work, his soccer practice, his family. It was frustrating. So freaking frustrating because he had other priorities. Other things took precedence for him over me. And so we always kept fighting, arguing with each other.

"But still there was hope. That one day he'd get to leave his town, his family, and be his own man. He'd have time for me then. I'd be his priority. And everyone knew that he was going to go pro one day and I knew when that happened, my parents would accept him. And for a little while, it did look like our life was getting on track. We applied and got into the same college. He got a soccer scholarship. There was talk of scouts already lining up to see him play.

"But then, only a couple of months into our first semester in college, his mom died; she had cancer. And he decided to move back to take care of stuff. His siblings. And..." She shakes her head, breathing sharply. "And I didn't want him to move back. I wanted him to choose me. For once. Just choose me, choose our future together. Choose his career, our love. We'd worked so hard to be together. We'd gone through so much, and yes, I was selfish. I wanted him for myself. I gave him an ultimatum. I told him that if he chose his family over me again, it was over. I wouldn't wait for him. And he didn't care." She laughs sadly. "He left anyway. He chose his family over me. He said he wouldn't even dream of making me wait. He said that his family was everything and if he didn't go back, then he wouldn't be the man that I fell in love with. And I was so angry at him. So angry that I didn't stop him."

Callie told me about their mom's cancer. That Conrad had been the one taking care of their mom and he hadn't even wanted to go to college in the first place. But their mom insisted and so he went.

"B-but his mom had just died," I say, stumbling. "He had to go back."

"Yes," Helen says. "But he didn't have to stay there. He didn't have to abandon everything. His career, his place in the pros. He didn't have to abandon everything that he ever worked for. He didn't have to abandon *me*. I was so alone in a new city, without the guy who promised to be there for me. But he did. He gave all that up. All of it. And now he's stuck being a soccer coach. He ruined his own life."

For his family.

He did that for his *family*.

For his brothers and Callie, and he did it all alone, didn't he?

He did it all by himself. He could've had someone, her, the woman he loved — that he still loves from the looks of it — by his side but...

"So you didn't go with him?" I ask again, but I'm not sure why since I already know the answer. "You let him... You let him go alone."

That irritates her, my question, and it shows on her frowning face and in her tone. "Yes, Bronwyn, I let him go. I'm the bad guy here. I'm selfish. You can think whatever you want but I wasn't going to drag myself down with him. I wasn't going to be foolish like him and destroy everything, including my family, when he was choosing *his* over me."

But who chose *him*?

If he was choosing everyone, if he was taking care of everyone, then who picked him?

Who took care of him?

I'm not sure how I'm even sitting up straight when every part of my body is trembling and shivering and shaking. When pain attacks my chest and my belly in waves.

When all I want to do is run out of this room and find him.

When all I want to do is hug him and tell him that...

That I choose him.

I do.

Even though I know it doesn't matter that I do. Even though he wouldn't care.

But still.

"But anyway, a few years later, my parents introduced me to Seth," she continues. "And we fell in love. We got married. But when I moved back, I... I contacted Con. I invited him to my wedding. I don't know why I did that. Maybe because he was my first love. He was the man I was going to marry one day but didn't. He was the one who got away. He was the guy who left me. And I just... when I came back I realized that I still have feelings for him. Those feelings I had for him just never went away."

"You should tell him," I blurt out.

She frowns at me. "Tell who what?"

"Seth," I explain. "I mean, there's no way that this could be easy for you. But you need to tell Seth that you love Conr — Coach Thorne — and that you want to be with him."

Yes.

Exactly.

This is what she should do. Especially when she has feelings for Conrad.

Maybe she didn't choose him before, when his mom died and he had to leave everything behind and choose his family over his own wishes — and God, just the thought of it, of him going through the loss of a relationship along with his mother makes me want to start sobbing — but she can do it now.

She can choose him now.

Can't she?

"What?"

"I know it will break his heart. Seth's," I tell her, my mind racing with all the possibilities. "I've seen you two together. He's completely in love with you. But this is worse, isn't it? Letting him think that you love him back when you love someone else, and even though it might not mean much, but I will be there for you. I will support you —"

"But I do love Seth," Helen cuts me off.

Now it's my turn to be confused. "What?"

"I do," she replies. "I do love my husband."

"But you just said..." I shake my head, even more confused now. "You just said that when you came back, you realized that you still love Coach Thorne."

Helen regards me with something I don't understand. "Yes, but I'm not going to leave my husband for him."

"But I don't..."

Sighing, she sits back. "You're young, Bronwyn. You're idealistic. But you're still from Wuthering Garden. You still know how our town is. How divorces are viewed. I can't just leave Seth. He handles my father's business. Our families are business partners."

"No, I understand. It's going to be so difficult. But I think –"

"I'm not going to ruin everything just because I have feelings for my ex-boyfriend."

My hands are fisted in my lap and there's a tightness in my chest as I'm trying to make sense of everything she's telling me. "So you're staying with Seth then?"

"Look," she begins, irritated, even more so than before. "Even if I leave Seth for Con, there's no future here. My parents would never agree to me being with Con. His pro days are over. He's stuck here, in this town. In this job. He chose his path years ago and I can't walk on that path with him. I can't marry a nobody. I can't do this to my parents. I need to use my head."

I think I get it.

I think I finally understand everything.

Up until now I thought that there was no choice. That they *had* to do this.

They had to meet in secret, had to sneak around, had to carry on their relationship in private because they loved each other so much. Because they were compelled at the hands of love.

But now I think I was wrong.

I was wrong because they do have a choice.

Helen *does* have a choice.

"So you're saying that you want both of them," I state at last, my heart pounding painfully in my chest. "Your husband *and* your ex-boyfriend."

She scoffs at my tone, which she follows with a mocking laugh. "Are you judging me?" Another laugh. "God, you're so young. Anyway, I don't expect you to understand this right now, Bronwyn. Maybe one day when you've grown up enough, you might be able to see where I'm coming from. In fact I'm pretty sure that you'll be in the same position as me. You don't think you're above me or anyone else from our town, do you?" She runs her eyes over me. "I know you've always had difficulty blending in. With your art and things. And I personally subscribe to the notion that you should do what you want, but you can't be that naive. You can't think that given the same situation, you wouldn't do the same thing as me."

Would I?

Would I do the same thing as Helen?

Leave the man I love when he needs me the most.

Maybe I *am* young and I *am* naive but I don't think I could do that. I don't think I could leave the man I loved. Not for anything. Not for my town. Not for my parents. Not for the one thing I've always loved: art.

If I loved a man, I would choose him over everything.

I would choose him over myself.

I'm not sure what that makes me. Definitely not above anyone else from my town or otherwise. It probably makes me a fool. Maybe even pathetic, because you can't live your life based on your heart.

But it's okay.

I'll be a fool and I'll be pathetic but I don't think I could ever leave the man I loved.

"Besides, all of this is moot anyway," she says after a few moments.

"Why?"

"Because it's over." Then, "Not that it ever began, but still."

I swallow, my heart thudding in my chest, louder and hungrier than before.

"Between you and… Conrad."

I let his name slip. Deliberately.

To humanize him. To make him even more real in her eyes.

Just so she would stop plunging the knife in his heart. In *my* heart.

"Yes," she says in a cutting voice. "Apparently, he's like you. Idealistic and foolish. So no matter how many times I call him or text him or *beg* him to be with me, he won't. And I know he wants to. I can see that he still has feelings for me. It's obvious, but still this time around, he's choosing his useless principles over me. Never me."

I knew it.

I *knew* it.

I knew he wouldn't do it. I knew that he would never do something like this.

And God, I'm so relieved. I'm so fucking glad that he made the right choice that it takes me a second to realize something.

Something awful that makes me bite my lip and fist my hands really hard.

"So he's…" I whisper, "still alone?"

Because if he chose his principles over the woman he loves, then he's still alone, isn't he?

As alone as he was at that wedding party.

As alone as he must've been when they broke up years ago.

As alone as… ever.

Helen scoffs. "Conrad Thorne is alone because that's his own choice. I've given him chances over chances. You can't help someone if they don't want to be helped. So I don't think you need to worry about him. He can handle himself."

# CHAPTER THIRTEEN

At St. Mary's, we have a ritual.

Every Friday, at midnight, my girls — Poe, Salem and Callie — and I sneak out of the dorms and go to this bar, Ballad of the Bards, in Bardstown. To hang out, dance and just generally have fun.

Well, not Callie anymore because she moved out a few weeks ago.

And also recently, not me either.

I haven't been to the bar in a few weeks. Four to be exact — well more than that, almost six weeks, if you count the Christmas and New Year's break, but still.

Because for the last however many weeks my outing privileges have been suspended.

Which means I couldn't go off campus.

Not that sneaking out in the middle of the night is a St. Mary's sanctioned outing, or that anyone would've known if I had chosen to go out.

But still I chose to remain in my room.

Because he wanted me to.

He was the one who took my privileges away and I didn't want to disobey him.

I know it's kind of silly but I haven't been able to bring myself to go, much to both Salem's and Poe's chagrin. But that self-imposed restriction lifts tonight because the winter break is over and I officially have my privileges back.

And so the first destination is Bardstown.

*His* town.

I've been here before, of course. To this bar, obviously, along with various stores and restaurants with Callie and my other girls over the past year, but I never knew that I was in his town.

Like he was in mine back then. The night I met him.

So this is special.

Tonight is special.

"I think I'll dance."

I've shocked my friends with my declaration.

Even though this is a dance bar — a very unusual kind because instead of dance music, they play music with violins and bass and lyrics that speak of lost and tragic love, hence the name '*Ballad*' of the Bards — I don't usually dance. I usually bring my sketchpad, sit in a corner and draw while Salem and Callie, both dancers, enjoy the music and Poe, strictly *not* a dancer because her boobs hit her face every time she does, flirts with guys and tries to sneak drinks past the bartender.

Salem blinks at me. "You'll dance?"

I nod, watching the crowd slowly swaying on the dance floor and feeling the urge to do the same myself. "Yup."

"But you never dance." That's Poe.

I shrug. "I know. But I want to."

Salem and Poe look at each other first before glancing at me warily. Then Salem bursts out, "Oh my God." She turns to Poe. "She doesn't have her sketchpad."

Poe glances down at my hands and gasps. "Oh God, yes. How did I not notice this before? Where's your sketchpad?"

"Back in my room." I don't give them a chance to protest anymore and take off my parka — magenta, with yellow flowers that I've painted on it myself — throw it on the high table we're standing at and grab Salem's arm. "Are we dancing or not?"

And then I drag her onto the dance floor.

Because again, tonight is special.

Not only because I'm in his town while *knowing* I'm in his town, but also because for the first time ever, I have an urge to feel these sad songs.

I have an urge to live in them.

Callie and Salem are huge fans of this music and they've always talked about their love for sad songs. Probably because they've both felt heartbreak and longing.

I never understood it though.

Not until *he* came to St. Mary's.

Not until I realized that he's felt it too. He's felt the heartbreak, the longing.

He's felt the loneliness.

So I want to feel it too.

I want to feel *his* pain.

I want to feel these thorny, stinging emotions. I want to steal them from him, absorb them into my skin that he thinks is velvet and my body that he thinks is fragile and small.

And color myself all pink for him.

So I close my eyes and take a deep breath.

I try to feel the woman's raspy voice and her words of a tragic love. Before I raise my arms and push my fingers through my light brown tresses, loose and long.

I slowly sway my hips and bend my knees.

Before I drop down on the ground and part my thighs.

And as I come up, I'm flowing with the music. I'm flowing with her words. I'm flowing with his pain.

I'm flowing with him.

So much so that I feel a sting behind my eyes. I feel the tears. They fall down my cheeks, hot and sad, and I let them.

I let them make my cheeks wet for him. I let myself cry for him. I let myself hurt as I throw my head back and gyrate my hips.

Until someone grabs my arm and my heart jumps in fright.

I pop my eyes open; it's Salem, who leans over and whispers in my ear, "He's here."

I blink at her. "What?"

"The guy you were dancing for." She throws me a grave look before adding, "*And* crying for."

My eyes widen when I understand her meaning. "Conrad?"

Her smile is tiny and kind of sad. "I knew it. I *knew* something was going on with you and him." She looks behind me. "Okay, we don't have much time. But we're gonna talk about this later." She gives me a quick hug then. "Good luck."

With that she leaves and I spin around.

And there he is.

At the edge of the dance floor.

Taller than everyone. And so easily noticeable.

Even though the space is dark with only meager lighting, he's easy to make out. He's so easy to stop and make way for.

Because that's what people are doing.

They're stopping mid-dance to look up at him, to part and build a clear path for him.

I think it's his eyes. That are making them do that.

They are glittering in the dark. Shining with something that can only be described as predatory. And dominating.

Or it could be his shoulders, so wide and straight that people and obstacles have no choice but to move out of his way. Because he seems unstoppable.

He looks like a force to be reckoned with.

A force that won't stop until it gets where it wants to go.

To me.

And I can't help but brace myself for the impact.

I can't help but welcome it with heaving breaths and my soft, receptive body. And when he does get here, I tilt up my neck to look at his sharp, beautiful features. "Hi."

He sweeps his shiny eyes over my face for a second and clenches his jaw.

Then, "Follow me."

## CHAPTER FOURTEEN

He's staring at me.

He's *been* staring at me for the past thirty seconds.

Give or take, I mean.

Not that I mind really, because I'm staring at him back. This is the first time I'm seeing him after the break. Actually, I wasn't expecting to see him until Monday, when school actually starts, but still; even though we hate St. Mary's – except me – we usually come back to campus earlier since most of my girls want to stay home as less as possible.

Anyway, when he said to follow him, I did.

Of course I did, and now we're in a room at the back of the bar. It's a small office-like space with a desk, a leather couch and a dresser set by the wall.

I'm by the dresser and he's still by the door.

In fact he's blocking the door.

Like he did back at his office.

He's leaning against it, his arms folded across his chest and his thighs almost sprawled.

And since the space is empty except for the two of us and is extremely well lit, I notice, for the first time ever, that his clothes are different.

Except for that one time last year when I saw him in a suit, I've only ever seen him in coach-ly things: workout t-shirts and pants, hoodies.

But tonight he's wearing jeans.

Navy blue like his eyes, and a dark gray sweater with sleeves pushed up to his elbows and exposing his strong arms, dusted with dark hairs. But the thing that has my full attention is the white shirt that he has on underneath.

I can only see the collar — straight and starched — peeking out from under the rounded neck of the sweater.

But that's enough.

That's enough to make him look so... *mature*.

So authoritative and older.

Good and responsible.

And so I can't take it anymore.

I can't take this heavy silence.

Clenching my thighs together where his name is buzzing, I say, "H-how was your break?"

He was in the process of looking me over, going from the top of my head to the bottom of my feet.

Because, well, *my* clothes are different too.

Except for that one time that he saw me in a ball gown — which he doesn't remember; though I did remind him of that night under that tree, before break — he's only seen me in my school uniform. This is the first time that he's seeing me in something that I actually love wearing: a pink, maxi-length dress.

It's sleeveless, with a V neck and an uneven thready hem. And purple flowers that are scattered all over. That I, myself, have painted on, like I did with my parka.

But that's not all.

I'm wearing other things too.

And before I distracted him with my words, he had his eyes on one such thing.

My arm bracelet. Silver with trailing, tinkling chains.

"I like your sweater," I say when he doesn't respond to my friendly question. "Callie's Christmas present, right? I know. She was knitting it at school." Then because he still doesn't choose to say anything and keeps staring at me, I go on, "Remember that white hat that I always have on? She made that too. Also the sweater. That pink one."

Nothing.

He doesn't respond to that either so I have to continue, swallowing first. "I like jewelry. Lots of it." I shrug and when I do, there's a tinkling produced by the two necklaces that I'm wearing and my arm bracelets. Plus the other three bracelets around my wrists. "As you can see. And hear. And since we're not allowed to wear jewelry at school, I tend to go all out when I can."

I do.

Plus my mom doesn't like my taste in jewelry very much and the fact that I get it from thrift stores mostly, so that's another incentive to wear a lot of it when I can. Especially during my outings from St. Mary's.

Since he's still choosing to hold his silence, I don't stop talking. "And of course, drawing on my body."

Because that's the other thing he was staring at before I started talking.

The flowers around my elbows and shoulders.

I have other art on my body as well, under my clothes. Like his name.

Which thank God he can't see right now.

"I'm into self-decorating. And I know what you're thinking. You're —"

"You do?" he says at last.

My lips part at his voice.

Low and deep as ever.

My favorite.

"Yes," I reply.

He tilts his head to the side. "So what is it? What am I thinking," he pauses before adding, "Bronwyn."

He does that, doesn't he?

Takes a pause before saying my name.

I'm not sure why. Maybe to intimidate me.

But it only makes me want to hear my name from him even more.

"Uh, you're thinking that if she's into self-decorating, then why not tattoos? But the thing about tattoos is that they're permanent. I mean, when you're not getting a temporary one. But I like to think of my body as my canvas. So I love drawing things. On it."

His features change during my explanation.

His eyes get darker. His jaw gets harsher, and even though I don't know what it means, the pulsing in my thighs — and between them — gets more intense too.

That ticking pulse skips a beat when he slowly shakes his head in response. "Try again."

And again I clench my thighs, staring at his set-in-stone features. "Uh, you're thinking" — I lick my lips — "what am I doing here. At this bar."

His shining eyes narrow. "Bingo."

Shit.

Damn it.

It's not as if I didn't know that he was thinking that.

Of course I knew.

Because before anything else, he's my teacher. My coach.

And he's caught me again.

This time while breaking curfew.

But I was so happy to see him after such a long time and I... I just didn't want to bring St. Mary's between us. But it's always going to be between us, isn't it? So I fist my hands and steel my spine to explain my presence at this bar, at this time of night.

"Yes, about that. It's... I know it's strictly against the rules. Like, way outside of the rule book. But please, *please*, don't punish my friends. They already don't have very many privileges and I promise — I *do* — that after this, I won't let them break any other rule. You can count on me."

"I can count on you."

"Yes, you can." Grimacing and sighing, I continue, "I realize that my word doesn't mean a whole lot right now. Given everything that has happened and everything that I have done. But I promise. I really, really do. Please."

He studies me for a few beats, my pleading eyes, my parted lips, before saying, "And what about you? Are you going to break any more rules?"

"No, of course not. Me neither." I press a hand to my chest. "I won't break another rule, I promise. But I understand that I've already broken this one, so if you want to punish someone, punish me. You can take away my privileges again. Outing, computer, TV, whatever you want. You can punish me however you like. Just please don't... do anything to my friends."

He waits a moment to respond.

He uses it, that moment, to run his eyes all over me again.

"I can punish you however I like," he repeats my words but in a rougher, lower tone.

And I can't help but think about that day under the tree.

About all the ways he said he'd punish me and all the ways I'd tell him to stop.

So much so that along with my thighs and the place between them, I feel the throb in my ass as well. I feel the burn and I step back to press it against that dresser. His eyes turn even darker at my action and I whisper, "Yes. However you like."

His nostrils flare at this. And his chest expands as he says, ignoring my invitation, "Who taught you to dance like that?"

"What?"

He jerks his chin at me. "Out there. On the dance floor. Who taught you to move your ass like that?"

Oh.

That's extremely random.

But I reply anyway. "No one really. But um, my mom sent me to dance classes my freshman year. Although it was a total disaster."

"Why?"

"Because I wasn't interested in it. I was going through my oil painting phase back then. You know, before I settled on something less complicated like watercolors, because watercolors are more..." I stop rambling when he narrows his eyes and get back on track. "But anyway, I used to always have like, a book open before practice, or I'd be watching tutorials online. I'd be totally distracted. I'd miss steps or do the wrong ones. The number of times André had to come over and correct my posture was," I sigh, "not funny. I was his worst student ever."

I was.

Like I'm *his* worst student. Player. Whatever.

I think I'm just bad at everything else in this world except... art.

"André," he clips, somehow even angrier than before.

"Yes."

"So he's responsible for this."

I frown. "Responsible for what?"

"For you" — he dips his chin, his eyes boring into mine — "dancing like a stripper."

"What?"

"Tell me something. Did this *André* also tip you? For shaking that ass. Slip you a twenty dollar bill every time he came to correct your goddamn posture? So very many times, according to you, that it's not fucking funny."

I draw back at this, at the venom in his voice. "You're... That's —"

"No actually, what I'd like to know is why *is it*, that men are always sniffing around you, and you're the last person in this whole goddamn world to know about it." He leans forward then, his teeth clenched. "Why is it that assholes like your dance teacher and your fucking art teacher, Mr. Pierre, and whoever the fuck Robbie was, are always salivating like dogs over your tiny *self-decorated* body and you never have a clue? What I'd like to know, *Bronwyn*, is what the fuck goes on in that bubblegum pink brain of yours?"

"You're insane," I say with a screeching voice. "Mr. Pierre is..."

I trail off.

Because... Because how does he know about Mr. Pierre? How does he know the name *Robbie*? How does...

And then something drops inside my body.

Something heavy and warm and liquid that makes me part my lips. It makes me press my thighs together and curl my toes.

"You remember," I breathe out. "You *remember* that night. You remember..."

Me.

He keeps watching me, his eyes dark and intense. "You."

I jerk out a nod, wordlessly.

"I do, yeah," he rumbles. "I remember you."

"B-because I reminded you?" I ask. "The other day."

"No." He shakes his head. "Because I never forgot."

And then I'm glad I'm standing stuck to a dresser because I know if I wasn't, I would've lost my footing.

I would've fallen down to my knees because they're trembling.

They're trembling so badly.

As badly as my heart.

As *badly* as all the places where his name is written on my self-decorated body.

In fact, all those places *hurt*.

They hurt with the intensity of my shivers. With all these thorns that I've drawn in his honor pricking at my skin. "You never forgot."

"No," he says, his voice thick. "I didn't forget a girl I met on the side of the road. I didn't forget that she was sitting all alone on the curb in the middle of the night. And that she was drawing roses on her thighs. I didn't forget any of that. I never did."

I open my mouth to say something when I run the words he just said through my mind.

The same words he said under that tree. The same words I've been hearing over and over in my dreams: *as pink as the roses you keep drawing on your thighs.*

"You saw that," I say, my eyes wide. "You saw that I was drawing roses on my thighs that night."

"I did."

I lick my dried lips. "But I hid them. I covered them with my dress as soon as I heard your footsteps."

"Not fast enough, no."

Like I wasn't fast enough the day he saw me sketching his eyes. And then I remember something else. Something that he'd said, at the library, referring to my dad.

*He made you cry...*

"You also saw that I was crying."

That makes him clench his jaw. "Yes."

I bow my head because suddenly it seems too heavy for my neck to hold up. Suddenly I feel so many emotions that my whole body feels too small to hold them.

There were so many clues.

So many hints, but I never picked them up.

But then why didn't he say anything?

Why didn't he tell me before?

I want to ask those questions of him, but he speaks and I look up. "I also remember that you were supposed to go to a posh boarding school. Where every rich kid went."

"Yes," I say, staring into his denim blue eyes.

"But you're here. At St. Mary's instead."

"Yes, because I drew —"

"Because of me," he says, speaking over me. "Because of *me* you did the thing that you did and ended up here. At a prison-like school. With barred windows and brick walls. At a school with a million bullshit rules and a fucking privilege system. Which I took away from you, by the way. I was the cause for all this. For you ending up at a reform school in the middle of fucking nowhere because you ran into me one night. Because I *inspired* you." He scoffs. "I've hated the fact that my sister goes here. I've *hated* the guy who was responsible for that. But turns out I'm exactly like that motherfucker, aren't I? Because I'm responsible for sending my sister's best friend to this hellhole."

I get myself unglued from the dresser as soon as he finishes.

Actually I was already unglued way before he finished talking. I'm now a quarter of the way across to him. And in the next couple of seconds, I make the whole journey.

I reach him and stand so close that I can feel his heat, smell his spicy sweet scent.

My thorn.

So close that I have to tilt my head way back to look up at him, into his angry, regret-filled eyes. "You did inspire me. I was ready to give it all up. I was ready to go to that boarding school. I was ready to do everything that my parents wanted me to do. I was ready to break all my dreams because no one understood them. No one supported them. But you told me not to. You told me to be what I wanted to be. It's not your fault that I chose to make such a big show out of it, though. I could've been subtler. I could've been —"

His head is bent way down too so he can look into my wide and what I hope are grateful eyes as he cuts me off. "Were your parents *subtle* about their objection to your art?"

I swallow, shaking my head. "Not really. But —"

"So then as I told you before, what you did was right," he says, boring his eyes into mine. "What you did was fucking justified."

Warmth floods my chest at these words.

At his anger on my behalf.

"See? You're the only one who's ever been angry on my behalf," I tell him, so happy that I finally get to tell him how wonderful he is. "The only one who's ever been so proud of me for doing what I did. Except for my friends here. Whom I met *because* I came here. To St. Mary's. I know this place has a lot of rules, but I love it here. For the first time ever, I have friends. I never had friends, back in my town. No one even *wanted* to be my friend. I was never invited to any parties. I was never invited to sit with anyone at lunch even. People moved away from me at school because I was always untidy and my fingers were always dirty and ink-stained from all the drawing and sketching.

"But look." I show him my dirty hands, looking at them myself. "Here I can draw and no one cares. Everyone knows that I'm Wyn, the artist, and they all accept me for who I am."

I glance up at him to find that all this time he was looking down at me and not at my hands. "I can't do that back home anymore. I can't draw. I'm not allowed to after what I did with my dad's car. Which I completely get. They think I'm dangerous with all the paints and stuff. But do you understand what I'm saying to you? I can be myself here. I belong here. I have a *best friend* here. *Three* best friends. And it's all because I ran into you one night."

He keeps looking down at me with the same angry sort of look and I keep my smile in place.

To melt that frown between his brows.

To show him that I'm really, truly happy and it's all because of him.

"You're not *allowed* to draw back home."

"I'm —"

He shakes his head, his eyes narrowed. "Your fucking parents don't quit being pieces of shit, do they? Well, maybe I should give them a reason to —"

I put a stop to it this very second.

By reaching up and placing a hand on his mouth.

Holy fuck.

I'm touching his mouth.

I'm touching his very warm and soft and plush mouth.

Such an anomaly on his otherwise all hard and sharp face.

But I ignore all that.

I ignore his flashing blue eyes even as I say, "That's all you got from that? I said all those wonderful, *true* things but you picked up the wrong thing to listen to. And no, you're not doing anything to my parents. My dad's the DA, okay? He can do things to you. So don't even joke about it. The moral of the story is that you're wonderful, period. And I love St. Mary's, and I never would've gone here if not for that night. If not for you."

My hand still covers his mouth and maybe that's why his eyes look so pretty and so dangerous.

Maybe that's why they feel like the center of my world in this moment. And so when something passes through them, a dark sort of amusement, I feel it in my belly.

I feel it all over my skin and I take my hand off his mouth as if electrocuted.

"I'm wonderful," he says, staring down at me.

I fist the hand by my side, the one with which I touched his lips. "Yes."

*You're also my thorn.*

His jaw clenches as if he heard me. "Then you're crazier than I thought."

*And also your flower.*

His jaw clenches again as if he heard that too before saying, "And I can do things to your dad too. The kind where he'd be limping for the rest of his life. So you don't need to worry about me."

My skin breaks out in goosebumps at his confidence.

Arrogance.

The sheer masculinity.

Swallowing, I ask, "Why didn't you say anything?"

He knows what I'm talking about.

He knows I'm asking him about pretending to forget when he never did.

"Because it doesn't matter."

"What?"

His features rearrange themselves in his usual blank, cool look as he explains, "It doesn't matter that we met one night and I walked you back home. What matters is that I'm your coach and you're a student at St. Mary's."

Damn it.

Again.

Again he brought St. Mary's between us when I was happy to have forgotten its existence. I love that place — I do — but I'm really starting to hate it.

I'm really starting to hate how he creates this distance between us.

This professional, respectable, *appropriate* distance.

But I'm not going to let him do that anymore. I'm not going to let him create any sort of distance between us.

"I don't care about that. I don't care that you're my coach," I say vehemently. "Because you're not just my coach, are you? You're the man who changed my life and I know you."

When his eyes narrow, I continue in a determined voice, "Yes, I do. I know all the things that I wanted to know back then. That night. Things you never told me. I know the sister you were talking about back then, because of whom you stopped to check on me. That sister is Callie. I know you have three other siblings, three brothers, all younger than you. I know the town you live in. I'm *in* your town. And I know what your name is and what people call you."

His jaw clenches at my last statement.

A little throwback of his own words, the ones he said to me at the library the day he so thoroughly crushed my heart.

Because he wanted to push me away.

I'm not letting him do that anymore though. Not again.

So I keep going. "You kept it from me. That night. Didn't you? You didn't tell me your name. You didn't tell me anything about you. Maybe you wanted to keep a distance between us, but guess what, I don't care. And I *know* now. I know everything. " I take a deep breath and just say it, "I know that you're not having an affair with her. I *know* that."

My information jars him.

It makes his chest undulate with a sharp breath. It even makes him shift on his feet as he bites out, "She *talked*."

And since I'm not letting him get away anymore, I put my hands on him.

I place my hands on his forearms and clutch them. "And I know that you were right."

"Right about what?"

"That I'm just a teenager."

His brows snap together. "What?"

And I can't hold it in anymore.

All these things that I've been thinking ever since my meeting with Helen before the break. All the things that I've been *feeling* while dancing out there.

All the pain and heartbreak.

His heartbreak.

"Callie would talk about you, you know. All the time," I begin, looking up at his beautiful face, strong shoulders, my fingers digging into his warm flesh. "She'd tell me all the things that you did for her, for your brothers, for your mom before she died. All the sacrifices you made. And I thought... I thought I *understood* that. I thought I understood what you gave up and I admired you for it. God, so much.

"And then I finally saw you. And I found out who you were. That you're not only the man who changed my life but also the brother my best friend kept talking about and I was... amazed. I was so freaking amazed, Conrad" – his body tightens up even more when I say his name, and in response I move closer until the toes of our boots are knocking together – "and I *still* thought I understood everything. But I was wrong. I didn't. Not until I saw you with her, under that tree. You looked so... still, so lifeless. That's exactly how you looked back then, at the wedding. So no, I never understood. I never understood anything until then. Until Helen told me everything and I realized that I've always admired you for your goodness. I've always admired you for your ability to do the right thing. But I never..."

I let my sentence hang because something is poking me in my throat.

Something prickly and thorny.

Something painful that won't let me speak.

That won't let me go on because all I want to do right now is break down.

All I want to do right now is cry.

For him.

For all the things he's gone through. Alone.

Taking care of his family, his little siblings. His mother. Giving up his ambitions for them.

Giving up the woman he loved — loves.

For not only going through the blow of losing his mother but also a relationship.

I want to cry for all the times he's chosen others over himself.

"But you never *what*?" he asks when I don't go on, his voice as tight as ever.

And I somehow push the lump of emotions down and continue, still looking into his eyes. "But I never understood the cost. Of all your sacrifices. I never grasped the effect that they had on you. I admired how you changed everyone else's life without realizing that in the process, your life was changing too. I think..." I shake my head, digging and digging my fingers into his forearm. "I think we overestimate the strong people. We think that the strongest of us don't suffer. Because the strongest of us are always taking on responsibilities that others won't and doing the right thing when the world doesn't. But they *do* suffer. They do feel the pain. They do get lonely. In fact I think the strongest of us need more comfort, more warmth. More softness."

I squeeze his arms again. "And I think... I was wrong about the thorns too. They're my favorite thing to draw because I always thought that thorns are there to protect the roses. And that may be true. But I think there's more to it than that." I go up on my tiptoes and stare and *stare* into his eyes, hoping that he will hear me, and he stares back, looking like he may be listening. "I think thorns grow where the roses are because they're starved for softness. They're hungry for all the soft, fragile things after living a sharp, prickly life. A thorn needs the softness of a rose. And I think that's why a rose is so soft in the first place. Because a thorn needs it to be."

It's true, isn't it?

That's what I've been thinking about all through the Christmas break as I missed him, missed St. Mary's.

I've always seen him as such a pillar, with such strong architecture – a monument of his family – that I forgot to take a peek underneath.

I forgot to look under his big brother, hardass coach persona.

I admired him so much that I forgot to understand.

And I so callously, so naively preached to him about doing the right thing with Helen.

God, I'm an idiot.

I'm such a fucking idiot.

"It must be so hard for you to say no to her," I go on then. "And yet you did. You did say no. Just because you wanted to do the right thing and I was so freakishly stupid to tell you what to do and —"

He unfolds his arms then.

Finally.

Breaking out of my hold.

He looks down at me with flashing blue eyes and such a tight jaw that I think he must be hurting himself and so my hands go to his body again. I put them on his torso, on his contracting and expanding stomach as he says, "You want to know why I said no to her? Why I refused her offer? You heard her story. Now let me tell you mine. I said no to her because I don't fuck a woman and send her home to another man. If I fuck a woman, I keep her. For however long I want to. And she's not allowed to look at other men. She's not allowed to be *looked at* by them either" – he looks me up and down, my jewelry, my roses – "or shake her tight stripper ass for someone other than me. If I fuck a woman, she knows to get on her back at the crook of my finger and spread her legs. She knows to arch that back too and open her hole for me. And if instead of on her back I want her at my feet and if instead of her hole, I want her pink mouth, she knows to drop everything and get the fuck on her knees. And open that fucking mouth.

"If I fuck a woman, Bronwyn, her world revolves around me, do you understand? I'm the center of her gravity. I'm the blood in her veins and the beats of her heart. I'm the man for her and no one else. So the reason I said no to her is because I'm a possessive motherfucker who never learned to share his toys. So I kindly ask you to not waste your teenage sympathy on me. Because it's not about doing the right thing. It's about doing things my way."

His words, so graphic and so intense, explode in my belly like firecrackers.

I feel heat and colors running through my veins. So much heat, sticky and heavy, collecting in my lower belly.

In the place between my thighs.

I know that wasn't his intention though.

It wasn't his intention to make my belly quiver or my thighs clench together. It wasn't his intention to make my limbs go restless and heavy.

I know he was trying to scare me but there you have it.

Not to mention that he's right.

He's so absolutely right. To want that.

For himself.

For someone to choose him and him only.

To do all the things his way, and I feel that so much in my chest and my belly and all over my body that I do what I've been wanting to do since Helen's office.

Since forever.

I hug him.

I hug this strong, special man who's still staring down at me with a frown and a clenched jaw and I don't even care if he ends up rejecting it.

But he doesn't.

Somehow he doesn't reject it.

Somehow he lets me.

He lets me put my arms around his sleek waist. He lets me put my head on his chest, on his ribs. And then he lets me hear his heart beating and beating under my cheek.

The only indication that he is alive.

Because as soon as I hugged him, he went rigid as a stone. Frozen.

So as I hug him, I listen to his heart beating, making sure that he's alive and real. I feel his warmth, cozy as a blanket. I squeeze his body, trying to feel the density of his muscles, the hardness of them as I give him my softness.

My thorn, and I'm his flower.

His wallflower.

"What the..." he asks, his words vibrating under my cheek, and I close my eyes. "What the fuck are you doing?"

I squeeze his body. "Hugging you."

I feel his fists clenching by his sides even though my eyes are closed. "Why the fuck are you hugging me?"

"Because you need a hug."

A moment passes in silence.

Then, "Let go of me."

I rub my nose in his sweater. "No."

"Let go of me, Bronwyn."

"No."

His chest moves on a sharp breath. "I'm getting —"

"I hate it," I say, squeezing him again.

"Hate what?"

"All the things you went through."

Another movement of his chest, and this time I feel the hair on my head flutter as well, with his big sigh as he mutters almost to himself, "Jesus Christ."

I burrow my face in his chest even more, smelling his spicy scent. "I'm so sorry. I don't even know what to say."

"Good," he clips. "You don't have to. Just stop clinging to me like a fucking spider monkey and let me go."

I hug him even tighter as I say, "A flower."

"What?"

"I'm a flower, remember? Not a spider monkey."

This time his sigh is bigger. "A wallflower, yes. Erysimum."

"What?"

"That's the correct nomenclature." A second later, he says, "You belong to the cabbage family."

I snap my head up, only to find that he's already looking down at me, his eyes dark and shiny, his jaw tight but his features rippling with something.

Something intense.

"H-how do you know that?" I ask.

He hates the question but still replies, "Google."

He Googled wallflower?

He did, didn't he?

God, he did.

And... and he wants me to let him go.

He wants me to not hug him.

He's crazy.

My thorn is crazy.

Squeezing my arms around his waist again, I whisper, "You were alone. When your mom died. You could've been... with someone."

*With the woman you love.*

His jaw clenches. "I didn't need anyone. I *don't* need anyone."

"Everyone needs someone."

"I don't," he says, his expression stubborn, almost like a little boy's. "I never have."

I fist the back of his sweater and press my body to his, fully aware that he's not touching me at all. He's not hugging me back. His hands are fisted at his sides.

"It's not fair," I say.

"What's not fair?"

"That you had to give up so many things."

I expect a surface answer at this. I expect him to brush off my concern, but he doesn't.

He studies me first, my upturned face, my loose hair. My necklaces, even the art on my shoulders. He takes it all in before coming back up to my face and saying, "It's my fault."

I freeze for a second.

Unable to comprehend what he's saying.

Unable to understand why he would say that, and maybe he can see the confusion on my face because he goes on to explain, his navy blue eyes boring into mine, "All the things that I wanted, all the things that I dreamed about for myself were out of reach. They were out of my league. I tried to be more than who I was. I tried to reach for the stars: soccer, a rich princess of a girlfriend. I knew stories like that didn't end well. I knew that. Especially for someone like me. Someone who was born on the wrong side of the tracks. Someone who didn't have a lot to begin with. But I wanted it all anyway. I dreamed about them anyway. So if I had to give it all up, if my dreams are broken, then it's no one's fault but mine."

My heart squeezes then.

It squeezes and squeezes and I don't know what to do.

I don't know how to process this.

Is that what he thinks? That his dreams are broken and that it's his fault.

That he has no right to dream.

That's bullshit.

That's fucking bullshit.

I squeeze my arms around his body again, with as much pressure as I'm feeling in my own heart as I say, "That's not true, okay? That is absolutely not true. This is your life and you *can* dream. You *should* dream. You should —"

"You'd mentioned that you needed my help," he says abruptly, cutting me off.

"What?"

He moves his jaw back and forth as if mulling it over. "That day at the library. You said that you needed my help with your art. Your college applications, portfolio, whatever."

A few moments pass as I try to make sense of where this is going.

Where did this even come from?

Then he adds in something else. "I might have some time. Next week." Then, "Probably next Saturday."

I move my eyes over his sharp face, his beautiful features as I finally make sense of what he's doing. He's talking about the painting thing that I so completely thrust out of my mind.

And maybe he's doing that to distract me from what we were talking about before.

But I see that even if I want to go back to it, he won't let me, so I say, "To let me...To let me draw you?"

"Yes."

"Because of my college applications."

His eyes drop to my lips. "For your college applications."

That's when I realize something else too.

That my dress, my jewelry, my body art aren't the only things he's seeing for the first time. There's also something else.

On my lips.

My lipstick.

My pink lipstick called Pink and Shameless.

Something that I completely forgot about. My mother always wanted me to wear lipstick and make-up, and while I still don't wear make-up, I have gotten into wearing lipstick. Courtesy of Poe. Which my mother is always happy to see when I go back home.

And this lipstick gives me an idea.

The fact that he's staring at it.

So I stretch myself up on my tiptoes and press up against his body even more. His eyes snap up and I think he's confused. There's a frown between his brows and I think he's about to say something but I don't give him a chance. Before he can utter a word or take even a breath in, I kiss him.

On his jaw.

I press my lips against his smooth skin and leave a lipstick mark.

Like she did.

And even though it's not a stain on his soul like I wanted it to be, I'll take it.

I'll take the perfect pink mark on his pretty jaw.

"It's called Pink and Shameless. My lipstick. It's my second favorite."

His eyes flash at my words and his jaw clenches.

As if he can feel it.

The mark I've left on there.

Then, "Let's go." At my frown, he explains, "I'm driving you and your friends back."

## CHAPTER FIFTEEN

"Talk."

I look up from my book and find Poe — who's just said that — and Salem, sitting across from me on my roommate's bed.

"Now," Poe adds impatiently.

"Yes. About everything," says Salem as impatiently as Poe. "But especially about last night."

Before I can say anything at all, Poe bursts out, "Did we really get to ride in his truck? I mean..." She pretends to swoon and sprawls down on the bed.

Salem laughs. "I know. And he didn't even punish us." She stares at me with wide eyes. "Can you believe that? The most hardass teacher at St. Mary's, who took your outing privileges for *four whole weeks*, caught us last night. And he didn't even say a word about it. Like, what is that? You *have* to tell us what's going on."

At Salem's mention of last night, I bite my lip.

After he agreed to let me draw him and I kissed his jaw — God, I *kissed* him — he took us back to St. Mary's in his big black truck. And they're right: he didn't say a single word to us. Except to ask us about the drop-off point. Which is the woods behind St. Mary's.

And then he walked with us — I knew he would — to the spot in the brick wall, from which we usually sneak in and out. Poe and Salem went over first and, when it was my turn to go, I faced him and said thank you.

To which he responded, "Remember your promise. Behave." I remember biting my lip then too and I remember him glancing down at it before saying, "No more late-night adventures with your friends. Or I'll come for you."

I'm not sure he realized what that '*I'll come for you*' would do to me.

Because now I want to go on late-night adventures even more.

But anyway, now it's Saturday morning and my friends have questions.

I knew they would.

And honestly, I want to give them answers. I *want* to talk to them.

They're my best friends. I want to share all the things inside of me and so I shut the book and sit up. "Okay, but you have to promise me that you won't tell Callie."

My heart twists.

I feel like such a betrayer. Especially when she's always been such a close confidant. She was the first person, the *only* person, I told about that night. She's always been so involved and so excited about that one crazy incident in my life.

And now I'm keeping things from her.

Such important things.

I know I should tell her especially now that he remembers me – he *remembers* me – but I'm still not ready to risk it. I'm not ready to risk the damage it may or may not cause our friendship. I just need more time to figure things out.

Poe rolls her eyes at me. "Duh. Of course. Why else do you think we've never brought it up during school hours?"

"What?"

"We know, Wyn," Salem tells me, swinging her legs back and forth. "That something is going on between you and Coach Thorne. Remember on the dance floor last night? I told you I knew."

Right.

She did tell me.

I completely forgot about that in the midst of everything, and now something occurs to me. "Do you think Callie knows?"

Salem waves my worries away. "No. She doesn't know anything. The only reason *we* know is because ever since he arrived, you've become quite the bad girl."

Poe grins. "Yes, and I'm so proud of you. You're finally a St. Mary's rebel." She puts both her hands on her chest and sighs happily. "All my hard work and bad influence is finally paying off."

I stick my tongue out at her. "Yes, that's it. I couldn't resist your charm, Poe."

Poe flicks her dark hair. "No one can."

Salem looks at me expectantly. "So? Tell us everything so we can help."

I blow out a breath, close my eyes and then tell them.

Everything.

From the beginning.

How we met over a year ago and how he changed my life and how I've been obsessed with him ever since. How it was such a jarring shock that he turned out to be Callie's brother. Who in turn became our new soccer coach.

And then I tell them about Helen. About his past with her and what I discovered.

I know I promised him — also her — that I would never tell anyone. That I would never gossip. But this isn't that.

This isn't gossip.

Because after last night, I've decided something.

I've decided that I'm going to help him.

And I need *their* help with that.

When I finish, there is complete silence. They are both staring at me like they think I'm joking. That whatever I've told them can't possibly be real.

Poe's first to break the silence. "Holy shit."

"Holy fucking shit," Salem breathes out.

I wring my hands in my lap. "Yeah."

Poe raises her hand in a gesture that says she needs a minute to process this and I give it to her. Then, "You're here, at St. Mary's, because of him."

"Well, not really," I reply, still wringing my hands. "I mean, he didn't twist my arm and make me vandalize my dad's car. I just did it because he inspired me that night. To be an artist. He set me free, really. I know none of the girls want to be here at St. Mary's. But this is my happy place."

At this, Salem smiles slightly. "And now he's here."

"Yeah."

She shakes her head. "That's some serious..."

"Voodoo shit," Poe supplies.

"I was gonna say Fate," Salem replies. "This is some serious destiny happening here. I mean, I thought Arrow and me were destined. Like you know how he came here when *I* came here? But we've got nothing on you guys."

Arrow Carlisle, our former soccer coach and Salem's boyfriend, did arrive at St. Mary's at the same time as Salem. And I do think that it was destiny. Because before that Salem had been in love with him for eight years and he never noticed her.

Not until St. Mary's.

"I'm not sure about Fate," I say, shaking my head, not knowing what to say to her observation.

"Are you serious? This is definitely Fate." Salem grimaces. "Although I don't like the fact that he likes Miss Halsey."

"He doesn't just like her," I correct Salem. "He loves her. He loved her years back when they were in high school and I think he loves her *now* years later. I mean he went to her wedding. And I saw his face. It was... it was so frozen."

"And she gave him an ultimatum and let him go when his mom died?" Salem asks.

My heart squeezes in my chest and so I can only nod.

This is the one thing, in everything, that's making me writhe in pain.

That's making me want to curl into a ball and sob.

The very fact that she left him when he needed her the most.

I can't cope with that. I don't know how.

"And she's really not willing to leave her husband for him?" Salem goes on. "Even though she said she has feelings for him and she's been wanting to get back together?"

"No. Not right now at least," I say.

"Wow, I did not expect that from her," Poe asks, disbelief clear in her voice. "I mean, she's a fucking guidance counselor. Aren't they supposed to be like, the epitome of morals and stuff? Look at the hypocrisy here. They can take away *our* privileges just because we didn't turn in our homework on time and she's ready to be unfaithful to her husband with no repercussions. Plus you *know* her. She used to babysit you when you were a kid. You're like... *friends*."

I don't want to think about the infidelity thing right now.

Except that I know it's hard.

In our town and our society, it's very hard, divorces. And complicated and difficult and... I can't imagine all the tough choices she will have to make and all the people she will have to hurt in order to do this, to choose Conrad over Seth.

But then...

But what about him?

The man who's left all alone in this mess.

The man who's always been alone.

"And she teaches history," Poe continues. "History is like the most boring subject in the world. I fucking hate history."

Both Salem and I get distracted at this and Salem asks, "Okay, why do you hate history?"

Poe takes her time replying. Then with a sharp sigh, she says, "Because *he* teaches it."

"He's a history teacher?" I blurt out.

"*Professor*," Poe corrects reluctantly. "He teaches history at a college."

Okay so now, we're completely and thoroughly distracted from the matter at hand because Poe has dropped a bomb on us.

"Wait." Salem frowns. "But you always said that he didn't do *anything*. Like he was this retired, lazy old man who got custody of you after your mom died and who's in control of all your finances until you graduate from high school. So we're all supposed to hate that evil old man who doesn't give you money and who sent you here as a punishment."

Exactly.

That's what she told us about her guardian. That he's this cruel old man who deserves to die at her hands or under her Prada heels.

Again, Poe makes us wait for her answer.

She looks at the ceiling, glances down at her nails, blows on them like she's getting a manicure. Then she sighs and at last pays attention to us. "I may have exaggerated his age a little bit."

"How exaggerated?" I ask suspiciously.

She purses her lips. "A lot."

Salem goes, "Well then, how old —"

Poe cuts her off. "He might not be as old as I led everyone to believe. But he *is* old, or old*er* than us. And he does have control of my finances until I graduate. Which happens in two months, and he did send me here as a punishment. So yeah, sue me for making him sound like a senile old man who was born with the dinosaurs."

Salem and I look at each other for a second before she asks, "Does he really wear tweed coats with elbow patches, Poe?"

"Yes!" Poe says emphatically. "So can you really blame me after all?"

"Can we please, *please*, see his photo?" I beg but before she can say anything, I go, "Wait, is his name really what you told us? Or did you lie about that too?"

"No, I did not lie about that," Poe says. "I couldn't make up that stupid name even if I wanted to."

"So can we finally see his photo now?" I ask again, beyond intrigued now.

I can't believe Poe has been lying to us about her guardian's age. I always wondered that she shared everything about him, so why wouldn't she share his photo as well? And now I know why.

"Yes." Salem jumps up and down in her spot. "Please? *Please?* I mean, we know everything about him now. Can we?"

Poe looks at her and then at me before saying, "Yes, you can. At his funeral. I'll be sure to pick out a picture where he looks particularly... *dashing* or something, okay? Now can we please get back to Wyn's problem?"

I sigh.

Because yes, we do need to get back to me.

And Salem nods. "Yes. Right. Sorry." She focuses on me. "So what are you going to do?"

My distracted, scattered thoughts come rushing back and I shake my head. "I don't know. I just... He's lonely, okay? He's lonely and alone and he says that he doesn't need anyone but that's not true. Even Helen said that he was alone by choice and that he doesn't need anyone. But he does. He does need someone. And I want to give him that. I want... He's done so much for others. He's given up so much. For his family. For his siblings. He's always made them the center of his universe, you know? He's always chosen others over himself, over his career, over his love and I... I want it to be his turn now. *His* turn to be chosen. His turn to be happy, to have joy, to be the center of someone's universe."

That's what he said, didn't he, at the bar last night.

And I want to give him that.

I want him to have that.

I want to give him everything *he* wants.

"So then give him that," Salem says.

And there's the problem.

The problem I need their help with.

*How* to give him that?

"Well, I would like to. It's just that..." I swallow, feeling a little self-conscious. "I don't know how. Like, what do I do to make that happen? What *can* I do?"

"You're joking, right?" Salem asks in disbelief.

Well now I'm not just self-conscious, I'm downright embarrassed as I squirm on my bed, tucking my hair behind my ear. "No, I'm not. How can I possibly do this for him? Like set him up on a date?"

As soon as I say it, I want to throw up.

I don't want him going on dates.

I didn't even *like* seeing him with Helen, the woman he loves.

The woman he actually wants but can't have because she's married.

I don't think I can watch him go on dates with other women. But isn't that selfish of me and shouldn't I...

My friends' chuckles break my thoughts and I ask, "What?"

"You want to set him up on a date?" Salem asks, chuckling.

"I'm... I don't..."

"She doesn't know," Poe says to Salem, smirking.

Salem looks at her for a second before coming back to me and studying my confused face again. "Oh my God, she doesn't."

Poe chuckles. "Nope."

"Yeah, she's got no clue," Salem says sadly, shaking her head.

"Okay, time out, all right? What *don't* I know?"

Poe loses her shit then and starts laughing. "You're so cute when you're pissed off."

Salem laughs too but her words are a little more helpful than Poe's. "Wyn, honey, you love him."

"I-I'm sorry?"

Her laughter dies down to a smile as she says, "You're in love with him. You've possibly been in love with him since the moment you saw him."

I shake my head. "I'm not."

"Really?"

"Yes. I'm *not* in love with him. Yes, I'm obsessed with him. I also might have a little bit of a crush on him. And yes, I've thought about him ever since that night. But that's only because he changed my life. It's only because he inspired me and told me to dream and be what I want to be. And I..." I blink, feeling moisture well up in my eyes. "I can't imagine a world where he's not happy. Where he's not smiling. He doesn't smile, did you guys know that? I've never seen him smile. He's always angry and frowning and my whole body hurts when I think of him that way. When I think of him all alone. My chest *aches* when I think about all the dreams that he's had to give up. About the fact that he thinks it's his fault. That he has no right to dream and I... I want it to end. Now. I'm not letting him be alone anymore. I can't. So that's why. It's not... love."

It can't be.

Right?

No, it can't. I can't be in love with my best friend's *brother*. That's even worse than all the secrets that I've been keeping from Callie.

So much worse.

And on top of that, he's a teacher here. A *teacher*.

I can't be in love with a teacher. That's like, no privileges till the end of time. Not that I care about privileges. But I can't be that much of a rebel either. I can't disregard rules so blatantly.

Plus he's in love with someone else. That's the worst kind of love: to be in love with someone who loves someone else.

Besides, God forbid if *he* ever found out.

That me — a *teenager* — is in love with him. A teenager who's his sister's age and his student.

He would kill me.

He already wants to half the time, so no.

I can't be in love with him.

It would be a disaster. A tragedy. A catastrophe.

There's so much working against me already and I can't.

I can't. I can't.

I'm *not*.

My heart pounds in my chest and my palms turn clammy and just for good measure, I repeat, "I'm not... I can't love him. I can't. I absolutely cannot and—"

"Okay. Fine. That's fine," Salem cuts me off, trying to calm me down. "You don't love him. My bad. But I do think I have a solution to the problem. In fact, I think you solved your own problem back there."

I finally catch my breath then and ask, "What? How?"

She looks at Poe and they both give each other a look before Poe goes, "You want to kill his loneliness, right? You want to make him smile. You want to make him happy."

"Yeah."

She shrugs. "Well, there's only one way to kill the loneliness."

Salem nods. "Yup. And you guessed it."

I think about it and then, "Stop it. No."

"I mean, loneliness goes away when you have company, right? And you have company when you go on dates."

"Exactly. You need to get him laid," Poe insists.

Salem swats her arm. "That's gross, Poe."

"What, it's the truth."

Salem shakes her head and focuses on me. "Look, you want to make him happy, right? You want him to be chosen, to be the center of someone's universe. Now it could be either you or some other girl. I did something similar with Arrow back then. And I decided that *I* wanted to be that girl for him. So now you need to decide. Who you want it to be."

"Me," I blurt out as soon as Salem finishes. "I want..."

It to be me.

I want to do it.

Despite all my protestations about love and all, I know in the center of my being that I want it to be me.

I want to be that girl.

For him.

Because I already am, aren't I?

I already am that girl whose universe revolves around him. I already am the girl whose gravity is centered on him.

And isn't it fair that *I* do this for him? Me and no one else.

He changed my life, my thorn. And so it's only fair that I get to change his, his flower.

"You want what?" Salem asks.

"I want to be that girl," I whisper, my heart thrashing in my chest. "For him."

Salem smiles. "I know."

I look at her. "But he thinks I'm just an annoying teenager. His sister's best friend."

"So it's up to you then. To show him that you're not," Salem tells me. "It's up to you to show him that you're more than that."

"Exactly," Poe agrees. "Show Coach Thorne that teenager or not, his sister's best friend or not, you're going to rock his fucking world. Show him that you're his dream girl."

Dream girl.

My heart leaps and flies in my chest.

At the thought of being his dream girl.

But I can't, can I?

He already has one.

Strangely, it's okay in this moment though.

Because I know I can't be his dream girl, but I can be the girl who chooses him.

I can be the girl, the artist, who fills his life with colors and joy. The girl who takes away his loneliness.

I'm not his dream girl, but I can be his consolation prize.

# CHAPTER SIXTEEN

The weather has finally turned.

And St. Mary's is a winter wonderland.

A wonderland made of pretty white snow. It covers the earth, the concrete buildings, the stone benches, the brick wall. The forest behind the school.

And even the soccer field that I'm standing on is white and snowy.

I've never been a fan of the snow.

It feels monochromatic. I like spring or fall better, when flowers are blooming or leaves are turning and it's an explosion of colors.

Not today though.

I don't think snow is monochromatic at all.

I think snow is wonderful.

And so is the man walking on it.

At first glance, it might look like he's monochromatic as well. He has a black hoodie on, along with a pair of black workout pants. Plus a pair of black running shoes.

But.

You have to look closer. You have to squint your eyes as you walk toward him and make out all the pretty colors. Like the winter flush on his high cheekbones, the warm golden brown of his hair. The red of his lips.

And then there are his eyes, that are on me as he walks toward me as well.

Navy blue.

See? He's colorful.

You just have to look at him.

And I have.

A lot.

Especially here from my spot where I draw him every morning and where I'm back this Monday morning as well. Although I have to say that it doesn't feel like a typical Monday morning, and it's not only the snow.

And I express that to him when we reach each other.

"Hey, oh my God," I say, gasping and putting a hand on my chest in mock surprise. "Haven't we met somewhere before?"

He stares at me for a second, something playing at the corners of his eyes. Something like amusement. "Have we?"

I bite my lip to stop my smile as I say, "Uh-huh. I definitely think we've met before."

That amusement increases as he rumbles, "I don't know. You're going to have to remind me."

I narrow my eyes at him and that amusement expands even more to cover the side of his lips, and they twitch as I tell him, "Well from what I remember, I saw you on the side of the road, wearing the biggest silver watch known to mankind, trying to help a damsel in distress like about a year and a half ago."

His eyes flick back and forth between mine, amusement still lingering on his features, before he protests, "It's not the biggest silver watch known to mankind."

I chuckle. "It so is. Have you looked at that thing?"

"And she wasn't a damsel in distress."

"What?"

He glances over my calf-length magenta parka with yellow flowers. "I don't save damsels in distress, remember?" He lifts his crisp blue eyes. "She was a wallflower. A wallflower in a yellow ball gown."

God.

*God.*

Him saying *ball gown* in that deep voice of his makes something move in my stomach. The fact that he remembers me, that he remembered me all this time, makes something move in my stomach too and all I can do is shake my head at him. "You're a jerk."

Then his mouth lifts in a half smile and I forget to breathe. "And here I thought I was wonderful."

He smiled.

*Smiled*.

Even though it was only one fourth of a smile — a super fucking glorious one at that, that made him even more gorgeous than he already is —I'll take it.

I'll take it and I'll run with it.

Before I can pull myself together and comment on it, he jerks his chin at me. "Flowers, huh."

Heart pounding in my chest, I look down at my parka. "Yeah."

"You draw them on yourself?"

"Yes."

"Because I'm guessing you're also into…" He tilts his head to the side in thought. "Clothes decorating. Or whatever the fuck that's called."

"Close. Fabric painting. And yes, I'm into all sorts of decorating." Before he can say something else, I blurt out, "I'm also into your smiles." When he frowns lightly, I jerk *my* chin at him, his amused lips. "You should do that more often."

Now it's his turn to shake his head at me, his lips still pulled up in that quarter of a smile.

But before he can say anything, I ask him the thing I meant to ask him as soon as I saw him. "Can I see your house?"

That clears off his amusement and makes him frown. "What?"

I'm slightly sad about that, about his tiny smile vanishing, but it's okay.

I'm going to give him more smiles.

I just need to get this done first. So I clear my throat as I explain, "I mean, can I draw you in your house? This Saturday."

"In my house."

"Yes. In your personal space I mean. I think it will help me capture the essence. Of you."

He studies me in silence for a beat or two. "It's for your college applications, correct?"

I hesitate for a second as I tug at the strap of my messenger bag that holds all my art supplies and my sketchpad. "Yes."

"Fine."

"What?"

"You can capture it. The *essence*." He takes a pause before saying, "Of me."

"I can?"

"That's what I said."

I shake my head in wonder. That was easy. And here I was tossing and turning all night, trying to imagine all the scenarios where he'd say no and then I'd have to convince him somehow.

Smiling, I say, "Thank you. It'll be great. You'll see."

He hums at that. "What's your favorite food?"

His out-of-the-blue question throws me a little. "What?"

He shifts on his feet as if slightly uncomfortable. "What do you like to eat?"

I draw back. "What do I like to *eat*?"

"Is that a hard question?"

"No." I shake my head. "Uh, I guess Mexican. I like Mexican food."

He nods. "I'll pick some up then. And twelve thirty."

"Twelve thirty what?"

"I'll pick you up Saturday at twelve thirty. Be ready."

He's said so many things in so few words that it takes me a few seconds to make sense of it all. And when I do, something moves in my chest again.

Something warm and cozy.

Like his sweater from the other night when I hugged him.

"Are you saying that you'll pick up Mexican food for me on Saturday because it's my favorite? And that you'll also come pick me up at school at twelve thirty?" I ask to clarify.

"If you're expecting me to cook for you at my house, then you're going to be sorely disappointed," he says, thrusting his hands inside his pockets. "In all my years of packing lunches and cooking dinners, I'm afraid I never really learned the skill. And yes, I'll come pick you up at the school, because you don't really know where I live, do you?"

That warm cozy feeling in my chest moves down to my stomach and I shake my head. "You don't have to do any of that. I can just take the bus and I —"

"You're not taking the bus."

"But I —"

"End of discussion," he clips in his most authoritative voice.

The voice that makes his name on my thighs sing. "End of discussion? Really? How *old* are you?"

"Thirty-three," he replies, in the most shocking turn of events. Or rather, the second shocking turn of events, because the first one was when he smiled. Before I can absorb the fact that he actually did tell me his age after refusing to for such a long time, he continues, "Twelve thirty Saturday. Don't be late. I don't like to be kept waiting."

He's ready to leave after that but I take a step closer to him. "You can't."

"What?"

"You can't come pick me up."

"And why's that?"

Because the whole reason I'm going to his house is to make his life... easier. I'm going to his house because I'm doing it.

I'm going to be that girl for him.

The girl who's chosen him. Who has made *him* the center of her universe.

Which means I need to spend time with him – hence the house. So I can show him. That I already *am*. That girl.

And seduce him.

Yes, I'm going to seduce my new soccer coach.

Who also happens to be my best friend's brother.

The best friend I'm betraying by doing this, and I hope to God that she understands when I tell her everything.

But anyway, if he comes to pick me up at school like he said he would, people will talk. There will be rumors, gossip. His reputation might come into question.

That is *not* making his life easier, and I'm not going to let that happen.

I crane my neck up and stretch my legs to get up in his face. "Because if you come pick me up, then people will see you. Girls will talk. You're a teacher here. You can't pick me up, put me in your truck and drive me away. Students here can be really vicious. You've seen how things are for Callie, right? You'll go through the same thing. Your reputation will be a joke."

In fact, just the other day, some girls were bothering Callie during lunch and Conrad caught them himself. In his usual scary fashion, he stared them down before taking their TV privileges.

Good.

He steps closer to me. "Has someone been bothering you?"

"What, no. Of course not. But you can't —"

"I want you to tell me if they do," he goes, his eyes grave. "Do you understand?"

"But that's not the point. I'm fine."

"You're not fine. You're *here*, in this hellhole, because of me. And no matter how much you love it here, I want to know if anyone, a student, a teacher, a fucking security guard, is bothering you. I want to know if your parents are bothering you."

"My parents."

His jaw is clenched in anger. "Yeah. Your mom, your fucking dad, whoever. Someone bothers you, you're going to tell me."

My chest feels so tight then. And my heart too big for it as I breathe out. "Anyone in the world?"

"Fuck yes. Anyone in the world. Do you understand, Bronwyn?" His cheekbones are slashed with agitation. "If someone fucking bothers you, I want to hear about it."

I duck my head then and catch my breath for a few seconds.

I even press a hand to my stomach because there's a ruckus in the depths of it.

He's causing a ruckus in my body.

Because he's being exactly who he is: a thorn protecting his flower. And so I need to protect him too.

I need to protect my thorn.

At last, I look up and whisper, "I will. But only if you promise that you won't come to pick me up. Please. You have to understand. For your own sake. I told you at the tree. I would never let anything happen to you."

His nostrils flare.

Distaste ripples through his features as if he hates St. Mary's even more. I get it. I do. Despite my love for it, I hate this place sometimes as well. Especially when it stands between us like this.

Finally he sighs sharply. "All right."

"Really?"

"Yeah. For *your* sake."

"What?"

He bends down a little as he says, "I want you to understand something: I don't care about my reputation. Fuck my reputation. The only reason I came to talk to you that day about *her* was because she was going to. And as I said before, I don't want anyone bothering you in this godforsaken place that you love so much, so I decided to step in. And that's the only reason why I won't come to pick you up."

My breaths are all scattered right now. At the revelation.

About why he talked to me that day.

He hurt me by his questions. Even though I knew I shouldn't have taken them personally. But I'm so relieved now.

So... glad and overwhelmed.

Because he did it to protect me.

Even when he was pretending that he didn't remember me.

"Conrad, I..."

I'm not sure what I was going to say but his name on my lips makes his eyes flash as he continues, "At the *gate*."

"What?"

He grinds his jaw. "I'll be at the bend of the road. Just up ahead."

"But —"

"I'm not letting you take the bus," he says again, his eyes dark and determined.

And I'd argue more, but honestly I don't want to.

I don't want to argue with him.

When all I want to do is hug him again.

Kiss him.

Thank him.

But since I can't do any of those things right now, I nod and give him what he wants. "Okay."

"Good."

With that, he steps back, ready to leave, when I notice something about him.

Something so very, *very* crucial.

I can't believe I didn't see it before. I mean, I was waiting for it, or rather hoping and willing it back.

Maybe it's that his hoodie kept it hidden from me, but...

"Your hair," I breathe out and he halts in his tracks. "It's long. Like, longer than before."

It is.

It's not as long as it was that first night, but it's longer than it was when he arrived here. In fact, now that I'm paying attention, I can see the strands curling at the end, grazing the neck of his hoodie. I can even see a few flicks over his forehead when he raises his hand and pushes them back.

I shake my head, my eyes wide. "Are you... Are you growing it *out*?"

He looks... embarrassed.

That's the only way to describe it. That's the only way to describe the way he averts his eyes for a second and breathes out, frowning. And the way he pushes his fingers through his hair again.

"You could say that," he replies finally.

My heart expands in my chest. Expands and expands.

And *expands*.

"Why?" I ask.

His eyes come back to me, flashing. "Because I thought it's time I felt the air. In my hair."

# PART 3

# CHAPTER SEVENTEEN

I'm in his house.

I'm standing in the living room, taking everything in with what I know are wide, *wide* eyes.

But I can't help it.

This is his house. His *home*.

He lives here.

My thorn lives here, and the very first thing I know right away — that I knew right as soon as I stepped through the door — is that this house, this place has character.

Not the kind that comes from crown molding or vintage light fixtures or a classic black and white tile backsplash, no. It's the kind of character that comes from living here.

Living here for years and years, so that the house takes on your personality. That you can tell just by looking at it that a family, a loving family, calls this place their home.

Four brothers and their loving sister.

The fact that the sister is my best friend, Callie, I'm trying to ignore. Although it's hard because her signature is everywhere: in the colorful throws on the couch, the blue rug under the coffee table, that knitting basket by the fireplace.

But I'm trying to focus on the other people who live here as much as I can.

From everything that Callie has told me about her brothers over the last year, I can figure out that the big bookcase by the far wall is mostly used by Stellan, who's a big reader. There are a few framed vintage car posters scattered around this large space that I think are courtesy of Shepard, who loves cars. And under the huge TV — which I know that all the brothers chipped in to buy because sports! — sits a complicated gaming console which I think definitely belongs to Ledger but from what I hear is fought over by all the brothers alike.

Well, except one. I *think*.

Who for some reason is standing by the door, leaning against it, his arms folded.

And whose signature is in everything and everywhere.

Organization.

How everything is neatly arranged, the books on the bookshelf, the cushions on the couch. The fact that all the posters are straight as opposed to even slightly tilted or off-center.

I know he's responsible for that.

For overseeing everything and everyone.

Conrad.

He's also the one who brought me here.

Like we discussed, or rather, like he reluctantly promised me on Monday, he was waiting for me at the end of the road that cuts off the highway and leads to St. Mary's. The forty-minute ride to his house was done in silence. And if it was a usual situation, I would have made some conversation.

But it wasn't.

I mean, he was driving me to his house, where I'm now going to put my plan into motion.

So I stayed quiet and I stared.

At him, a lot.

From the corner of my eye, of course.

I stared at his strong hands that were gripping the wheel in a way that I wanted them to grip me. And his jaw that was set in a firm line that made me want to stroke it and loosen it up.

And then there was his hair.

That *has* grown out, very noticeably too, and that was really hard to look away from.

Anyway, we're here now and we've yet to say a word to each other.

But it's okay.

While I was nervous before, I'm not anymore.

I'm calm.

His house, a glimpse into his life, has made me calm.

So when I'm done running my eyes over his living room, I settle them on him and say in a bright voice, "Are you going to just stand at the door the whole time? This is your house. You can take a walk through it if you want."

At my words, something enters his eyes, something that I now recognize as amusement. "I wouldn't want to get in the way of all *your* watching."

"I know I'm being a creep but this is amazing." I smile with pleasure. "I love your house."

"As opposed to your mansion that can fit three of these things," he says drily.

"Oh, you mean the mansion where I'm not allowed to draw?" I raise my eyebrows. "Yes, I think so."

He watches me for a second before tipping his mouth up on one side, something that I still see as victory, his quarter of a smile.

"Point taken." Looking around his own house he murmurs, "This place is a dump. But it's home. It's always been home."

"You know, you think I'm this rich, snotty *teenage* princess," I tell him. "But I'm really not."

"Yeah?" he rumbles. "How about a rich, snotty teenage wallflower?"

"No," I say, my heart drumming in my chest. "Just a wallflower."

And I'm going to show him that.

His wallflower.

But for now, I want to see more of his house.

So I fold my hands at my back and turn around to keep taking my walk. There's a hallway down from the living room with a couple of rooms off it and a flight of stairs that goes up. But before that comes the dining room, and when I glance at it, I feel like I've hit the jackpot.

Because photos.

Tons and tons of them. They are hanging on a wall, almost covering it, and instead of going down the hallway, which was my original plan, I detour and make my way up to the pictures.

As soon as I reach them, a smile breaks out on my lips.

I haven't even analyzed them or focused on one, but just the whole mosaic of smiling, laughing faces fills me with so much joy.

I pick a photo at the center, then and slowly and carefully make my way outwards from there.

Most of the pictures are of Callie, right from when she was a baby up until as recently as this summer, I think. In each one of them, she's surrounded by her brothers. And in each one of them, they're goofing around.

Especially Ledger and Shepard, with their bunny ears and grinning faces.

Stellan too, but not as often. His smiles and poses are more subdued. More in line with gravity and arrogance, even with a lopsided smile or a smirk.

I guess I can see who he takes after.

His oldest brother.

Only I can't find him anywhere.

Unlike his signature, which was pretty apparent back in the living room and also here with everything tidy and clean, I haven't been able to find his photo and I think I've gone through more than half of them.

I search for him in the other half, and just when I'm about to lose hope, there he is.

Off to the side, as if letting his family take center stage while he keeps to the shadows.

But he can't, can he?

He's too shiny for that. Too magnetic. Too much the force that binds this family together.

Too much the authoritative oldest brother.

And this photo of him — a few actually, all lumped together — are fucking magical. They're a time machine, taking me to his past.

Because in them, he looks to be in high school.

In fact in a couple, he's playing soccer.

He's on the field, wearing a green and white uniform – school colors I presume – and he's almost mid-air. His one leg is thrust out as if he's running, the other behind him and folded at the knee, ready to deliver the strike, with both arms spread out for balance.

Someone caught him mid-strike, didn't they?

And I am so grateful to them because gosh, he's magnificent.

He's larger than life here.

Even though he's frozen in time and space, I can still see the wind whipping his long-ish hair — actually, his hair then was even longer than it was the first time I saw him — and his soccer jersey. I can almost feel his own heaving breaths, his utter focus on the ball, because his mouth is slightly parted and his brows are snapped together.

And then there are a couple where he's with his team, I think.

They're all grinning at the camera, holding a trophy, and he's in the middle of the huddle.

Although I don't think he wants to be. In the photo at all, I mean.

Because he's the only one who's throwing a subdued lopsided smile to the camera, making me think that he'd rather be anywhere else. But I can see the happiness in his blue eyes. I can see that he's proud of what he's done, what they have done together as a team.

My heart is pounding in my veins.

Roaring.

Watching him like this. This happy, this handsome. And just looking at him, I get this ache in my chest.

This longing to *be* there.

In the past where he is.

To be able to actually watch him play, sitting on the bleachers.

And suddenly this longing is so big and deep that I curl my toes.

Because I hear him come into the room.

I hear his footsteps, drawing close.

Closer and closer until he's behind me.

Until I feel his heat at my spine.

I feel his presence tingling the small of my back. I even feel my hair fluttering, my long, long hair that goes down to my ass, moving slightly, *softly*, strands rustling together.

As if he might be touching it, rubbing it between his fingers.

Swallowing, I raise my hand to touch one of his pictures, where his teammates are holding a soccer jersey for the camera. "They call you Thorn, don't they?"

It's on the jersey that they're holding.

*His* jersey with his name on it.

But instead of spelling his last name with an 'e,' they simply have 'Thorn' in thick black letters.

I feel his breath on the back of my neck and my fingers tremble on his picture. "Yes. Or at least they used to."

"Used to?"

"In the beginning," he tells me. "But then my brothers came along and they were Thornes too. So now I'm something else."

"What?"

His chest expands, or at least I feel it as he says, "The Original Thorn. Just OG."

I bite my lip harder. "I love it."

"Yeah?"

"Yes." I stroke his name through the glass frame. "It means that you're the first of your kind. The first thorn. The original."

And I can't help but want to be the first flower.

The original flower.

Just to match him.

"And probably the sharpest," he murmurs and I feel a pull on my scalp.

Like he tugged on my hair.

Is he... Is he touching my hair?

*Touching.*

He hasn't yet.

Except for that one time when he pushed me out of his office with his fingers wrapped around my bicep, he's always kept his hands away from me.

So I should turn around. I should ask him, but I'm afraid.

I'm afraid that he'll stop if I do.

So I let him.

I let him touch *me* — my hair — in secret.

"And so the most protective," I whisper, feeling warm in my chest. "You look so happy here. So proud and so full of joy."

I don't expect him to make a response but he does and it cuts me.

It makes my fingers shiver on that lopsided smile that I'm tracing.

"I was a fool."

My spine tingles with heat and I very vehemently protest, "No, you weren't."

He lets out a puff of breath. "Yeah? You see that guy. Right next to me?" I feel him tipping his chin at him. "He plays for the New York City FC." Another puff of breath. "He couldn't dribble for shit. I taught him that. Me. And the guy next to him? He couldn't even make the team on the first try. I practiced with him for weeks before the second tryouts and voilà. He was on the team. And then he went on to play in college. And I'm still here, *teaching* things to people. I'll probably be teaching things to people for a long, long time."

I want to turn around then.

I want to look at his mature face rather than the teenage one I'm staring at right now. Because the former is more precious to me.

It's more dear and more beautiful.

More *mine* somehow.

I want to tell him that he's not a fool.

He was a dreamer, and he still *can* be.

But it's as if he senses it, my intention to turn around, and steps even closer.

So much so that I feel his hard chest grazing my shoulders. He even raises his arm, his left one, his bicep brushing against my cheek as he rasps, "And that, over there, is my mom."

It's so hard to focus when I'm surrounded by him.

When he's actually made it so that I'm surrounded by him.

When he's actually made it so that every breath that I take is that of the sweet roses and prickly thorns.

But I do.

I focus and I promise myself that once I've shown him that I'm that girl and I've filled his life with joy, I'm also going to make him a dreamer again.

I will somehow make him dream.

*Somehow.*

"Your mom," I whisper and I feel his short nod on the top of my head. "She's beautiful."

His mom has the biggest, most beautiful smile ever. She's grinning at the camera as her children surround her.

Well, except for the man behind me.

As with all the photos here, I think he's chosen to take a back seat and be the sibling behind the camera. And my heart just bursts with all the tenderness for him.

All the warmth.

"She is," he agrees, his arm still raised and his fingers on the picture.

"She looks like Callie," I whisper, rubbing my cheek on his bicep that flexes at my touch. "Or rather, Callie looks like her."

"She met my dad in high school," he says, his chest shifting with a breath. "They were both seniors when they fell in love. And before the year was out, she got pregnant with me and dropped out. My dad dropped out as well. They got married, got jobs, had me. I think we were happy for a little while, or maybe I'm just making things up because I want to believe that. But then they had more kids, and my dad started drinking. He started cheating on my mom. He'd flake out on his job too. He'd get fired, get another job, do the same thing and get fired again. So my mom had to pick up the slack. Which means as amazing as she was, she didn't have much time for the kids. And so I had to step in."

A pause here.

I'm afraid to move. Breathe even.

I'm afraid to blink lest he stop. Lest he realize that someone is *listening* to the story that he's telling. That someone is hanging on his every word, cherishing it like a treasure, a gift.

"I was happy the day he decided to leave," he continues. "I know my mom wasn't. Even though he was dead weight, an asshole, a drunk, a cheater, my mother loved him. My mother not only loved him, she gave up everything for him. Her school, education. Chose to have five kids with that piece of shit. Chose to have me. Do you know why that was?"

"Why?" I ask on a whisper, my body still strung tight and immobile.

"Because she was a teenager." He lowers his arm with that. "When she met and fell in love with the wrong guy. And teenagers usually don't know what they're doing. They fall in love. They dream. They make mistakes that sometimes affect everyone around them. So Callie doesn't just look like my mother. She *is* my mother."

He steps away then and I spin around, finally getting to see his face.

And it jars me in the chest. In my stomach.

As if I'm seeing him after years.

Those jutting cheekbones that are slightly flushed and those shining eyes. His red lips that look wet and parted like he's been tracing them with his tongue all this time.

Even though it feels like I've just woken up from a dream, I lift my chin and frown at him, ready to defend my best friend. "You're right. Callie *is* like your mom. Which means she's going to be an amazing mother and her baby is going to be like one of her siblings. Hopefully like you. Because you're wonderful. Not so much right now, but still. And you know what else?" I widen my stance and fist my hands. "Maybe your mom made a mistake picking your dad, but I think *Reed* is different. *Reed* is going to be an amazing dad. And I know that because Callie fell in love with him once. And I know they're having problems now but Callie would never have picked him if Reed wasn't worthy. And so I trust her decision. Even though she's my age, a *teenager*. So you should cut them some slack. You should probably give them a chance to show you that they can be more. That they *are* more. Because apparently us, teenagers? We can surprise you sometimes.

"Oh and just so you know, dreams aren't only for teenagers. Dreams are for everyone. There's no age or limit to dreams. And dreaming doesn't make you a fool, it makes you a visionary and —"

"What's your deal with long hair?" he asks abruptly, putting an end to my tirade.

"What?"

His eyes are still shining but along with that glint, they weirdly hold amusement as well. Much stronger amusement than when he was watching me take in his living room, much stronger than any other time before that even. "Your hair."

My breaths are heaving and I'm sure my face is flushed at the moment with my irritation. But still I look down at it.

My long brown tresses are half over my shoulder and half flowing down my back. I'm not sure why we're talking about my hair all of a sudden but I glance up at him and say, "Yes?"

He flicks his eyes to it for a second before saying, "It's long."

I frown at him as I run my fingers through the strands. "I know."

"You could use it to climb down a tower. Or at least a tree."

I blink, my fingers coming to a halt. "Are you saying that I've got Rapunzel hair?"

"No." He shakes his head slowly. "I'm saying *why* do you have Rapunzel hair?"

I narrow my eyes at him and his amusement only grows.

"That Disney movie knowledge," I ask then, raising my eyebrows. "Is it because you've got a sister my age?"

He thrusts his hands down into his pockets. "Yes. Who also happens to be your best friend. The one you were defending so prettily just now."

Despite my ire, I blush at his *prettily* and now his lips are twitching.

Which I have to say melts that ire of mine some more.

"Because I like it, long hair," I decide to answer him, curling a strand around my finger. "Because it's one thing my mom and I agreed on. That long hair looks pretty. On a girl." But maybe my ire hasn't melted all the way because I make sure to look at his gorgeous hair and point out, "Not on a *boy* though."

If I thought he'd be offended, then I was wrong.

He's far from offended.

He smiles and I'd even call it half a smile because it's bigger than all the other smiles he's given me so far and my heart almost bursts in my chest.

"Well, good thing that I'm a man then." He glances over to my hair again before saying, "And as much as I hate to admit it, I'd say that your mom was right."

# CHAPTER EIGHTEEN

It's time.

We're in his bedroom and I take my clothes off.

Or at least it feels like it.

In reality, it's only my sweater. But since I'm doing it under *his* scrutiny, it feels like I'm getting naked.

Because it's intense and exposing, his scrutiny.

With the way he's watching me from across the room, it makes me feel like he's the artist and I'm the muse.

But that's not the case, is it?

The case is that *I'm* here to paint him.

I'm also here to do something else, something far more difficult than sketching him on paper.

So that's why back in the dining room, where after looking at all the photos he told me to sit at the table because we were going to eat — the Mexican food that he'd picked up for me because it's my favorite — I said that I wanted to paint him in his bedroom.

And in order to convince him to say yes, I told him that it was even more of a personal space.

A space that belongs to him and *him* only.

So it will be good for the essence. That I was trying to capture.

And all he said was fine. Like he did back on the soccer field when I proposed this crazy idea of letting me sketch him in his house.

But anyway, now we're here.

In his bedroom, and when I'm done taking my sweater off, I let it drop on the foot of his very Spartan-looking bed with its dark-colored blanket and crisp white sheet.

To gather my courage, I run my hands down my pink dress, making my bracelets clink and my arm chains tinkle. I even go so far as to graze my fingers over the elaborate four-chain necklace — with pink stones to match my dress — that I'm wearing.

My entire outfit, my dress and my ornaments, has been carefully picked out by Poe, since she's the fashion queen. And up until now I thought it was a little too much, a little too exposing, with only thin spaghetti straps holding the dress up and a wide square neckline that shows off a ton of my almost D-cup cleavage. Not to mention the length. The hem hits me somewhere mid-thigh, leaving my legs bare.

But I don't think that anymore.

Because as exposing as his gaze is, as naked as it makes me feel, I love it.

I *love* that he's staring at my shoulders, which are decorated with flowers. I love that he's watching my chest go up and down with rapid breaths. I love that his eyes take in the shine of my necklace, the little trails of my bracelets.

I love his eyes on me.

And I can't wait to show him. More.

I can't wait for his eyes on the rest of my body, that's even more decorated — with his name — and hidden under my skimpy dress.

But all in good time.

For now, staring into his dark eyes, I say, "Your turn." As eager as I am, I still stumble when I say the next words. "Could you take off y-your sweater for me please?"

I don't know what I was expecting here.

Maybe I was expecting him to make a protest. Or maybe clench his jaw in that angry but delicious way of his.

But nothing happens.

His expression remains the same — as intense and watchful as ever — as he snags the back of his dark gray sweater, all sexily, and pulls it off in one go.

I swallow then.

I have to because my mouth has gone dry.

At the fact that when he took off his sweater, he rumpled his long-ish hair a bit and now the strands are hanging over his forehead, brushing the corners of his eyes and cheek.

At the fact that while I carefully dropped mine on his bed, he *carelessly* throws his aside.

A direct contrast to his very neat and organized habits.

Not to mention, I can finally see his shirt, of which only the collar was visible until now.

White and crisp.

"Uh," I clear my throat. "You can take a seat now." I motion with my chin. "On that armchair. Just behind you." Then, "Please."

He does that as well.

All gracefully and smoothly.

Although I'm not sure how because he doesn't even look where he's going. Because his eyes are still on me, all steady and staring as if he's waiting for me to tell him what to do next. But somehow he simply, slowly sets himself down on that brown leather armchair with a high back.

And I swallow again.

Because again, my throat has gone dry.

At how kingly he looks right now. How godly. Sitting like that on his high-backed throne-like chair. With his jean-clad thighs sprawled, his large body slightly bent over as he rests his elbows on them.

And how even though he's sitting and his face is dipped, his eyes are up and lifted.

On me.

God.

Okay.

Okay, I can do this. I can *do* this.

This is the easy part. Sketching him is the *easy part*. The rest, I will think about when the time comes. So I run my eyes over him and look at him objectively.

Like an artist would.

Thankfully his room has good lighting. In fact, the location that I've chosen for him sits directly in the path of that light, which means he's glowing.

Perfect.

This is *exactly* how I want to draw him. All natural and effortless.

Taking a deep breath, I pick up my sketchpad that I already took out of my messenger bag and take a seat of my own on the edge of his bed. "Okay, this is good. I like the light in here. Just... hold the pose." I flick through pages to get to an empty one. "If you start to get tired, let me know and we'll stop. Although, it shouldn't take long. All I'm trying to do today is get the pose down, do the big stuff. The details and everything will come later."

Biting my lip, I take one last squinting look at him before I begin.

The room fills with the scratching of my pencil on the thick paper. The clinking of my bracelets when I get a little aggressive with the lines of his body. Or the chime of my necklace when I shift to get a better look at the shadows that are playing on his features.

In all of this, he sits there, all silent and unmoving.

My own personal Greek statue.

With animated eyes and an intense face.

He sits there and he lets me draw him.

For a long, *long* time.

I'm not sure how much time has passed when I finish getting the last — for now — of the angles and slopes of his bent body down or how he even knows that I'm done, but the moment I am in fact done, he speaks his first words.

"Show me."

I look up at his raspy voice.

He's still bent over, his eyes displaying the same quiet but heavy look, even though he clearly knows that I'm done and he can move.

I squirm in my seat. "Uh, it's not done yet. We might still have to do like, a few more sittings. And then I have to do the colors and I need to get..."

I trail off because he clenches his jaw.

Which is fine; he does that all the time.

But this time he also gives me a look, or rather his eyes turn commanding, slightly narrowed and even more intense. And paired with his tight jaw, he doesn't need words.

To order me. To make me do things.

I do it.

I have to.

Even though I'm a tiny bit afraid to show him my efforts.

I know he already saw me draw those roses on my thighs that night, and then again, his eyes in my sketchpad. But this is different. This is him seeing something in its entirety and I'm nervous.

I want him to like it.

I walk over to him on trembling legs, my ornaments clinking. He straightens as I draw closer and when I reach him, he widens his muscular thighs.

As if in invitation to step between them.

Or more like a command if he's issuing it, and I do that too. Happily.

And I do it in a way that the sides of my naked thighs brush against the coarse fabric of his jeans. And when they do, his muscles flex. They twitch and leap and so I bend my knee and rub it against his tightly strung thigh even more before offering him my sketchpad.

Which he takes, his eyes darker than before.

Once he has it in his large hand, his gaze drops away from me for the first time since we entered the room. And he sees it. How I see him.

A warrior. A god. A protector.

The original thorn.

*My* thorn.

A few moments pass in silence with his head bent and his eyes glued to my sketchbook. And when I can't take it anymore, I ask, both hesitantly and eagerly, "Do you like it?"

He looks up then.

And I have to fist my dress at the sight of his face.

All tight and pretty and brimming with things.

Things that are reflected in his blue — bluest ever — eyes and in the leaping muscle on his cheek. In his fingers too. That have tightened on the sketchpad so much that he's crinkling the paper, bending the thick pad.

"I'm keeping it," he says in a voice that's brimming with things as well.

Throbbing and thick.

"But it's not done yet," I say, feeling each jump of the muscle on his cheek in my own belly.

In the place between my legs.

"I'm *keeping* it," he repeats, bites out almost.

"But I —"

"It's mine, isn't it? My sketch."

"Yes. But it's for my…"

I can't say it.

For some reason, I *cannot* say it.

Even though I've said it to him so many times before.

His eyes flash as he completes my thread. "For your college applications."

A hot blush creeps up my neck, my cheeks, and I jerk out a nod. "Yes."

"That you submitted a month ago."

As always, he hasn't raised his voice.

It's very rare for him to do that. But I still flinch.

I still try to get away from him.

But he doesn't let me go.

He *keeps* me where I am as he tightens his thighs around mine. His knees digging into my soft flesh and his eyes warning me against moving even an inch.

"Didn't you?" he asks when all I do is stay silent and drag short puffs of breath.

"You know," I whisper.

"That you don't need my help," he says in his soft, silky voice. "Yeah, I know. I know when most college applications are due. I went to college. Even if it was years ago. And even if it was only for a little bit."

I *have* been lying to him.

Back at the library when I first brought it up, it was a lie then too; I'd already submitted my applications. I only said it so he'd agree, but he didn't. And later when he did, I didn't want to tell him the truth. I could have. I *should* have. I know that. But I needed this time — I *need* this time — with him so I can do the thing I want to.

But of course he knows. *Of course.*

It was a stupid, careless lie to begin with.

"So then why did you…" I fist and unfist my dress. "Why did you agree to do it? I'd abandoned all plans of ever getting to draw you after the library. After you…"

*Hurt me so badly.*

Regret flickers over his features at what he did back then and I want to tell him that I've forgiven him for it. The moment he apologized. But he squeezes his thighs around my legs and says, "Because I've been lying to you too."

"What?"

He licks his lips. "About not remembering you." Then, "I pretended that I didn't. And while I still stand by it, I wanted to... give you what you wanted. Before, when I was still lying. In exchange for all the bullshit I put you through. So consider us even. And now you have what you wanted. You've drawn me." A jaw clench. "So I'm keeping this. Because you don't need it."

"And you do?" I ask.

His eyes move over my face as he says, "Yes. It's mine."

*Mine.*

*His.*

This sketch is his, yes. But I'm *his* also.

I've been his for over eighteen months now, haven't I?

And I think I'm going to be his for the rest of my life.

My thorn.

Who gave me what I wanted because he lied to me. Because he deliberately misled me and put me through so much turmoil. And while I do understand why he did it — I hated it though; I still do — I didn't know that I needed this.

That I needed this apology from him, this acknowledgement of his wrongdoings.

Of his own lies.

And now that I have what I didn't even know that I wanted, I'm going to give him something of me.

My heart.

Because I love him.

I'm in love with him, aren't I?

God.

I'm in love with this man. I always have been.

Salem and Poe were right.

And I was wrong.

I was wrong to think that I wouldn't risk my friendship with Callie. I wouldn't risk breaking any more rules of St. Mary's. Or my college goals. Or risk *myself*, my heart, my sanity. Because he's in love with someone else.

I would.

I would risk everything for him. *Everything.*

I would choose him every single day and every single time.

I would choose him over myself.

And so I unfurl my fists and let love fill my body.

I let purpose fill my body too.

To love him. To care for him like he just did for me. To be his flower.

"I don't have what I want," I say.

"What?"

There is zero hesitation in me when I lean forward and put my hands on his shoulders. Like the muscles of his thighs, they leap and strain under my soft touch. And his gaze drops down.

It goes to the wide square neckline of my pretty pink dress. It goes to my cleavage.

And nothing, not one thing before this, has felt *this* right.

Him watching me so shamelessly. So raptly.

Him watching the flush on my skin. The goosebumps. Him *noticing* how tight and swollen my breasts are under my dress when he's so close to them. When he's staring at them with a singular focus.

So much so that his mouth parts.

And he drags in a deep breath at the sight of my heavy breasts, and then I can't stop myself.

From dropping down at his feet.

"What the…"

He finally comes out of his stupor, jerking in the chair so violently that my sketchpad slips from his lap. "What the fuck are you doing?"

Bringing my hands down to his tight, *tight* thighs, I whisper, "Telling you that I don't have what I really want."

His jaw snaps shut for a second before commanding, "Get off the fucking floor now."

Shaking my head, I rub my open palms up and down his thighs and they tighten even more if possible. "I want something else."

His hands fist on the arms of the chair, the tendons on his wrist standing taut. "Get off the floor. *Now*."

I dig my fingers in his taut muscles. "No."

He watches me then. With such a... violence. Such an angry, belligerent look that I bite my lip, feeling slightly guilty for aggravating him again.

I bite my lip harder when he opens his mouth and then shuts it before doing it for the second time. Followed by closing his eyes and taking another deep breath.

As if controlling himself.

Like he did back at the tree.

When he *has* controlled himself, he opens his lids, his eyes looking as violent as ever, and he says, "Just when I think..." He pauses, his fists tightening. "Just when I think I've made you understand, I've made you *behave*, I've fucking gotten your bad behavior under control, you pull something like this. You..." He pauses again, this time to pinch the bridge of his nose before banging the armrest with his fist. "Get off the floor right now. Get *off*. And get the fuck *over* your teenage obsession, you understand? Right the fuck now. I'm warning you, or I'll make it hurt more than I did before. Trust me on that. Fucking take my word on that, Bronwyn."

I clench my thighs at how... teacher-ly he sounds.

How stern and authoritative.

How fucking sexy.

I peek at him through my eyelashes, which only manages to aggravate him more. "This is not teenage obsession."

"Yeah, then what the fuck is it?" he snaps, almost glaring at me.

"This is me... thanking you."

That makes him go still.

That makes him stop breathing as he bites out, "What?"

I swallow.

I dig my nails into his unforgiving thighs as I tell him what I knew I would have to. In order to convince him. It's not a lie but it's not the whole truth either.

Especially now.

Especially when I've just admitted to myself that I'm in love with him.

"I know you think you're my soccer coach and —"

"I fucking am."

"And that you're older than me. Much older. And you've got a sister my age, a sister who's my best friend." He grinds his teeth here. "But you're more than that. To me. You're the man who changed my life. Who set me free. Who gave me things I didn't even know I wanted." This has never been truer than it is now after how he apologized for lying. "And I'm more as well. To you. I'm the girl you helped. I'm the girl you saved. That night. In so many ways. And so I want to give you things too."

His eyes are shooting fire at me, all heated and enflamed and blue as he asks roughly, "What things?"

I go back to massaging his thighs, which flex again. "Things that you want. Things that you said the other day, at the bar. You said that the woman that you fuck..." I pause here — I have to — because his nostrils flare at my F word. "You said that she gets on her knees. For you. Whenever you want. And I... I want to do that. I want to be that girl. For you. Whose entire world revolves around you. Whose center of gravity is you."

"Me."

I nod, my heart pounding in my chest. "Yes."

He studies my face for a few beats. The rose on my shoulders, my four-chain necklace. My Rapunzel hair that I know he was touching back there.

Before looking back into my eyes and rasping, "So this is gratitude then."

No.

It's love.

But it's okay if he thinks that. I don't need him to know the truth.

I just need him to let me love him like a woman. Even though I'm a teenage girl.

"Yes," I whisper the lie.

"So you want to thank me," he rumbles, his eyes going back and forth between mine.

"Yes."

"On your knees."

My breath comes out hiccup-y. "Yes. Or on my back."

His nostrils flare with a large breath. "Or on your back."

"Like you said."

"Like I fucking said," he repeats my words and I nod. "Is that why you wanted to draw me in my house? In my *bedroom*. So you could thank me like I fucking said."

"Yes."

His jaw starts ticking as he glances down for a second before asking, "And this dress. You wear this rosy pink dress for me too?"

"Yes. For you."

"So you've set the stage," he clips, his jaw pulsing. "Brought me to my bedroom; waved your ripe and milky and jiggling tits in a skimpy fucking dress under my nose; gone down on your knees in front of me. And you've done all this so you could thank me like I *motherfucking* said. Am I getting this right?"

My breasts — milky and ripe and jiggling — heave at his words.

They shudder and become even more ripe.

And he notices that, his eyes going down.

"Yes," I whisper.

At this, he glances up. "Do you remember what else I said?"

"What?"

He finally leans closer to me.

So close that I have to make space for his body. I have to bow my spine and arch my neck as he comes at me.

And I do it all happily.

I happily let him hang over me like a dark, masculine threat.

"I said that when a *girl*," he says, "is at my feet, she *knows* to open her pink mouth, doesn't she?"

My mouth tingles at his graphic words and I nod, my hands clutching his thighs. "Yes."

"Are you going to open your pink mouth for me, Bronwyn?"

"Yes. I will."

"Yeah? Your pink and shameless mouth, isn't it?" His eyes drop to my lips for a moment. "That was the name of the lipstick you wore that night, yeah?"

I dig my nails on his smooth jaw. "Yes. Pink and Shameless."

"Your second favorite."

I bite my lip at his memory. At how well he remembers what I said to him.

How well he remembers that night, even.

"It is."

"What about this one?" He motions with his jaw. "Is this your favorite then?"

"Uh-huh." I nod. "Pinky Winky Promises."

His cheekbones go even tighter. "Pinky Winky Promises."

"Yes."

It's a dusky, more rosy sort of pink that goes with my dress.

And it *is* my favorite.

"So is your mouth *pinky* promising me," he says, his jaw moving tightly, his thighs still flexing, "that it will give me a good ride? That it will give me the ride of my fucking life?"

"Yes," I answer eagerly. "It is. I pinky promise."

He shudders at my enthusiastic reply.

He shudders and breathes a long, *long* breath.

And then he does something that I've been waiting for ever since I met him.

Ever since he stepped into my life wearing that suit and silver watch and with his gorgeous hair.

He unfurls his fists that were planted on the arms of his chair and brings his hands forward. And then he touches me.

He actually, legit touches me with them.

Not just my hair like in his dining room, but *me*.

He not only touches me, he grabs me.

He buries his fingers in my hair and fists them again. Only this time instead of air, he's clutching my hair and pulling at it so my neck is even more taut and bent.

And that's only one hand.

His other goes around my neck. It goes on my four-chain necklace. Which he picks up from my chest noisily, before he clutches it in his fist too.

And once he has me in his hands, all tightly and domineeringly, I smile.

I put my hands on his taut biceps as my body goes liquid and soft. And I can't help but feel like I'm finally complete.

I'm finally his flower because I've broken his barrier; my thorn is touching me. He's fisting and pulling on things, making it sting so beautifully.

Poetically.

I know I have a long way to go still. But I will take this.

I will rejoice.

"How about before you pinky promise me anything," he begins, his voice as rough and sexy as his touch, "you tell me what it is you're promising me, huh? Tell me what I'm saying to you, Bronwyn. Tell *me* what I want your pink mouth to do."

My heart is pounding in my chest, racing and flying. With so much love for him. So much affection.

With how clueless he is.

Does he really think this will shock me? Him asking that question.

I caress his harsh biceps — the veins of which I can feel even through the fabric of his shirt — as I whisper, "You want my mouth to suck your cock."

His breath is so violent at my frank words, so gusty that it flutters the hairs on the top of my head. And his hand around my necklace shakes so much that he makes the chain tinkle so gloriously.

"My cock," he growls.

"Yes." I bite my lip and glance down at his lap. "That I think is big. Because *you're* so big. And I can't wait."

Another shudder runs through his tight frame and he tugs at my hair again, making me look up. "Stop fucking staring at it."

"But —"

"And it is huge."

"How huge?" I ask with wide eyes.

He gnashes his teeth at my question. And I think that he won't answer but he does.

In fact, he paints a picture that has me panting.

"It's the cock of a thirty-three-year-old man," he rasps, "that won't fit in your eighteen-year-old mouth. It's a beast that your *eighteen-year-old mouth* will struggle to take in, let alone suck it like I like it. It's wider than your tiny wrists and longer than that rosy as fuck face of yours, do you understand? You put your face under my dick, Bronwyn, and I'll cover it from your chin to your forehead and still have inches left. Do you understand what I'm saying to you?"

I'm not only panting now, I'm salivating.

I swear to God, I am.

I'm also clenching my thighs, clenching and pressing them together, because I really can't wait now.

I really can't wait to have that thing, his beast, in my pink mouth.

"I do, yes," I whisper, fisting his shirt. "And now I really can't wait."

"You really can't wait," he lashes out, his fingers twisting in my hair. "You *really can't wait* to fit my dick in your rosebud of a mouth, yeah? To open that rosebud of a mouth and stretch it wide for me. You can't wait to thrust out your tongue and have me in there. Is that what you're saying? Have me stretch you, like a rubber fucking band. Because I will. I will stretch your lips. I'll fucking smear your pretty lipstick all over your chin. Your favorite fucking lipstick, all over your goddamn chin, *wrecking* all your pinky promises. So think before you talk. *Think*, Bronwyn."

"I am."

"You are."

"Yes." I swallow, licking my rosebud of a mouth. "And I understand that maybe I won't be able to do it in one go. But then... But then I can practice."

"Practice."

"Yes. Maybe I can start by only sucking on the head," I whisper, so eager, so fucking eager to do it. "Licking it, making it all wet and slobbery. And then when I can do that well, maybe you can... maybe you can give me more. And I can do it, too. Everyone says that I'm a good student. That I'm a hard worker. I learn fast. You read my file, remember?"

He is silent for a couple of seconds as if absorbing what I said, as if mulling the idea over in his head, before saying in a voice that sounds abraded, sanded down, "Yeah, I did. Bronwyn Littleton, good girl of St. Mary's."

I want to nod my head but he's got such a grip on me that I can't move it, so I inject all my determination and eagerness into the spoken word. "Yes. And I know I misbehave sometimes and I can be trouble. But I promise that I'll learn fast. I promise that I'll suck your dick like you like it. Because you're my thorn and I'm your wallflower."

That makes him growl.

A very low growl, somewhere down in his chest.

"My wallflower," he repeats. "Mine. And she wants to thank me. By sucking my dick like I like it."

"Uh-huh."

His fingers flex in my hair again. "I like it a lot, you understand? I *need* it a lot. I need my dick sucked every day, three times a day. You up for that?"

I lick my lips again, this time my mouth watering to the fullest. "Yes. Yes I am."

He pushes his chest into mine, bumping our noses almost. "I need it before the first bell, yeah? Before you go to your class and listen to your teachers like the good girl you are. And then again, during lunch. I need you to suck my dick before you eat your lunch, so the first thing that goes into that pink mouth is me. And then I need it one more time. After the last bell and before you go back to your dorm to do your homework. Can you do that?"

"Yes, but..."

"But what?"

"I can't... I can't do it in school."

His cheekbones jut out more at this. As if he's angry at this prospect, that I can't suck his dick at school.

As if he was looking forward to it.

*Please God, let him look forward to it.*

"And why not?" he asks.

"B-because someone might see us."

His forehead drops to mine, his furious eyes ever so close. "Yeah, my fucking reputation."

I unfurl his shirt and go up to his face, his sharp and peaked and beautiful face that I just spent a long time staring at and sketching. I touch it and I press my forehead against his as I whisper, "Yes. I know you don't care about it but I do. I can't... I can't let anything happen to it. Or to you. I have to protect you."

"Protect me."

"Yes," I whisper, caressing his face as softly as I can. "You're always protecting others. Someone has to protect you. And it has to be me. Because I'm your wallflower."

Something moves over his features at my words, something other than this tightness, this agitation that he's displaying. Something like... softness mixed in with disbelief.

Like he can't believe someone wants to protect him.

But it comes and goes so quickly that now I think I was imagining it. "So how about I lock my office door as soon as you drop down at my feet?"

At his words, my knees mash against the floor as I say, "But still. We can't take the chance."

He hums deep in his chest before proposing another idea. "How about I lock the door *and* hide you under the desk too? How about as soon as you come into my office and get down on your knees, I make you crawl. I make my wallflower crawl across the floor in her school girl uniform and she gets under my desk. Will she suck my dick then?"

My breasts are moving up and down his chest, my nipples scraping against his muscles. "Under your desk."

He nods, rolling our foreheads together. "Yeah, under my desk. So if by chance someone does come in, they don't see."

"They don't."

"No." His voice is barely human now. "They don't see that Coach Thorne's got a teenager under his desk. They don't see that he's getting his dick sucked while school's in session. And the student who's got her rosy mouth wrapped around his beast is none other than the good girl of St. Mary's. Bronwyn Bailey Littleton. The wallflower. *His* wallflower."

"Okay, yeah. I will."

"Yeah?" His eyes are both bright and drugged, probably like mine. "So they don't see how hard his wallflower is working his dick. His throbbing, beet-red dick. They don't see how eager she looks, how her tits — tits that quite possibly belong on a milkmaid in a fucking porno — are all swollen under her schoolgirl blouse and how wet she is under that skirt. Maybe she's dripping on the floor, making a puddle at my feet. Like she's dripping down her chin and making a puddle at the base of her throat. Is she? Dripping, Bronwyn."

"God, yes. She is. *I am.*"

"Yeah, she is," he keeps going, rolling his forehead against mine. "She's dripping and *dripping* down her chin and it keeps coming. It keeps coming because Coach Thorne doesn't care, does he? He doesn't care that his wallflower is slobbering all over his cock because all he cares about is going even deeper. All he cares about is going down to her throat so *he* can see. He can see the fat outline of his cock in her slim throat. So he can see how he's wrecking her. Owning her. Touching her tight teenage stomach."

My stomach spasms. "Yes. Yes, please. Conrad, I —"

"Not anyone else though."

"No."

"No one is allowed to see what Coach Thorne does to his wallflower under his desk. How mean he is to her. How he dumps his load in her throat and sends her to lunch everyday with her belly full of his cum."

I nod. "No. No one."

Suddenly the pain in my scalp goes up and my head is yanked back.

Suddenly he's all over me, angry and fuming, his frown so big and black, his long-ish hair flicks down to his furious eyebrows.

"Stop saying yes," he fumes.

"What?"

He shakes his fist in my hair. "Stop fucking saying yes to every dirty thing I'm saying to you."

"But I —"

"Enough. You're not allowed to say yes anymore. Do you understand?"

"Conrad, I —"

"Shut the fuck up," he thunders. "For once in your life, shut your fucking mouth, Bronwyn. Because it's time to stop talking and start listening: painting time is over. I'm putting you in my truck and taking you back to St. Mary's and you're not allowed to *talk*. You're not allowed to say even a single word to me. You're not *allowed* to let *me* talk. To you. The way I just did. Like you're a filthy slut I picked up from a bar instead of an innocent wallflower of a girl that I met on the side of the road and walked back home, understand?"

"You're not allowed to get down on your knees in front of me. And you're not allowed to wear this fucking dress ever again. If I ever catch you wearing this rosy goddamn dress, waving your stripper ass and your milkmaid fucking tits under my nose, I'll take it off you myself. I'll tear it down the middle and rip it off your tight little body in front of the whole school. The whole world, you got that? And we'll see what happens to my fucking reputation then. So this here, this is the end. I'm putting a stop to it. There will be no gratitude here, all right? I don't want it. I don't want you to thank me. I don't want you to talk. I don't want you to think. I don't want you to say my fucking name."

# CHAPTER NINETEEN

The Original Thorn

No. No. No. No.

A thousand fucking times no.

I'm not doing it. I'm not *fucking* doing it.

I'm not taking what she's throwing at me. I'm not.

She's young.

She's my sister's age.

She's my sister's best friend.

She's my *student*.

With every pounding step I take on the pavement as I run and run and fucking run and probably won't stop running all night tonight, I repeat this mantra.

I'm not taking her. I'm not taking what she is so eagerly giving.

No one and I mean *no one* has ever aggravated me the way she has. The way she does.

Not anyone that I've ever met. Not even Helen.

Still I'm not doing it.

I'm not.

It doesn't matter that every chant in my head is followed by her sweet voice: *you want my mouth to suck your cock.*

It doesn't matter that every chant is followed by a waft of the scent of her soft, soft hair: roses.

It *doesn't* matter.

## CHAPTER TWENTY

There's a mailbox on the door of his office.

It has a thin slot where you can pop things in — things like memos and documents and letters — and those things will slide down and drop to the bottom. And sit there safely until he opens it with a little key that's given to every faculty member, and retrieves them.

That's where Salem used to put her letters for Arrow.

Back when Arrow was our soccer coach.

Yes, she used to write him secret letters. Secret and sexy. Because she was trying to seduce him.

God, we're definitely the St. Mary's rebels, aren't we?

Salem for falling in love with Arrow and seducing him when he was the soccer coach here; Callie for getting pregnant, the first girl to do so while still at St. Mary's; and now me.

For falling in love with the *new* coach and seducing him.

Because I am.

I haven't given up on that. Of course not.

I know he wants me to.

Which I expected.

He wouldn't be the man I fell in love with, all good and moral and professional even when he doesn't need to be, if he didn't fight against it.

If he didn't try to push me away and scare me.

Which he tried to do – again – when he drove me back in frothing silence that day.

After the painting/failed seduction session, he put me in his truck and drove me back. Although I did notice that *before* putting me in his truck, he tore the page — the page with his sketch that I'd made — out of my sketchbook, folded it neatly and put it in his pocket.

Which sort of made me smile.

But anyway, not once did he look at me, let alone talk to me on the way back.

Not once did he stop clenching his jaw or taking long breaths.

I know that what I'm doing right now, *today*, might make him do all those same things again.

But I have to do it.

So standing outside of his office first thing Monday morning, I reach out, ready to drop something — the thing that I've brought him — into that tiny little slot on his mailbox.

But at the last second, the door swings open and the person whose mailbox I was trying to get into is standing there himself.

Wearing his usual black hoodie and track pants and his typical big frown.

I bring my hands back, hiding the thing from him, which he notices with a flick of his navy blue eyes. Before I can say something to him about it though, he asks, "What the fuck are you doing?"

He does it on a growl.

Thick and deep.

And I have to clench my thighs like I always do. Before smiling and saying, "Hi. Happy Monday."

His jaw clenches.

"So I wanted to drop something off."

"What?"

"Uh, it's just something I wrote," I tell him, still keeping my hands back. "And I wanted to slide it in your mailbox."

He studies my face that I hope appears upbeat and sunny to contrast his black mood. "Something you wrote."

"Yes." I nod. "Because you said that I'm not allowed to talk to you. The other day."

At the mention of the other day, his jaw clenches again and it stays that way for a few seconds before he loosens it and growls, "You're talking now."

"Right," I say, still smiling. "I realize that. And that's why I wanted to drop it off. The thing I wrote, in your mailbox. But then you opened the door and I —"

"I don't want it."

"What?"

"I don't want it," he clips. "Whatever it is that you wrote."

I finally bring it forward. "But I was just going to give it to you now —"

"It's *pink*," he says with clenched teeth, looking extremely offended.

I look down at the envelope in my hand, which is indeed pink.

Or rather a shade of it.

I spent the entire day yesterday, or at least the six hours that I was allotted for my outing, to look for these envelopes. I wanted to get the perfect shade, so I went to every gift shop and bookstore in St. Mary's and the neighboring towns: his town, my town even.

I finally found it in his though.

"Not really. It's more rosy," I say, licking my lips. "Like my lipstick the other day."

Pinky Winky Promises.

The one he said that he'll wreck if I try to suck his cock.

Just the thought of it makes me clench my thighs again and it's such a big clench that he notices. His eyes go to my pressed thighs before moving up and resting for a second or two on my rapidly breathing chest.

I have a cardigan on, so I can't show him the effect he has on my nipples, but I wish I could.

Then he'd know.

That I've been thinking about him all weekend.

I wonder if he was thinking about me.

He brings his now smoky eyes up. "You can take it back."

"But I wrote it for you."

"And I'm not interested in reading it."

I take a step closer to him and, sliding into his earlier role, he moves back.

Which hurts me.

Because this *is* taking a step back, isn't it? From all the progress we've made.

But I don't let it stop me — I can't — and so I take another step closer and I keep doing that until his back is to the door and he has nowhere to go.

Until I've trapped him.

Which is laughable because I really can't, but at least for now, he's not going anywhere.

"But I can't take it back," I tell him, looking into his uncompromising face. "It's about a dream I had."

It really is.

And all the things I've been thinking about since Saturday.

When I got back and told Salem and Poe about what happened, Poe immediately told me to sneak attack him on Monday and jump his bones in his office. Salem proposed a subtler approach though. She reminded me that she wrote letters to Arrow and so maybe I should do the same.

And then it clicked.

My dreams.

Maybe I should tell him about them more.

Like I did at the tree that day.

His chest expands on a breath. "A dream."

"Yes." I nod. "And the only person I want to tell is you."

"I'm the *last* fucking person you want to tell it to."

"Please?"

At my soft, pleading voice, his fists clench and his chest stops moving for a few moments.

Those few moments turn into hours and days and weeks until it starts up again, his chest. With a sharp, sighing breath, and he takes it from me.

He takes the dream I brought him, the pink paper looking so fragile in his large, scrape-y hand.

So perfect.

"Thank you," I whisper with gratitude.

Another sharp breath. "Just go to class."

And that's that.

He has my letter now and I go to my classes walking on clouds.

I'm also walking on tenterhooks for the rest of the day. On pins and needles and thorns, imagining his reaction.

Wondering if he has read it yet.

If he's mad about it.

Maybe I should go to him. Maybe I should see for myself what he's going through and if I can do something about it.

But then I don't have to.

Because he comes to me.

Or rather, he comes to our table during lunch.

I'm sitting next to Callie while Poe and Salem are sitting on the opposite side. And usually, I keep my head down when he comes.

But today I do look up.

Just to see if he's read it yet. Just to see what his reaction is if he has.

And the answer to that question is… nothing.

There's no reaction. None whatsoever.

He's as calm and cool as ever. As concerned about Callie and her lunch and her classes as he usually is, which he should be, of course.

But I was hoping that he'd have some reaction.

I was hoping that he'd give some indication that he's read the letter and not just crumpled it and thrown it away.

Disheartened, I look away from him and go back to my food.

It's okay.

It's totally okay if he hasn't read it.

Maybe he will. Later. Or maybe he won't.

And that's okay too.

I'll just have to keep writing them until he gives in and reads one. And then I'll keep writing him some more until I convince him.

Until I make him see that I'm his flower.

I'm just not sure why I want to cry. Why I want to stab this piece of carrot over and over.

"So Reed. He's good with cars, yes?"

His voice makes me stop and look up.

Conrad's standing by the table, his hands down in his pockets, his features arranged in their usual neutral, *unaffected* way. Well, except when he's looking at me and frowning.

And when he's talking about Callie's ex-boyfriend and the guy whose baby she's pregnant with, Reed Jackson.

"Uh, yeah," Callie says hesitantly, as flabbergasted as me and Poe and Salem that her brother is willingly mentioning Reed.

Who *is* good with cars.

Remember the car Callie drove into the lake and because of which she ended up here? Reed built that car himself. So yeah, definitely good.

Conrad jerks out a nod. "I need someone to look at my truck. Do you think he'd be up for it?"

Callie's eyes — as blue as her brother's except for a lighter shade — go wide, as she nods her head. "Yes, of course. I-I mean, I don't see why not."

"Good. I'll bring it to your house this Saturday." Then, "And I'll bring lunch."

"What?"

His jaw clenches for a second before he sighs and shifts on his feet. "As a thank you. For hopefully looking at my truck. And for..." Another sigh. "Taking care of you."

I realize what it is then.

I realize what he's doing here.

He's giving them a chance. He's giving *a teenager* a chance. Not that Reed's a teenager, but still. His sister is, and he's willing to let them show him how well they can handle this situation.

And he's doing it because of what I said, isn't he?

He is.

He *so* is.

And so when he steps back, ready to leave, without even looking at me through this whole encounter — he never does, but still — without even acknowledging my presence, I blurt out, "Please don't leave."

My hands fist, one clutching the stabby fork and the other set in my lap, at my stupid, *impulsive* words.

Although they do stop him.

My words halt him in his tracks and his eyes, denim blue and *glittering*, settle on me. *And* narrow. Making my heart soar and pound in my chest like a happy bird.

"I-I mean, why don't you, uh, eat with us?" I say, stumbling, tasting thick, sweet love on my tongue. "You never eat with us."

Poe and Salem, like the good friends they are who are in on my secret, nod. Callie nods too but more cluelessly and thoughtfully as if this is a good idea that's only now occurring to her.

Her brother, however, doesn't know all this.

Because he's not looking at them.

He's looking at me and he's doing it in a way that makes me think that he'll never look away.

"Eat with you," he rumbles, rasps even, staring steadily at me.

I let go of the fork and bring my hand down to my lap so I can clutch them both together. "Yes. I mean, it's lunch and you're going to eat anyway, right? So might as well do it with us."

Again, Salem and Poe nod. Callie too. And again he's oblivious to all that because his eyes are glued to me.

From my messy braid, on the verge of unraveling, to my heated cheeks.

"Actually I'm not," he says at last.

"You're not what?" I ask, tucking my strands back.

"Going to eat this afternoon."

"Oh. Why not?"

He lets a beat pass before answering, "Because I have to catch up on some correspondence."

"What?"

He nods gravely, shifting on his feet. "Correspondence. Emails, letters. That sort of thing."

Now my heart isn't beating at all.

It has slowed down.

It has also dropped from my chest and down to my stomach.

Like a flower dropping off the stalk and falling to the ground. Waiting to either be picked up by someone's kind fingers or be crushed under someone's boots.

"Letters," I say, trying to keep my voice calm and natural.

"Yeah," he replies, and is it me or has his voice gone even lower, rougher. "I received a letter this morning and I've been..." A pause, then, "Thinking about it."

"Oh." I swallow, twisting my hands in my lap. "Have you?"

"I've been thinking about how to answer it. How to get my message across."

"Your message?"

"Yes." A thoughtful frown appears between his brows but his eyes — at least to me — appear darker, shinier. "See, it's troubling. The contents of that letter. And I've been trying to think of a solution."

I want to smile then. At his '*troubling.*'

But all I do is blink innocently and ask, "Can I help? With figuring out the solution. I'm good with them. Solutions, I mean."

"And here I thought you were just the artist."

"I'm —"

"Thanks for the offer though." He at last gets moving, taking another step back before he says, "But I think this one I'm going to have to figure out on my own."

With that, he leaves and I think I'll combust in my chair.

Especially when Poe looks at me and winks.

And Salem giggles in her soup and Callie murmurs something along the lines of her big brother acting extremely weird.

"I don't think he's ever said the word 'correspondence' in his life before," she says. "I don't even think he *likes* receiving correspondence."

# CHAPTER TWENTY-ONE

He read my letter.

He *did*.

He did. He did. He did.

And so the next day, I stand in front of his office with another dream for him, wrapped up in rosy pink, with a smile. And again like yesterday, he opens the door before I can slide it in his mailbox.

In fact he opens the door *way* before I've even reached my arm out to put the letter in.

He opens it as soon as I get there.

Like he knew I'd come. Like he was waiting for me.

"Hi," I whisper. "Happy Tuesday."

My greeting, like yesterday, like *always*, makes him frown and I, like always, keep going. "I have another dream for you. This one picks up right after the first one."

His chest moves sharply with his breath. "Get in."

"What?"

"Get inside my office."

I press the letter to my chest. "But I... I have class now."

His teeth clench, his features set in stone. "And you'll go to your class. After I'm done with you."

After he's *done* with me.

Sounds ominous.

But okay. Fine. I can take him.

"All right," I say and pass him by.

As soon as I cross the threshold, he shuts the door and locks it too.

Spinning around, I face him and find that his eyes are running over my body.

Slowly, methodically. Lazily.

This time of day, I'm all put-together and tidy.

Though that doesn't mean that I'm neat and tidy on the inside.

I'm all chaotic actually.

I'm all heated and restless.

All because he's watching me like that.

When he's done making me a mess, he looks up. "Stand over there."

He jerks his head in the direction of *'over there.'*

It's the bare wall adjacent to his desk that I wanted to paint that first day. I wanted to paint it with colors and flowers so he could have something interesting to look at.

Something that might give him joy.

Now I go to it, on trembling legs and buzzing thighs. And stand with my back to it.

I press my back to it even, not only to give myself some balance but also to become a painting myself.

A flower stuck to the wall.

For him.

It's as if he can hear my silly, fanciful thoughts.

Because his eyes flash and his chest moves up and down in a couple of rapid breaths before it calms down and he thrusts his hand, the one with that big silver watch, inside his pocket.

Only to bring it out a second later with his fingers clutching something.

The rosy envelope identical to the one that I'm holding in my own hand.

My letter from yesterday.

"Read it."

I lick my lips and ask, "What?"

He puts the letter that he was holding in his hand on his desk and slides it over to me. "Read the letter."

I look at the letter sitting on his desk.

It's folded in the middle and its edges are crumpled and look handled. I ask, glancing up, "You want me to read the letter I wrote you?"

His jaw ticks. "Yes."

"But I —"

"If you can write it," he says almost bitingly, "you can read it too. Now pick it up and read what you wrote to me."

That's when I get it.

I get what he's asking me to do.

I want to laugh then.

Smile at least.

This is his solution? For the trouble that is me.

He thinks this might put me in my place, reading my own words out loud to him. Like I'm a wayward child.

He's an idiot.

An adorable, angry idiot.

Fine, I'll do it.

So instead of laughing or smiling or shaking my head at him, I step forward to pick up the letter from his desk. "Okay. If that's what you want."

The muscles on his biceps go taut at my words and I can totally see that in his navy blue t-shirt and no hoodie.

But then he casually props his hip against the edge of his desk and folds his arms across his chest. "Whenever you're ready."

At this I duck my head and I do smile as I open the envelope and retrieve the sheet of paper.

Which is as rosy pink as the envelope *and* it has a rose printed in the right-hand corner.

Taking a deep breath, I begin.

. . .

"Dear Coach Thorne,

I'm pretty sure you're fuming right now. I'm pretty sure you're also frowning at this letter. Maybe you want to hunt me down across campus and take my privileges away. Just so you know, I'm okay with that and if you go looking for me, I'll always be easy to find.

But bear with me.

There's a purpose to this letter.

So the other day I had a dream.

About you.

Which as you know is a common occurrence.

But anyway, I had a dream that I was sketching you. Like I did Saturday afternoon.

We were in your house, in your bedroom in fact. You were on the same armchair like you were that day and I was on the bed. The only difference is that instead of wearing that white shirt, you were wearing... nothing.

I mean, you did have your jeans on. The navy blue ones. That I think match the color of your beautiful eyes.

But not the shirt. The white one, with such crisp collars that make you look all sexy and dominating.

And so I could see you.

I could see your body. The tight slopes of your chest. The curves and bulges of your shoulders. I could even see the ladders and the ridges of your ribs and abs. And that V.

Oh my God, I think you have a V.

You do, don't you?

And I could see that. I could see everything.

And because I could see everything, I think you could imagine what I was going through.

Not only in the dream but also in my bed.

Where I was tossing and turning. All heated and restless.

My panties were all sticky and riding up the crack of my ass. My nightie was all twisted up around my stomach. And every time I moved, my tits ached. The nipples scraped against the fabric and it was so painful. Like they were on fire.

I was on fire.

*And I think I moaned. Multiple times, in fact, and I did it so loudly that I woke up my roommate. Who was pretty mad about all the ruckus I was causing.*

*But that's not the point.*

*The point is that even though I had a dream about you that made me all wet and swollen and achy, so much so that I had to touch my pussy after my roommate went back to sleep, I still didn't break your rule. Because when I came with your name on my pink lips, I called you Coach Thorne and not Conrad. Like you wanted me to.*

*See? A good girl.*

*A fast learner. A hard worker.*

*Your Bronwyn (your wallflower), whom people call Wyn and whom you mistakenly think is trouble.*

*PS: Please notice that even here I've addressed you as Coach Thorne and not Conrad."*

When I'm done, my fingers are trembling.

And I have zero shame in saying that my legs are clenched tightly. Zero fucking shame in saying that I'm even rocking my hips here and there, moving my ass against the wall, biting my lip, breathing heavily.

It takes me a second to focus my drugged gaze when I look up.

Only to find that *his* gaze matches mine.

That his navy blue eyes are glittering and dark. His pupils have swallowed his blue eyes whole.

And he isn't even propped against his desk anymore, no.

He's standing straight, his feet shoulder-width apart and his hands fisted at his sides. And the body that I was talking about is moving, shifting with his breaths.

I stare at him, my body drenched in lust and my pussy weeping in my panties like it was when I had that dream and I can't help but whimper, "Conrad, please, I need —"

"Read the next one," he clips, his voice tighter, more guttural.

So much so that it scrapes down my body, his voice.

As if it were hands.

"But I —"

"Read it."

I'm not sure how I manage to do it, but somehow, someway, I lower the first letter and swap it with the one that I wrote to him today and begin.

"D*-dear Coach Thorne,*

*I hope you survived my last letter and that this letter won't make you as mad as my first one must have. Because again if you bear with me, you'll realize that it has a happy ending too.*

*I'm still sketching you in your bedroom and you're still in that armchair. I'm still on your bed and you still don't have your shirt on. But this time, you're angry about my clothes.*

*That rosy pink dress that I wore for you on Saturday.*

*The one you said that I'm not allowed to wear anymore. Because of how tight it is and how short. Because you think it clings to my stripper ass and my milkmaid tits.*

*And I promise —"*

That's all I manage to get out.

Before he's on me.

Before his body is crowding me against the wall and his arms are planted on either side of my head, making sure that I don't go anywhere.

"Stop talking," he says in a voice that's even more abraded than before.

"W-what?"

The frowny groove between his brows grows deeper. "Fuck the letter. Fuck it."

I agree.

So I crumple the letter in my fist and let it float to the floor before answering, "B-but you wanted me to read it and I was. I was doing it for you. I'm your wallflower."

"Stop talking. Stop *saying* these things to me."

"But I —"

"It isn't working," he growls. "This whole thing isn't working. This whole *idea* was fucking bullshit. Making you read your pinky letters out loud, the letters you shouldn't even be writing to me in the first place. It's not making you *understand* that you shouldn't talk to me this way."

I press my body to him then. I press my chest to his harshly cut ribs and fist his t-shirt. "But I'm yours. And you're the only person I want to talk to this way. And…"

I trail off because like Saturday he touches me again.

He takes his hands off the wall and buries them in my hair, messing up my neatly arranged braid in the process. He digs his fingers in my scalp and tugs my head back, his mouth so close to me.

As close as it was back in his house.

Actually no, even closer.

And my eyelids flutter at his proximity. They flutter at the fact that he's touching me again and it's glorious.

Even more so now than before, somehow.

But then something else happens that's even more glorious.

Something that tips my world on its axis.

Because he picks me up.

Off the floor.

I don't even know how that happened. Because one second his hands were messing up my braid, tugging my head back, and the next, they're on my waist.

They're *squeezing* my waist and he's picking me up off the floor, my Mary Janes floating in the air before he plasters me to his body. But he doesn't stop there. His hand goes down to my ass and he hauls me up even more.

So that my thighs are hooked around his slim waist and I'm trapped between him and the wall.

My hands go to his shoulders, where I fist his t-shirt and ask, panting, "What are you doing?"

"Putting my hands on you," he growls, both his hands on my ass, squeezing and kneading the flesh over the skirt.

"Why?" I ask, not that I mind.

I'm just... flabbergasted at this turn of events.

Flabbergasted that my thighs are wrapped around his hips, where they can't stop squeezing him. Where they can't stop rejoicing in his hard muscles.

*I* can't stop rejoicing in the fact that I'm plastered to him, to his body. To the lattice and network of his muscles.

"Because I'm going to teach you," he says, his fingers digging into my ass.

I squirm. "Teach me what?"

He leans closer, his chest pushing against mine, scraping against my hard nipples. "The ways of the world. And what happens when you push a man to his limit."

He finishes it with the tightest squeeze ever and I get it. I so get what he means – his words reminiscent of what he said to me at the tree weeks back – and I open my mouth to say something to him when he follows that squeeze with a smack.

On my ass.

A loud, lashing smack that rings in the room and that jiggles not only my ass but my entire body.

That makes me jump in his arms too.

Not to mention it makes me bite my lip. Hard. So hard.

Because it hurts.

It *hurts*.

And he knows it. He knows because he rumbles, "Hurts, yeah?"

I hate to say yes.

I hate to prove him right but I can't hide it. It's written on my face, in my grimace. So I jerk out, "Y-yes."

His eyes turn mean as he says, "Well then, maybe this will get my message across. Maybe this will make you understand that you can't say these things to me."

No it won't.

Nothing will get his message across because his message is bullshit. "It's not —"

Another smack. That one not only steals my words but also makes me arch my back.

And makes me moan too.

"Remember what I told you Saturday?" he asks, his heated eyes roving over my features. "You're not allowed to talk. You're not allowed to say anything except what I tell you to."

I push against his chest, breathing heavily. "You're being mean."

He shifts between my thighs then and God, *God* something happens.

Something delicious and amazing that turns the burn on my ass into something... sexy.

Into something needy and full of lust.

Because when he shifted, his ridged torso brushed against the perfect spot. Against my clit, and that just changes the whole game. And I didn't even know that I could feel that right now.

Until he moved against it.

Until he told me with his body.

Until he gave me what I wanted.

Like he always does.

And he knows that too. He knows that he hurt me and so now this is his apology. Because he shifts again, hitting that spot which he accompanies with another slap on my ass and rasps, "Yeah. And I'm about to get meaner."

God, he's wonderful, isn't he?

Even when he's being mean.

There is no way I'm going to stop now.

No. Way.

"Conrad, I... Please..."

He squeezes my ass and growls, "Repeat after me: I will not write inappropriate letters to Coach Thorne."

And *Jesus Christ* even that goes straight to my core.

It hits me in my pussy.

His rough, authoritative words. And all I can do is moan and squirm.

Which obviously doesn't satisfy him because he smacks my ass again. "Say it, Bronwyn. Say the fucking words. Say, 'I will not write inappropriate letters to Coach Thorne.'"

I'm not sure how *this* will get his message across.

Making me writhe against his body like this. Making me hump his stomach like a slutty, horny girl.

But writhing against him, I do give him what he wants. "I will not write inappropriate letters to Coach Thorne."

My submission makes him breathe deep and he smacks my ass again. "I won't tell Coach Thorne about my dreams."

It makes me leave his t-shirt and go for his hair. "I won't tell Coach Thorne about my dreams."

"Coach Thorne doesn't want my letters," he says, smacking me again, making me rub up and down his stomach even more.

"Coach Thorne doesn't want my letters."

He shudders, his chest scraping against mine as he issues his next command. "I won't tell him that I tossed and turned in my bed."

Fisting his hair, I increase my rhythm. "I won't tell him that I tossed and turned in my bed."

"I *won't* toss and turn in my bed, period."

"I-I won't toss and turn in m-my bed, period."

He leans into me then. As if he can't hold himself up anymore. His fingers massage my ass, both giving and soothing the pain, his nose landing somewhere below my ear.

And then he smells me.

He smells my skin and growls.

And I tilt my head to the side, twisting in his arms, giving him more access.

"I won't let my nightie ride up my stomach when I sleep," he growls in my skin.

Whimpering, I try to repeat what he said, "I won't... I won't let my..."

But I can't.

Because now that his nose is there, on my throat, he's rubbing it.

So softly. So gently.

So in contrast to what his fingers are doing. So in contrast to what his lips are saying to me.

It makes me feel like I'm really his flower.

That my skin is velvet and he can't get enough of it.

Of me.

"Say it, Bronwyn," he reminds me as he noses the column of my throat. "Say, 'I won't let my nightie ride up my tight rosy stomach when I sleep.'"

"I won't..." I swallow, pressing the back of his head to bring him even closer. "I won't let my nightie ride up my t-tight rosy stomach when I sleep."

"I'll keep it pulled down and tucked around my little body."

"I-I'll keep it pulled down and tucked around my little body."

"Yes," he says, at the center of my throat now, his mouth open and breathing. "So it hides my pussy, that tight rose between my legs."

My pussy — my tight rose — spasms and I swear I almost come.

I almost lose it.

"So it... it hides my pussy, that tight rose between my legs."

His chest shudders again. "Was it pink? Your nightie."

I roll my head back and forth on the wall as I answer him in a daze, "Yes. M-my favorite."

"Did it have flowers on it?"

"Yeah."

"You paint them yourself?"

"Uh-huh. Roses."

Another shudder, a spasm, this one more violent than the previous ones as he says, "I'll stop wearing my favorite rosy nightie to bed."

I wind my arms around his neck, still undulating in his arms. "I'll stop wearing my favorite rosy nightie to bed."

His fingers that are still on my ass but have stopped doling out punishment for quite a while now go to my thighs. They massage my thighs over my skirt, right where his name is, and I moan.

I moan and bury my own nose in his hair.

"I'll throw my favorite nightie away," he says, his lips on my braid now.

"I'll... I'll throw my favorite nightie away."

Rubbing his lips in my hair, he growls, "I won't cream my panties thinking about Coach Thorne."

"I won't," I hiccup, "cream my panties thinking about Coach Thorne."

"Were they pink too?" he asks, rubbing my skirt up and down, nosing my braid.

"W-white. But with pink lace."

A puff of breath on my hair and I squeeze my arms around him. "Tell me how wet they were. Your white but with pink lace panties."

"*So* wet."

"Yeah? Were they stuck to your pussy?"

"Yes."

"I bet they were so stuck that you could see it, yeah?" he whispers. "I bet you could see the shape of your rosy pussy through your wet panties. I bet your rosy pussy was so swollen that she was bursting out of your panties too. Gushing and dripping, making everything sticky."

I nod, rubbing my cheek against his. "Yes. Everything was all sticky and hot."

Everything *is* sticky and hot.

Everything is swollen and achy. Everything is drenched in lust and my cream.

And I just want to come.

I just want him to make me come and I go to tell him that but he has other plans.

He wants something else from me, because he lets go of my thighs and brings both his hands up to my face. He grabs it and makes me look into his lusty, feverish eyes. "Tell me about the happy ending." When I only blink at him and at his gorgeous, heated face, he licks his lips and explains, "Of that second dream."

Panting, I whisper, "You burn it."

He gets it.

He gets what I'm talking about. "The dress."

"Yes." I lick my lips. "Because you hate it so much and because it makes you so angry. You tear it off my body like you said you would and you... you burn it."

"Good," he growls. "Because I don't want to look at it and wonder. I don't want to wonder if that tight little rose between your legs, that tight little *forbidden* rose is as pinky and rosy as your fucking dress is."

I want to tell him that it's not forbidden.

My rose is his.

I want to give it to him.

But he doesn't give me the time to respond. Because somehow he moves me, maneuvers me against his body in such a way that I shatter.

Even through the layers of clothing, his and mine, he manages to touch that spot on me, on my pussy, so that I break into pieces and come.

My breaths are all gone.

My heart's all gone too.

I know I'm never getting it back, my heart, but he's kind enough to give me my breaths back.

He's kind enough to open his mouth over mine, drag our misty, steamy lips together, and breathe into me.

Only it stings.

Because he's not kind enough to close those lips of his over mine and give me what I really want.

What I really need.

His kisses.

And he keeps doing that.

He keeps hurting me with his sweet breaths for days.

Because every day I write him a new dream and every day before the first bell when I go to give it to him, he tells me to get inside his office. He stands me by that same wall and asks me to read them out loud.

And then he hauls me up in his arms and spanks me.

He tells me to say things.

Or at least it starts out that way because his spanks, his growling words, his body, the way he smells me, the way he forgets to punish me in the middle of it all and simply kneads my flesh, simply feels it, forms it, molds it in his large hands, make me come.

Only there are no kisses and no budging on his part.

But I'm still not giving up.

I'll never give up.

If I have to show him every day that I choose him, I will.

Only I don't get to.

Because on one such day, I'm not at St. Mary's like I thought I would be.

They take me away.

## CHAPTER TWENTY-TWO

"We're home, Miss Littleton."

The voice wakes me up and I realize that the car has stopped moving.

Blinking, I look out from the window into the darkness and find that we're indeed home. "Right. Sorry." I straighten up in my seat. "Thanks, Charles."

Charles, our driver, nods in the front seat and I pick up my backpack from the carpeted floor of my dad's car, ready to get out. But as soon as I open the door, I remember something and stop.

"Oh, I forgot this," I say to Charles and dig into my backpack, looking for something. "I made this really cute sketch for Janie. Martha said that she's into Spider-Man these days." I find the sketch that I had framed today. "Tell Janie that she made a great choice. But Iron Man *is* the man. I refuse to watch any more Marvel movies because they killed him in the last one."

I mean, Tom Holland is great but Robert Downey Jr. is a total dreamboat. That beard, that arrogance. His dry sarcastic remarks. That only comes with age and experience.

Charles takes the sketch from me for his granddaughter Janie; Martha's his daughter and one of our staff members with perfect hands *and* one of my very good friends.

Charles looks at it and smiles. "This is wonderful. But you didn't have to do that."

I flush with pleasure; Charles, and of course Martha, have always been supportive of my art. Even so, I didn't start showing off my sketches and making stuff for Janie — even though I've always wanted to — until I was sent to St. Mary's and learned what acceptance looks like.

So now I try to make things for Janie every opportunity I get.

Shrugging, I say, "Meh. It's no problem. I hope Janie likes it though." I point to the sketch. "I also made her a tiny Iron Man in the back. Just to, you know, nudge her in the right direction."

Charles laughs. "I'll be sure to tell her that. I know Janie will love it. Appreciate it, Miss Littleton."

Picking up my backpack, I open the door of the car wider, ready to hop out. "Just so you know, my offer still stands." Charles frowns and I explain, "To call me Wyn instead of Miss Littleton. In case you forgot."

"After you reminding me about twenty to thirty times in the past year alone? Of course not, Miss Littleton."

I narrow my eyes at him. "Ha. Ha. Goodnight, Charles."

He chuckles. "See you Monday, Miss Littleton."

Yes, Monday.

When I'll get to go back to my actual home, St. Mary's.

Waving goodbye to Charles, I finally climb out of the car and shut the door behind me.

I sling the backpack over my shoulders, ready to hit the shower and wash this long, *awful* day off my body.

The only thought that's keeping me going right now is that it's done. What my parents wanted me to do and had me miss school for. Now I won't ever have to do it again. And on Monday Charles will be here at around six in the morning and he'll take me back to St. Mary's. Plus the next weekend visit isn't until my dad's birthday, which is still weeks away.

I'm walking down the driveway of my house, lugging my backpack on my shoulders, when I hear it: the sound of a car door shutting with a bang and sharp, thudding footsteps.

Followed by my name, "Bronwyn."

In his voice.

*His.*

For a second I stare blindly at my well-lit house.

I also come to a halt, freezing in my spot, my heart thudding as loudly as those footsteps that I can still hear.

The footsteps that are growing closer and closer with each beat of my heart.

Until they stop and my heart stops with them.

Only for it to slam back to life because I hear my name again, this time with an edge of impatience. "Bronwyn."

I spin around and there he is.

As if stepping out of the past.

Tall and broad and shrouded in darkness, he stands exactly where he did the night he walked me back home.

If I didn't know better, I'd think that this is a hallucination.

That he's an apparition.

But I *do* know better, and when he starts to walk toward me, as crazy as it may seem, I realize that he's here.

He's really here and he's coming closer.

He's crossing over to me, his steps purposeful and long, his eyes flashing, glittering in the dark. And when he reaches me, my backpack slides off my shoulder and falls to the ground.

"Conrad? What…" I can't seem to form words right now. "What are you doing here?"

He's staring down at me, his gaze sweeping over my stunned features. "Are you okay?"

"What?"

"Are you fucking okay?"

I don't understand the urgency in his voice but still I reassure him, "Yeah, of course. Of course I'm okay. Why would you think that I wouldn't be?"

He doesn't answer right away.

Instead he takes his time studying my features some more. As if to make sure that I'm not lying about being okay.

And I still don't understand why.

I still don't get what's happening here.

Then, "You didn't show up this mor —" He stops himself before saying, "You didn't show up for soccer practice."

"Oh."

That's all I can say as I frown up at him, still confused.

Wondering if missing soccer practice should warrant such a reaction from him.

Should it though?

I mean I know he's my soccer coach but is that really why he came, because I missed practice?

"What the fuck happened? Your parents did something to you?"

"What, no." I shake my head, my heart squeezing that he's always so on edge when it comes to my parents. "They didn't do anything. Well, except pulling me out of school today. But anyway, they wanted to take me away."

"Take you where?"

"Uh, to New York. For a campus tour," I explain. "Well, it was mostly for this event my dad was invited to, at the school. It's his alma mater and they were throwing this charity thing with my dad as the guest of honor. So they took me along as well. To meet all the people, see the campus, that sort of thing. In fact, I'm just getting back. But someone from my dad's office called the school and let them know that I'd be missing today."

Which I hated, by the way.

I hated missing school.

I hated not going to his office this morning. I hated it because I missed him.

So much.

"Campus tour," he clips, his jaw ticking.

"Yes," I reply.

"Your dad's alma mater."

I jerk out a nod. "Yes."

"How's the art program there?"

I bite my lip at his casual tone, which completely belies his dark features. "They don't have one."

"They don't have one."

"No, but —"

"So it was a complete waste of time." Then, "For you."

I grimace. "It wasn't a waste of time. It was a good campus. It's just that I'm not going there."

"They know that yet? Your *parents*."

I grimace harder. "Not really." When his chest moves sharply, I put both my hands up. "I told you. I'm waiting for the right time. I'm waiting for my acceptance letter, okay? And until I get one there's just no point telling them about it and upsetting them. Especially when I don't even know if I'm going to get one and —"

"Of course you'll get a fucking acceptance letter," he interrupts in a lashing voice.

And my heart soars in my chest. At his utter belief in me.

In my dream.

"You think so?" I can't help but ask.

I mean, I know this is what I want to do and I *know* I can do it but what if...

What if I can't?

What if it's all in my head?

What if I'm not good enough to go to art school?

"Do I *think* so," he asks, his voice as lashing as before — actually more so now. "Fuck yeah, I think so. I think so because you work hard for it. *And* you're talented as fuck." He steps closer to me, his head bent, his eyes full of fire and belief. "Do you know how rare that is? To be talented at something and also be disciplined enough to make something out of it? It's fucking rare. So *rare* that I can count on one hand all the players I've coached who're not only talented but are also smart enough to recognize that. The rest of them are just little shitheads who don't know what to do with the talent they were born with."

I open my mouth to say something to him then.

Something like *I love you*.

Or like *why can't you love me back? Why do you love someone else?*

And it's so huge, that urge, that I have to clench my teeth to keep the words inside.

Because if I don't, he'll leave.

And he'll never come back. And I'll never get a chance to show him all the things I want to.

I'll never get the chance to be his.

Not even for a little bit.

"Where are your parents?" he asks abruptly, pulling me out of my thoughts.

"What?"

"If they took you to New York today and you're just getting back, where are they?"

"What, why?"

"Because the right time is now."

"What?" I squeal almost, completely horrified.

"Come on," he says, looking up at the house. "Let's go tell them. Let's tell them that you're going to art school. And so they should stop pulling you out of school like this and wasting everyone's time."

Oh my God.

Oh God.

He's crazy.

He's absolutely crazy.

I'm not telling my parents right now.

I can't.

They were so happy today. Well, as happy as they can be with me, but still. This was the first time my dad introduced me to people and didn't grimace in a year. Since I vandalized his car.

I can't tell them right now and ruin everything.

I already did once.

I need time.

I need to gently break the news to them.

And this is not gentle. This man here, breathing wildly, glaring at the house I grew up in.

"No," I tell him and he focuses on me. "Absolutely not. You're not talking to my parents about anything. It doesn't matter. It was one campus tour and now it's over. I won't have to do it again."

When he opens his mouth I stop him again. But this time I do it with both my words and my hands. I put them both on his chest and splay my fingers. "They're my parents, Conrad, and I can handle them myself. I've done it for eighteen years. It's going to be fine. Once I have my acceptance letter, I'll tell them then. You don't get to make this decision for me, okay? So back off."

Now he's glaring at *me*.

His chest all big and hard under my palms. Scary.

But I don't care.

He absolutely does not get to make this decision for me.

I will make it myself. I will choose the time and the place to do this.

He finally loses the stubborn look on his face and takes a deep breath. Which makes me take a deep, relieved breath too.

"You're coming with me."

I'm confused by his command. "What?"

"I'm assuming since you got out of the car all alone, your parents aren't here," he explains. "Are they?"

"No."

My dad's in DC because he got a call last minute about a meeting that he had to attend. In reality, I think he's flown over to meet his girlfriend or mistress or whoever she is. And when my mother realized that, she booked herself a spa for the weekend and didn't return from New York at all.

"And what about your army of servants? Are they going to take the night off and leave?"

"Yes, except for..." I shake my head. "Wait, how do you know about my army of servants?" But before he can answer me, I go on, "First of all: please don't call them servants. They all work here, for my parents. They're making an honest living and their job just happens to be keeping my parents' house. Calling them servants is demeaning. And second of all: as I said, they work for my parents, so they're not mine. Also there's no army. We have like, five or maybe six people working on our property." I scrunch my brows then. "Wait, there's two more. But one of them only comes two days a week so I don't know if you can call him full time or what but —"

"Bronwyn," he warns.

And I shut my mouth, realizing that I'm rambling. "Right. Sorry. But how'd you know?" I narrow my eyes at him, fisting his sweater. "Because you think every snotty rich teenage princess has an army of servants?"

If he says yes to that, I swear I'm going to hit him.

But he doesn't.

"No, I guess we've already established that you're not a princess." Then, he averts his eyes for a second before saying, "I might've... talked to one of them."

"You *talked* to one of them?"

He sighs. "When I got here, yes. One of them opened the door when I knocked — a woman. And when I asked about you, she told me that you weren't here and that you were due back in an hour or two."

I'm... astonished.

I'm fucking astonished.

At least as much as I was when I saw him here, standing at the end of my driveway, if not more.

This is surreal.

I quit studying his features then and look away from him because I remember something: the sound of a car door shutting when he first called out my name.

I look in the direction of where he came from and notice the polished glint of his truck.

Snapping my gaze back to him, I ask, my heart starting to race in my chest again, "So you've been... Have you been waiting for me to come back home? For the last hour or two."

My question, hesitant and hopeful, makes him clench his jaw. It makes his heart roar in his chest too.

Just like mine.

I feel it under my palms.

Only I don't know the reason behind it.

Is it the same as mine? The reason.

Is it because he's as ecstatic to see me as I am to see him? And because he missed me as much as I missed him?

This is why he came, didn't he? Not because of stupid soccer practice.

"Come on, let's go."

That's all he says and I fist his sweater even more tightly than before. "But I need to know. I need to know if you were waiting for me. And if you were, did you miss me? I —"

"Your incompetent fucking parents aren't here," he speaks over me. "And I'm not leaving you in this house. Without parental supervision."

My heart that was racing and roaring in my chest comes to a screeching halt.

And my lips part as I drag in large gulps of breath. "Parental supervision."

His heart, on the other hand, is well and alive. It's still beating away, roaring and thundering in his chest.

"Yes."

I rove my eyes over his sharply defined features, looking for something, *anything*, to tell me that the conclusions I'm drawing in my head right now are wrong. I even ask him, "You came here to check on me because I missed soccer practice?"

A blast, a thunder goes off in his chest then. "Yes."

"Because you thought my parents did something to me."

Another thundering beat. "Given your parents' history, it was an obvious conclusion to draw."

I twist my fists on his chest. "And now you want me to go with you because they're not here. Because you think I need parental supervision."

His eyes bore into mine. "Yes."

"And that's the only reason and nothing else."

"Yes."

"Right." I nod. "Okay."

I keep nodding as my fists go loose around his sweater. As they let go of it.

I also keep nodding when I step away from him.

Which I notice that *he* notices.

His eyes snap down to my feet, to my winter boots, as I take another step away from him.

"You should leave," I tell him.

At my voice, he lifts his eyes. "Not without you, no."

A third step away from him. "I'm not going with you."

His nostrils flare as he warns like he usually does, "Bronwyn."

I shake my head as I keep moving away from him. "I'm not going anywhere with you. I want you to leave. Now."

"Stop moving away from me," he growls.

I don't.

"Leave," I say sternly and his fists clench. "Now." Ignoring my command, he takes a step forward and I put my hands up. "If you come near me right now, I'm going to scream. I'm going to fucking scream this place down, do you understand? I want you to leave. Leave, Conrad."

Of course my threats don't scare him.

Of course he ignores them like they don't matter. And why wouldn't he?

Nothing I do matters to him. Nothing I do makes a difference.

Nothing I do will *ever* make a difference, will ever make him see that I'm more than a teenager.

That I'm more.

And I was stupid, so stupid to think that he came here because he missed me.

"I've been very patient with you," I tell him, my hands still up and my feet still moving back. "Extremely patient. But it doesn't matter, does it? Because you'll never look at me as anything but a teenager who needs *parental supervision*."

In an epic role reversal, he's the one still moving closer to me as he says, "You *are* a fucking teenager."

His words pierce my skin, my heart as I say, "I know. I know I am, and what a huge crime it is that I am, isn't it? What a huge *fucking* crime it is that I'm eighteen." I throw my hands up and let out a broken laugh. "And if I could do something about it, if I could do something about my age, I would. Trust me, I would. I would make myself whatever age you think is appropriate for you. Because I've done everything else. *Everything else.* To make you see that I'm more than just a teenager. I mean, I've done everything that you've asked for. I stand there every morning, doing your bidding, reading my letters out loud to you to show you that I'm more. And all you do is punish me for it. And you don't even deign to kiss me. And you *won't,* will you? I realize that now. Because you're prejudiced and judgmental and an epic asshole. You're an ageist. That's what you are and I hate you. So you need to leave or I'm going to throw *such* a teenage tantrum the likes of which you've never seen in your entire thirty-three years of life, Coach Thorne."

With that I spin around, ready to leave.

Ready to go up to my room and cry.

And cry and cry.

Because I don't think I'm going to stop any time soon.

Crying.

For myself. For my age. For the fact that I'm in love with an asshole who will never see me as anything but a teenager. And I...

My thoughts seize up then.

Because I feel him at my back. I feel his heat, sudden and jarring, his breaths, and then I feel his grip.

I feel his fingers grabbing hold of my bicep and then I feel them squeezing my flesh, putting pressure on it until he spins me back around, pulling me toward him. And I go crashing into his chest.

And then I both hear and feel him growl, "Stop fucking walking away from me."

I'm ready to push him away like I was ready to leave and cry.

I am.

I even plant my palms on his wildly breathing chest so I can shove him away.

But at the last second, like a fool, like a *fucking* fool, I look up and blurt out, "If I was older," I ask and lick my lips. "Would you kiss me then?"

His eyes are sweeping over my features with the same urgency again. Although this time I think his urgency has a different flavor.

A different edge.

This time his urgency is laced with a strange desperation.

"No," he whispers, shaking his head slowly.

So now is the time then.

Now is the time to push him away since I have my answer.

But for some reason I can't look away from that desperation in his glinting eyes. "Not even if I was nineteen?"

His fingers on my bicep flex. "No."

"Twenty?"

"No."

I should stop now.

I should.

Every no is such a knife to my heart. Every no makes me bleed. Every no pricks me like a thorn.

And yet, like a pathetic masochist, I keep going. "Twenty-one?"

"No."

I finally gather the self-preservation to push him away but by then I'm already trapped.

By then, his other hand is in my hair and the one that was grabbing my bicep has grabbed onto my face.

And he's dug his fingers into my body.

He's dug his stinging, scrape-y, perfect fingers into my hair and my cheek and that desperation has leached into his voice as he says, "The other day you told me something. You *told* me that if I went looking for you across campus, you'd be easy to find. But you lied, didn't you? Because when you didn't show up this morning, to stand there and do my bidding and read those rosy pink letters of yours, I went looking for you. I looked for you in the hallways, in the cafeteria, in the library. I looked for you in every classroom. I searched every inch of those snow-covered grounds. But you weren't there. You were here. You were on your useless goddamn campus tour."

"You looked for m-me?"

"Yeah." He leans even closer to me, tugging my neck, my face back so he can really look at me and make me look at him. "And the reason I wouldn't kiss you if you were older is because I'm going to kiss you *now*. Not when you're nineteen or twenty or twenty-one. I'm going to kiss your eighteen-year-old-mouth right *fucking* now because I'm done not kissing it. And you might hate me for it. You might hate me because I'm going to do it like I'm pissed off at your mouth. Like I'm fucking angry at it. But that's only because you've got a criminal mouth, Bronwyn. Your pouting, plump, *pinky* mouth is a sexy little criminal for saying sexy little things to me. For torturing me. For driving me *in-fucking-sane*. And for being the star of my every X-rated thought."

And then he does it.

He kisses me.

He's *kissing* me.

His mouth is on me. And it's warm and wet and soft.

So, *so* soft.

But it's also commanding, his mouth.

So commanding and dominating. Possessive and punishing.

But.

But.

He can't kiss me. Not now. Not *here*.

And I should tell him that too. I should tell him that he can't kiss me here.

That someone might see. That we might get caught.

But as it turns out, I don't have to say anything to him. He gets it all by himself. He gets it because he wants to protect me as much as I want to protect him.

We're two peas in a pod, aren't we?

And so like he always does in his office, he hauls me up. He puts his hands on my waist and gives me the boost that he gives every morning. And since my body is so used to his actions, it goes up.

My feet leave the ground and my thighs settle around his hips, spreading.

Settling my pussy on his stomach and lighting me up.

And when he's settled me on himself, he begins to move. He begins to take me somewhere and I wonder where, in the back of my head, as I twist in his arms, my fingers clutching his sweater, his mouth moving over mine.

Turns out it's not very far.

He comes to a halt after only a few steps and then things shift a little. I tighten my thighs around his when I feel him going down.

When I feel him lowering himself to his knees and laying me down on the ground.

On soft grass.

Like I'm his bed of roses, his bed of pretty little wallflowers, and he lies down over me.

And I sigh in his kiss.

I sigh because now I can kiss him back. Now that we're hidden and safe and secure, I can kiss him with all the love in my heart. My kisses won't ruin things for him.

So I do.

I kiss him back.

And soon as I do, he comes alive.

His mouth becomes aggressive, like he was waiting for me to participate. He was waiting for me to kiss him and now that I am, he forces me to open it, my mouth.

Like a flower.

So he can get inside.

So he can pierce me like a sharp thorn. And when he does, I move against him. I bloom like my mouth is blooming.

I wind my arms around his neck and pull him closer.

To pull him all over me. To give me his weight, to press down on me, while I wind my thighs around his waist and rub my pussy on his stomach. Because I can't *imagine* not being pressed down by him. I can't imagine not being his wallflower and getting crushed under his weight.

And I guess he thinks the same way.

Because his grip tightens around me at my actions. His grip becomes crushing and pervasive.

As if he's everywhere, all at once.

His mouth is gripping mine all possessively. His fingers are gripping my cheek, squeezing to open my mouth wider. They're somehow also gripping the back of my head to pull me even closer to him.

To his harshly breathing body, to his expertly kissing mouth.

And I moan.

I moan so very loudly. Because this is what I wanted.

This is what I *needed*.

To be laid on the ground and spread out like this. To rub my swollen bruise of a pussy on his stomach like I do every day. To hump my wet and weeping and soppy pussy on the ridges of his abs so I can leave tearstains on his shirt.

And from the looks of it, he needed that too.

He needed it badly.

He might have needed it for weeks now.

And then I feel something else.

Something between my thighs. That something is rubbing and pushing into me through the layers of clothing for the first time ever and I don't know what to do except push against it.

His cock.

His big, hard cock that he said would cover me from chin to forehead if I ever put my face under it.

That beast of a cock is between my legs now and like his mouth, he hasn't let me touch it yet.

He makes me rub my pussy on his stomach like a shameless slut every morning but he doesn't let me rub it against his dick.

And I've tried.

I've tried so many times over the past days.

Every time I slide lower than where he wants me to be, he smacks my ass. He smacks my thighs too, where I still write his name every night, and these days, soon after our office sessions. Because I like the thought of drawing pretty roses on my stinging, pink skin courtesy of my thorn.

But not tonight.

Tonight along with his mouth, he gives me his dick as well. He not only gives it but he rubs it up and down the juncture of my thighs. He rolls his hips, hitting the right spot every time.

And I move with him. I dance with him.

All happy and lusty and so fucking drugged on his kisses.

And he likes the way I'm dancing and writhing for him because he groans.

He groans into my mouth, egging me on, moving his hips, humping them against me like I hump my pussy in his office. All desperately and lustily and in a way that makes me think that he wants me to orgasm.

And so I give it to him.

I jerk under him.

I jerk and twist and I come.

I come in my parents' front yard like I come in his office every day, my body spasming, my limbs tightening around him even more, my head thrown back and my moans reaching the sky.

Only tonight his lips are there to calm me down.

His lips are there to kiss the blush on my cheeks, to blow on the sweat on my forehead. His fingers are there to trace the shape of my chin, my nose.

And his eyes, all glittering and possessive as he stares down at me and asks, "Are you on the pill?"

My heart pulses.

My pussy pulses too.

And panting, I break out a dazed nod. "Yes."

"I want you to know that I'm clean."

"Okay."

He licks his lips, his eyes roving over my face as he says, as if to himself, "Nothing has worked. Not one thing has worked. *Nothing* that I've done has made me want you less. I know I shouldn't. I know that. I shouldn't even think about you, let alone want you the way I do. You're barely eighteen. You're my sister's best friend. You're my student. So I'm going to try one last thing."

"What?"

He stares into my eyes as he rasps, "I'm going to take you."

Again a pulse runs through me and I jerk under him. "T-take me."

"Yeah," he whispers, his thumb caressing my cheek, his breaths fanning over my lips. "I'm going to take every inch of you. Every rosy little inch. And then I'm going to eat you up. I'm going to drink you down. I'm going to inhale you. Inject you in my bloodstream. I'm going to fucking *live* you, Bronwyn. Until I don't want to anymore. Until this crazy irrational desire is gone. Until I'm not looking for you at school or driving down to your town and knocking at your door like an addict. Just because I didn't get to see you today. Just because I didn't get my fix. So you're coming with me. Because you're my pretty little wallflower and I'm done being insane over you."

# CHAPTER TWENTY-THREE

I'm in his house again.

In his bedroom.

And standing at the door, he's staring at me.

He's actually *leaning* against the door — the doorjamb, his arms folded across his chest *while* he stares at me with intense and possessive eyes. Same as they were back at my house, in my parents' front yard.

"You know, you could've just *asked*," I say.

It's as if he wakes up at my voice, blinking.

And I realize that he wasn't. Blinking, I mean.

He hadn't all the while he was staring at me. Which has been pretty much the whole time since we arrived at his house about twenty minutes ago. And as soon as we did, I toed off my winter boots, my magenta parka with yellow flowers, and made a beeline to his bedroom and he simply followed me.

"Asked what?"

"Where I was," I explain. "Back at St. Mary's. You could've just asked someone where I was. Instead of looking for me. In every classroom. And in the hallways." I widen my eyes, all teasingly. "And on the soccer field. At the library."

Amusement flashes through his eyes. "And the cafeteria."

"What?"

His lips twitch. "I also looked for you in the cafeteria."

"Oh right. Forgot that one. My bad." I raise my eyebrows at him. "So? You could've saved yourself the trouble and just asked someone."

"I did."

"Who?"

"One of your friends."

This time my eyes go wide in serious shock. "Not Ca…"

His narrow, however, something flashing in them. "Are we protecting my reputation from my sister too?"

I bite my lip. "No. It's just that…"

"Just what?"

I grimace, kicking myself for bringing this up now of all the places and times. What if he changes his mind now?

What if he realizes that we can't do this?

*Great, Wyn. Just great.*

"It's just that she knows. About my Mystery Man. That's what I've been calling you. Before I knew…" I stare into his eyes. "Who you were. But anyway, she knows that I met someone and he changed my life and… But she doesn't know that it's you. She doesn't know that we've met before and I-I feel like I'm betraying her by not telling her. But I'm afraid if I do tell her, she might…"

"She might?"

"Freak out? I don't know. She might hate me for keeping all these secrets from her. And besides," I swallow, still staring into his eyes, "everything is much more complicated now, right?"

*Because I'm with you. Here.*

*Because I was waiting and waiting to be taken. And because you've finally taken me.*

I don't have to say that to him. He gets it already.

It's clear on his features, which are set in tight lines as he stares back at me.

"Not for you, no," he says at last.

"What?"

"It's not complicated for you," he explains, his taut biceps flexing. "It's complicated for *me*. Because I'm the one who brought you here. I'm the one who took you. Despite…" His jaw clenches. "Everything. So now, this secret is mine. It belongs to me. I'm the one betraying her. So if my sister wants to hate someone, she can hate me. Not you."

"But I —"

"Not you, Bronwyn," he says sternly. "You understand?"

I swallow again, my heart twisting.

This isn't what I wanted.

I didn't want to give him any more burdens. Or responsibilities.

"You're mine now," he continues. "So your secrets are mine. I don't want you worrying over something like that. She's your best friend and she'll always be your best friend. I'll make sure of that."

Even after he's gone, he means.

That's what he means, doesn't he?

After this is over. After I've done my job and filled his life with all the colors and all the joy. And after he stops wanting me, he'll make sure that I don't lose my friend.

Because that's why he brought me here. To get me out of his system.

To fuck me out.

I fist my hands at my sides. I suck my belly in.

Because the pain is immense.

And it hits me from nowhere.

But I ignore it because I love him, and I'll give him whatever he wants. I'll choose him over myself and this pain.

Swallowing, I whisper, "Okay." Another swallow, this time with a tremulous smile. "Thank you."

His features bunch up for a moment as he takes in my smile. As if he's thinking the same thing. As if he's thinking about the end before we've even begun.

But it goes away quickly and he says, "It was your other friend."

"Which one?"

"The one who's always" — he shakes his head with a slight grimace — "giving me looks."

An almost-giggle shocks me out of nowhere. "Poe?"

"Yeah."

"So she told you that I was home?"

"No," he clips. "She told me that it was for her to know and for me to find out. Where you were."

This time I let the giggle escape. "She didn't."

"She did. In those exact words."

His eyes turn soft when I laugh some more. "So how'd you find out?"

"Your other friend," he replies, still leaning by the door. "The one who knows how to play soccer. The *only* one who knows how to play soccer."

"So Salem then. That's how you knew to drive to my house?"

"Yeah."

"And so you did."

"And so I did."

"And knocked at my door and asked about me."

He unfolds his arms then. "And knocked at your door and asked about you, yeah."

"And —"

He takes a step toward me. "And *waited* for two hours."

Shaking my head, I take a step back. "I knew it. I *knew* it. I *so* knew you were waiting."

"And then I watched you flirt with one of your fans," he says, his voice taking on a dangerous edge, his eyes pinned on me as he keeps moving forward.

My feet stumble but I keep going back, edging closer to the wall by his bed. "What fan?"

His jaw tightens for a second. "The guy you were talking to. *Laughing* with. In the car."

"Charles?"

"So there's a Charles now too."

"Oh my God, you're insane," I say, laughing. "Charles is like... He's my friend. And he's old."

"Yeah?"

"Yes."

"How old?"

A current goes through me at his words, the familiar question he's asking me. At the look in his eyes as he advances on me while I keep moving back.

"Older," I whisper.

"How much older?"

I bite my lip. "Much." When his eyes flash even more, I say, "He's probably sixty. He's got a granddaughter, Janie. I was giving him a sketch that I made for her. She's into Spider-Man, but I'm trying to make her a convert and turn her to Iron Man."

I'm not sure why but his chest undulates at this information. It shifts, and his fists clench as if something, some great emotion, is moving through him. Then, he mutters as if to himself, "She never quits, does she?"

"Quit —"

"What's this one called?" he asks, tipping his chin at my lips, moving closer and closer.

My lipstick.

I'm wearing one now.

After he made me come and explained all the things to me, he was ready for us to leave. But I told him that I needed a few things before we could go. So I ran inside the house, grabbed the things that I needed, which included this lipstick that I'm wearing, and ran back out to go with him.

Martha did catch me coming and going but when I told her that I was going to a party and she saw the clothes I had on — yes, I've changed clothes too; I prettied myself up for him — she let me go without batting an eyelash.

Anyway now, I reply, biting my lip, "Red Addict."

His eyes flare slightly.

*Until I'm not looking for you at school or driving down to your town and knocking at your door like an addict.*

That's what he said to me, so I painted my lips that color, dark maroon-ish red, for him.

"Do you like it?" I ask.

At my question he shudders and his voice turns all thick and growly. "Get over here."

I don't.

I keep going. "What about my dress?"

His eyes go to my dress. It's a maroon dress to match the lipstick. It's lacy and shows more cleavage than the one I wore on the day I sketched him. And when I took off the magenta parka and revealed it to him, I thought he'd say something. But he hasn't yet.

"Bronwyn, get the fuck over here."

I don't obey him though. I keep walking back until I can't.

Until I touch the wall.

The wall that is as bare as that office wall I stand against every morning. Except I didn't get to do that today.

So I stand here.

And with scattered breaths, I say, "I have a dream for you."

He comes to a jerking halt at this, his features drawing up tight and severe.

"I wrote something for you on that rosy pink paper. A dream I had last night," I say, fidgeting with the fabric of my dress. "But I didn't get to give it to you today. And now I don't want to. I don't want to give you something I wrote on a piece of paper. When I really want to give you something else, a different kind of dream."

By the time I'm done, his body has become the tightest that I've ever seen it.

All bulging muscles and ridges under his dark sweater.

"A different kind of a dream," he repeats in an abraded voice.

"Yes," I whisper, fisting the fabric of my dark dress and sliding the hem up.

His gaze immediately drops to my hands. And latches on.

I watch him beginning to breathe faster, his chest expanding and contracting as I say, "I've been wanting to, but I... I was waiting for the right time. I was waiting for you to want it, want *me*. And it turns out that you do want me. And that you were pretending. You're so good at that, at keeping all your thoughts and emotions in check. At making me think what you want me to think, even if it's not true. I hate that, and we're going to talk about that at some point."

Things flicker and move in his eyes at my words but I keep going, both with my words and the hem of my dress. "And so I want to give you, show you, something that I made. Something that I make every night. Something that I decorate with sharp thorns and pretty roses. A piece of art. On my body. That I've been hiding under my clothes. From everyone. From you."

He swallows when I pause again, bringing my dress to right there.

Right fucking there.

One micro-inch up and he'll see it.

He'll see the things I do to myself. How I write his name.

This is the last barrier, isn't it?

I've broken down all of his and now this is mine. My one little barrier.

That I've been wanting to break down for some time now and so it's a relief.

A euphoria to be able to show him.

And I do.

I pull my hem up and up, and then I take my entire lacy dress off, revealing my body to him. I even take my panties off and toe them away, leaving myself all decorated and naked.

"I don't want to give you a dream written on a piece of paper when I can give you one written on my body," I whisper, my eyes bold and shameless, my Rapunzel hair falling down my bare spine in a light brown curtain.

For a second, nothing happens.

He's frozen, unmovable in the face of my bare body. In the face of my thorns and roses.

My heart thuds and *thuds* in my chest and I feel like a chill is setting in, turning my heated skin blue.

But then it happens.

Piece by piece. Bit by bit.

He begins to thaw. He begins to heat up, even.

It starts with his eyes, dark blue that appear even darker right now. Heavier, more intense, more alive. And a second ago they were focused on my hands, but now they are... unfocused.

They are frantic.

They are everywhere.

Like his hands were when he was kissing me.

On my thighs where his name is written in elaborate swirls. On my lower belly, where I've written his name in a stabby font. Then they jump to the side of my ribs where I've used a combination of both. Followed by the place just under my breasts and then on my belly again, where I've drawn a rose around my belly button, and on the petals, I've written his name again in a tiny script.

And while his eyes are on the move, circling, sweeping and going back and forth on my body, the muscles on his are shifting as well.

Shifting and expanding and rising and falling.

As he takes wild breaths. As he parts his mouth. As his pulse ticks on the side of his neck.

And then there are noises. A growl, I think.

Coming from deep inside his heaving chest. Probably originating somewhere in his contracting and expanding stomach.

Finally it reaches — this phenomenon that's happening to him, this thawing and heating up — his legs.

Because they move.

No actually, they lunge.

They leap across the distance between us and before I can even blink, he's right there. He appears before me, so close to me that his sweater-clad chest *almost* grazes the tips of my breasts.

And then that almost graze becomes an overwhelming firecracker of a touch when he leans over and snags an arm around my naked waist. When he yanks me to him, bends his knees and hauls me up. And when he does all that, my naked soft body, my naked soft skin slides and writhes over his scrape-y jeans and his woolen sweater.

Making me gasp.

Making me restless and hot.

And so so wet.

As wet as the kisses he's giving me.

Because he is.

As soon as he's made me climb his body, he puts his mouth on me. And of course I latch on. Of course I suck on his plump bottom lip and he sucks on mine with equal vigor.

And he takes me somewhere. Like he did back at my house when he had me in his arms.

Not only that, he also tips and tilts my world — again like he did before — but this time, my back hits warm sheets instead of cold grass. And yet again, he's all over me.

He's settled over my naked body, his muscular, unforgiving chest pressing into my plump tits and his jean-clad thighs rubbing against mine. And his mouth still kissing and biting and sucking as his hands feel me up.

As his hands, as rough and delicious as his clothes, roam over my body.

They squeeze my naked tits. They press into my delicate ribs before moving down and kneading my ass. Before moving down *further* and massaging my thighs. Actually they're tugging on my thighs, pulling them over his waist, and I wind them around his hips tightly. I even cross my ankles at his back and move.

I rub my naked pussy on his clothes as he breaks the kiss and goes to my throat.

Where the first thing he does is sink his teeth in and bite.

And I jerk as if someone has electrocuted me.

I also moan loud and clear and tilt my head to the side to give him more space, more skin to bite on. To suck on, which he does a second later.

He sucks on my soft flesh like he's drinking from it. Like he said he would.

He also rubs his nose on my skin like he's breathing me in.

Before bringing his mouth on my chest. On my tits to be exact.

Not at the nipple though. Where I realize I need him the most. But at the slope of my breast, at the meaty part, which he immediately sinks his teeth into again as my back arches up with pulsing currents.

And then he begins to suck my plump flesh.

I arch up and into his mouth as he sucks and sucks. With such force — God, with such a pull — that his cheeks hollow out. I notice that; I do. His sharp cheeks form pits and his high cheekbones go higher as he sucks and tugs my heavy tit up and away from my body.

Before letting it go and making it bounce and jiggle.

And a red bruise blooms on my pale skin.

Before I have the time to take a breath, he dives in again. He does the same to my other tit before going for my nipples. Those throbbing, painful things that have needed his attention for ages now.

And then he moves lower.

To my ribs, my waist, my belly.

That I have also decorated for him, with a belly chain — the only piece of jewelry that I thought would be appropriate. I didn't want anything on me except his name.

He tugs at the chain now. He pulls at it as he goes down to my belly button.

Meanwhile, I'm writhing under him, moaning, getting wetter and wetter.

All steaming and hot.

But when he hits my lower belly and I feel his shoulders rubbing against my thighs, when I feel his chin rubbing against the top of my very wet mound, I fist his hair.

I pull at it and twist against him as I say, "Conrad, wait…"

He doesn't.

He's busy painting my skin with his teeth and giving me love bites.

"C-Conrad." I pull at his hair again, going up on my trembling elbows. "What are you… What are you doing?"

At last, he looks up and what I see makes my elbows slip and sends me back down on the bed.

What I see is a man possessed.

With dark eyes — pitch black — and a harsh face.

A face with so many sharp, thorny edges that if he hadn't said that, back at my house, if he hadn't claimed me as his flower, I'd still feel like one.

I'd still feel all velvety and soft and feminine in the face of his sheer masculinity. His sharp and intense possessiveness.

Even his hands are possessive and masculine the way they're holding my thighs open for him.

I can see his chest going up and down against the bed as I ask again, "What are you doing?"

He licks his dark red lips. "Apologizing."

"What?"

"For lying to you again." He runs his eyes up the length of my body. "For making you hide from me."

My heart twists at the reminder. That he did, in fact, lie to me again.

"You looked for me."

"Yes."

"You came to my house," I whisper. "You wanted me. All this time." I fist his hair some more. "But you pretended not to."

Regret flashes through his features. "I did."

I shake my head, my nails digging into his scalp. "You're a jerk." Then with narrowed eyes, I say, "Coach Thorne."

At my 'Coach Thorne' something happens to him.

Right in front of my eyes, he expands and becomes larger. His muscles bulge out and the hollows of his face become sharper. He becomes more beautiful, more lethal.

Somehow more mine.

As he clenches his jaw and growls, "Yeah, and now I'm going to fucking apologize for it."

With that, he goes back to my pussy.

He rubs his nose over my creamy lips, smelling them. Taking in their scent. Almost snorting my scent in. And then he licks.

God, does he lick.

He licks my whole snatch, sucks it into his mouth and makes me come.

It's embarrassing how easy I am.

How slutty that one lick and I'm there. I'm coming in his mouth but I can't hate myself for that. I've been waiting for this moment for so long and he had me all revved up.

He had me on the edge so my rose just bursts in his mouth and he drinks it all down.

He even thrusts his tongue inside and I feel a pressure. Very little, but it's there. It tells me that something is inside of me, making me fist the sheets as I writhe on his mouth, my belly chain jiggling and making soft noises.

Conrad is making noises too but they aren't soft.

God, no.

They're growly and horny and I swear I feel them in my pussy. And Jesus, I come again.

For the second time.

Or is that the third, I don't know.

And I don't have the brain power to count because as soon as he makes me come, he rises from between my thighs.

Like a Greek god of some kind, a Viking warrior with his long, dark blond hair in his eyes, and he gets up on his knees, his mouth all wet.

And swollen.

Then like the day I painted him and asked him to take his sweater off, he reaches over and snags the back of his sweater before pulling it off his body and throwing it away somewhere.

But what gets my breaths wild and crazy and makes my stomach tremble is the fact that, staring down at me, he begins to unbutton his shirt. Actually, he starts with his cuffs, which somehow makes everything even hotter.

Because for some reason, it makes him look so mature and grown up, starting at the cuffs, revealing his big silver watch.

Then he moves on to his top button and right in front of my eyes, he goes through them so gracefully, so fast and yet so slow that by the time he's done and he's pulling the shirttails out of his jeans, I'm a mess.

I'm a creaming mess.

Not that I wasn't before.

But I'm pretty sure that I've already orgasmed again because my channel won't stop pulsing. My channel won't stop gushing. And somewhere in the last few seconds, I probably blinked or something because the next thing I know, his glorious, rippling, muscled flesh is revealed.

And Jesus Christ, he does have a V.

But before I can marvel over it, he comes down at me.

Not all the way though.

He leans over me, both his hands on either side of my face, his long hair making a super sexy and masculine curtain over his forehead and my arms reach up to him.

My hands grip his biceps and I even raise my thighs and wrap them around his hot, naked sides like some kind of shameless, horny gymnast.

In a very guttural and deep voice, he says, "I'm an asshole, Bronwyn. Your Coach Thorne is a cruel selfish asshole. For doing that to you. For putting you through bullshit again."

I roll my head from side to side. "No, please. I just... I just want..."

"Especially when every day I stand by that wall. And I smell it."

"What?"

"I stand by the wall where you stand and rub my nose on the bricks, hoping to catch a whiff of you. And when I do, I fucking open my mouth and drink it down. Your Coach Thorne drinks you down and then he bangs his head on the wall for doing that. For doing something so depraved. And then, even though he's cursing at himself, hating himself for wanting his forbidden little wallflower, he goes to his chair. He sits on it and he opens her rosy pink letter. He opens it and reads it himself."

I'm shuddering now, arching my back, digging my nails into his biceps. "C-Conrad, please."

"And when I do my dick gets hard. It gets hard*er*," he tells me, his stomach contracting. "Because it's usually already hard the moment you enter through the door and it stays that way until you leave. But when I read your letters, Bronwyn, when I see those words written in your delicate, flowery handwriting, I lose my shit. My dick throbs. It pulses and drop after drop of pre-cum slides down my cock. But I don't jack off, no. Because I'm punishing myself, see. I'm fucking punishing myself for wanting something so young and sweet. But I was wrong, wasn't I?

"Because all this time I was punishing you too. I was torturing you. Making you wait, making you suffer under my hands when every night, you *make* yourself for me. You decorate yourself. You write my name on every inch of your body so sweetly. You make flowers on it. My wallflower makes flowers on her body for her thorn and instead of cherishing that, instead of kissing every inch of her body, I make her flesh burn. I color her pink and bruised. But not anymore, you got that?"

"Conrad, you don't —"

"I'm not going to let you hide from me. Not from me," he says, his biceps bunching under my hands. "Not like you've had to do with others."

My heart squeezes again.

I know what he's referring to. I know what he's getting at, my parents, my town, and I just... I just want him here. On me. In me. Close to me.

"Conrad," I whisper because that's all I can do in the face of so much love pressing down on me.

For him.

"I'm not going to let you keep any more secrets," he insists. "Nothing will come between us, Bronwyn. I'm going to destroy everything that does. Even that tiny piece of flesh."

"T-tiny piece of flesh?"

He lowers himself slightly, his arms straining, bending as if he's about to do a push-up. "That tiny piece of flesh that I'm obsessed with. That keeps you tight and pure."

My channel pulses for the millionth time tonight.

Or maybe it never stopped.

"My virginity?"

He lowers even more at this and I arch my back, my bruised nipples grazing his hard chest. My pussy rubbing on his bare stomach now that he's lowered enough for me to do so.

"Yeah. Your virginity." A puff of breath escapes him. "And I'm not only obsessed with it, no. I'm not only constantly, *constantly* thinking about sticking my tongue down there, inside your rosy hole, so I can taste it, that tiny piece of flesh. In my fucking mouth. Before I rip it with my dick. Like I just did."

"Y-you..."

"Yeah. And it tastes as good as your pussy. Rosy."

My channel pulses, remembering that pressure inside me when he stuck his tongue inside. And I keep rubbing my wet, creaming hole on the tight ridges of his abs as I ask, "W-what else are you thinking about?"

"I'm also thinking about the fact that it's there for *me*," he rumbles, his fingers fisting the sheets. "That you've *kept* it, your hymen, all unbroken and intact for me. I'm arrogant enough to think that all these years, you've kept your legs closed and your skirts down to your knees so you can keep it all safe. From the rest of those assholes, those motherfucking fans of yours, because you've been waiting for me. You've been waiting for me to come and take it. You want *my* dick to steal it from you and make you bleed. And then you want my dick to paint your rose down there, your pretty pinky rose, with my cum. Me and no one else. That's how arrogant and *selfish* I've been, Bronwyn. That's how selfish and cruel your Coach Thorne is, who makes you stand by a wall and read out those letters and makes you hide your body from him."

My hands fly to his face, sweaty and tight. "I want it too. I want it. And I did. I kept it for you. I wouldn't let anyone take it."

"Yeah?" He skims his lips over mine and I suck on them like hard candy.

I nod, letting go of his lips with a pop. "Yes. Only you. Only my thorn."

Finally he drops down on me and whispers in my ear, "Yeah, you kept your pussy all rosy and pure for me. Locked up tight against all those horny bastards who given the chance would pound you seven ways to Sunday even if you didn't want it. Because you're mine, aren't you? Because you're made for me."

I'm so delirious right now that I nod again.

Wordlessly.

And then he goes over to my ear, licks my earlobe as he whispers, "I'm sorry, Bronwyn. I'm so fucking sorry."

I want to tell him that I'm not mad at him anymore. That yes, I wanted to talk about his lying but I don't now.

Now all I want is him.

But he disappears. He takes himself away from me.

Only for a second though.

Before I can even blink my eyes open and think of forming some coherent words, he's here and I can feel the tip of his cock, nudging my opening.

Suspended on his elbows, he bends down and places a soft kiss on my lips, whispering, "My wallflower."

And enters.

He slams his cock inside of me and I arch my back. And I swear to God, I come again.

My channel pulses around the one thing it's always wanted, him. And I guess one thing he's always wanted is me as well because he groans and drops completely down on my body.

My thorn.

Cradling my face, he tucks his head in the crook of my neck, hugging me, his lips breathing and shushing me. As his dick is all lodged inside my creamy, formerly virgin pussy.

That for being so recently virgin, is behaving so... gustily.

I'm not sure if it's the fact that I've orgasmed so many times tonight that my pussy is all lubed up and open. Or maybe it's the fact that I'm still coming around his length.

But I don't feel the pain.

Yes, there's pressure. And there's fullness. So much of it. But I've craved it for so long, I've ached for it for so, *so* long that I don't mind it. I don't mind feeling full or stretched out.

In fact I like it. I like that he's jammed up inside of me, that my core is full of him like my heart.

So I move.

Because I don't need him to stop. I don't need him to shush me or make me feel better. I already do, with him inside me.

I tell him that by moving under him, arching and writhing. And he looks up.

Making my heart twist.

His eyes are drugged, his pupils dark and blown up. His features are dark too, tight and straining. There's a dotting of sweat on his forehead, from holding himself back I think. Even if I did feel any pain, it would be gone now in the face of his care and his struggle.

"Bronwyn, stop mo..." he trails off, his words slurred.

It's okay.

He doesn't need to talk. I'll take care of him.

So I smile like the flower I am.

His wallflower.

And cupping his cheek, I whisper, "My thorn."

His eyes hone in on my smile then. His body hones in on my movements and he goes alert.

He comes alive over my twisting body and on my fifth or so movement, he moves with me. And I gasp, gripping his waist and inching up my thighs even more.

So I'm more open for him.

So he can take me. He can take whatever he wants.

All of my juices. My nectar.

All my love.

And he does take it all.

At first, he's up there, watching me, his jaw all tight and his hair in his eyes. His sweaty muscles rippling over me, moving and sliding like his cock inside my pussy. But then after a few strokes, he comes for my rosy mouth and picks up speed. He establishes a fast rhythm and begins to really move. Really pound my pussy, *really* making me feel him.

Again, I wait for the pain but there's only pleasure.

As if when our bodies are joined, everything is right with the world. Everything is smooth and soft. Everything is roses. When we are like this, kissing and touching each other, all the pain, all the torment is gone.

It's like a dream.

Our dream.

So all there is in this dream is pleasure and him and his lovely thorn kisses.

And he keeps giving them to me even when his hips are slamming into mine. Even when I can hear the *slapslapslap* of the flesh. The *chinkchinkchink* of my belly chain.

Suddenly all of this comes to a halt when he jerks over me, his entire body going rigid.

And he groans, his mouth still stuck to mine.

I hug him tight then. Tighter than ever.

Because I know he's coming.

I know he's coming inside his wallflower.

# CHAPTER TWENTY-FOUR

I open my eyes to an empty, dark-ish room.

At first I panic.

Not because I don't know where I am — I definitely know where I am and what just happened — but because of what time it is.

On the drive over, I told Conrad that I'd have to get back to my house at the end of the night so my parents don't figure out my absence. He never said anything about it though. Only clenched his jaw and flexed his fingers on the wheel.

So I'm worried that I'm late and everything is going to fall apart now. Barely two seconds after everything has begun.

But when I glance at the blinking clock on the nightstand, it says that it's only 2 AM and I sigh.

Before I focus on the next problem.

Where is Conrad?

Because I know he fell asleep with me.

I remember that once we were done, he withdrew himself. Went to the bathroom to freshen up — still naked; I *specifically* remember seeing his gorgeous back rippling, his extremely tight and muscled ass bunching as he walked — and brought me a hot towel. He cleaned me between the thighs even though I told him that I could do it myself. His reaction was to snap his eyes up and keep holding my thighs open with his possessive hands and growl, "You're mine."

That's it.

I took it to mean: you're mine to take care of and clean up.

So I let it be.

And then I remember that after the clean-up was done, he pulled up his jeans with his back to me — I definitely stared at his ass then — went inside his bathroom again and brought back a bottle of pills. He gave me one along with water and when I asked why, he simply said, "For the pain."

I wanted to argue because there was literally no pain. But the look on his face was super determined so I took that too.

And then he came to bed at last.

He gathered me in his arms without a word, pulled a blanket over us and made me fall asleep on his chest. He wouldn't even loosen his arm from around me — again something I remember specifically — because it made me smile and rub my nose on his bare chest.

After that is now.

I don't know when he woke up and left the bed.

So I pull my naked body up, push aside the blanket and climb down. Or try to. Because when I swing my legs over to the floor, I wince.

Yikes.

My body is all sore. My breasts feel heavy and my nipples throb with a dull ache. But my thighs... they are in actual pain. Not to mention, there's some *major* soreness in the place between them.

I squirm in the bed to test things out and yeah, I wince again.

I guess Conrad was right then.

As always, he knew what I needed.

Which makes me smile slightly, even through the pain, and more determined to go find him.

So I carefully get myself out of bed and pad around it, wincing here and there. But by the time I search for my dress, which is strangely nowhere to be found, I'm okay to walk. I do find his sweater though, lying on the floor where he so sexily discarded it. So I wear that and go in search of him.

The house is quiet and the hallway is dimly lit. There's light coming from the kitchen and the living room, but I turn in the direction of a door that's open down at the end of the hallway. I'm assuming that's the backyard and I'm right.

It is and that's where I find him.

Playing soccer.

Or rather, just kicking the ball into the net.

He has tons of them, lying at his feet, spilling out of a netted sack, and he's kicking them one by one.

As I step out and go over to the railing to watch him closely, I realize that he's kicking them in a way that hits the net at different spots.

First he stares at it, the net, as he spins the ball between his two hands, before bending down and putting it in front of him. Then he goes back a few steps before jogging forward and striking the ball, which goes flying and hits the net where he wants it to. Sometimes it's dead center; sometimes it's on the left or on the right. And sometimes he hits the pole on top and when that happens, the ball comes bouncing back and he kicks it again. And again it tears through the air and hits the net.

It's breathtaking.

The way he plays. The way his body moves and ripples under his gray t-shirt, which he must've put on when he woke up.

And God, at one point he does a flip in the air, his long hair fluttering around his face, his magnificent body going sideways, his strong leg striking the ball, and I lose my breath.

I lose it and I stand here, all shivering and in awe.

And maybe he can hear my thoughts, the frantic beats of my heart — I wouldn't be surprised because they're so loud; they're like firecrackers in my body — because he turns, his chest panting, his lips parted and dragging puffs of breaths.

"Bronwyn," he says, raking a hand through his hair and pushing it off his forehead.

I grab the railing tightly. "Hi."

He abandons the ball and his one-man soccer game and begins to stride toward me. "You okay? Why are you up?"

Instead of answering him, I watch him like a perv.

I watch his hair that despite being pushed back is hanging on his forehead. I watch his massive, glorious chest, his tapering torso. Those lightly swinging arms as he walks, those thighs.

When he reaches the bottom step of the back porch, I move to stand on the top step. "You're amazing."

He frowns, his eyes moving up and down my body. "Bronwyn, what the fuck are you doing? It's cold. Get back inside."

"You're out here too."

His frown only grows and before I know it, he's bent down, snagged his arms around my bare thighs and my waist, and picked me up off the porch. He's hauled me up in his arms and my thighs — in pain or not — wrap around his waist.

Wrapping my arms around his neck, I ask breathily, "Now what are *you* doing?"

"Taking you back inside," he replies, his one hand splayed on my spine and the other on the back of my head. "Where it's not cold."

I'm not even sure how he's doing that, walking me back inside when he's not even watching where he's going.

When he's watching me.

But I don't care as long as I'm in his arms. So tugging the ends of his sweat-damp hair, I ask, "Did you hear what I said? You're amazing."

"I heard you."

I tug at his hair again. "So it's a compliment."

We're inside the house now and, still carrying me, he shuts the door behind him with his foot and deposits me against the hallway wall. I assume that he'll put me down and I don't want him to so I go to pull him closer.

But he's there already.

He pushes closer on his own, plants himself between my thighs before *planting* his hands on my thighs too.

Way up on them.

Where his name is written, among other places.

Actually he's not content to simply touch it. He pushes up the hem of his sweater, which was somewhere around my mid-thigh until he exposes his name.

He exposes the thorns and roses that I've made for him.

And in the process, exposes the rose between my legs too.

When he's done opening me up like that, exposing all the parts of me that he wants to feast his eyes on, he looks up. "Compliment."

I squirm between his hard, sweaty body and the wall as I say, "Yes."

"Like interesting hair, you mean."

"Uh-huh." I nod, my channel pulsing. "Do you think..."

"Do I think what?"

"Do you think I could ever" — I stare into his eyes — "come watch you play?"

His fingers flex on my thighs. "No."

I frown, playing with the ends of his hair. "Why not?"

Clenching his jaw for a second, he replies, "Because I don't play anymore. Remember?"

"But you coach," I tell him. "I'm sure you play with them sometimes."

"I don't."

"What, why not?"

Another clench. "Because I don't want to."

I study his features, trying to figure out if he's telling the truth. I'm not sure if he is. Given how I *just* saw him playing in the middle of the night. "Maybe you should. Because I think you love it." Tugging on his hair again, I add, "Enough to play it by yourself. In the middle of the night."

"I *like* playing it by myself. In the middle of the night."

I narrow my eyes at him. "Is it the same thing as your 'I don't need anyone because I've never needed anyone and I'm happy alone'?"

Because that's what he said back at the bar when I hugged him for the first time.

"How's the pain?"

Of course.

That's what he does when I ask deep questions, distract me.

But I'm not giving up. "There is no pain. So you play every night?"

He throws me a look. "There is no pain."

"Nope." I shake my head and tug on his hair again. "So? Do you?"

His eyes go back and forth between mine, his fingers digging into the soft flesh of my upper thighs. "Yes. And stop lying about the pain."

"I'm not lying," I say. "So if you play every night, why can't you play with your team and all the guys you coach?"

He shifts between my thighs, rubbing his torso over my naked pussy, making me gasp. "Stop lying about *lying*. And I told you: I like playing by myself and I don't sleep much anyway."

"Why not?"

Sighing, he warns, "Bronwyn."

I widen my eyes. "Conrad."

His grip flexes on my thighs again. "Do you need another pill?"

"No," I reply just to be stubborn because he's being that way.

He leans closer then, his palms moving even further up, his thumb super-duper close to the seam of my core. "I saw your pussy, Bronwyn. It is trashed. All dark pink and puffy. I saw the blood on my dick too, and on the sheets. That's why I gave you the pill. Now, I want you to tell me if you need another pill or not."

I do, I think.

But I'm not going to tell him that until he tells *me* his answer.

"I'll tell you if I need another pill or not," I say, lifting my chin, "if you answer my questions." Then, pointing my finger at him, "Truthfully."

He stares at me, almost belligerently, but I wait him out.

Then, "I don't sleep much because the house is quiet. Too quiet. I'm used to... more noise. So as my brothers left one by one and then Callie left, my sleep went away too. And I'm not going to play with my students because it reminds me too much."

"Of what?"

A big breath. "Of the past. Of how I used to play with my team. And I don't like looking at the past."

My heart twists then.

It twists and twists in my chest.

It squeezes and contracts and becomes half the size of a normal functioning heart. I don't even think it beats. Not in the normal way at least.

It beats in a broken way, in an aching way.

For him.

And I feel a sting in my eyes. A great lump in my throat as I open my mouth to say something. I'm not sure what I could say though. What I could possibly say to him at this, but I don't have to.

Because he gets there first.

And he gets there with a frown.

"Are you..." He studies my face with what I can only assume is confusion. "Are you *crying*?"

A tear falls down my cheek the moment he says it but still I shake my head. "No."

His hands snap away from my thighs and cradle my cheeks. "Bronwyn. Stop fucking lying to me."

"I'm not lying."

Wiping the onslaught of tears off my cheeks, he says tightly, "And stop *fucking* crying." He adds sternly, "Right now."

I fist the neck of his t-shirt. "That's not how you make someone stop crying, Conrad. You can't yell at them." I hiccup. "T-that's not how it works."

His face ripples with pain and an onslaught of emotions. Just like my onslaught of tears. And his forehead drops over mine, his fingers dragging, squeezing my cheeks as he rasps, "Bronwyn, please, all right? Stop crying. Just stop crying. Please, baby."

I cry harder at his 'baby.'

This is the moment he chooses to call me by something other than my full fucking name.

*This.*

When I'm already so emotional over him.

When I'm already so in love with him that I'm bursting at the seams.

I wind my arms around his neck and press my forehead into his. "I hate it, okay? I told you. I hate that you're alone. I hate that you're even playing alone like this. Remember what you told me? I'll always be an artist no matter what. And you'll always be a soccer player. Just because you're a coach and you teach things now doesn't mean that you aren't a player anymore. You don't have to go pro to find joy in it, to play with a team. You can still do that. You can still make new dreams and find new joy. I promise you. You can."

He presses his mouth on mine then. To kiss me.

To kiss my tears and probably to shut down any other words I may have about this.

But I can't not kiss him back.

I can't not show him that I love him every chance I get. So I do.

I kiss him back with all the desperation, all the love inside of me.

And all the lust too.

Because as his mouth moves over mine, his hips slide against my pussy. My sore, beaten-up pussy blooms and creams and juices herself up for him.

Breaking the kiss, he pants against my mouth, "I know I trashed your pussy earlier. I know I beat her up but I —"

This time I cut him off with my kiss that he latches on to, hungrily, desperately, before I whisper, "Do it, please. Fuck me."

In the dim lighting, his eyes appear bright and feverish. Frantic.

As frantic as his hands that go down to open the zipper of his jeans. I'm no slouch either. I tighten my thighs around him and arch my body. I even go so far as to drag my hand down and rub my pussy to spread the wetness around.

To open my rosy lips and make things easier for him.

Although I don't think I needed that. Because I'm already so open, so wet and creamy.

And so he slides inside of me so easily.

Like a dream.

Yet again, I feel very little pain.

There's soreness from before but it isn't enough for me to push him away. It isn't enough for me to tell him to stop.

Besides, if he did, I'd die.

So I bring him even closer and breathe with him.

And as he breathes with me, I promise him — silently, secretly and once again — that I'll fill his life with so many colors, so much joy, so many dreams that he'll never be alone.

Even when I'm gone.

# CHAPTER TWENTY-FIVE

The Original Thorn

I have three brothers and a sister.

Four siblings in total.

People often ask me who my favorite sibling is. It's a stupid question; I love all my siblings equally. But I don't stop them if they want to speculate. And according to the most popular of their speculations, it's Callie.

They say Callie is my favorite sibling among the four.

And Stellan is my favorite brother.

It's an obvious assumption to make: Callie's the youngest of us all. She's my baby sister. I was the first one to hold her in my arms; my mother was resting after a hard delivery and my father was nowhere to be found. He came back a week later to tell us that he was leaving.

So of course Callie is my favorite.

She is my heart. She's all our hearts actually.

We've all loved her, all four of us, since the day she was born.

The other speculation, that Stellan's my favorite brother, is an obvious one again. Even though he's eight years younger than me, being three minutes older than Shepard, he's the next in line.

He's always been my right hand.

He's the most similar to me. If I'm not there, he's in charge. He's the one running things and the one the rest of them answer to. So again, it's obvious.

But the truth is that no matter how much I try, I can't pick a favorite brother.

It's like picking a favorite organ.

There is no favorite organ. They're all equally important. They all keep you alive. So my sister might be my — our — heart, but my brothers are an equal part of me.

And right now I want to strangle each one of them.

It's Saturday and my brothers are all visiting from New York. It was a surprise visit. They called and said that they were at the house while I was out getting groceries.

Although honestly, not as surprising as all that.

Now that Callie's pregnant, they like to come down as much as their schedules allow. And given how busy their schedules are — Shepard plays for the New York City FC, Ledger just got picked and Stellan is the assistant coach with them — it's kind of amazing they're still here every other weekend, a testament to how much we love our sister. How much we want to take care of her and check on her.

And how much we don't trust Reed fucking Jackson to do it.

How we're all just waiting for him to screw up like our father screwed up with us.

Although I have to admit that so far he hasn't. So far he has surprised us. And well, I can personally attest to his great automobile mechanic skills too.

But that's not the point.

The point is that I've just returned from my grocery run and now I'm going to kill my brothers.

The only reason I'm still standing at the door and haven't made my move yet is because I'm in shock — in fucking shock — at what I'm seeing and I haven't decided who to go for first.

"Tits," Ledger says, his eyes flicking back and forth across the TV screen and his thumbs pushing on the buttons of his controller relentlessly. "Definitely tits."

"What?" Shepard shakes his head, doing the same. "Fuck tits, man. Tits won't keep you warm on a cold night."

"Yeah? And an ass will?"

"Uh, yeah. You can fuck an ass."

Ledger side-eyes Shep. "You can fuck tits too, genius."

"I know. But a hole is a hole, my friend," Shep says sagely.

"Right. Whatever." Ledge shrugs. Then, "Hey, Stellan. Your turn."

Stellan, who's been focusing on his book, asks distractedly without lifting his eyes, "My turn at what?"

"To answer the question."

"What question?"

Ledger shakes his head in exasperation. "Tits or ass. You have to pick one. And that's all you get for the rest of your life."

"I pick" – Stellan flips the page – "you both shutting the hell up and leaving me the fuck alone."

At this, Shep laughs so loudly that he misses the shot and Ledge takes the lead. At least, that's why I think Ledge is cackling like a dumb witch.

"Leave him alone, Ledge," Shep says, getting back into the game. "Stella is moping."

"Call me Stella one more time and I'll be *mopping* the floor with you," Stellan responds drily.

Which only makes Shep wiggle his eyebrows. "Ooh, word play. Stella's feisty tonight."

Ledger frowns at Stellan. "Why the fuck are you moping?"

Stellan opens his mouth to respond but of course Shepard gets there first. "Because a chick he likes picked me."

At this, all festivities come to a halt.

Ledger pauses the game. Shepard protests with "I was winning, dumbass". And Stellan slams the book shut with a snap, appearing ready to punch Shep.

"What chick?" Ledger asks.

Again Shepard gets there first. "This insanely hot chick that he's been eyeing but of course she's been eyeing me. Isadora."

"I'm fucking warning you," Stellan says gravely.

Ledger raises his hand. "Let me get this straight: a chick named Isadora picked Shepard over you. What, is she crazy?"

Shepard smacks Ledger on the head. "Fuck you, man. She's got taste. I'm clearly the better catch."

Ledger smacks Shep back. "Yeah, if she wants to *catch* chlamydia maybe."

Shepard frowns, sitting up straight. "You fucking —"

"What the fuck is that?" I boom then, not interested in listening to their bullshit any longer, clenching and unclenching my fists.

All three of them jump in their seats and snap their gazes over to me.

And when they see where my eyes are planted, *their* eyes widen.

They scramble to take their feet off the table. Shepard and Ledger shove aside their controllers, and Stellan throws his book on the table.

Where it skids and ends up touching the very thing I'm staring at.

"Where did you find those?" I ask when no one has said anything. "And what the fuck are they doing on the coffee table?"

They all wince in response and look at each other, guiltily.

Which just pisses me off even more and I thunder, "If no one answers in the next five seconds, I'm coming to smash all your noses into your faces. So you better open your holes and start talking."

Shepard's the first one to break, as he points his finger at Ledger. "He did."

Ledger's eyes snap wide as he addresses Shepard. "What the fuck, dude?" Turning to me, he says, "It wasn't me, Con. I don't even go into your room let alone..." He waves in the general direction of the object. "Bring something out of there. I don't want to die. It was Shep. He was turning the house upside down looking for batteries, went into your room, opened the drawer of your nightstand and found them there. And he's the one who brought 'em out here."

Shep slaps the back of Ledger's head. "Yeah, and who said it's about time Con got some, huh? Who was it who said, as soon as he saw the pair of panties in my hands, that thank God our big brother got laid?"

The word 'panties' finally breaks me into action.

I stride over to the coffee table and pick them up. Bunching them in my hand, I shove them in my back pocket, away from their beady eyes.

That's when my favorite brother decides to break his silence. "So whose are they?"

I swivel my gaze over to Stellan, who's watching me with shrewd eyes. "What'd you just say?"

He shrugs. "I'm just asking. It's very rare that you have a girl over. So who is she?"

I clench my fists, debating whether to strangle the brother whom I've always been closest to — well, as close as I can get with anyone really, given the fact that he's still a big eight years younger than me — or just knock his teeth out so he'll stop talking.

"Clean this shit up," I tell him before pinning my eyes on the other two morons. "And you two. If I see either of you for the rest of the weekend, I'm going to forget that you're related to me, you understand?"

With that, I stalk out of the room and get away from them before I really do something drastic.

Hours later and after a tense dinner with my brothers, I find myself awake in the middle of the night as usual. But instead of kicking the ball around as I usually do, I sit on the rocking chair on the back porch and stare into the darkness.

"Beer?"

I hear the voice from behind me and without even looking, I know who it is. He's the only one who's brave enough to come talk to me when my mood is shitty.

Walking around the old rocking chair that I'm sitting in, Stellan drops down on the one next to it and props his feet up on the wooden railing before saying, "As a truce?"

I glance at his truce and raise the bottle that I do have resting on my thigh. "Not in the mood for it."

"Whiskey, huh."

I shrug and take a gulp of it in response.

"Things must be dire," he goes on. "For you to pick up the hard stuff."

Dire. Yeah.

They *are* fucking dire.

My only response is to drink another gulp of whiskey.

He sighs and sips his beer. "So have you thought about it?"

"About sparing your life another day? Yeah." I glance at him. "I think I'll let you live."

He chuckles, shaking his head. Then, "How long are you going to keep avoiding it?"

My fingers tighten around the bottle because I knew he'd bring it up. He always does.

"I'm not avoiding it," I reply. "I'm saying no. You just don't know how to take it."

"Con, seriously," Stellan says gravely. "You can at least come up and check out the facilities. They're fucking top of the line, all right? You know that. And FC wants you. They really fucking want you."

I know.

New York City FC wants me as their coach.

They've wanted me for a long time now. And they've tried everything to get me. Up until a couple of years ago, they'd call me every other month. They'd show up at Bardstown High. Once or twice, they've even showed up at this house. And every single time I've turned them down.

I thought they got the message when they stopped trying.

But now that Stellan works for them, they've started up again. Not that I've budged from my position, but they've recruited Stellan in their crusade to hire me.

"I know they want me," I tell him. "And they know that I'm not interested. I've never been interested. So why don't you stop doing their dirty work for them and tell them, yet again, that I'm not taking the job."

Stellan's jaw clenches, much like mine, and I realize that he's not going to let this go.

He's *my* brother.

"I'm not doing their dirty work for them. Fuck them. I'm trying to convince you that this is the right move for you. So I'm basically trying to do your job here: thinking. Coaching a pro team is where you belong."

Irritation seeps into my voice as I reply, "I don't care about the pros, all right? I haven't in fourteen years and I've got no desire to go back. And besides, Callie is here. She's fucking pregnant. I need to be there for her."

At the mention of Callie's pregnancy, his jaw clenches again and I completely agree with that display of emotion.

We're all worried about her.

For her future, for the baby.

"Yes, and we're all here for her," he says. "And when she does have her baby, we'll be there for her then as well. And then she'll go to college, Con. She'll probably end up at her dream school. She'll live her life. And we'll be there for her through all of that. *But* it doesn't mean that you don't get to live *your* life. There's no reason for you not to even consider their offer."

Our sister is a ballerina, a fucking fantastic one at that, and her dream school is Juilliard. When she got pregnant and decided to keep the baby that was my major concern. That she might have to give up her dream, but as it turns out, through none other than Reed's support, she's still trying to reach for it.

And I know, I know it in my heart, that she'll get it.

She's talented. She's hard-working. She's phenomenal.

Like her best friend.

My entire body jolts at the thought.

My heartbeat jacks up too.

Like it somehow, for some reason, always does.

But I ignore it, such an irrational, severe reaction at the mere thought of her. "The *reason* is that I'm not interested."

"So what, are you going to be a high school coach for the rest of your life?"

Pain attacks the base of my skull at his words.

Viciously, brutally.

Bitingly.

It's never far away, the pain.

But sometimes it grows teeth. It scratches me with its claws.

"Why, is it not good enough for you now?" I snap out, my fingers squeezing and squeezing the bottle. "That I'm a high school soccer coach? Now that you've all got your places in the pros?"

As soon as I say it, I know I shouldn't have.

I know my brother didn't mean it that way.

And I know that *he* knows that I didn't mean what I just said in a wrong way either.

If I'm sure of anything in this world, it's my bond with my siblings.

We've been through a lot together.

An alcoholic father, his abandonment, an overworked and tired mother, her illness, her death. The uncertainty of what was going to happen when Mom died. Although I've always made sure that I banished those worries for them, but still.

They know that I love them. Not only that, they know that I'm proud of them.

I'm fucking proud of them for dreaming and *achieving* those dreams.

For going out there and living their lives. *Making* their lives.

They also know that if they hadn't, I would've pushed them even harder than I did. I would've moved heaven and earth, mountains and valleys to give them their dreams.

Because I know the pain.

I *know* the regret, the desolation of broken dreams.

"Jesus, you know I didn't mean that, Con," Stellan says, apologetic, even though he doesn't have to. "You know that. All I meant was…" He sighs, taking a pause, pinning me with a grave, frank look. "Listen, you're my big brother, all right? I fucking love you. I fucking look up to you. You're the best man I know. And it guts me, okay? It guts me that you're here, all alone. When we're all out there. When we're all living our lives. I know you couldn't before. I know you had obligations. You had *us*. We've been your biggest obstacle, your biggest hurdle. And you gave up so much for us. You gave up your entire life for us. Your career, your education, everything, and if I could change that, Con, I would. I fucking would. But I can't. All I can do is try to make you see that you don't have to be here anymore. You don't have to hold back. You can live your life. You need to live your life. And you need to be on that team because that's your place. Besides, the coach we've got now is shit."

"That your professional opinion as an assistant coach?" I quip.

"Fuck yeah," he says, sitting back in his chair. "I'm telling you. You belong there."

I belong there, he thinks.

That I should be living my life out there.

Once upon a time I thought like him as well.

I thought that my life was out there. That this town isn't all there is. I thought that I'd get out of this town, do what I was meant to do — play soccer in the pros; something I found accidentally when I was five or so and gotten fortunate enough to work with the coaches who nurtured my talent — and get my family out of this hellhole.

I dreamed that my mother wouldn't have to work from sunup to sundown. My siblings wouldn't have to feel neglected because of it. I dreamed that we'd all live in a big house, always have enough Christmas presents, go on vacations. I dreamed that we'd be happy.

But then my mother got sick and kept getting sicker. Whatever little happiness our family had, it kept inching away from us. Hospital stays, doctor's visits, medication, chemotherapy, radiation. I actually had made up my mind not to go to college at all, but my mother kept insisting so I went.

Until they called me back because she died.

And all my dreams of getting my mother out of this town, giving her the life she deserved, giving my siblings the lives they deserved, vanished. My own dreams, the kind of life *I* wanted to live, vanished.

I was sad about that, yeah.

I was devastated.

But then I shut that door. I buried the pieces of my broken dreams because I had work to do.

Because even though my dreams were broken, I could still help my brothers, my sister, realize theirs. They were young. They were untouched. They were yet to realize their potential.

So I did everything that I could to make their dreams come true.

I pushed them, encouraged them, cheered them on, bandaged up their scrapes, picked them up when they fell.

And one by one they got everything that they wished for.

That they deserved.

So this is my life now.

In this town. In this house. Taking care of my siblings, even if they have all outgrown me. And that's fine. Every parent wants their kids to fly and yes, I realize that they are not my kids but I've taken care of them like they are.

This is where I belong.

"You're not a hurdle," I say then, emphatically. "Or an obstacle. You are my family and I did what I did, I do what I do, because I love you. Not because you're some fucking obligation." Pausing to take another sip of whiskey, I add, "And I'm fine. I'm living my life. So you don't have to worry about me."

Because over the years I've realized that some people don't get to dream.

Some people don't get to spread their wings and fly. Some people are rooted in the ground like trees.

Solid and dependable and strong.

People like me.

I'm that tree. I've always been that tree.

I tried to uproot once. I tried to dream once and it fucking blew up in my face. I'm not doing that again. I'm not dreaming or reaching for the stars or whatever the fuck it is they say to inspire people.

Nothing is worth that pain.

Not one thing in this world is worth going through that pain again.

Anyway, Stellan seems to have given up because his only response is to sigh and shake his head. Which is great. I could use some silence.

To reflect on what I did.

Last night.

But as it turns out, I'm not going to get it. Because after only a couple of minutes, my brother speaks up. "So is she special?"

"What?"

He throws me a smirk and I narrow my eyes. "The girl with pink panties."

I sit up straight. "What the —"

"Well, I have to say she's got great taste," he says, cutting me off. "I mean, there's something about pink lacy panties that just does it for a guy, you know. And —"

"I'm fucking warning you, Stellan," I growl. "You talk about her like that, you won't be talking ever again."

The bastard chuckles and sips his beer. "So she's special then."

"Shut your fucking mouth."

He chuckles again and shrugs. "I'm happy though."

I clench my teeth.

"Aren't you going to ask me why?"

I remain silent, digging my fingers into the bottle. Somehow very aware of the fact that I still have her panties in the back pocket of my jeans. Very fucking aware that I picked them up this morning — they were shoved under the bed — and they felt like gossamer or something similar in my rough fingers before I carefully put them in my nightstand instead of *not*.

Instead of just... throwing them away.

But as it did this morning too, the thought is revolting to me. The thought of carelessly discarding them or anything that belongs to her is... unacceptable.

Clearly it was a huge mistake.

Putting them in the nightstand.

Where anyone, my asshole brothers, could find them. They're staying close to me now, in my back pocket. At least for this weekend.

Only so I can guard them.

That's the *only* reason.

On Monday, I'll give them back to her and that will be it.

I viciously drink another swallow of whiskey at the fact that this is *again* somehow an objectionable thought.

Giving them back.

Fucking *Christ*.

I hate what she does to me. *Hate* how she twists my insides like this and I don't understand the reason why.

I've never been able to.

"Well, I'm going to tell you anyway," Stellan begins. "It's because —"

"Don't."

"It's because it's not Helen."

That gives me pause.

I was in the process of taking another sip of the liquor, the bottle almost tipped up to my mouth, but I lower it and glance at my brother.

He's sitting there, all casual like, sipping his beer as if he didn't say something noteworthy.

As if he didn't drop a bomb on me.

My relationship with Helen is not a secret from my siblings but it's not a well-known fact either. I was with her briefly when I was about seventeen, eighteen, and all my brothers were kids back then. Stellan and Shepard were ten, Ledger was eight and Callie was merely four.

The twins did have some idea, but I don't think Ledger and Callie even knew that I dated someone back then. Plus our relationship didn't last very long anyway, so no, it's not a very well-known fact.

And there have probably been one or at the most two occasions when Stellan has broached the subject. The first time I remember specifically was just after Mom's death, when I moved back home and he'd asked about her. I remember being shocked that he even knew and I told him that it wasn't something he needed to worry about. The second time was probably years after that and by that time Helen was so far behind in my past that I don't even remember what I said.

So I'm not sure where this is coming from.

Why would he even mention her name now?

But I know that he's baiting me for some reason and despite knowing that, I take it. The bait.

"What the fuck is that supposed to mean?"

He glances at me then. "Nothing. It's just that you never acted like that. So possessive and angry. When you were with her."

"You were fucking ten when I was with her. What do you know about how I acted?"

Shooting me a look, he replies, "I know you were unhappy. I know you were stressed all the time. Juggling work, soccer, us and her. I know there were days when you'd sneak out at midnight, after we'd all fallen asleep and Mom was gone for her night job or whatever, and come home at dawn or something. There were days when you'd be dead tired. I saw it on your face. And yes, I was ten, nine even, a kid myself. But you're forgetting one very important thing, big brother – we never had much of a childhood, you and I. Shep has always been carefree. Ledge was a baby. Callie was actually *the* baby. I know you consider me a kid too but I'm not. I don't think I ever was. I'm your right fucking hand for a reason. So fuck yeah, I know."

He tips the mouth of his bottle to me as he continues, "And I also know, even though you never told me — not that you would because you never talk when the topic of conversation is you — that she got married the summer before last. And she works at St. Mary's now. I've actually been watching you for the past year. More so now that you work at St. Mary's too. Just to see if you were doing okay. Because when you're not doing okay, you have a habit of biting people's heads off. Like you did tonight. And that's why I'm happy."

I'm stunned.

I'm... I'm not really sure what to say, except, "I didn't... know I was that transparent."

"Not to others, no. But to me, yeah."

I'm transparent to my little brother.

Me.

The guy who brought him up.

How is that... I can't even compute that so maybe that's why I say this: "Maybe it *is* Helen."

He howls with laughter and I'm not going to lie, it pisses me off a little.

"Helen? Yeah, right." He laughs again as he continues, "She's married. You wouldn't touch her with a ten-foot pole. Because you know what cheating does to a home. You've seen our father. You're the man who wouldn't even touch hard liquor because our dad was an alcoholic" – he shoots a pointed look at the bottle I'm holding – "well, except for when the situation is extremely dire. I've never seen you hungover or drunk. You're too good, too moral for it. So no, it's not Helen. And I'm very fucking happy about that."

He is right. At least about one thing.

About me not doing what my father did: cheat and drink.

I don't drink hard liquor except for when the situation is extremely dire. And everything has been extremely dire ever since I started at St. Mary's.

So have I underestimated him then, Stellan? Like I've underestimated so many others.

He's always been the most mature and aware of my brothers. And yes, that's the reason why I've always felt comfortable leaving him in charge of things. But he's still my younger brother and I've shielded him from things, protected him like the rest of them.

But I didn't know that he noticed things.

That he was more attuned to his surroundings than I thought.

"It's not Helen's fault," I find myself saying, *confiding*. "We just never got the chance to be happy. I was a shitty boyfriend to begin with. I never had much time for her. I made promises to her but I broke all of them. I made her wait. I made her hope. So the fault is mine."

It is.

Along with making myself dream, I made her dream too.

Of a better life. A better relationship.

I should've known.

I should've known not to.

"Fuck no," Stellan emphasizes. "It's not your fault. So maybe you didn't have time for her. But it wasn't by choice. What happened wasn't by your choice. You didn't want to be responsible for us. You didn't want Mom to get cancer. But what Helen did, she did it by her own fucking choice. She broke up with you when you were at the lowest point of your life. When you needed her the most. So fuck her, all right?"

I shake my head. "I couldn't have asked her to walk with me on this path. I was dragging her down and she did what was right for her. My pro career was over before it ever began. She came from a filthy rich family. They never would've gone for me. So I can't blame her for looking out for herself."

And neither did I blame her for getting married to that guy.

Because the truth is that we'd moved on.

I had — *have* — a life as small and as boring as it may seem. A job, responsibilities. Yes, I haven't strictly dated anyone but I've been with women. I'm not a fucking monk. If over the years I've wanted company, I've sought it out. It wasn't as if I was waiting for her or pining for her.

So no, I do not blame her.

Both for moving on and for wanting to look back.

Because I've wanted that too.

But no. I don't ever cheat and I'm not going to break this rule for anyone. Not even Helen.

"But I can," Stellan responds with clenched teeth. "For not choosing you. For not loving you the way you deserve. A woman who loves you, Con, doesn't leave you out in the cold. She walks with you in the snow and on thin ice if need be. And if this new one can —"

"This new one is fucking eighteen years old," I snap out.

Stellan pauses for a second. Then, "What?"

I grind my jaw. "She goes to St. Mary's."

I'm not looking at him but I know he's looking at me. I know that his mouth has fallen open and he's staring at me in shock as he breathes, "Holy fuck."

Yeah, holy fuck is right.

Even so, it doesn't capture the depth of wrongness, the depth of the crime that I've committed.

And the reason for that is that it doesn't feel like one.

It doesn't feel like a crime.

It doesn't feel wrong. The fact that I've been thinking about her all day. I've been smelling her all over the house. I've been staring at that spot of blood on my sheets. I've been fucking jacking off to her.

That's what I did all day today before my brothers got here.

I jacked off to that red stain on my bed.

To the fact that she cried for me last night. She wants to protect me. She wants to be my flower.

Mine.

But that's not all.

Last night, before I very reluctantly dropped her off at her house, I studied her body while she was sleeping. I traced her skin with my fingers. All the places she'd written my name. All the roses and thorns she decorated her body with.

For me.

In my name.

Not to mention, I played with her hair too.

Because she drives me crazy. She drives me *fucking crazy* like no one has ever done before.

Fuck. Fuck. *Fucking* fuck.

"Dora."

Stellan's voice distracts me from my furious thoughts and I snap my gaze to him. "What?"

His jaw is ticking. "I know you overheard our conversation earlier. About Isadora. I call her Dora though."

I frown. "The girl who likes Shepard?"

"Likes Shepard." He scoffs before biting out, "I saw her first."

Oh fuck.

I have a bad feeling about this.

A bad fucking feeling.

Even so as I've always done, I keep my calm and ask, "And?"

I can see the tightness on his features as he stares into the darkness for a few seconds.

"Doesn't matter," he says after a while, shaking his head. "He was right. She did choose him."

"But you wanted her to choose you."

Another few seconds pass.

Then he takes a large pull of his beer before he says, "I mean, why do I even want her when she doesn't want me? If she wants my shithead brother she can fucking have him."

"But," I prod again because with Stellan you need to.

Ledger and Shep are usually more open. Callie too.

He swallows. "I do want her." Glancing at me, he says, "I want my twin brother's new girlfriend."

My own jaw clenches as I look at him.

As I study his face, his features, his tells.

This one's going to hurt.

I can see that.

And like always, my own chest feels tight when my siblings want something but can't get it. My own chest feels suffocated as I say, "You need to get away. Come back here. Home."

That might be the only way to get over the pain.

My solution makes him smile and shake his head. "I knew you'd say that. Because you're always thinking about us. I'm going to be fine though." Another shake of his head. "The point I'm trying to make, big brother, is that you're not the biggest asshole here. For wanting an eighteen-year-old student. So you need to cut yourself some slack."

Slack.

No. I can't.

I can't because she's too young. Too shiny, too precious.

And I know I've underestimated her as well. Which is why I know she's going to do great things in life.

Maybe I should let her go. I've had her once and the only reason I did that was to drive her out of my mind, my system.

But even the thought of that, the thought of giving her up right now, is somehow even more objectionable than throwing away her panties.

Even so as I sit here, I promise myself. I fucking *promise* that I will let her go.

That I won't keep her.

I will end this one day.

One fucking day.

Because even though my name is written on every inch of her soft, velvet, wallflower of a body, she's not really mine.

# CHAPTER TWENTY-SIX

I can't wait to see him.

I'm not sure what the protocol is here. But when I wake up Monday morning I can't stop grinning.

Since Charles is driving me back to school from Wuthering Garden, I know I'm going to miss my early morning sketching session. So I won't be able to see him run laps around the soccer field.

Which makes me a little sad.

Because I wanted to see him. Talk to him, before school starts, away from everyone else.

I wanted to make sure that it was real.

What happened between us.

And that he made love to me not once but twice.

I know. I know there's no love involved here. I know that. I'm too young for him and he's in love with another woman and he'll never love me but still.

To me it was making love because *I* love him.

Because I'm the wallflower to his thorn.

So no one can dampen my enthusiasm right now.

Especially because after that second round of sex in the hallway, where he wouldn't stop kissing me, wouldn't let me breathe anything other than the air from his lungs, I made him breakfast and completely surprised him.

After he told me the other day that he wasn't much of a cook, I decided that if given the chance I'd cook for him.

Because I'm a kickass cook.

We had a cook for a couple of years who became my friend and who taught me things. So I can cook pretty much everything. And since it was late night, which could be stretched and called super early morning, I made him pancakes and a spinach omelet.

I'm not going to lie, he was a little bit shocked.

"I know what you're thinking."

"Yeah? What am I thinking, Bronwyn?" he asked, standing at the threshold of the kitchen, propped against the wall like he always is when he watches me in his space.

"You're thinking, *Conrad*" — I widened my eyes, which made him break out his quarter of a smile — "that how is it possible that Bronwyn can cook? A *teenager* who doesn't know the ways of the world. How on *earth* is it possible? But I'll have you know —"

That was all I could get out before he was on me.

Before he picked me up again, his mouth kissing the fuck out of me like he can't bear the thought of ever breaking our kisses, and laid me down on the kitchen island.

"But you do know the ways of the world now, don't you?" he said over my lips. "I taught you. I'm teaching you. And I'm going to teach you more."

I grabbed his hair. "Are you saying I'm not a teenager anymore?"

"You fucking are," he said before roving his eyes over my face and continuing, "but you're different. You're more."

I grinned then.

Slowly and surely.

Because oh my God. Did he really just say that?

And I went in to ask him, to confirm, but he proceeded to kiss me again before going down and kissing me down *there* too.

Oh, and I also figured out, while I was making pancakes for him and he sat at that same kitchen island, staring at me with his wet, red lips, what happened to my dress.

Apparently he threw it away.

And when I asked him why, this was his response: "Because I told you what would happen if you wore a dress that could barely contain your milkmaid tits and your stripper ass." His bright eyes darkened as he ran them up and down my body. "I told you that I'd rip it off. But since it was already off your body, I just picked it up and thew it in the trash."

Once I got over that shock, I asked, sputtering, "What am I... What am I going to wear on my way back home?"

His gaze turned possessive then. "My clothes. And you can't say no."

It sent a shiver running down my body. A strong, pulsing shiver.

"I can't say no."

He shook his head very, very slowly, with a smirk stretching his lips up on one side. "No."

"And why not?"

"Because" — his eyes went on the move again, looking at my bare legs that partially showed off the art on my body — "my name is written all over you. Which means I own you. Which *means* that if I want to see you in my clothes, you're not allowed to say no."

So there.

I'm not allowed to say no and I don't even want to.

So *of course* I've been grinning since Friday.

Which Salem and Poe definitely notice. And since they can both guess why, they grin with me. Salem throws me winks and Poe shoulder-bumps me whenever Callie isn't looking.

Which, despite everything, does put a damper on my enthusiasm a little bit.

She has every right to know why I'm so happy today. Not only because she's one of my best friends, but also because the reason for my happiness is her brother.

And yet I'm hiding things from her.

I know Conrad said that she'd always be my best friend, but now I'm not so sure. If I had gone to her before and confessed everything, I still could have saved our friendship. But now after so many secrets, especially the one that happened on Friday, I know I've lost my chance.

I know I've screwed things up more than they needed to be.

I'll tell her soon though. I will.

I must.

But for now I need to see him.

So instead of going to class with my girls, I make an excuse and run up to his office.

As I said, I'm not sure of the protocol here. Do I wait for him to find me or should I go find him myself? So I'm just picking the best option.

Only he's nowhere to be found.

Or at least he's not in his office.

Plus the door is locked, which is very unusual. It makes me think that maybe he never arrived at St. Mary's today. Which is highly unusual too because he's never missed a day since he started.

The earlier buoyancy and lightness that I felt starts to vanish then.

But the worry really starts to set in when he doesn't show up for lunch either. Which he does like clockwork. Every single day, to see Callie. And I get so restless that I almost ask her where her brother is.

I mean, just asking about it won't raise suspicion.

I can ask about Conrad, right?

But as it turns out I don't have to. Salem does it for me and she does it so casually too. "Where's Coach Thorne?"

Poe nods, again all casually. "Yeah, he's usually here by now."

God I love my friends.

I love them to pieces.

Callie, who's totally oblivious — which I can't help but repeat in my head and regret a million times a day — shrugs. "Oh, he's not here today. He's not going to be here this week."

"What?"

My voice is so high and squeaky that I shock even myself and the fork that I'm holding clatters down on the tray.

Callie watches me with a frown. "Wyn, are you okay?"

*Seriously, Wyn? Seriously?*

I'm such a big idiot.

"Yes," I tell her in a much calmer voice as I pick up the fork with a slightly trembling hand. "Sorry, that came out way louder than I thought. I just... Yeah, I'm okay."

I'm saved from giving any sort of explanation because Poe and Salem come to my rescue again. Poe looks at me worriedly before pouting in her usual way at Callie. "Well, why not? Now what am I gonna do for eye candy?"

Salem rolls her eyes. "Who's going to do our soccer practice today then?"

Callie now sufficiently distracted, replies, "Oh, he's helping at Bardstown High this week. Their new coach pulled his knee and they have a big home game this Friday so they've asked him to pitch in. He's going to be over there this whole week."

This whole week.

This *entire* week.

I won't get to see him. I won't get to talk to him.

I won't get to... touch him.

Not that I was going to. Not here. Not where people could see, but still.

He won't be here for a whole week.

I'm not sure why it's hitting me so badly. So much so that I have to clench my teeth, fist my hands in my lap, swallow repeatedly to gulp down my oncoming tears.

I mean, he will be back in a week.

He's not *gone* gone. This is temporary.

But the thing is that everything about us is temporary. This whole relationship — if you could even call it that — is temporary.

It's here now but it will be gone one day.

He'll either crush me like the sharp thorn he is or I'll scatter on my own like the petals of a flower.

So I have very little time to live.

Very little time to be his.

And so the rest of the day passes in a fog. A depressing gray fog.

Even so, I tell myself that I'm overreacting. That things are still okay. So what if I don't get to see him today and for the rest of the week?

I can survive a week. I'm not that desperate or pathetic.

Until the last bell rings and I somehow see him in the courtyard as we come out of the front door.

That's when I realize that I *am* that pathetic. I *am* that desperate.

Because just the sight of him, in his usual dark sweater and blue jeans, jumpstarts my heart. It jumpstarts my lungs too. As if I'm breathing for the first time ever since I set foot in St. Mary's this morning with all the hopes of seeing him.

And before I can think of the consequences and all the reasons why I shouldn't, I take a step toward him.

He looks up at that very second as if he was watching the door, waiting for me to come out after the last bell.

And all the despair, the stupid concern about the correct protocol, vanishes.

Because his eyes, those navy blue eyes, glitter with possessiveness.

Ownership even.

He takes a step toward me then, his fists clenched, his chest shifting with a long breath, and a smile blooms on my lips.

But then it dies.

Because his progress is halted by something.

A red nailed, delicate hand that wrote him that note.

Helen.

The woman he loves.

She puts a hand on his chest and stops him from taking another step. Which is when I notice that he's not alone. He's standing with a group of teachers, Helen included, as they all chat and laugh about something.

Not to mention, I'm not alone either, am I?

I've got my friends around me — Callie is standing right next to me in fact. The courtyard is full of teachers and students.

*Of course* we're not alone.

For a second I forgot that.

And Helen's here and she's saying something to him with a smile. The only thing is that he's not paying attention to her. His eyes are glued to mine and that cut jaw of his clenches.

But I look away.

I can't keep staring at him like this. Like my heart is breaking. Especially when he's staring back, and if I don't rein it in, he's going to know the secret that I'm taking to my grave with me.

Even though he doesn't want me to hide anymore, this is the one thing I can't tell him.

Plus there's Helen and Callie and all the other people who can't be a witness to this.

So I try to focus on what my friends are talking about. But it proves to be a struggle because I keep going back to him and every time I do, he's staring back.

Until Callie shocks me with her question. "Hey, what's up?"

I blink. "What?"

"What are you looking at?"

"Nothing."

"Are you sure? You were staring pretty hard at something."

God.

Yikes.

I duck my head and tuck a stupid wayward strand behind my ear. "Uh, no. I was just... thinking about something."

She gets concerned then. "About what? You know, you've been pretty quiet these days. Is something going on, Wyn? You can tell me, you know that, right? I mean, you *have* to know that. I love you."

Oh God.

She noticed.

And here I thought I was being smart. I was being all slick and secretive about things.

Somehow I gather enough sense to smile and make up a bullshit reason. "I know. It's just I'm stressing about art school applications. It's the end of February now and I haven't heard anything back. So I don't know if they liked my sketches or not."

What a wretched lie.

Not that I haven't thought about it, about getting acceptance letters. But it's still early to hear anything back and besides, that thought is not even remotely on my radar right now.

But she buys it.

And that makes it even more of a wretched lie. That she completely buys my concern and proceeds to make me feel better about it. Not only her, both Poe and Salem come to console me. I know they're doing it for Callie, to make her feel included in this web of lies that I've created.

So when Callie leaves for the day, I breathe a sigh of relief.

I also take one last look at him.

He's still here of course, standing at the same spot, and Helen's right next to him, laughing and chatting. As are the rest of the faculty members. Only he's focusing on them now instead of me and I don't know why but that hurts even more.

I mean, he couldn't very well stand there and stare at me, right?

A *student*.

So I should probably stop this urge to cry.

As I walk down the steps, I should probably stop seeing that hand, *her* hand, on his chest in the back of my mind or obsessing over what he's doing here when supposedly he should be at Bardstown High.

They work together. Of course they're going to be close to each other.

Of course.

"Bronwyn."

I come to a jerking halt as he calls my name. From somewhere behind me. My friends come to a jerking halt as well.

In fact one of them holds my hand.

I look up to find it's Salem.

Her golden eyes hold a hint of sadness but her smile is encouraging. I know she saw it too, him with her. And given that she's gone through something similar with Arrow, she is lending me her support.

Poe's support comes in the form of a whisper. "Chin up, buttercup." She scrunches up her nose. "Or something like that. I was trying to be supportive without being inappropriate. But anyway, go get him. We'll wait for you in your room."

Just then we hear him come closer.

Before he addresses me, or rather my back. "Can I talk to you for a second?"

My heart begins to thud, and when Salem squeezes my hand one last time, ready to let me go, I hesitate for a second. I grow fearful for some reason. Even though I've wanted to see him, be with him since the moment he dropped me off back home on Friday.

But my friend gets that too.

She squeezes my hand again and whispers, "You can do this. Trust me."

I let her go then.

Because she's right. I can do this. Whatever this is.

I can be brave.

Breathing deeply, getting all my emotions under control so I look serene, I turn around to face him. And grow weak in the knees right away.

Because he's got the same look in his eyes that he did before.

Only he's much closer now and so the effect is more potent.

It's thicker and heavier.

This possessiveness in his eyes.

"Hi," I say softly.

His jaw clenches for a second — much more tightly than usual — when I greet him before he says, "You okay?"

For some reason his deep voice hits me differently today.

It hits me with much more force and I swallow, nodding. "Yes."

"You got to school okay this morning?"

"Yes."

"Good."

"This isn't the first time I've gone on a visitation weekend," I tell him to put him at ease, because his '*good*' didn't sound so convincing.

His jaw moves again. "And this isn't the first time I've wanted to ask that question."

I clench my thighs then and blurt out, "I went to see you this morning. In your office. It was locked though."

His features ripple with an unknown emotion. "I'm not going to be here this week."

Jerking out a nod, I say, "Yes, Callie told me. You're helping out at Bardstown High."

His chest moves with a breath and he shakes his head in disgust as he says, "The new coach apparently pulled his knee. While *standing* on the field. Fucking incompetent asshole. And they called me in as a favor. Instead of asking someone else on the faculty to take over. Now I have to waste my time on a team that's never winning another game because their new coach does his job as well as he stands."

I bite my lip at his irritation. "But it's your team, right? I mean before you came here. You practiced with them."

"So?"

"So maybe it all happened for the best. Callie told me it's an important game this Friday. Maybe you can help them win," I tell him with a slight smile. "You can remind them of all the stuff you taught them before. Maybe this is the best thing their new coach has done for them. Pulling his knee and stepping aside. So their old coach can help."

He's silent for a few moments, his eyes flicking back and forth between mine.

And the more they do that, the darker they get and I can't help but part my lips.

Glancing at them for a moment, he lifts his gaze and says roughly, "You don't quit, do you?"

Goosebumps rise all over my skin at his rough, tender tone. "Quit what?"

"Being so fucking sweet and rosy all the time."

My chest expands then. Making my breaths all scattered and weird.

And I can't help but ask, "W-what are you doing here?"

*Why were you standing so close to her?*

As soon as the thought flashes through my head, I get a bad feeling.

A very, very bad feeling.

A *crushing* feeling.

Maybe he came here to see her. Because he won't get to. For the next week.

Maybe he...

"I didn't," he begins, pulling me from my dark thoughts, "I didn't know she'd be here. When I came. And I'm not... We're not..." He sighs then, stumbling and trailing off before he picks up the thread and states, "We've been practicing all day. Because that's how bad they are and... I couldn't pull myself out until this afternoon."

"Okay."

He pins me with his gaze for this next part, "Or I would've been here sooner to..."

"To do what?"

A beat passes as he shoves his hands down into his pockets. "To tell you."

"Tell me?"

Another breath. "That I'm not going to be here this week."

I study his face for a second, his eyes, trying to understand what he means. Then, finally it clicks and I breathe out, "You came here to see me."

At my words, he takes a step closer to me. "It was unexpected. Their call. I didn't have the time to tell anyone. You."

I take a step closer to him as well even though I know it's dangerous to do that.

I must look all lovestruck and love-drenched as I stare up at him. But it's so hard, *so* hard, to stay away from him when he's just made me bloom.

Like he did Friday night when he came to my town, my house, to look for me.

"When can I..." I ask, swallowing. "When can we..."

*Be together.*

That possessive glint in his eyes shines bright, brighter than before. "Friday." He pulls something out of his pocket, a pink permission slip, before giving it to me. "Here."

I take it and see that it's an overnight pass. For the entire weekend.

Snapping my eyes up, I frown. "But it's not a visitation weekend."

"It is," he says, "if I want it to be."

Right.

Of course, faculty members can give out visitation weekend passes outside of visitation weekends. Not that every student can get them. Only a handful like me with the highest of privileges.

"I didn't like it," he continues in a low, rough voice and I look up, suddenly all happy.

"What?"

"That I had to drive you back. After. Sneak you back into your house like some sort of a thief."

I hug the pink slip to my chest. "Is that why you were so mad on the way back home?"

Because he was.

All angry and grumpy, answering my questions with a grunt or heavy silences.

"Fuck yeah," he bites out. "This time I'm not letting you leave my bed. You're going to stay there. With me. And when Monday comes *I'll* drive you back to St. Mary's after your fucking visitation weekend."

I bite the inside of my cheek to stop from grinning. "Okay."

He studies my face for a few moments, as if memorizing my features because he won't get to see them for the next week. I do the same, feeling both sad and happy in this moment.

Before I feel a light tug and I look down to see the source of it.

It's him. His fingers.

That are rubbing the tail of my braid.

I watch his large fingers move. Once. Twice.

And then one more time before he steps back and shoves his hands down into his pockets again. "I'll pick you up Friday. At seven. Same spot as before."

With that he turns around and leaves.

And I let my smile out.

Friday then.

# CHAPTER TWENTY-SEVEN

It's Friday.

But I'm not where I'm supposed to be.

I'm not waiting for him at the bend of the road at seven as he asked me to.

I'm actually waiting for him at Bardstown High. Or more like *watching* him, on the soccer field, from the stands. Along with hundreds of other people, because the game is on.

It's been on for the last hour and we're drawing to a close soon.

*And* we're winning.

It's crazy that I'm calling the team 'we,' when I don't go to this school and neither am I from this town. Also I've never had much interest in sports to call any team 'we.'

This team feels like 'we' though.

Because of him.

Because he's their coach. Well, ex-coach, but he's coached them this week and he's the reason that they're winning.

He is.

Because he's magnificent.

And he's not even playing.

He's standing on the sidelines, his feet shoulder-width apart, his arms folded across his chest as he watches the game with a very cool face. Occasionally, *extremely* occasionally, he calls things out to his players. While a couple of people around him, which I'm guessing must be the assistant coaches or whatever, are shouting and cursing, looking all sorts of animated.

But he's the star of the show nonetheless.

Actually no, he's not the star. He's the king.

He's the god these players are trying to impress.

Because they are.

Every little while, they look at their coach, not the surrounding clowns, but him, the head coach, waiting for his approval, his feedback.

Which he gives with a short nod and a slight tip of his lips.

And it just makes me feel so proud. At the way people respond to him. The way he inspires them, changes their moment, their day, their life just like that.

That's why I came actually.

Because I wanted to watch him in his element.

I also wanted to surprise him, but mostly I came to watch him around his dream, around soccer. And I have to say that he *absolutely* shines.

So much so that I want to capture him in my sketchbook right here, right now. To *show* him. To make him see that even though he's not playing like he always wanted to, he still manages to make this game better. And I have a feeling that it gives him pride as well. When they do something right. When they reach their potential.

Because the moment they win the game, he smiles. And for the first time since the game began, he claps. He moves from his spot and strides over to his players, who all welcome him into their midst like they missed him.

Missed his guidance.

Although he doesn't stay with them for long. He stands among them for a couple of minutes before disengaging and breaking off from the crowd. I watch him shake his head and refuse what I assume are the invitations to stay, maybe even to celebrate with them.

And then I watch him glance down at that big silver watch of his and I know.

I know why.

I know he's refusing them because he needs to get to me. He needs to drive over to St. Mary's in exactly fifty minutes to go pick me up, and that's when I move.

I was already standing, clapping with the hundreds of spectators when the team won, and now I push through the crowd. I make my way through the rows of people who are all trying to leave and are blocking my path until I'm at the end of the row, and then I'm bounding down the stairs and dashing over to the exit, to this archway kind of thing that leads into the stadium.

Where I know he's going to come out of.

In fact, he's there right now, at the mouth of it, as soon as I reach it.

I can see him striding through the flood of exiting people and I'm about to call out to him when my view is blocked. By a group of guys. Who from what it looks like are also trying to exit.

I bump into them in my hurry. "Oh, I'm sorry."

"It's okay," one of them says but instead of moving out of my way he continues, "Are you lost?"

"Uh, no," I tell him, trying to get past him. "I just need to..."

The second guy, this one taller than the first one, asks, "Do you go to school here? What grade are you in?"

I step back from them. "No, I don't. I'm just... I need to get to someone."

The third guy joins in and I move back again, bumping against someone. "We can help you find them, if you like. This place could get confusing if you don't know where you're going."

"Yeah, and I don't think you're here with someone, right?" the second guy chimes in.

I draw back. "What?"

"Sorry, that came out creepy." The second guy laughs nervously as the other two groan. "It's just that we were sitting in the same row and —"

"Bronwyn."

At my name, I breathe out in relief.

Not only because the sea of boys — who were frankly starting to creep me out — part, but also because he's here.

He *saw* me.

Apart from being freaked out by these strange guys, I was starting to get antsy that we'd miss each other.

He's standing only a few feet away, all tall and frowning, as he stares at me. And I throw him a small relieved smile. Just then one of the guys says, "Oh hey, Coach Thorne. Good game."

The second one grins. "Fucking great game, dude. I thought this season was doomed."

The third one says something as well but I barely pay attention to him.

I'm only paying attention to Conrad, who I don't even think heard the first two guys speak. Because his entire focus is on me, and then he begins to stride over and my heart gets louder than the stadium, which is still cheering at our team's victory.

He bulldozes through them, barely saying a word while they keep talking, to get to me.

But when one of the guys steps in front of him to say something, he snaps his gaze away and points it at him. And right in front of my eyes that heated denim blue turns into such an icy shade that I shiver. I shiver at the chill Conrad blasts that guy with for getting in his way.

Which makes that boy scramble to get out of Conrad's way, and then his focus is back on me again.

Then his eyes are heating up again too.

And when he reaches me, they're flashing and intense. So intense that I feel a pull toward them, toward *him* and I crane my neck up as I whisper with my heart in my throat, "Surprise."

His nostrils flare at my soft voice.

Before he grabs my hand and begins to stride again with me in tow.

I don't get a chance to say another word after that. Or check out my surroundings as I jog behind him, my backpack slung over my shoulders.

Not that I would even want to look at the surroundings right now.

Or even talk.

Which is a surprise, because I always want to talk to him.

Right now though, I'm happy being pulled along and taken places. I'm happy with his rough fingers digging into my wrist in a way that makes me think that he's just as afraid of losing me as I am of getting lost in this strange, crowded place.

Soon we're in the parking lot and quickly we cross it and at last, we're at his truck.

Still holding my hand, he snaps the door open and pulls me forward. He puts his hands on my waist and dumps me in his truck, all silently and broodily. Just as my thighs hit the leather seats, he shuts the door with a bang and rounds the vehicle.

Through the windshield, I see that the muscle on his cheek is ticking and my heart ticks along with it. I place my backpack that I packed for my weekend stay with him on the floor, between my knees, and buckle my seatbelt just as he enters the truck.

Still without a word, he starts the ignition, backs out of the spot, and then we're off.

I'm not sure where we're going — I'm thinking back to his house? — but I know that I want to get there fast. I know that I want to go to a place where we're alone.

Truly alone.

And I think he feels the same as me.

He feels the same desperation.

I think all his agitation, the speed with which he's driving and the fact that he just ran through a yellow light, is because he wants to get wherever he's going fast as well.

And I'm proven correct in the next few minutes, when he doesn't even get to where he's going.

Unless his destination was in fact a random spot on the dark highway, at which he goes off the road and drives into the woods. He drives until we're a little further in and the road isn't as visible through the thick trunks before he brings his truck to a jerking halt.

By the time he gets out, I'm already untethered, both literally — my seat belt is off — and figuratively because I'm ready to melt with all the restlessness. So when he opens the door and wraps his hands around my waist again, this time to get me out of the cab, I'm thankful.

I'm so thankful to him that my arms go easily around his neck. And then he shuts the door again and settles me against it, hauling my thighs up, tightening them around his body before going for my face and cradling it.

"How did you get here?" he asks thickly, his eyes staring into mine, into my soul even.

My own hands settle on his cheeks too, my fingers tracing his long hair, moving it out of his gorgeous eyes. "I took the bus."

His chest pushes into mine with a breath. "The bus."

I nod, arching up against him, rubbing my heavy tits against his chest after the longest week I've ever had in my life. "I know you don't like that. Me taking the bus. But I wanted to see you. I wanted to see the game. I know it was important and I know you thought you guys wouldn't win, but look, you did. And I told you —"

He squeezes my cheeks, cutting me off, as he rasps, "Fuck the game."

And then he kisses me.

He captures my mouth in his and pushes his tongue inside. And I latch on to it. I latch onto him.

Not that I wasn't before.

But it's like his lips, his kisses, have jolted me back to life and I'm alive for the first time in days.

I'm alive and *breathing* for the first time since Monday.

When he gave me that pink permission slip.

I've been sleeping with it tucked under my pillow. Counting days and hours and minutes.

Pushing away, I break the kiss and tell him that. "I came as soon as I could. As soon as they would let me out."

I did.

He was going to be there three hours later but I made sure that I was out those gates the moment I was free to go.

His response is to growl as if unhappy that I broke the kiss, that I took my lips away from him. And so he goes back for them. He goes back to kiss me and in between the sucks of his mouth and nips of his teeth, he says gutturally, "I thought I was seeing things."

I fist his hair. "When?"

He sucks and sucks on my lower lip, making it sting, making me all wet and squirmy in his arms, rubbing my body shamelessly. "When I saw you. Back there."

"You weren't."

He presses his forehead into me, his eyes dark and stormy, his mouth panting over mine. "I should go back. I should fucking rip their eyes out for looking at you. For talking to you. For even *thinking* about you."

I shiver again at the violence in his voice. "I think you scared them pretty good already."

His jaw tightens up as lust wars with anger in his eyes.

Or maybe they're both fueling each other, I don't know.

"They *smelled* it on you, you understand? They smelled her," he growls.

I fist the back of his sweater as I rain down soft kisses on his tense features. "Smelled what?"

At my question, he has to breathe deep.

He has to fist my hair and pull my head back, making me stop.

As if he doesn't want my softness right now.

When he says, "Your pussy."

My pussy pulses at the mention.

So strongly that I jerk and undulate in his arms, rubbing not only my tits but also my core against his body. And so all I can respond with is a needy moan.

Which only grows louder when he drops his head and runs his nose along the column of my throat, growling again, "They could smell your pussy. They could sniff out that she was freshly broken. As fresh as a week ago. They could smell that up until seven days ago, no one had touched her. No one had even laid their eyes on her. No one had tasted her. No one. Before *me*." He licks my skin at this, as if imagining doing that to my pussy. "No one had seen her rosy color. Or how pink she is. Pink and Shameless. Just like your lipstick, yeah?"

I nod, all happy and horny that he noticed the lipstick that I'm wearing right now for him, that he remembered the shade, as I tilt my neck to the side, giving him more access to lick and bite and suck.

And he goes for it.

He pops my soft flesh into his mouth and sucks and sucks, growling again before he continues, "No one knew how tight she is either. How small. Like a fragile flower. A sweet fucking rose. No one knew that before last week, Bronwyn. Before me."

"Yes."

His body tightens again, vibrates with all the pent-up aggression. "And they could sense that. They wanted that. They wanted their turn at it."

"But you —"

He's back on my lips again, breathing wildly, staring into my eyes with a fever. "And guys are horndogs. You understand what I'm saying to you? They'll fuck any pussy that's thrown their way. *Any* pussy. But this here" — he rolls his hips against mine, making me moan again, making me flutter my eyes closed — "this is prime pussy. This pussy is magic. It's what dreams are made of. Because when it was wrapped around me last week, when it kept coming and coming and pulsing around me, *strangling* me, I saw stars. I fucking saw pink glitter and unicorns. Your rosy fucking pussy made me see double, Bronwyn.

And they wanted that for themselves. They wanted *my* wallflower. And for that, for just *thinking* that, they deserve to die. They deserve to be torn apart limb from fucking limb. And I should go do that. I should take my time with it."

He bangs his hand against the truck, shaking the entire cab as he finishes.

I tighten, tighten, *tighten* my limbs around him then.

I practically fuse myself with him as I say, "No, you're not going anywhere. I won't let you. Because it doesn't matter what they thought. It doesn't matter if they wanted me for themselves. I'm not theirs."

"Fuck no, you aren't," he snaps, his eyes almost taken over by anger. "You're mine. *Mine.*"

"I am. And so you need to take care of me. And you need to let me take care of you. Because it's been a week, okay? A whole week without you. I missed you." I sweep my eyes all over his face. "I missed you so much."

The fever lingers in his eyes for a few seconds, the violence, until it's all replaced by lust.

Dark and hot.

"Yeah," he rasps, looking over my features as well, and that's enough.

For me to know. For me to be happy.

His acknowledgement that he missed me.

That he wouldn't give me last week. When he came looking for me.

So I smile slightly and he captures my lips again.

And I arch my spine and thrust my tits into his chest, while pressing on the back of his head so he can kiss me even deeper. To make up for the past week.

But the more he sucks and the more he makes it sting and hurt so good, the more achy I get. Achier than before.

Heavier and more swollen, more lust-laden.

So much so that I get the strength from somewhere deep down to push him away, to take his mouth off my lips and even get down from his arms.

Then I kneel.

At his feet.

My tits jiggling under my sweater dress and my knees hitting the icy cold ground.

And when I'm in position, I look up.

I look at his tall and large body. His bent face, his bright eyes. That long-ish hair of his, hanging over his forehead, his harsh cheeks.

And I say, "I need your dick."

He stills.

"In my mouth."

When all he does is stare down at me with parted, panting lips, his fingers clenched at his sides, I put my hands on his thighs and say, "I know it's big and it won't fit in my mouth. But I still need it and you can't say no."

Finally he breaks his silence. "I can't."

I shake my head. "No. Because if I'm your wallflower, then it means you're my thorn too. And so if I want to suck your beast of a dick with my flower of a mouth, I can. You will let me. You're not allowed to say no."

His thighs flex at my words.

The words he said to me in his kitchen last week.

The words that mean more to me than he could ever imagine.

So I go for it then.

I go for his jeans, ready to unbutton them, as I rub my cheek over that tent in his pants, hot and throbbing. Which makes it throb some more, my soft cheeks.

But he grabs the back of my neck and stretches me up. He bends down and levels me with his lusty eyes so he can growl over my lips, "You want to suck my cock, baby?" I nod, all lit up at his endearment, and he presses a hard, possessive kiss on my lips before continuing, "You can suck my cock. But remember what I told you. Remember that my beast of a cock is going to wreck your flower of a mouth. It will wreck and stretch your pinky lips before it does the same to your throat. Remember that I warned you. *Your thorn* warned you about his dick."

He presses another possessive kiss on my mouth before straightening up and leaving me to do my thing.

And I do.

I *do* do my thing as my hands jump and leap to open his jeans. To tug at them, lower them and get out his cock.

And when it's out, I hate to say it but I forget about everything.

I become all selfish and self-centered.

A bratty teenager.

A teenager who has no concept of the woods, the winter, the wildly breathing man standing over her. She only needs this thing, this red throbbing thing in front of her.

She wants to lick it and suck on the head. So she does that.

I do that.

I jerk forward to put his wide purple head in my mouth and it throbs like a heart on my tongue. So I do it more. Pressing my hands on his thighs, I suck and suck on the head of his dick, making it throb, making him all tight and growly.

Until I get bored with it. As if I'm playing a game and now I want to play another one.

Now I want to see if what he told me was true or not.

So I wrap my hands around his thick trunk and put it on my face. From chin to forehead. And he was right. He *was*.

It covers me whole and there are still some inches left. His purple head goes past my forehead and I smile. And moan.

I also slap my cheek with it, rub my nose along the underside of his dark rod. As I lick that vein.

That thick vein that I think — I *think* — I felt throbbing when he was inside of me last week. I think it expanded when he came and I'm so eager to see if it does the same when I make him come now.

In my mouth.

So I abandon this game too.

Which is just as well because I think I've made him angry with my callous games. I've made him all aggressive again with the way he's staring down at me with slitted eyes and clenched fists.

So I bite my lip and give him a look of contrition through my eyelashes.

But that only makes him growl even more.

It only makes his dick jump in my hands and ooze pre-cum, which I catch with my tongue, swirling it around the head, licking it clean, my whole body shivering at his salty, musky taste.

And then I don't let go.

I don't let his dick leave my mouth after that. I keep it on my tongue, my lips stretching around it as I suck and suck. As I lean forward and push it inside more.

At which point his fists unfurl and his hands grab the back of my head, fisting my hair. Not pushing on me, no. But just there, like a dark but cozy threat.

A threat that makes me even more excited to keep going.

To shove him even further into my mouth, and after a few tries and some gagging, I do get to do it. I do get him deeper, touching the roof of my mouth, the back of it.

But a second later, I'm ripped off from his cock and pulled up. And before I can even blink, he spins me around and hauls up my ass.

My hands go to the windows of his truck and I turn back, panting. "But I…"

He's in the process of shoving up my dress and pulling down my lacy panties when he looks up, all mad and obsessed. "No more, you understand? We're not playing this game anymore. We're *not* playing 'Let's see how goddamn crazy we make Conrad with Bronwyn's dick-sucking mouth.'" He finishes that with a tight slap on my ass that makes me moan as he continues, "I'm over that now."

I fist his sweater as I stare back at him with somehow both drugged and eager eyes. "But did you like it? Did you see? I almost took it all. I almost —"

He cuts me off by coming for my swollen mouth again like he can't bear to hear me talk right now. Like he can't bear to be away from it, from giving me his kisses.

His lovely thorn kisses.

"Yeah, baby, I saw," he both coos and growls then, his mouth sucking on my lips. "And it was fucking phenomenal, yeah? And one day I'll come in your mouth and watch myself drip down your chin. Or maybe I'll come on your tits" — he reaches forward to grab one and squeeze over my dress — "hose them down with my cream. And then I'll stand over you and watch as you rub my cum all over your milkmaid tits. So you smell like me. But for now, I need a ride in that prime pussy, okay? It's been seven days. Seven fucking days and I have thought of nothing else. Nothing else, Bronwyn. Not the game, not practice. Just getting inside that pinky pussy and beating it up."

How can I refuse him then?

How can I be a bratty selfish teenager and tell him to let me suck his cock when he needs my pussy so much?

When this is all he's thought about.

So I kiss him back and whisper, "Okay."

A wave of emotion runs over his features at my easy acquiescence before they go harsh again, dripping with demon lust, and I feel him position himself at my soft, soppy entrance.

I feel his head nudging my hole for a second before he pushes it in.

And keeps going and going until he bottoms out.

Until it feels like he's up in my belly, nudging my womb.

He groans then, smacking my ass again as if he can't contain his pleasure. And I swear, I swear to fucking God, I feel that vein I was playing with swell up and throb. My one hand twists in his sweater and the other slips on the window as I go up on my tiptoes, arching my ass even further so he can go up even higher.

And then I'm moaning in his mouth because he's kissing me as he starts moving.

As he starts pumping into me.

Slowly, lazily at first.

Because I think he's giving me time to adjust. Because I'm still almost a virgin, see. I'm still all tight and fresh because I've only had him twice on one night. Last Friday.

So despite being all crazy to get to me, to get at my pussy, my Conrad is giving me all the time in the world.

He opens up my channel with his thick cock, all careful like.

All sweet like.

While he keeps me soft and cozy with his kisses.

And slowly, I start to push back.

I start to bounce my ass on his dick.

Which is what he was waiting for.

He steps back from our kiss and adjusts our positions. He bends me down even more, making me put both my hands on the glass window, and hikes up my ass so he can really get at it. And then he's moving. He's sliding in and out. He's pumping and pounding as he rides my prime pussy, his tight abs bouncing against my ass, against the spots where he spanked me, making this fuck even more delicious than our first.

Meanwhile all I can do is bounce back every time he comes for me.

All I can do is feel it spreading, this heated, liquid lust.

Until I'm all covered in it.

Until I'm right there, on the edge.

And until he leans forward, his big chest breathing at my back, his hands that were holding on to my hips now wrapped around my waist, straightening me up and plastering me against him.

It changes the angle at which his dick is hitting me and I gasp out, "God, Conrad, I…"

"You like that, huh?"

"Uh-huh."

He brings a hand up and grabs my throat, his lips whispering in my ear, "Yeah, my wallflower likes it. She likes it when I wreck her pussy too. When I beat it up so good that she can't help but come on my dick. Are you going to come, Bronwyn?"

I nod my head. "Yes."

But it doesn't happen.

Not right away.

Even though I thought it would.

I don't fly over the edge, until he pushes me. Until he smacks his hand on my ass, the loudest, most biting slap so far, and I come.

I fly and scatter like petals.

But he keeps me collected.

He keeps me gathered and tethered in his arms as he comes as well.

Inside me, all thick and hot and lashing.

By the time he rights my clothes and bends down to put my panties back on, depositing me in the cab after, I'm all sleepy and sated. But I do remember to say, "Congratulations."

When he frowns, I smile sleepily and move his hair out of his eyes. "You won the game. I knew you would. Because you're wonderful."

There's a tightening of his features for a second or two as he stares at my disheveled, sleepy self like *I'm* wonderful. Like I'm the most wonderful girl in the world.

Before he kisses me again and whispers, "Go to sleep."

# CHAPTER TWENTY-EIGHT

I spend every weekend with him.

Well, not *every* weekend.

Because I go to a school where our every move is monitored and accounted for. And even though I'm one of the few girls who has the most privileges, I still can't abuse them willy-nilly.

So we have to pace ourselves.

We have to be careful.

Even though it's hard after that one-week separation.

So instead of *every* weekend, Conrad gives me a pink permission slip every couple of weeks. That I can use to go out and stay with him. And on those weekends, he waits for me at the bend of the road in his truck to take me to his house in Bardstown.

And can I just say that I love his house?

I know it's old and I know that he's lived in it all his life. Which means he isn't much of a fan, but still.

And just because I *want* him to love it more, I'm giving him a new one.

A new home, I mean.

By painting his walls a new color.

Especially his bedroom walls.

Standing in the middle of his bedroom on one such weekend, I tell him, "You know, I wanted to paint your walls."

Again he's at the door, leaning against it with his arms folded, as he watches me walk freely around his domain.

Or he watches my thighs; specifically, the art on them.

So recently I've had a fashion consult with none other than Poe, the fashionista among us. I told her that I wanted something short and slightly more revealing and sexy. She obviously figured it was for Conrad — which it is — and lent me a ton of her clothes. It's a good thing that we're sort of the same in the chest department. Hers are bigger than mine though, but since I'm taller than her, her short dresses are slightly shorter on me.

Which is even better than good.

Because in her short, made-shorter-on-me dresses, I can show off the art on my body.

I can show off his name that I still write every night in my dorm room.

Which is what he's staring at: his name peeking out from under the hem of my red dress.

Lifting his eyes, he says from his spot by the door, "Paint my walls."

I clench my thighs a bit at his voice, at the dark glitter in his eyes. At the fact that he hasn't stopped staring at me ever since we arrived at his house and I took off my magenta parka.

"Yes." I nod, raising my eyebrows. "I hate to tell you this but your walls are bare. Especially the ones in your office. I noticed it the first day I was there."

His eyes narrow at the mention of that first day. The day he took my privileges away. "You mean, the day you took a walk through my office like it was your personal amusement park."

Right.

I try to look contrite as I say, "Yes. Which I'm still really sorry for, by the way."

But I think I fail because my apology is what gets him moving. My apology gets him to unfold his arms, lean away from the door and take a step toward me.

And just to rile him up, I take a step back.

He watches my bare, pink-nailed toes, my ankles adorned with silver anklets before glancing up at me. "Are you?"

"Yes," I reply right away, biting the inside of my cheek to keep my excited smile at bay. "But that's not the point I'm trying to make here."

He takes another step toward me. "And what *is* the point you're trying to make here?"

"The point I'm trying to make is that I wanted to paint your walls that day," I tell him, moving back. "I wanted to give you something pretty and colorful to look at while you sit in your boring chair and do all the boring coach-ly things."

His lips twitch at 'coach-ly things' as he runs his eyes up and down my body, looking at my pink toenails, my red dress, my golden arm chain with red beads, my necklace made of red stones. "Something pretty and colorful, huh."

I blush. "Yes. Like flowers."

That gives him pause.

His smooth, predatory steps falter as well.

"Flowers," he says, looking slightly offended.

I come to a stop because I'm at the wall now as I reply, "Yes. Flowers."

He stares at me a beat. "Well, I'm glad you didn't."

"And why is that?" I ask, raising my chin. "Are you too much of a man to like a flower, Conrad Thorne?"

At this something astonishing happens.

Something that takes my breath away for a second or two and makes me forget what we were talking about.

He chuckles.

*Chuckles.*

Like really.

I don't think I've ever heard him or seen him do that before. Because I would've remembered. I would've remembered how deep it is. How low and rough, just like his voice. How it makes his Greek god face glow.

And it makes me think that I've been aiming too low.

I've wanted to make him smile and I always felt victorious when he did.

But I should've aimed for *this*.

I should've aimed for his chuckles. Amazing and beautiful and sexy chuckles.

I'm so entranced by this wonderful turn of events that it doesn't even register when he resumes walking and makes it all the way over to me. Not until he puts one hand on the wall up above my head and leans over. Not until he says, all thickly and with amusement at the same time, "No, Bronwyn Littleton, I'm not too much of a man to like a flower. In fact, there's this one flower I really like."

I go to say something at that but only a gasp comes out because he touches me.

With his other hand, he touches me *down there*.

And if it were over my dress, I would probably be okay.

But it's not.

Somehow he's managed to get his other hand *under* my dress, and on my pussy. Somehow he's managed to hook his fingers around the crotch of my panties and pull them. Up against my channel, up against that little bundle of nerves.

"This pretty little rose," he rasps, his eyes almost burning me alive. "Right here."

I clench my thighs and arch my back so he can use my panties to rub me harder. I even go so far as to rock against his movements as I say breathily, grabbing his bicep, "I'm going to do it."

"Do what?"

"Paint your bare walls. With f-flowers."

At this he fists my panties and pulls them harder, making me jerk. "Yeah?"

"Yes."

He moves his hand from the wall and puts that one on my body as well, on the back of my neck to pull me up and closer. "And do you know what I'm going to do?"

"Fuck me?"

His jaw tightens slightly at my shameless reply. "Yeah. Because you need that. You also need me to remind you of a very important thing, don't you?"

"What thing?"

Another hard tug with his knuckles rubbing against my clit. "That you're not allowed to move away from me. You're not allowed to move away from Conrad." A shiver runs down my spine when he says that and I'm on the verge of closing my eyes but he squeezes my neck and continues, "But first I'm going to take care of this dress."

I'm up on my tiptoes now, all stretched up and teetering on the edge of an orgasm and all he's done is play with my clit. "You mean r-rip it off my body and throw it in the trash?"

That's the other reason why I went to Poe for a wardrobe consult.

To rile him up a little.

His eyes go back and forth between mine. "That's why you wore it, yeah?"

"Yes. And also because I'll get to wear your clothes after."

"Well, if you dressed up so prettily for me," he says, his fingers still clutching and twisting my panties, "then it's only fair I give you what you want. But I think I'll keep my clothes this time."

"Why?" I ask frowning.

"Because I think I prefer you naked. Only so I have something pretty and colorful to look at."

He kisses me as soon as he finishes, and I come as soon as he touches his mouth to mine.

I still can't believe how easy I am when it comes to him.

How easily he makes me come and fall apart.

But anyway, the next day he takes me to buy paint and supplies so I can start giving him a new home.

Which I hate to say that even after several weeks is still lagging behind.

I'm so freaking behind on my plans.

Because as much as I want to work on giving him a pretty picture of bold and colorful flowers, he just won't let me do it.

He keeps distracting me.

Something that I never ever thought Conrad Thorne, the epitome of authority and control, would be capable of.

But every Saturday morning after we have breakfast — which *I* make because I've also decided to cook for him every chance I get because he really does suck at cooking — and I put on my baggy denim overalls to get to work, he comes into the room and watches me.

And it's not a normal... watching.

It's not as if he's doing something while watching me. Like reading a book, for example, or something where every once in a while he'll glance at me before going back to his actual activity, no.

He *actually* watches me.

He either stands at the door in his usual way, arms folded, or sits at the edge of his bed, bent over, his elbows resting on his spread thighs as he runs his eyes over my bejeweled and decorated arms or my exposed midriff in the bra-style crop top that I wear under my overalls.

And every second he's there, *watching me*, I can't think.

I can't work.

I can't even breathe properly.

And when I ask him what it is that he thinks he's doing, he always tells me, "Staring at something colorful and pretty."

Which always, *always* melts me and then there's no point thinking about work.

What I need is to crawl over to him and kneel at his feet.

What I need is for him to unravel my topknot that I usually wear for work and set my Rapunzel hair free.

And then I get his dick out and suck on it. Suck on it and suck on it until I've taken him completely — I've been practicing — and until he goes so crazy that he fists my hair and pulls me off his rod. So instead of my mouth, he can stick it in my pussy, right there on the floor, among all the colors and paints.

But that's not all.

That's not the only time he distracts me.

He also distracts me when I'm painting *him*.

Which I've started to do a lot more, and that's saying something because I already sketched him twenty-four seven.

These days though it's more fun, because I don't have to hide it from him anymore *and* because my creative juices are always at their most potent. Especially in bed, when he's just made me come.

For some reason his orgasms act as an aphrodisiac.

The nectar of the creative gods.

They inspire me, his dick, his body, his kisses. They give me this epic itch, epic *need* to sketch and draw and fill the world with colors and confetti.

So I put some music on his phone — usually this one slow and sexy song about a girl who's in love with this guy and she's getting drunk with him as she counts constellations like freckles on his body — and turn to my favorite thing to draw: him.

Oh, and I also get to pose him.

Yes!

I get to pose the man I'm in love with.

I get to play with his hair, all messy and pretty after our lovemaking. I get to move it, style it, arrange it over his forehead however I like. I get to tell him to sit back on the white pillows, his chest bare and sweaty, the ridges of his abs expanding and contracting with his breaths, his thighs spread under the white sheets.

Sometimes I ask him to put his arm over his head, stretching the sculpted muscles of his pecs and tightening his biceps. And sometimes when he doesn't do it right, I go in and arrange him myself. Actually, I arrange him myself even when he does it right.

Because I'm a fiend for his body.

And also his silver watch.

Which I always tell him to wear. Especially during sex and painting sessions.

When I mentioned it the first time, he was confused. "My watch."

Sprawled on him after sex, I smiled. "Uh-huh."

"You have a thing for my... silver watch," he asked again, tipping his chin down to look at me, all sexily.

"Yup." I nodded, kissing his sweaty chest. "It makes you look all sexy and dominating. Authoritative." And then I lowered my voice a little. "'Do you know what time it is? It's 11:15.'"

I chuckled and he grabbed my hair, pulling my head up. "Is that supposed to be funny?"

Widening my eyes in mock fear, I said, "No, sir."

His fists tightened in my hair and his lips twitched. "You're the..."

"I'm the what?"

His eyes roved over my flushed features. "You're the strangest person I've ever met." Then, pulling me closer to his lips, "And if you call me sir again, I'll make sure that's all you ever get to call me."

And then he kissed me and fucked me.

All with the silver watch on his wrist.

Because he lets me do everything my heart desires.

He lets me touch him, poke him, prod him with the blunt end of my pencil, stare at him for hours as I sketch him, trying to get all the details right. He indulges all my quirks and I indulge his: drawing him while naked.

Because he likes to look at me too.

Apart from his usual watching, he likes to look at the artwork on my body. His name decorated with roses and thorns.

In fact, he's taken to writing his name on me himself. And he's so sneaky about it.

Like he won't do it when I'm awake or when I'm watching, no.

He writes his name on my body when I'm sleeping and he writes it in places that I can easily find. That I can easily make out in the mirror when I go to shower after I've woken up: my collarbones, in the valley between my breasts.

And when I do find it, I smile and make roses around it. Just to tell him that I saw and that I loved it.

He also likes my jewelry.

That he tells me to keep on even when he rips my dresses off my body.

He actually bought me one too.

Yeah. A belly chain.

Sort of like the one I wore the first time we had sex. His is simpler, a delicate chain made of gold, no dangling, tinkling things. And I love it more than I've ever loved anything in my life.

It's totally him.

And so I wear it all the time.

Even at school, under my uniform.

But anyway, he likes to play with my jewelry like I play with his muscles.

He likes to reach out and flick a finger at my dangling bracelets, making them clink. Or stick his pinky in the little holes of my necklace and pull.

Sometimes he does it with my hair too, curls it around his large masculine digits and pulls.

And when he does that while I'm sketching him, I slap his hand away and tell him that I'm working.

That I'm trying to focus.

"You shouldn't be moving around anyway," I say, my eyes on the sketchbook, my pencil moving. "You're supposed to be my model. You're supposed to stay put, Conrad."

He doesn't listen.

He goes for my loose hair again and picks up a strand to rub between his fingers.

Finally I snap my eyes up to tell him to cut it out.

Only to find that his gaze is burning.

It has gone all dark and horny and the next breath I take is shaky.

My next words are shaky as well. "Conrad, stop."

Again he doesn't.

At my protest, something possessive flickers through his already heated eyes, something arrogant too, making me burn even more.

"I can't believe this," I say then, trying to be all strong in the face of his somehow both mature and boyish arrogance. "I thought you were good. I thought you followed all the rules. You were this uptight, disciplined, goody two shoes who would never even think of distracting someone from serious business."

Propped up on pillows, he should look relaxed and lazy. And he does to some extent. But at my words, it seems as if his body thrums with a current. It vibrates with a thick pulse of domination as he tugs at my hair again before going for my wrist as he hums, "Maybe for you I'm different. I'm bad. Maybe for you, Bronwyn, I'm trouble."

My breathing has gone all haywire now, given that he's repeated what I said to him from so long ago. And even as I say these words, I don't mean them at all. "I have to finish this."

"Yeah?"

I nod my head as primly as I can while sitting naked in front of him, with my breasts exposed and heaving, and with only a pillow in my lap and my sketchbook open on it.

"Yes," I whisper. "Because I'm an artist and I need to get this sketch done."

He tightens his fingers around my wrist and gives it a pull, a slightly forceful tug, and there I go.

I'm jerked toward him, my sketchbook sliding off my pillow, my pencil falling from my fingers, as he leans forward too, coming off his pillows.

As he descends over me, all massive shoulders and dark eyes.

"Let's see how much of an artist you are," he rasps, bringing his other hand forward and clutching at my necklace. "Let's see if you can finish this sketch on your knees. If you can color within the lines when I'm giving it to you doggy style. When I'm making this tight body shake and your pinky pussy talk." His lips are breathing over me now, his fingers flexing around my wrist. "Come on, Bronwyn. Let's see if my pretty little wallflower can make art when I smack her tight ass and ring all the bells on her body."

I kiss him then.

Because fuck art.

He can smack my ass and ring all the bells on my body any time he wants. Also spoiler alert: I couldn't.

Color within the lines, I mean.

When he was giving it to me doggy style.

God, I love these weekends with him.

I absolutely love them.

I love painting his house. I love painting *him*.

I love making him watch Disney movies — yeah, I make him watch Disney movies. He was disgruntled about that in the beginning but once I told him that they are my favorite, he agreed. They're not actually my favorite though. I mean, I like them, but I like watching them with him more and laughing at his pained expressions.

I love waking up in his bed, kissing him whenever I want to, being kissed whenever he wants to. I love going out with him, because we do go out. Not where we can be recognized. Just on long drives.

He also brings me to his soccer practice.

Just for the record: That wasn't an easy thing to achieve.

I didn't even know that he was still helping out at Bardstown High. I thought they borrowed him for that one week and that was it. But apparently he's helping them over the weekends.

Which he told me very reluctantly after disappearing twice on Saturdays while I was staying with him.

So naturally my first question was if I could come see his practice. To which he definitely said no. But I kept at it and kept at it and one weekend, he gave in. On the condition that I'd sit on the bleachers, out in the open, and watch him. As opposed to finding a discreet place somewhere, hiding away from all the players, and watching him.

Which was my plan, of course.

Because I don't want people to ask him questions about me, about what I'm doing there and how he knows me and all that. I'm not sure how I was going to accomplish 'hiding' in a wide-open field, but I was going to figure something out.

But he shut it all down and said that he'd take care of it.

And he did. Take care of it, I mean.

He told everyone that I was his student from St. Mary's and that I'm an artist and I'm doing a series of soccer related portraits for my college portfolios. And so as a good teacher, he'd given me permission to sit in on his practice. And since Coach Thorne has such a stellar reputation, no one even batted an eye at his lie.

So since then I've been to his practice a few times.

I sit at the bleachers with my sketchbook open, watch him command a group of about twenty teenage guys.

I watch his eyes light up when a player does something right and how when they don't, he goes into his inspiring coach mode. Where he guides them, patiently works with them and doesn't let them quit until they're on the right track. Oh, and if they fuck around, he easily slips into his hardass coach mode as well and lets them have it.

I watch it all with the same feeling I got back at that game.

That Conrad might... *like* this. He might like his job. He might like coaching and guiding and *teaching* people.

Only he doesn't know it.

Maybe because he's too angry at it. That he *had* to take this job years and years ago instead of fulfilling his pro dreams.

So as I watch him, I draw.

I sketch all that in my sketchpad and later when we get to his house, I show him all my sketches.

I show him how he shines and glows when he's around soccer. When he's coaching kids and guiding them, making them better players. I tell him how wonderful that is. How wonderful and amazing and awe-inspiring that he touches so many lives on a daily basis.

He lets me turn the pages of my sketchbook and ramble about things, point at things, until he doesn't.

Until he grabs the back of my neck and takes my mouth.

I know he does that to distract me. To shut me up, because I don't think he likes hearing these things.

But that doesn't mean I'm going to quit.

I'm going to keep telling him, making him understand that even though his dream of being a pro soccer player didn't pan out, he can still find joy in this game. That even though this was a job he *had* to take years ago, it doesn't mean that he has to hate it for that.

But most importantly, I want to tell him that he doesn't have to wake up in the middle of the night every night and go kick the ball around in his backyard all alone.

Because he does that too.

And I honestly think after spending several weekends with him over the last couple of months that maybe I'm making progress. That maybe he can see that his coaching job could be his new passion.

But then one day at practice, a couple of people arrive and it immediately sours his mood. Immediately and visibly. And I realize that I'm so far away from my goal that it's not even funny.

When I ask him about them at his house later, he ignores me. But by now he should know that I'm not going to budge. And I don't. Not until he tells me that they were from New York City FC.

"Okay," I say, frowning. "So what did they want with you?"

He doesn't like the question because he not only clenches his jaw, he stomps over to his fridge, snaps it open and grabs a Gatorade from it. Which he then proceeds to drink down in its entirety in one swallow.

Standing at the kitchen island, I wait for him before prodding again. Because by now *I* know that he needs to be pushed in doses. So when he's done and he sets the bottle down on the island with a thud, I go, "Conrad. What did they want with you?"

He breathes sharply, staring at me. "They want me as their coach."

"Their coach?"

He clenches his jaw before almost lashing out, "Yes."

I stare at him wordlessly for a few seconds before asking, "But like, isn't that a good thing?"

His response is to clench his jaw again.

But I don't let it deter me. "Conrad, oh my God." I skip on the spot. "That's amazing. They want you. They want you to coach their team. It's a pro team. Oh my God. How are you not jumping up and down right now?"

He eyes my happiness for a second before clipping, "Because I'm not interested."

"I'm sorry?"

His chest moves with a sharp breath. "I'm not fucking interested in taking the job. I have never been interested in taking that job."

I blink, trying to clear out the cobwebs of confusion. "Wait, this isn't the first time they've offered it to you? The job."

Another breath, but this is more of a sigh, like he's tired of having this conversation. Which we've only just begun. He picks up the plastic bottle of Gatorade that he's just emptied and dumps it in the recycle bin before saying, distractedly, "No, not the first time. And definitely not the first time that I've turned them down."

"But why?" I grab the edge of the island. "Why would you do that? Why would you turn them down?"

"Because I'm not interested," he repeats as if he's memorized these lines, as he tries to walk past me.

I stop him though.

I grab his hand and halt him in his tracks.

Looking up at his rigid profile, I ask again, "Conrad, tell me, okay? Why? Why would you turn them down? You love coaching. You *do*. I've seen you. With your players. I've seen how you are with them. How passionate you are about teaching them and making them better players. I saw you at the game that day. You smiled when they won. You never smile, Conrad. That's a big deal. You love this and I know you think you can't have new dreams or a new passion. But you can. You just have to embrace it and —"

He snaps his gaze at me. "Don't."

"But —"

"No," he says all curtly, his voice an echo of how he used to be with me back then, when he first started at St. Mary's, all distant and aloof. "I'm not taking that job because I'm not interested. I'm not interested in swapping one shitty job with another. I'm not interested in leaving this town again and going back to New York like I did fourteen years ago. I'm not *interested* in uprooting my life again, do you understand? This is my life. *This* is my place. And this is my job. End of discussion."

With that he leaves the kitchen and marches over to his bathroom to take a shower.

While I stand there jarred.

I stand there hearing his words over and over again. The determination in them. The absolute refusal to even consider a wonderful opportunity in his life.

And I realize that maybe he'll never get it.

Maybe I'll never be able to convince him.

Maybe there aren't enough weekends in this world, in *our* world, to make him understand.

And there aren't, are there?

Because I won't be here next weekend.

# CHAPTER TWENTY-NINE

I stare at myself in the mirror.

I'm wearing a rose pink ball gown type of dress with a slit on one side. It's strapless and fits me like a glove. Especially over the chest area.

Which my mom particularly likes.

"Turn around," she says and I do. She runs her eyes up and down my body and I have to smooth my hands over my thighs to hide their tremble. "Okay, I think this should work. We've finally found a color that doesn't make you look like a corpse." She squints her eyes. "Or maybe the lighting is good. In which case, I'm glad that we had to move the party to our house instead."

It's my dad's birthday party and we usually have it at the country club, where my dad invites the whole town and everyone he knows. Everyone he's ever known, actually. But a pipe burst at the last minute and my mom had to change the venue. She was extremely stressed about it all day yesterday but at least now she looks happy.

Which almost makes this whole dress worth it.

Because honestly, I don't like it.

I don't like how revealing it is.

How in order to wear it, I had to carefully and diligently scrub the exposed spots where I had written his name. I actually don't like the fact that I have to expose my skin at all. Where people can see. Where they can run their eyes over my undecorated skin and I have no control over that.

And it's not as if I haven't worn such dresses before.

I have.

But now I only want to show him. Now I only like *his* eyes on my body, my thorn's.

And I miss him.

I miss him so terribly.

The man who thinks I'm rosy skinned while the rest of the world thinks I'm ghostly.

I already knew that I wasn't going to be able to spend this weekend with him — it's my dad's birthday and also because we'd already spent the previous weekend together — and so during the week, everything felt dismal.

Everything felt out of sync and upside down.

Something that happens every time I know I won't be able to spend three glorious days with him. Or rather two and a half days.

Because it's not as if we can be together at school.

The only time that we do get together is when he runs his morning laps. That's when I get to see him unabashedly, sitting under the tree, wearing his hoodie — remember the hoodie he gave me that one time? Yeah, I've been wearing that a lot, trying to feel his arms around me. And he loves to see me in it because I know he stares at me back.

But the rest of the time we keep our distance.

I already pushed my luck back when I'd go to his office and read him those letters. I'm not going to do that anymore.

And since last weekend we had our sort of first fight — over the reps from New York City FC — and I realized how far away I am from my goal, I hated this week even more.

Not to mention, I found out something yesterday evening that I can't wait to share with him.

So yeah.

I'm not in a party mood, but it's my dad's birthday and I'm going to try to be a good daughter.

To make up for the fact that I'm really not.

In my pink dress and strappy silver heels, I climb down the stairs of my house to go to the backyard where all the guests are gathered. Standing at the French doors that lead to the massively decorated area, I survey the crowded scene, trying to decide which way to go.

I should actually find my mom and see if she needs something done. This whole venue thing has thrown her for a loop, and...

All my thoughts vanish when during my survey I find something.

Someone.

Tall and broad and sporting long-ish hair.

He's also sporting a suit.

Not the one he wore that night. This one's different. This one's probably new. And even though I'm super attached to his old suit because that was the first outfit I saw him in, I like this one too.

But that's not the most noteworthy thing here.

The most noteworthy thing — apart from the fact that he is somehow here — is that he *isn't* standing in a dark corner, away from everyone, staring at something with a heavy stillness.

He is away from people, yes. And he does look frozen.

But he's staring at *me*.

And his eyes are moving. His eyes are flashing and shining as they take me in. And when he's done running them up and down my body, he brings them back to my face and I can't stop myself.

I can't stop myself like I do at school.

I can't stop myself from dashing to him, from running over.

And he can't stop himself either.

Because as soon as I move, he does too.

Although he's more controlled about his steps I think. He's more controlled and graceful about the way he strides across the space, without making people turn their head so as to see what's happening.

Not me though.

I think a few people do stare at me, at my jogging form, but in this moment I don't care.

In this moment I need to get to him and when I do get there, I almost throw my arms around him. I almost jump into *his* arms. But then I hear a burst of laughter in the distance and somehow reality comes crashing back.

The reality of where we are.

The reality of what I was going to do.

He sees it happen on my face and his jaw clenches. His features tighten up, but thrusting his hands down into his pockets, he takes a step away from me.

With heaving breaths, I ask, "What... What are you doing here?"

He stares at me for a few seconds more. Like his first scrutiny wasn't enough. Like it didn't satisfy him when he was doing it from afar. He needs to do it, study me, from up close.

And when he's done, I'm heaving even more.

"I was invited," he replies.

I frown. "What?"

He shrugs. "The entire St. Mary's faculty was."

Right.

Of course.

When I said that my dad invites everyone he knows, I mean he invites *everyone*.

Every. One.

Including the faculty members of St. Mary's. He'd invite the faculty members of my previous school as well. And I've never been happier about it. Never been so on board with including every single person in this town and all the neighboring towns.

So much so that I smile. "I completely forgot about that."

This is fantastic.

This is *epic*.

I missed him so much and now he's here. And no, I won't get to spend too much time with him or talk to him outside of what's appropriate, but I can still see him. I can still bask in the knowledge that he's at this party.

I might even be able to give him my news now instead of waiting till Monday.

And I'm about to say something to that effect when he says, jerking his chin at something over my shoulders, "That your dad?"

"What?"

He's staring at something over my shoulders with a thoughtful expression. "I'd like to meet him."

My eyes go wide at his words.

And I step in his path the moment he moves in what I now know is my dad's direction. "What are you doing?"

Conrad roves his eyes over my face, his gaze going to my hair.

It's an elaborate up-do that took my mom's hair dresser close to an hour to do. I raise my arm to touch it, touch the plaited and braided and bound strands.

That frankly look ridiculous instead of sophisticated.

And painful.

And tight and confining.

At my action, he murmurs, "You should take down that nest in your hair and let it go free."

"What?"

"You know, just so you could feel the wind in your hair. I think you'd like that."

With that – throwing my words back at me – he leaves to go meet my father. And of course I can't let that happen.

Because knowing Conrad, it's not going to be pretty. And my dad is going to make it even uglier.

So as soon as Conrad starts in the direction of my father, I do the same. But instead of walking like Conrad, I'm jogging. Again. I'm drawing people's eyes but this time, I care even less than I did before.

I have to get to my dad before Conrad does.

I'm not sure what I'll do when I get there but I need to be there. So I put all my strength into it and get there probably four seconds before Conrad does, startling my dad.

He was talking to a group of people with a glass of champagne in his hand and as soon as he senses me there, he turns to me abruptly, a disapproving frown on his forehead.

"Dad, hey," I say, trying to control my breathing.

"What —"

I cut him off as I see Conrad in my peripheral vision, coming to stand next to me. "Uh, I'd like you to meet someone." Smiling nervously, I turn to Conrad. "This is my soccer coach, Coach Thorne. And this is my dad, Jack Littleton."

My dad glances over at Conrad with a smile.

A pleased, friendly smile.

That usually tells people that my dad is an approachable guy. Polished and high society, yes. But he's also a people person. A public prosecutor.

Conrad doesn't think so.

He doesn't offer my father a smile in return.

In fact it takes him a couple of seconds — seconds in which I wring and wring my hands in front of me — to accept my father's handshake.

"Coach Thorne," my dad says, pumping Conrad's hand up and down, looking thoughtful.

Conrad throws my dad a short nod. "Mr. Littleton."

Even though his tone was polite, I still swallow in nervousness. Because I can see the chill in his eyes. I can see how cold they appear right now.

My dad is none the wiser though as he says, "Thorne. Conrad Thorne, correct?"

"Yes."

My dad's smile grows. It actually becomes quite genuine. "Of course. Of course. I heard that you joined St. Mary's. Such a pleasure to meet you. How are you enjoying the party?" He lifts his glass. "There's champagne. And cake, of course."

Conrad gives my dad's champagne flute a look. "I think I'll leave the champagne to you. And I don't like cake."

My dad's eyes narrow slightly and I'm beginning to grimace but he lets it go and says, "Suit yourself. Although I do have to tell you that you've been quite the topic of conversation for the last few months. Actually you've always been a topic of conversation among people."

"Is that so?"

"Yes, and why not?" My dad chuckles. "You're the best soccer coach we've seen in years. Everybody wants you on their team. Every school in this town and for four towns around. In fact, every school in this state. And if that's not enough, I hear pros are constantly knocking at your door." My dad takes a sip of his champagne as he goes on, "People were really surprised when you accepted an offer from St. Mary's."

Conrad thrusts his hands down into his pockets. "Yeah, that's me. I like to surprise people."

My dad chuckles again. "Well, I hope you're enjoying your time at St. Mary's." He looks at me then. He actually wraps his arm around my shoulders and gives me a side hug like a proud father would. "I hope my daughter here isn't giving you too much of a hard time. She can be very hopeless at sports if I do say so myself."

Anger flashes through Conrad's features and he opens his mouth to say something — definitely something scathing — but I don't let him. "Yeah, soccer isn't my thing, sorry."

My dad chuckles again, squeezing my shoulders before letting go. "Well, it doesn't need to be. You should probably focus more on your grades than wasting your time kicking around a muddy ball." He glances at Conrad at this. "No offense, of course."

Conrad is seething.

I can see that. His jaw is clenched so tightly and his eyes are shooting fire. And it's not because of my dad's offhand comment about soccer, and I'm proven right in the next second when Conrad finally finds an opening and says, "From what I understand your daughter is into art. She's an artist, isn't she? So yes, she doesn't need to focus on something she isn't interested in."

Irritation flashes through my father's eyes but he manages to tone it down and say, "Yes, it was quite the phase, wasn't it?"

He shoots me a glance and I duck my head, blushing with embarrassment.

"A phase," Conrad politely murmurs.

My dad sighs before explaining, "Yes, unfortunately. Teenagers and their tantrums, right? What can you do?" He chuckles again. "But St. Mary's has been a godsend, hasn't it?"

My heart clenches but I smile nonetheless and nod. "Yes."

I mean, it has.

But not in the way that my dad thinks.

Conrad hums. "I don't know, Mr. Littleton, I think sometimes teenagers can surprise you." I snap my eyes over to him to find that he's looking at me before focusing on my dad. "It's hard to grasp, the concept. In fact, up until recently I wasn't even aware of it myself. But I'd like to say that I've grown. And now I think sometimes teenagers know exactly what they're doing and their tantrums aren't tantrums at all. Whether they are breaking curfew or vandalizing an expensive car."

While my heart is beating, beating, *beating* in my chest, my dad doesn't particularly care for Conrad's comments. And this time his irritation isn't easily gone. It seeps into his eyes a little and also into his voice. "That may be so. But I'd like to think that I know my daughter. That I know what's best for her."

Conrad's eyes narrow slightly as he says, "Yeah, I was afraid of that."

"Afraid of what?"

"That you'd think so. That you know what's best for your daughter."

"I'm sorry but" – my dad sips champagne again – "is that supposed to mean something?"

"Well between the two of us, you're the one who went to a law school," Conrad says, his eyes lethal and cold while his tone is casual. "Harvard, I hear. I'm sure you can figure it out. What that was supposed to mean."

My dad stares at Conrad in confusion or rather in thought before saying, "Are you actually ins —"

But he's cut off by a couple of new arrivals who want to talk to him and so he gets pulled away. And I breathe a sigh of relief. Actually I just breathe.

Because I haven't done that ever since Conrad started talking to my dad.

Looking up at him, I say, "What was that? Are you insane? You just insulted my dad at his *birthday party*." Then, "In a way that I don't think he really got, but still."

And I think that's because no one has actually insulted my dad to his face. Especially not at his own party.

Conrad was staring at my dad, but at my words, he focuses on me. "Public prosecutor, huh?"

"Are you listening to me? What —"

"Well, my deepest sympathies. To the public," he deadpans.

And then I have to press my lips together.

I have to.

Because I can't believe I want to laugh. And this is not a laughing situation. This could've been a disaster. And I tell him that. "I'm not sure what you were trying to do here. I've already told you to back off and —"

"What I'm trying to do," he bites out, cutting me off, "is make you realize that you need to stop."

"Stop what?"

He breathes sharply, looking down at me. "You said I inspired you that night, yeah? That I inspired you to stand up for yourself and for your art." He scoffs. "Then stop fucking punishing yourself for raising your voice. Stop punishing yourself for standing up. Stop fucking coddling your piece of shit parents because they can't handle who you are. Stop trying to forever please them because once in your life you did something for yourself. Stop *apologizing* for being an artist and *be* a goddamn artist."

I want to say something then.

I really do.

Only I don't know what to say. I don't know what I *could* say.

And before I get the chance to form some sort of a reply, I get pulled away like my dad. By my mother, and the night turns even more disastrous after that.

Because not once do I get to talk to Conrad.

Not once do I get to be close to him.

First, I'm busy helping my mom with the arrangements and things. And then when we get a moment to breathe from those, my mom pulls me in for introductions. At which point my dad joins in and then there's no escape after that; the media descends over us, photos and camera clicks and so many people. To make matters worse, when the music starts my mom sends me off to dance with the people she has introduced me to — a couple of college guys.

And it feels wrong.

It has always felt that way.

But before I'd tolerate it to keep the peace, to keep my parents happy, because they've already been so unhappy with me. But today this guy's strange arms and even stranger body make me almost sick. It makes me angry. It suffocates me more than usual.

It makes me look for him in the crowd again.

And there he is, standing at the edge of this little makeshift dancing area, staring at me. Staring at the guy with such ferocity. With a tightness that torments my own heart and I get it.

I finally, *finally* get it.

What he was trying to say. What he was trying to tell me, and he was right.

He was absolutely right.

I've always felt guilty for being who I am, an artist. I've always tried to apologize, to make up for my deficiencies as the daughter of a famous lawyer. And that feeling has only grown after what I did to my dad's car, and so I've been overcompensating for it. I've been trying to please them harder, keep the peace at all costs. I'm even keeping my decision to go to art school from them.

And with the arms of another guy around me and Conrad watching with seething fury, I realize that I'm not going to do it anymore. I'm not going to apologize anymore.

I need to stop.

Like he told me to.

God, I've been such an idiot.

So when he turns away from the dance floor, his demeanor tight and angry, I stop dancing.

I step back from the guy and, saying sorry to him, I leave the dance floor too.

I cut through the crowd, sweeping my eyes all over, trying to look for him. But he's nowhere to be found. So I leave the party area and head toward the house itself, toward the French doors where waiters and guests are coming in and out in the hope that I can catch him on his way out.

I'm in the hallway now, dashing through it, still looking for him, when out of the blue, someone grabs my hand rather tightly, effectively stopping my search and pulling me inside a bathroom. They close the door behind me with a bang and settle me against it and I'm so jarred, so shocked, that I let it all happen.

But then I wake up and I'm about to scream when a hand is pressed on my mouth and I realize — finally, *finally* — who it is.

I realize that it's the man I've been looking for myself.

## CHAPTER THIRTY

My already wide eyes go even wider at the welcome sight of him and my body goes loose.

As soon as it does, he takes his hand off and I breathe out, "Oh God, I was... You scared me."

He studies my flushed face with a tight jaw that only grows tighter the longer he stares at me. "I know."

I swallow, looking into his harsh and belligerent eyes. "I was looking for you."

"Why?"

I know he's angry. I know that.

I know seeing me with those guys made him furious. I know how possessive he is. How territorial. Last time some guys simply *talked* to me and he got agitated. He's definitely not going to handle well someone *touching* me, and that just makes me want to slap myself.

Because what was I thinking?

How did I think that it was okay to be my parents' puppet? That it was okay to do their bidding, not sketching when I'm home, going on unwanted campus tours, meeting people I don't want to meet, posing for cameras, dancing with guys I don't want to dance with.

Why did I think it would bring peace?

It *never* brings peace. No matter what I do, my parents are never pleased with me. They are never happy.

And look what I did in my foolish pursuit of that.

I suffered myself, yes.

But I made him suffer too. I hurt him.

The only person, other than my friends, who believes in me. Who supports me.

Who inspired me not once but twice now.

And I need to tell him that. I need to tell him that I'm going to stop.

So I grab onto his white dress shirt, my chest still heaving. "I'm sorry. Those guys... I didn't know who they were. My mom introduced me to them and —"

His nostrils flare and he slaps a hand on the door up above my head. "Your mom."

Even though he's all threatening and angry right now, leaning over me, covering me with his dark shadow, I feel safe for the first time since I left St. Mary's yesterday.

I feel whole.

I feel soft and feminine and pretty.

Twisting my hands in his shirt, I say, "Yes but I want you to know that —"

He leans even closer, his wildly breathing chest pushing into mine, as he cuts me off and says, "What about this dress? Your mom made you wear this dress too."

I hate, absolutely hate to admit it, but I answer him. "Yes. But when I wore it I was different and —"

Again he doesn't let me talk as he fires me with a sharp, biting question. "Why?"

"Conrad, please, listen —"

"Answer me," he bites out, his chest pushing into me more, rubbing my nipples with his harsh breaths.

I don't want to.

Because I know it will only stoke his anger. It will only agitate him more.

But I know he won't let this go.

So biting my lip, I tell him, "Because she thinks... she thinks my breasts look big and..."

"And what?"

"And guys like that."

My heart squeezes in my chest.

My belly squeezes too. Something deep inside of me just twists and writhes at the effect my answer has on him. At the utter fury and anguish I see in his eyes. And I try again.

I try to tell him, "But I'm not going to —"

"Why?"

"Conrad —"

"No," he thunders. "Fuck no. Not one word. I don't want to hear anything other than the answer to my question, you got that? I've just seen you with another guy. I've just motherfucking *witnessed* a teenage horndog touching what's mine. I told you guys are horndogs, yeah? So if you say anything other than what I've asked you, I'm going to lose it. I'm barely, *barely*, hanging on by a thread. Just answer why. Why does your mom want to dress you up in what guys like?"

And I can't refuse him.

I can't.

Because I realize that this is my turn to apologize now. It's my turn to make it up to him for putting him through the bullshit.

So I'll tell him later. I'll tell him that he was right and today is the day that I stop punishing myself.

For now, I'll soothe his anger. I'll give him what he wants.

I'll apologize.

"Because if I wear what they like, they might end up liking *me*. And if we get... together, my dad... it might help his campaign. With donations and networking and stuff. That's who Robbie was. Our parents wanted to set us up. Because his dad was an important potential donor. But when I... vandalized my dad's car, they backed off and..." I can't help but add, "You set me free from him too."

He breathes through his nose when I finish.

His chest is scraping and scraping against my nipples, starting up an ache down below.

In my pelvis. In between my thighs.

And I so want to stop talking about this. I so want to put my mouth on him. Kiss him, soothe him.

But I know he won't let me.

My apology needs to be on his terms.

"So she wants to pimp you out," he says, his voice thick, his fingers digging into the wood. "To the highest bidder. To the man who will pay your dad the most money to own you. Own your milkmaid tits and your stripper ass."

I shudder at his dirty words.

I shudder and spasm.

I also arch my spine up because the ache in my body, in my throbbing nipples, in my pussy, is at its highest. I'm all swollen and engorged and everything hurts at his filthy words, at his dark and dangerous presence.

"Conrad."

I use his name as a plea. A plea to stop this, to stop torturing himself and his furious eyes shift.

They move away from my face and go to my craned neck, my crazily fluttering pulse. Before moving down to my outthrust chest, my hard nipples, the outlines of which are clearly visible through my dress.

He mashes his teeth at the sight of them.

"She isn't wrong though, is she? Your *mom*," he says, his voice rough. "Guys do like big tits. And like your magic pussy, your tits are magic too. Your tits are what men jerk off to. What they fantasize about fucking when they're fucking their fist."

I let go of his shirt and grab his face at this. Cradle it, making him look up. "Conrad, I –"

His eyes are all dark and shiny. "Tell me something."

"What?"

"What if that man was me?"

"That man?"

He glances down at my tits for a second before focusing back on my face. "Yeah. What if I liked your tits? What if I liked them enough to pay for them? Your mom would let me?"

"Oh God, please, I'm sorry. I'm —"

"What if I pulled you inside a bathroom, pushed down your dress and stuck my dick between them? How much is that going to cost? What's the price of fucking your tits, Bronwyn?"

I bite my lip at the vicious current that rolls through me.

But he isn't done yet.

He isn't done jolting me with currents of lust as he continues, "What about your dad, huh? Your famous celebrity of a dad. Is he going to let me tit-fuck his daughter? While he's out there drinking champagne, celebrating his useless fucking life." He licks his lips, his eyes sweeping over my face. "If I had enough money, Bronwyn, would he let me buy you from him? Would he let me keep you?"

Keep me.

He's never said that before.

He's never even wanted that before.

And something about his question, the way he says *keep you*, in his guttural voice, makes my eyes sting. It makes me press my fingers on his sharp, thorn-y cheeks as I whisper, "No." He growls and I continue, "Because I'm already yours."

He goes still for a second at my frank reply. At my *honest* reply.

Of course I'm his.

He doesn't need to do anything to keep me.

That's not even the problem, is it?

The problem is that he doesn't want to. That's what he said in the beginning. That's why it all started, because he *doesn't* want to keep me. And that's why over the past weeks, I've never forgotten.

I've never forgotten who he loves.

Who he wants.

All my thoughts scatter when he comes for my mouth. When he captures it, traps it, sucks on it. When he assaults my mouth with his own and violates it with his tongue. When he makes love to it with his teeth.

And I'm not letting him go either.

I can't.

Finally I get to soothe him. Finally I get to take his frustration away and I can't wait.

I don't even care where we are.

I don't even care that we should be more cautious, more careful of our surroundings.

Because I have to apologize to him.

I have to give him my tits so he can fuck them. Because like me they are his.

So that's what I do.

I push him away and drop down at his feet. The place that I've come to love in the past weeks, to be on my knees for him, looking up. Looking at how my eagerness affects him, how he shudders and his features go dark and crimson. How his eyes become so horny and pretty with his hair hanging in them.

I scramble to unzip my dress and pull it down, baring my trembling rosy tits.

Staring up at his madly breathing, towering body, I palm my heavy mounds and offer them to him. "Look, they're yours too. I wrote your name on them, see? Because I had to erase it from other parts of my body. Will you fuck them? My tits."

Like always, a shudder goes through him.

A massive shudder, a spasm as he studies my kneeling, submissive form.

But today it's worse.

His shudders don't stop. His chest doesn't stop shifting and expanding with his breaths. He even has to reach up and wipe his parted lips with the back of his hand as a vein on his temple emerges, throbbing.

And then there's his dick.

That's throbbing too, making a big tent in his pants.

And I want it so bad. I want his beast of a dick between my heavy, achy tits so bad that I squeeze them. I knead the flesh, bring my heavy mounds together before pulling them apart as I whisper, begging, "Please Conrad. I hated dancing with him. I hated wearing this dress and baring my body to others. I *hated* it. Please, I'm sorry. Please fuck my tits."

At my final please, something splinters inside of him.

Something ripples through his entire frame and he reaches his arm out. He bends down slightly and buries his fingers in my hair, in my complex and painful updo.

Staring down at me, he growls, "I'm going to find a way to set you free, you got that? You're not doing this again. Not again. I won't let you."

And with that, he does set me free. He twists open my complicated updo that was held together by a pin and lets my hair fall down my back. He lets my heavy tresses breathe. He lets *me* breathe.

And then I'm on him.

I'm unzipping his pants faster than I undid my dress. I get his dick out even faster, more gracelessly than I scooped out my tits. And when he spits on his palm before rubbing the wetness on his dick, I knock his hand away.

Because it's my job.

It's my job to lube up his dick. To prepare it before he fucks my tits.

It's my cock. It belongs to me.

So I take over. *I* spit on his dick. I run my open mouth up and down his veiny rod. I lick it and suck it and make it all wet before I gather my breasts in my wet, sticky hands and make a valley for him.

A tight valley that makes him groan when he finally sticks his cock in it.

It makes his thighs and his slightly bent knees tremble. It makes him grab my breasts in his large hands and push them together, make the fit even tighter as he goes up and down.

As he pumps his dick, his large hands dimpling my flesh, his hips moving in the way that I love.

That makes me almost come just at the sight of it.

I hang my tongue out so at his every upward thrust, I can get a taste of his cock. I get to lick the pre-cum off his ruddy, swollen rod.

But after a few licks and a few moans that I can't keep inside, he lets go of my tits. He takes his cock away and sits me on the counter. That I didn't even notice was right there. Right by my side. So close, so easily accessible for him to sit me down and fuck me.

That's what he's going to do, isn't it?

He's going to fuck me.

So I spread my legs before he even has chance to push them apart. I haul my stupid dress up, exposing my thighs, my wet panties and also his name. Written on another part of my body.

He sees it and growls.

He digs his thumb into my flesh, right at the center of his name where I've made a rose, staring down at it.

And I tip his face up and whisper, "I'm sorry for putting you through my bullshit."

He takes in a sharp breath before claiming my mouth in a fierce kiss.

Before he's shoving my panties aside, exposing my hole and sticking his dick in.

That as always fits me so nicely and tightly and I barely ever feel the pain.

But he's always careful in the beginning.

No matter how many times we've done this.

He's always careful to pace his thrusts, to restrain his pumps until I'm all open. Until my walls are all soggy and soppy and soft like a flower. Only then does he pick up the speed. Only then does he give it to me and I feel him in my stomach.

And when his pumps have reached their maximum speed and force, he comes for my mouth.

He captures it in his and gives me his thorn kisses.

Tonight he does the same and the moment I feel him deep inside of me, I come.

I arch up in his arms, moaning and trembling, my channel spasming around his rod, making him come as well.

Making him all rigid as his dick throbs inside of me, lashing his hot cum, filling me up.

I'm not sure how much time has passed but when I feel his arms tightening around me, his thumb on the side of my parted mouth, I blink my eyes open to find him looking down at me with tenderness.

"Pinky Winky Promises," he whispers, his thumb tracing the curve of my bottom lip.

"I wore it for you," I whisper back, my fingers waking up and sifting through the thick strands of his hair. "I thought I wouldn't get to see you tonight so I wanted to feel that you were close. I also wore your belly chain."

He swallows. "Bronwyn, I —"

"You were right," I blurt out, stopping him. "When you said that I need to stop. I do. I do need to stop. All this time I kept thinking that if I did what they wanted me to do, if I made up for not being an ideal daughter, they'd be happy. That maybe they'd even come to... love me. So I took it all. I thought it was my due. To obey them, to do the things they want me to because I'm not all the things that they wanted in a daughter. But I can't do it anymore. And so I'm going to tell them."

I smile when I say this and he notices it with a frown, slightly angry on my behalf and also curious. "Tell them what?"

My smile widens and I squeeze my arms around his neck. "I got in."

"You..."

I nod enthusiastically. "I got into art school. NYU. I heard back from them yesterday and I wanted to tell you. But I was already back home and I've been dying. I've been absolutely dying to tell you, Conrad. And I thought that I'd have to wait till Monday, which totally sucked, but I can —"

He stops me with a kiss.

A hard, somehow both affectionate and passionate kiss.

Before he pulls back and God, he gives me the most breathtaking smile that I've ever seen from him. His lips all stretched up, his teeth showing.

And then he chuckles as his thumb rubs my cheek in the most precious way. "You got in."

I grab his wrist. "I did. I've also got a scholarship. And I wanted to tell you first."

He swallows at that, his eyes going liquid, staring at me like they sometimes do.

When I feel like the prettiest, most wonderful girl in the world.

"Are you proud?" I ask, even though I don't need to.

I can see it all over his face.

He chuckles again, his eyes turning even softer. "Yeah. Fuck yeah, I'm proud." He even comes in for another kiss. "My pretty little wallflower."

I bite my lip at his tender, *tender* tone. "And I didn't really have a plan about when to tell my parents. I know I kept saying that when I get an acceptance letter, I'll tell them then. But now it's here and I was panicking yesterday." I shake my head. "But I'm going to do it. I'm going to tell them that it's not a phase. And that I'm going to art school and they can't stop me."

A fierce expression colors his features then. A protective, possessive expression as he says, his fingers flexing on my face, "No they fucking can't."

I stare into his blue eyes. "And you made me see that. You just keep inspiring me, don't you?"

Another smile, this one smaller but no less beautiful. "No, it was never me. It was always you. There's just something about you. About the way you are. About how you see things and feel things. I..." Then, his eyes flickering over my features, "You could be..."

"I could be what?"

His jaw clenches with something. Something profound I think. Something extremely moving as he rasps, "I think... I think you could be someone's dream girl."

I go still then. He goes still too.

Still and frozen and... stunned.

Like he can't believe he said that.

The same thing that I said to him, back when I thought he was having an affair with Helen. And I said it because he was mine. He was my dream man.

He is.

A man so good and protective and so fucking loyal. A man who makes my heart race and my knees tremble. Who sees me and accepts me and supports me.

A man who *loves* me.

So does that mean...

Does he mean that I could be his dream girl?

Is that why... Is that why he said he wanted to keep me? Just now, just a little bit ago when he was angry.

When he begins to move away from me, I tighten my hold and blurt out, "Conrad, I —"

A knock at the door eats up my words.

It stops my breaths.

And then comes a voice that both jars me and makes me hold on to him harder.

"Con, you in there?"

Helen.

It's Helen.

Still on Conrad, my eyes turn wide and fearful. His eyes though are far from that. They're angry and hard, his jaw clenched. And it clenches more when Helen knocks again. "Hello? Con?" She mutters to herself then, "Damn it. Why's this door locked?" Before raising her voice again to repeat, "Hello? Is anyone in there?"

I don't even know what to do. I don't even know what to think.

I've lost all ability to function.

But he doesn't have that problem.

In a split second, he pulls my dress up, covering my breasts, then pushes the hem down, covering my thighs and my core. He even zips up his pants. Then, "Yeah, just a sec."

His loud, calm voice jars me again. It makes me even more afraid. It makes me feel like I'm going to be sick. And he can see that. He can see my apprehension, my utter panic, because he comes in for a soft kiss and whispers, "Trust me."

So I do.

I trust him as he brings me down from the counter and puts me against the wall by the door so when he opens it, I'll be hidden behind it. He straightens the rest of his clothes, runs his fingers through his hair to tame it and opens the door.

"Oh thank God," I hear Helen's voice say. "I thought I was losing my mind. Someone told me that they saw you go in there. Uh, what..." A pause. "Were you doing in there?"

The question of the hour.

The question that almost makes me hyperventilate. But something happens that instantly calms me down. That instantly spreads a rush of warmth all over my chest.

His hand.

He gives it to me.

Standing at the door, his right shoulder half-hidden behind it, he reaches his arm out and grabs my hand. He threads our fingers together, giving me something to hold on to, giving me a tether, reassuring me as he talks to the woman he loves.

And my eyes well up as it hits me again. What I put him through tonight.

Especially when he always does the opposite.

He makes *sure* to do the opposite.

Ever since I saw them together that day, when he came to St. Mary's to tell me that he wouldn't be there that week, he's been very careful about avoiding Helen. He's been very careful about not getting sucked into a conversation with her, or even if there is a conversation, it's when they are surrounded by people.

He's been very careful to stay away from her at every opportunity, going so far as to avoid her in hallways and around campus.

I've noticed it.

And even though I've never said anything about it to him, I know he does it for me.

I know he does it so as not to hurt me. He does it out of respect for me.

For his wallflower.

He's doing the same now. He's not going to fuck me and leave me. I know him. That's why he's given me his hand to hold on to.

And grateful, *so grateful*, I do.

"What do you want?" he asks in a flat tone.

A tone that I feel makes Helen hesitate. "I... I just, I was looking for you."

"And you've found me."

Another pause before she asks, "Are you... are you okay? You look a little..." I tighten my hold on his hand as I wait for her to finish. "If I didn't know any better, I'd think..."

When she trails off, Conrad squeezes my hand in response while saying to Helen, "You'd think what?"

I hear her self-conscious laugh. "Nothing. Just... I'd think you had someone in there."

I'm pretty sure my nails are going to break his skin any second with the way I'm gripping his hand. Not that there's any sign of distress on him, at my furious hold. In fact he only grips me harder.

"Well, you do know me better," Conrad says. "So what is it that you want?"

He uses his authoritative, cold voice that discourages all sorts of questions and it does the same with Helen. Because instead of prodding more, she asks, "Can I... Can I talk to you for a second?"

"Not really, no. Now's not a good time."

"But I —"

"We'll talk at school."

"Please, Con. I really need to..." She sighs again. "It's important, okay? It's about us."

His fingers flex. "Us."

"Yes. Please. I really... It's important that I talk to you right now."

Conrad doesn't say anything.

He lets the moment pass in silence and I think — *I have a feeling* — that he won't. Say anything, I mean.

I stare down at his hand, so solid and strong, slightly darker in shade than mine, and I realize that he won't leave with her.

Because I'm here. Because he won't do that to me. Not right now.

But Helen insists again and her voice is so... *pleading*. "Please, I have to tell you something."

My heart starts to thud in my chest.

Thuds, thuds, *thuds*.

And I let go of his hand.

I open my fingers and set him free.

Like he said he'd set me free from my parents. He doesn't have to – I can do it myself – but still.

Only he doesn't go anywhere.

Not for another three seconds.

In fact he tightens his hold. I can see his knuckles jutting out, almost bursting through the skin, so white and leached of all color. Like he doesn't want to let me go.

He doesn't want to give me up.

His pretty little wallflower.

And Jesus, I don't want to give him up either. I don't want him to leave me or go anywhere. I only set him free because I thought that's what he wanted. So I go to grab his hand again. I go to curl my fingers around his big, solid hand, but before I can do that, he lets go.

He takes his hand away and he sighs. "Fine."

And then he steps out of the room, closing the door behind him and taking her away, clearing the coast for me.

# CHAPTER THIRTY-ONE

I'm panicking.

I'm really fucking panicking right now.

But I tell myself to calm down.

I tell myself that nothing has happened. No tragedy has struck. No sky has fallen.

Yes, we almost got caught at my dad's birthday party. We almost ruined everything. Everything we've done to keep our secret safe, to keep each other safe. And I can honestly say that I don't care about myself. I don't care about the gossip or the judgement that I'm sure people will throw at me, but I do care about him.

I've only ever cared about him.

But.

The key word is almost.

We *almost* got caught. We *almost* ruined everything.

Conrad saved us at the last second. He averted the crisis.

So as I said, no major damage has been done. My thorn wouldn't let anything happen to me.

The only dramatic thing that happened over the weekend was that I told my parents.

I finally, finally took a stand.

And it had nothing to do with making graffiti or pulling a teenage stunt where I wouldn't have to face them and talk about it.

No, this time I talked about it.

I told them about art school and my scholarship and that I'm not going to the college of their choice. I told them this is what I want to do with my life and yes, it's different than what they want but I hope that they can support me. That I hope they can love me nonetheless.

As expected, they were angry. Very angry.

There were threats, loud voices, banging doors.

My mother couldn't even look at me the entire time I was home. My dad kept threatening that he would pull my scholarship, that he knows the dean of NYU and he can have the offer rescinded.

But I told him that it wouldn't matter if he did. Because there were other schools that I had applied to and I could get into one of them. And even if I didn't then that would be fine too. Because I'm an artist. I will always be one. A degree won't make or break me.

When that didn't work, I told them that I was eighteen.

An adult. I'm allowed to do whatever I want and legally they can't stop me.

Which finally penetrated my dad's brain.

I'm not happy about it. I've never wanted to fight with them, argue with them, especially after the graffiti thing. I've always wanted peace, but I can't do it anymore. I can't let them control me like they do.

Although I *will* say that making graffiti on my dad's car was way easier than actually confronting him like this. But I did it and I've never felt prouder of myself.

And I can't wait to tell him, the man who inspired me to do this.

Who says that it wasn't him at all. It was always me.

*You could be someone's dream girl…*

He said that to me.

Before his own dream girl knocked on the door. Before he left with her and I let him go.

So maybe that's why I'm panicking.

Because she wanted to tell him something.

Something about *them*. Something that sounded important.

And my mind, my heart hasn't stopped racing since that moment. Since the moment he left with her, effectively taking the threat away from me. Because when I came out of the bathroom after a little while and rejoined the party, I couldn't find them anywhere.

It's Monday morning now and I need to find him.

I need to ask him.

But I'm late getting back to St. Mary's, so I don't get the chance to catch him during his run or dash up to his office — which these days, I wouldn't normally do but it's desperate circumstances — and find him before the first bell. Which isn't ideal but it is what it is. I'll see him during lunch, and no, we won't be able to talk to each other but that's okay. Just seeing him will give me a measure of peace and I can figure out how to talk to him later.

Only he figures it out first.

He comes to our table at lunch, talks to Callie, brings her lunch and things. He hangs out a little while Poe and Salem join in the conversation and I as usual try to look unaffected.

But it becomes difficult when he glances at me with his denim blue eyes, cool and calm, and says, "Can I talk to you for a second?"

My eyes go wide and I almost drop my fork on the table. "Me?"

Nothing passes over his features at my clumsy actions. No sign that we know each other. Or that only a day ago, we almost got caught and that he said all those things.

He simply nods. "Yes."

Callie is the one to break the silence. Because even Poe and Salem are stunned like me. They both know that Conrad and I, we don't usually interact at school much. So this is a surprise — a shock — for them as well as me.

"Why?" Callie asks suspiciously.

He looks at his sister. "It's nothing you need to worry about."

Callie grabs my hand. "Of course I need to worry about it. She's my friend. Why do you need to talk to her?"

I go to tell her that it's okay, but Conrad clenches his jaw and clips, "And she's one of the players I coach. So if I want to talk to her, I will talk to her."

At this, Callie wraps her arm around my shoulders as if to protect me, ever the loyal friend. "No. I told you that you can't be mean to her about soccer. She doesn't like it, Con, okay? No one likes soccer." She glances at Salem then. "No offense." Before turning to Con, "Just leave her alone. She doesn't need a lecture from you about her skills."

Conrad opens his mouth to argue, I'm sure, but I put an end to this. "It's okay. I'll go." Callie turns to me, ready to protest, but standing up, I tell her, "It's fine. He's your brother but he's..." *The love of my life.* "My soccer coach and I can take criticism about soccer so it's totally okay." When Callie still keeps frowning, I bend down and give her a side hug, kissing her cheek. "I promise."

She sighs. "Fine." Then she turns to her brother. "Be nice to her."

She's going to be such a mama bear, I swear.

Taking in a deep breath, I straighten up and look at him. He still has that aloof expression on his face as he orders, "Follow me."

I would laugh if I could.

At his hardass, coach-ly command, but as it is, I'm a mass of anxiety and trembling muscles so all I do is obey and follow him.

We go through the cafeteria, the hallway, passing through the crowd that's oblivious to who we are and what we are to each other, and go up the stairs. I keep following him up until we reach the third floor, walk through the same, albeit less crowded hallway, until we reach his office.

There he unlocks the door, holds it open for me like a gentleman would, and waits for me to enter.

Which I do.

On trembling, shaking legs.

Then he closes the door and as soon as he does, I spin around, "Is everything —"

He faces me too, only he's not as abrupt as I was and his voice is as calm as it was in the cafeteria. "Yes. Everything is fine."

I wring my hands. "So no one knows? Like no one..."

His jaw moves. "No. No one knows anything." Then, in a tone that's super familiar and dear to my heart, he continues, "I don't want you to worry about these things. I'm not going to let anything happen to you."

My heart squeezes at his declaration that is as familiar as his ferocious tone. "I'm not worried about myself."

He clenches his jaw again before exhaling a sharp breath and saying, "Take a seat."

Ignoring him, I blurt out, "What did she want? Helen."

My question makes him stare at me for a beat or two before he says, "It's not important. Just take a seat."

I still don't listen. "But it sounded important. She wanted to talk about… you. Together. So what did she say? What happened? I couldn't find you at the party after I came out and —"

"It's not important," he repeats in a louder tone. "Now I want you to take a seat because we need to talk."

At this my already racing heart explodes.

I open my mouth to protest, to say something, *anything*, that might prevent this.

Whatever it is that's going to happen.

Because I know that it's bad.

I just know it.

But nothing comes out as he moves from his spot after issuing the command for the second time and strides over to his desk. He pulls his chair out and glances over at my still-standing form, making me realize that he's waiting for me to sit, which I do a second later.

Only then he takes a seat himself.

Because that's what he does.

He always waits for me to take my seat first before he does.

I know this because he does it at his house when we're about to eat at the dining table or at the island. Which makes me realize something strange.

Something crazy and completely irrelevant in this moment.

That in all the times that I've come into his office, I've never sat in a chair. I always either stood by one or stood by the wall. The wall where he made me read my letters to him.

The letters that I now know he keeps tucked away at the bottom of his dresser at home.

I remember smiling when I found them one day while looking for one of his t-shirts to wear. Along with that sketch that I'd made of him. That he'd insisted on keeping.

Oh and my pink panties, the ones I wore the first night we had sex.

When I asked him about it he told me – very grumpily and cryptically – that he was keeping them safe from pervs.

It's weird, this abrupt realization, and it makes me more panicked for some reason.

"Did you talk to your parents?" he asks, his shoulders rigid, fingers threaded together on his desk. "About art school."

I swallow, my own hands in my lap, fingers laced together. "Yes."

"And?"

"They're not happy about it. Which is expected. My dad threatened to have the offer rescinded. But I told him that I'd apply to a different school. That I'd keep applying everywhere until I got in and even if I didn't, it wouldn't matter because I'd still be an artist. Besides, they can't legally stop me. I'm eighteen, so."

I study the play of emotions on his face at this.

First comes anger and irritation at my parents' behavior, which is swiftly replaced by satisfaction and pride as he says, "Good girl."

Again it's so familiar, his tone and his expressions, so warm in this world that has suddenly turned cold, that I go to the edge of my seat and say, "Conrad, please. Tell me what —"

"I think we should stop."

"What?"

All the familiar expressions, all the familiar warmth is gone from his face. He's back to being aloof. He's back to being all professional and distant like he used to be as he says, "I think it's time we stopped."

"Stopped what?"

His denim blue eyes move across my face and I don't even care that I must look like an anxious mess right now. "It's over, Bronwyn."

It's only three words.

And one of them is my name.

So it should be easy to understand. It should be easy to grasp what he's saying to me.

But it's not.

So I go, "I beg your p-pardon."

I'm not sure why I've said it in that way.

I never say it. I never say 'I beg your pardon.'

But maybe it's his... harshness. His coldness that has prompted me to be more polite than I usually am. Just like his thorn sharpness that makes me go flower soft.

His nostrils flare then. As if he gets it.

As if he understands this strange, intimate dynamic between us.

A dynamic that no one else will ever get.

It's ours.

Then, "It never should've started in the first place. You already had a crush on me and I never should've done what I did. I should've known better. I should've fought *harder*. I should've —"

My hands fly over to his desk and grab onto the sharp edge of it. "But we're past that now. I broke all your barriers. I got through to you and I'm not sure why we're talking about this now. I don't…"

His chest moves under his white t-shirt with a sharp sigh. "We're talking about this now because it's over. Because we need to stop, and I —"

"Is it because of what happened?" I blurt out then, my voice high and, I'm afraid, nasal. "Is it because we almost got caught? But it was just one time. And that was only because we broke our own rule. We've been so good. We've been so careful all this time. You can't let one thing that happened ruin everything else."

His hands are still on the desk, all laced together, calm and composed. "It's not because of what happened. Because nothing happened. Because I'll be damned if I'd ever let anything happen to you."

"So then why are —"

"It's because it's time," he states firmly.

"It's time."

A short nod. "Yes. As I said, it never should've started. But it did and it has gone on long enough. So I've decided to end it here before it's too late."

I dig my nails into the wood. "You've *decided*."

"Yes."

"And who gave you the right to decide anything?" I ask with clenched teeth. "Why was *I* not involved in the decision? It clearly affects us both."

Silently, he stares at me with penetrating eyes.

And I swear to God if he says something condescending to me right now or refers to my age after *everything* that's happened between us and *everything* that we've been through, I'm going to do something really drastic.

I'm going to do something that will alert the whole school, the whole town, the world that there's something between us.

That we aren't who we say we are to each other.

He isn't just my soccer coach or my best friend's big brother. And I'm not just his student and his little sister's best friend.

He's *mine*.

He's my thorn and I'm his wallflower.

"I've made this decision on my own," he begins, again as calm as anyone can be, "because you're not thinking clearly right now. Because you're too emotional. Even now you're ready to cry. You're ready to cry over something that's not real. That has never been real. You're too attached. To me. To this whole idea of us… being together. When there's no us. There never was and it was my fault that I still encouraged this kind of behavior —"

"You didn't," I speak over him even though I know that I shouldn't.

That I should try to look as calm and composed, as unemotional as *he* does right now, especially when he's just pointed out that I'm ready to cry.

But how does one hold it together when their world has started to fall apart, brick by brick, wall by wall?

Even so, I take a deep breath and bring my hands down to my lap again, where I twist them, scratch at my own skin as I very calmly state, "I know that there's no us. I've always known that. I know this is not about romance or love or any of those things. I'm not that naive. I knew what I was getting into when it all started. I knew that you loved someone else. That you *love* someone else and you just want me for now."

"Exactly," he says as soon as I finish, as if he was waiting to say it, waiting with a counter argument of his own. "So how does it not bother you? How does it not bother you that I'm using you? That I've used you for my own purposes. To curb my own pain, my own loneliness. How does it not bother you that I've been selfish with you?" He pauses to drag in a sharp breath. "You need to aim higher than that. You need to aim higher than *me*. A weak, selfish man. You need to ask more for yourself, Bronwyn. You need to ask for the world from the person you're with because you goddamn deserve it."

"But I —"

"Or do you always want to get fucked in a bathroom while your parents are partying outside, oblivious to what's happening to their daughter?"

I had all the arguments prepared in my head.

I was waiting, *waiting* for a chance to spill them, to lay them out in front of him so he can forget about this whole 'it's over' thing and we can get back to normal.

*Our* normal.

But I don't remember any of them right now.

I don't remember what I was going to say after what *he* just said.

"What?" I breathe out, my hands loosening up, my fingers letting go of each other in my lap.

He shakes his head as if disgusted with himself before saying, "Look, the school year's almost over anyway. You're going to New York now. You're going to start a new life. A life away from this fucking school and your fucking parents. A life that's yours and *yours* only. You'll make it as beautiful and colorful as you make everything else. So as I said, it's time. We had to end it sometime and that time is now. There's no future here. There never was."

"What about her?"

"What?"

I lick my dried-out lips as I stare at him through a fog, from a distance almost, stuck at what he said only a short while ago. "Would you have fucked her in a bathroom in the middle of a party like you fucked me?"

His entire body tightens like a trap.

His clasped hands on his desk vibrate with how forcefully he's holding them together.

"What?" he bites out again, this time with much more fury.

I shake my head, almost talking to myself. "Of course not. Of course you wouldn't have. Because you love her. You have feelings for her. But I'm... I'm just a girl you're fucking. I'm just a girl you're using for your own selfish purposes. And I knew that and I was okay with that. I wanted it, didn't I? I begged for it. I practically *pleaded* you to use me. So what does that make me? If I wanted to get fucked in a bathroom while my parents were outside. If I wanted to get on my knees in front of you knowing that the whole world was just outside the door, *knowing* that you don't love me and that you'll never love me. It makes me a slut, doesn't it? It makes me a whore. I'm a whore and —"

I stop talking when my chair is abruptly turned around and there's a man, an angry, wildly breathing man, hanging over me, his dark blue eyes nailing me in my place, pinning me down.

Clutching the armrests of the chair that I'm sitting in, his features sharper than usual and slashed with anger, he says thickly, very thickly, "If you ever, *ever*" – he shakes the chair – "use that word in the same context as yourself, I'll punish you in a way that will make everything that has happened before, everything that I've put you through, a very happy and a very *distant* memory. If you ever put yourself down like that, if you even *think* about it, Bronwyn, I won't be held responsible for what I do to you. I won't be held responsible for what I'll do to the world." Another shake of the chair. "Nothing that happened between us, *nothing*, no matter how filthy or dirty for the narrow-minded world to understand, is remotely wrong. For us. It was fucking beautiful, you understand? It was beautiful and precious and *right*. It was us. You and me. It was between your thorn and my wallflower and I won't have you color it anything less than what it was."

My hands jump up to him then.

They leap up to grab his t-shirt, fist it tightly so he doesn't go anywhere. "So then why are you doing this? Why are you saying these things?"

Something ripples through his features, some kind of agony that I don't get but even now, I want to soothe it.

Even now as he's hurting me, crushing me under his boots, I want to take away his pain.

"Because it's time," he repeats yet again. "Because it's the right thing to do."

Taking his hands off the armrests, he wraps them around my fists, trying to dislodge my hold on him. But I don't let go. I can't as I say, *plead*, "This is not right. This is…"

Something occurs to me; something that I've been obsessing over ever since Saturday, that I was so focused on when I entered his office but that I completely got distracted from because of what followed and so I ask, "She said something to you, didn't she? She said something. What'd she say?"

He sighs, his grip on my fingers increasing. "Bronwyn, it's not important. It's —"

"No, tell me," I say, keeping my hold on him intact, *fighting* to keep my hold on him intact. "Tell me what she said. What did she mean when she said she wanted to talk about us?"

"Bronwyn."

Then, because I can't stop myself, I ask, "Are you… Are you going to her? Are you going to h-have…"

I can't even say it.

I can't even use that word when it comes to him.

But he understands it nonetheless.

He understands where my mind has gone off to and so he replies, "No."

And I breathe out a sigh of relief.

As much relief as I can feel in this moment when everything is still falling apart.

But I guess I did it too soon. I breathed too soon because he's not finished.

In the same calm voice with which he told me that we were over, he now says, "Because she's leaving her husband."

"She's..."

All the air, all the breaths that I've taken so far today, whoosh out of my body.

All the fight, all the strength.

And he finally manages to break free.

He finally manages to get away from the crushing hold of his wallflower and straighten up.

Looking down at me, he says, "So it wouldn't be an affair."

# CHAPTER THIRTY-TWO

The Original Thorn

I stare at the chair.

The one she sat in when she was in my office.

Bronwyn Bailey Littleton.

The artist.

My pretty little wallflower.

Well, she's not mine. She never was and now she's gone.

She's been gone from my office for about six hours now. I should leave too. Go back to my empty house, probably go to the gym, pick up dinner, get back to normal life.

Life before her.

The life I've had forever.

Before she barged into it and... changed everything.

But for some reason, I can't move from here.

I can't get myself to stand up from my own chair and leave.

I can't get myself to stop staring at it, her chair, either. And the more I stare at it, the more painful my headache becomes. The more painful and vicious the throbbing on the back of my neck becomes.

And I wonder...

I fucking wonder what she must be doing right now. On the other side of the campus. What she must be... *feeling*?

After what I said to her.

After all the things I said to her. But especially what I said to her at the end.

About Helen.

I didn't want to but she kept insisting and *insisting* and I just... I had no other choice. I had to say it. I had to lie and...

A knock sounds at the door, breaking my thoughts, making me realize that I've been grabbing the back of my neck in a stranglehold. I open my mouth to tell whoever it is at the door to fucking get lost when it opens and the last person I want to see right now stands there.

She not only stands there, she fucking walks in and closes the door behind her. Smiling, she says, "Hey, you're here late."

I watch her walk further into the room, approaching my desk.

Approaching that chair.

I watch her steps growing closer and her arm reaching out, to touch it maybe. To pull it out and sit in that chair herself and I snap, "Don't."

She snatches her hand back before it could make contact. "What?"

When I know, when I've made sure that her hand is back where it belongs, by her side, and she's not going to try to touch it again, I look up. "Have I asked you to sit?"

Her brows draw together. "Excuse me?"

"And neither do I recall asking you to come in."

She studies my face; I probably look how I feel: completely and utterly angry.

At myself.

"What is going on with you?" she asks, frowning lightly. "Is everything okay? What's happening?"

Taking a deep breath to control my temper, I tell her, "I'm going to save you the trouble and tell you — yet again — that it's not happening."

"What?"

Jesus Christ.

I don't have time for this.

I don't have time to deal with her drama, her constant and fake attempts to get my attention. To start things between us. I pinch the bridge of my nose before saying, "Look, I have very little patience left, all right? Very little. And this is really not a good time. So I want you to leave my office and never come back."

Anger makes her purse her lips, shake her head as she says, "Are you serious? Are you really fucking serious, Con? After what happened Saturday night."

Saturday night.

Right.

That night is going to haunt me for the rest of my life.

"What do you think happened on Saturday night?" I clip, trying to dismiss all my thoughts and ready to get this whole thing over with.

It pisses her off more that I'd ask her that.

But it's important.

She needs to understand what the fuck it is we're doing here. Or *not* doing.

Her charade has gone on long enough, but she crossed a line on Saturday and I'm fucking done.

"Okay." She smiles tightly. "Since you've forgotten so easily, let me remind you: on Saturday, I told you that I might be leaving my husband, my *marriage*. Something that no one ever does where I come from. Divorces are frowned upon. It's going to break my parents' hearts, their reputations. But I'm thinking about it because my husband might be cheating on me. My husband might be sleeping with another woman. I cried on your shoulders, Con. I was hurting. I needed a friend. I *need* a friend today and you're acting like a jerk. I need someone to get through this tough time in my life and despite what's happened between us in the past and last year, I thought you were that friend. I thought I could count on you to have my back. If I shared with anyone else from my circle, they'd all say that I was overreacting. That everyone cheats where I come from —"

"Like you were going to, yeah?" I remind her.

She hates that reminder even more. "I can't believe you're throwing that in my face right now."

I chuckle sharply.

Even though this isn't the time to laugh. This isn't the time to show restraint either.

Which is what I've done.

I straighten up in my chair. In fact I stand up. I leave the chair I've been sitting in for hours now, put my hands on the desk and lean toward her. "Let me make something very clear to you: I don't care if your husband is cheating on you. I don't care if he's sleeping with another woman. Because I *know* that it's another one of your ploys."

"What?"

I breathe in sharply and just let go. "I know it's another one of your excuses to get me to care. To get me to sleep with you. Which is what you've been trying to do ever since you came back into town two years ago. First, it was your endless texts and your phone calls and your invitations to meet you somewhere private. When those didn't work, you started to concoct plans, get-togethers with *teachers*, work-related parties and happy hours so you'd get a chance to be close to me. And when those didn't work either, you came up with this whole charade to get my sympathy. This whole drama about your broken marriage. Which if I'm being honest here, I'd say that even if it were true, I wouldn't care. But it's not. Because if it was, if you were really so broken fucking hearted, you wouldn't have tried to maul my mouth when I told you that I was leaving. So, Helen, I know. I am fucking aware, all right?"

When I went with Helen Saturday night, leaving Bronwyn in the bathroom, my only intention was to clear the coast.

Even though it... bothered me.

It bothered me very fucking much to let go of her hand. To leave her like that. Like she's some kind of a dirty little secret.

But I had to.

I had to protect her, take the danger away from *her*. So she could have an opportunity to sneak out and rejoin the party.

So I gave Helen what she wanted: going to a secluded spot where we could talk.

Well, to an extent.

Helen wanted to get out of there, go to a restaurant or a cafe or something. And I told her that the best I could do was out on the deserted street. So we went and we talked and when she started her sob story about Seth cheating on her and needing a friend, I made an excuse about having to leave.

Which shocked her of course, and so when despite her strong objections I turned to leave, she tried to kiss me. I firmly pushed her away because I'd had it with her.

I'd fucking had it.

For months, she's been trying to get my attention.

*Months.*

And while it was okay back when I wasn't... *involved* with someone, now it fucking pisses me off. Especially when she tries to get close to me at St. Mary's. Especially when she tries to stop me in the hallways, draw me into group conversations.

When she tries to touch me.

And when she does it in front of *her*.

It's not... *nice*. It's not...

Her rosy cheeks lose their color, all right? Her silver eyes lose their light. She stops smiling and laughing and I fucking hate that.

That's why I always make sure to stay away from Helen.

Not that I had any desire to be close to her in the first place; she's married for God's sake.

But these past few weeks, I've had an added purpose in doing so.

So this was a long time coming, this confrontation, and I'm glad the moment is here.

Helen clenches her teeth at my frank words, her hands fisted. "I did not try to maul your mouth. I was emotional." She runs her eyes up and down my body. "Something no one can accuse you of, apparently."

I press my hands on the desk even harder at her dig.

Not that she's wrong.

Emotions haven't been my forte for a long, long time now.

"Well, now that we've cleared it all up, you should leave," I tell her, hoping that I'll finally get some peace.

Although I'm not so sure if I will.

I'm not so sure that I'm ever getting peace.

"So why did you come?" she asks, folding her arms across her chest. "If you knew I was trying to get your fucking attention. If you knew I was trying to sleep with you, why did you pick up my calls and accept all my invitations back then?"

Yeah.

Why did I? Why did I accept all her invitations? Why did I meet her at the fucking tree?

I could've very easily shut her down.

I'm not known for gentleness or tact.

So why the fuck did I not?

In the beginning I thought it was desire. That I wanted to see her. Even though she's married and I'm not a man who looks back, I thought it was the undeniable urge to see an old, broken dream.

But it wasn't that, was it? It wasn't that at all.

I stare at her, at her face, her eyes and her lips, things that I once upon a time dreamed about as I say, finally, "Because I was guilty. Because I've always been guilty. For being a shitty boyfriend. For breaking my promises to you. For making you dream with me when I should've known better. When I should've been smarter. And I will always feel guilty for that. Always. And…"

I clench my jaw at this next part for a second, before continuing, "I went to your wedding. Even though when you called me with the invitation, I had no intention of going. I'd closed that chapter of my life and I'd closed it pretty hard. But I still went. And I think I did that because I wanted to punish myself. Because I wanted to watch you, someone that I had no right to want, someone that I had no right to dream about become someone else's."

Yeah, that's it.

Isn't it?

That's why I went to her wedding.

To see another one of my foolish dreams get taken away.

*Really* taken away.

To punish myself. To teach myself a lesson.

So that I never ever make the mistake of dreaming and reaching for things that don't belong to me.

Finally I straighten up and focus on her, noticing tears in her eyes for the first time.

And so I probably shouldn't say what I'm going to but I really don't care.

I really don't care about hurting Helen when I've already hurt… her.

"What we had is gone now, Helen," I tell her so she finally gets it and leaves me the hell alone. "It was gone the moment we broke up. Maybe we wanted each other once. But we don't want each other anymore. You don't want me. You just want the thrill I can bring you, into your boring life. And I don't want you. And for a while there, I thought it was because you were married. That I could never do what my dad did to my mother. But that's not true. That's not true at all.

"I'm not that moral. I'm not that good. I'm fucking selfish. When I want something, there's no power on this earth that can keep me from it. When I want something, I take it. I grab it. Without any thought of consequences or repercussions. So if I wanted you now, Helen, no one could've stopped me. Not your marriage, not your husband. Not the stupid fucking rules or stupid fucking morality."

It's true.

I didn't have the perspective to understand this.

To understand that I kept refusing Helen not because of some moral code but because I didn't want her.

I didn't understand the kind of man I really am.

Until I broke down, broke my own rules, and took *her*.

Even though I knew she wasn't – isn't – meant for me. She's too young. She's my student, my sister's best friend.

Not to mention, she's meant for bigger and better things.

She's meant for art school, isn't she?

I always knew that. I always knew that she'd get in. I always knew that I'd have to give her up one day.

And so it was time.

It was time to set her free.

So she could look to the future. *Her* future and start a new chapter in her life.

So she could cut down all the things that might drag her down.

Things like me.

A man who hasn't had a dream in fourteen years.

# PART 4

# CHAPTER THIRTY-THREE

I haven't sketched in days.

I thought I'd miss it. I have in the past.

Especially when I go back home and I don't get to sketch.

But I honestly don't miss it now.

I don't feel the need to create. I haven't in days.

It's like something has died inside of me.

Some little part, some little fire that made me want to pick up the pen and grab the nearest thing that I could draw on.

I'm not complaining though.

Death is good. Death is peaceful. Death is bliss.

It has given me a lot of free time to study and do my homework, prepare. I've always been very on top of things when it comes to my grades and such. And now I'm *really* on top of things. All my homework and assignments are done before anyone else's.

I've even started preparing for finals, even though everyone is relaxed because they are still a few weeks away. But I think you can never be over-prepared for something like finals.

So as I said, death is great.

It's when I come alive is the problem.

It's when my heart jumps and my breaths start up again. When life begins to rush through my veins.

That's when I feel the agony, the torture.

That's when I feel the pain.

The pain that I always knew was in my future.

That pain is here now and I feel it when he's close.

I feel it when I see him. When I hear him. When I hear his deep, authoritative voice.

Just because I'm no longer a wallflower, *his* wallflower, doesn't mean the world has stopped.

The world is very much moving forward and as I said, we have homework and classes and finals.

Which means school is on.

And which also means he's here.

He's still the soccer coach. He's still my best friend's very caring brother.

So of course I see him.

I see him in the hallways when I'm getting my books out of my locker. I see him when we're out in the courtyard and he's coming in for the day. Sometimes I see him when he's leaving for the day too.

And then there are lunches and soccer practice.

So over the days, I've developed a system.

A robust system where I only have to see him when it's absolutely necessary.

It's really not hard; I tried to do it before. Back when I still thought that I could control this thing inside of me and be a good friend, a good student.

So as per my system, I spend my lunches in the library, always pleading homework or studying for finals. I make sure to carry all my books with me so I don't have to go to my locker. I spend as little time as possible in the courtyard, especially when I know he'll be out there — being in love with someone punctual and who wears the biggest silver watch anyone has ever seen has its perks.

I can't do much about soccer practice but I do keep my head down and clench my muscles tight, *really tight*, so his voice doesn't hurt me as much.

Not that he speaks a lot.

He still lets Coach TJ speak for him and opens his mouth only when absolutely necessary.

So I'm doing... okay.

It could be worse. I could be alive all the time.

I could be crying and sobbing and screaming every second of every day.

As it is I only do it at night after my roommate goes to sleep.

So yeah, death is good.

Except my friends won't stop talking about it.

Or him.

When I told them what had happened — I had to, that very same day even; I was too broken up, too shaken to hide it — they couldn't believe it. They both thought that it was impossible Conrad would do something like that. They both thought that he was in love with me.

"I've seen the way he looks at you," Salem said. "That man is in love with you, Wyn. He loves you."

"Yes," Poe insisted. "Like every time he comes over at lunch, he's always staring at you. He can't take his eyes off you. I mean, it's a fucking wonder how Callie still doesn't know. That her morally good brother *who would never do such a thing* is in love with her best friend."

"Exactly." Salem nodded. "And it's not just lunch. It's all the time. Every time you're in the same space, he watches you, Wyn. He looks at you like he can't believe what he's seeing. Like he's so... *enchanted* or something. And frankly, I fought with Arrow about that when he came to visit last week. I was like, why don't you look at me like Coach Thorne looks at Wyn? Which totally confused him and he ended up buying me two huge buckets of ice cream but" – she shook her head – "the point is that Wyn, Coach Thorne loves you, okay? You have to talk to him. There must be something going on. You have to —"

"No," I said, clutching onto my pillow, wiping my tears off. "He doesn't. He loves her."

"Oh please, that's old news. Maybe he loved her before but he loves you now and —"

"He's going back to her."

Salem drew back. "What?"

"She's leaving Seth."

"What the fuck?"

That was Poe.

I nodded, hiccupping. "He told me."

"He said he was going back to her," Salem confirmed. "He said that to you. In those exact words."

"Y-yes."

He did tell me.

That was the whole point of that conversation, wasn't it?

That's why he ended things.

That's why he said it was time. Because he was going back to her. Because she'd finally decided to leave her husband for him and so he was breaking up with me — not that we ever had a traditional relationship, but still — to go to her.

So the discussion with my friends was ended.

Or so I thought.

Because since then Poe and Salem have established a system of their own. While I avoid him with a ferocity that I've never known before, they both basically stalk him.

And her.

They both keep track of his movements.

Like where he is, what he's doing. Who he's talking to. If he talked to Helen all day; if he was staring at Helen; were there any romantic vibes coming off of them, that one time they stood close together outside of the cafeteria.

Moreover, Poe has eyes and ears everywhere.

She has an elaborate network of gossips and spies and she's constantly monitoring her channels to see if they've picked up some teacher/teacher romance happening at St. Mary's.

"There's no way," Poe says one day, pacing back and forth in my room, while Salem sits on the opposite bed. "There is no fucking way something is going on between them. My sources haven't picked up anything." She keeps referring to them as sources, but we have no idea who they are; she never tells us. "*I* haven't picked up anything. They're hardly ever seen together. And did you notice how he bit Maisie's head off today at practice? Like, that girl just missed a pass. A fucking pass, dude. And he made her cry for that. He made her wish that she'd never been born."

He did make her cry.

Which I felt bad for.

I was playing worse than her and if I was still painting or drawing or creating, I would draw her something pretty. As it is I only gave her a hug after practice before I found myself a quiet corner to cry in. Something I rarely do during the day, but sometimes when I hear his voice, I can't wait until the middle of the night to cry.

Shaking her head, Salem says, "Well, it wasn't just a simple pass. We could've won if she had taken it. But point taken. I don't think anything is going on between them at all."

"Yeah, that man is too angry," Poe adds in, still pacing. "Too uptight and tightly wound. There is no way he's getting laid. There is no way —"

I shut my book then. "Okay, guys, time out, all right? I don't want to hear this."

"But, Wyn, I'm telling you," Poe insists, stopping in front of me. "We're *both* telling you that there's nothing going on between them. If she's left her husband for him, then she's done it for nothing. Because Coach Thorne ain't taking her back."

I open my mouth to reply but Salem speaks over me. "And Wyn, he still watches you, okay? He still fucking watches you. I mean when you're not avoiding him like the plague and are actually in the same space as him. And he asked about you, remember? I told you about that. That first day when you decided to eat lunch at the library. He asked about you. I still think that he lo —"

"Please, stop," I blurt out before she can say the L word; I don't think I'd be able to bear it and all my plans to hold off crying until the middle of the night would shatter. "I keep telling you that I don't want to hear this. And I want you guys to stop. Please. I know you guys are doing it for me but please, just stop. I don't care if something is going on between them or not. I actually want it to."

As soon as I say it, my heart starts beating again.

I'm jarred back to life, to pain.

And I'm not sure how I'm able to form any words right now when every part of my body is writhing, but I do. "He loves her. He's always loved her. And if he can have her, then he should. If she is what he wants, then they should be together."

"But Wyn —" Poe protests.

"No, please," I cut her off. "I just want him to be happy. That's all I've ever wanted. That's it. And if she makes him happy, then so be it."

That's the other thing that's keeping me going.

Apart from my little death.

The thought that he might finally have something that he's always wanted. That he might have her. He already thinks all his dreams are dead. He's already too angry about what life has thrown at him. So if he can have this one dream fulfilled, then how can I not want that for him?

Besides, Helen is finally doing the right thing. Even though we've never talked about these things after that one time and I get no indication from her about her personal life, I'm just glad that she finally knows what she wants to do.

And yes, sometimes I think that I should go talk to him.

Especially when I feel his eyes on me. And I do feel them. I *do*. But I guess it doesn't really matter.

He's made his choice.

And sometimes I also remember that I left so many things unfinished. So many things that I wanted to do for him that I never got a chance to bring to completion: that wall that I was painting in his bedroom; that movie I wanted to watch with him; that new Mexican dish I saw on YouTube that I wanted to make for him the following weekend after my dad's birthday; the fact that I never got to convince him to consider that job in New York.

I never got to convince him that having new dreams is okay.

That dreams can change and evolve and that new joy can still be found among the broken pieces of the old ones.

When I think about those things, I do want to go talk to him.

I do want to tell him that I love him. Or rather, I love him too and that I'll do anything to make him happy.

But that's the thing, isn't it?

This is what I have to do.

*This.*

Let him go to her. Let him be with her.

Because if he's happy with her, then how can I take that away from him?

Salem starts crying then.

Silent tears fall down her cheeks and she rushes over from the bed to come hug me. "Oh, Wyn. I'm so sorry. I'm so so sorry. God, I would never ever wish this pain on anyone, least of all you." Squeezing me tightly, she says, "You don't deserve this. You do not deserve this at all."

While Poe mutters, "Well if *this* is his happy face, then I don't want to even think about what he looks like when he's angry."

Despite everything, I chuckle as I hug Salem tightly.

She's the girl who knows this pain well. She knows how it feels. She went through it for eight years before she and Arrow got together. But she survived it.

So I can survive it too.

Besides, it's only a few more weeks.

Finals are almost upon us, and then we'll all graduate and go to college. I'll go to NYU. I'll start a new life in New York and slowly, things will get easier.

I'll start to feel better.

I won't pray for death so much like I do now.

But a few days later, it becomes *really* inconvenient that the man I love is my best friend's big brother, because my best friend decides to throw a little get-together.

Because we're all graduating soon, from St. Mary's School for Troubled Teenagers no less, the school that no one ever wants to go to. And we all got our acceptance letters — Callie got into Juilliard; I got into NYU; Salem got into this really great summer soccer camp over in California; and well, Poe will soon get to murder her guardian.

So technically everything is great.

And Callie wants to celebrate it at her new place she's been living in for the past few months because of her pregnancy. And if she was any less of my friend, I would've refused.

But I can't.

She's my best friend and she's the person that I've betrayed the most here.

I never got to tell her; another thing I didn't get to do before it was over. And that will always haunt me. The fact that she had the right to know but I still hid things from her.

Maybe I'll still tell her about it one day. When it won't hurt too much to think about.

But for now, I'm going to go back to being a good, loyal friend and support her by accepting her invitation.

It will be fine.

It will be like it is at soccer practice. I will keep my head down, stay busy with other people, and soon it will be over.

Only I don't count on something... bizarre.

Something so totally out of this world.

Her brother hitting on me.

Not the one I'm in love with. But her *other* brother, Ledger.

Ever since I arrived at the small get-together with Salem and Poe, he's been staring at me. I didn't notice it at first because I was busy *not* noticing things.

As I feared, *he* is here as well.

Tall and broad, wearing his usual white shirt and navy blue jeans. And since it's sort of springy weather, he doesn't have a sweater on and his top two buttons are unbuttoned.

I'm afraid to say that I noticed that right away. I also noticed that his hair has grown out since he last had a haircut. It already was when I was still with him, and when I pointed out that he needed a haircut, he proceeded to stare at me in his usual way before telling me that it was out of courtesy for me. Since I liked touching it, playing with it, fisting it during sexy times — only he didn't exactly say 'sexy times,' he used other colorful words.

"Frankly you're obsessed with my hair," he murmured, sitting at the kitchen island.

I threw a piece of bread at him. "What, and you aren't? Newsflash, Conrad: you're obsessed with my hair too. You're *beyond* obsessed with my hair. You touch it in your *sleep*. Yeah, I've noticed. You touch it when we're watching TV. You touch it when we're doing the dishes. You touched it the first time I came here and we were looking at those photos. Don't think you got away with that. I noticed that too. You touch it all the time."

By the time I finished, his whole gorgeous face was colored in amusement and his eyes were flashing as he said, "I do. And I am."

"You're what?"

"Going to touch it now."

And then he did. First when he pulled me in for a wet and hungry kiss and then when I got even hungrier and got down on my knees to suck his cock. He touched my hair then as well. He fisted it actually and used it to pull me on and off his thick, tasty dick and...

That was when I stopped noticing.

Things about him at the party, I mean.

And since everyone is here, all of Callie's brothers, Reed and his sister, Tempest — who's really kickass and has taken quite a liking to Poe — I got distracted by them.

Until I realized that I was being watched.

By Ledger.

Which came as an epic surprise for a lot of reasons, including the fact that I think I picked up a very strong vibe between him and Tempest.

So when he corners me in the kitchen — where I've gone to just take a second to myself before going out to where *he* is — and asks me out on a date, I'm speechless. I'm even more speechless when after my refusal, he keeps trying to convince me.

"What about her though?" I ask finally.

"What about who?"

I look him in his pretty brown eyes. He's got great eyes.

I would draw them if I still drew. And if I *could* draw anyone else's face.

Other than his.

"Tempest," I say.

That gets me a reaction. A pretty fierce one.

His brows snap together and his square jaw goes tight. His entire body goes tight as he replies, "What about her?"

"I thought... she was important to you. I mean, the way you were pretending to not stare at her and —"

"Tempest is nothing."

And that's my answer.

I know he's lying. And I know that I was right about the vibe that I picked up. There's something there, between them, and maybe that's why he's asking me out on a date. Because of her.

I smile at him sadly and say, "You know, it would be a great idea to go on a date. But you're..."

But I trail off because I notice movement behind Ledger's shoulders.

A flash of dark hair and stricken gray eyes.

Tempest.

She's standing at the kitchen threshold and from the looks of it, she heard everything. When she spins around and leaves, my heart twists for her, for the disdain and rejection she must've heard in Ledger's voice.

I'm about to go after her, maybe help her understand what's going on in Ledger's head, but I freeze.

Because she isn't the only one who heard things.

He heard them too.

The man I'm in love with.

He emerges from behind the light-colored wall and stands where Tempest was standing only a moment ago. And his features are... stricken as well.

Stunned and tight.

But only for a second though.

After that, he loses that stunned look and then there's simply tightness. A tight jaw. High and brittle cheekbones. Hard eyes.

With which he gives me a last look and leaves.

And then I don't know what to do. I don't know if I should go after him and tell him that...

Tell him what?

That I'm not interested in his brother. That he has no reason to be jealous or territorial. Because I know he gets that way. But then, that was before.

Before, when he wanted me.

Now he doesn't.

Now he's with someone else.

So I'm going to let it go.

Which is what I do for the rest of the party.

I mingle with people. I eat Callie's cupcakes. I help her with things because it's difficult for her to move around these days due to her pregnancy. Although I probably don't really need to help her, since Reed somehow always appears when Callie seems to need things.

But anyway, once things wind down, I do my share of the cleaning up. When Poe accidentally cuts her finger on glass — because in her words, she isn't made for manual labor — I rush to the bathroom to get the first aid kit.

Which is where he finds me.

Not only does he find me, he keeps me there for a little while as he enters and closes the door behind him. My back's turned as I root around in the medicine cabinet for some band-aids, but when I hear the soft click, I spin around.

And there he is.

Standing by the closed door, arms folded, eyes on me.

Like he always did. Back then.

And I'm not sure what I should do.

My robust system doesn't have anything in it about being shut up in a room with him.

In a room as small and confined as this.

So I have no choice but to focus on him. No choice but to look at him, *really* look at him.

Something that I haven't done in three weeks.

And God, I can't stop staring. I can't stop looking. I can't stop flicking my eyes over his features and wondering why they look so tired. Why do they look so strained? Why is he sporting stubble?

There was only one time when he looked like that.

Back when he said all those awful things at the library and he came to apologize for them at the tree.

And I can't help but wonder if this is because of what happened at his office and...

I shake my head to break my own fanciful thoughts. "I need to bring them the —"

He cuts me off. "How are you?"

"What?"

His jaw tightens for a second before asking again, "You okay?"

I'm not sure why he's asking me that. And why he's doing it in that intimate tone of his that both cuts me and soothes me at the same time. But I still answer with as much nonchalance as possible, "Uh, yeah. Of course." Then, with a slight smile, "How are you?"

His familiar response to my smile — the clenching of his jaw — makes me tighten my hold on the kit as he asks, "How are your classes?"

"Classes?"

"Yeah."

Again I'm not sure why he's asking me these things and why he chose to corner me in the bathroom, especially when it's in a house full of people.

People we both know and care about and who don't know anything about *us*.

"Classes are fine. The usual," I tell him. "Uh, is there something that you wanted?"

"And homework," he continues like I hadn't spoken.

Frowning, I reply, "I really think I should go. Poe cut her finger and —"

"She'll live," he says, his eyes flashing and flickering with something unknown. "You've been doing a lot of it."

"I've been doing a lot of what?"

"Homework," he explains. "You're always in the library. Doing homework."

I swallow again.

I remember what Salem said the other day, about him asking after me.

And I've tried to not dwell on it. I've tried to forget it, chalk it up to normal concern on his part.

I mean, he's not heartless.

He's just in love with someone else. And when he got the opportunity to be with her, he broke off his relationship with me. So when I stopped showing up for lunch, he got a little worried.

Nothing else.

But I don't...

I don't understand *this*.

I don't understand what's happening here.

Shaking my head, I reply, "Yes, I have been. But I've also been prepping for finals and —"

"They are still four weeks away," he tells me like I don't know.

"Well yeah, but you can never be too prepared for them, right? I mean, finals are finals, so."

He studies me for a beat, something like irritation passing through his features, as if he's annoyed at the thought of finals. "And your parents."

"My parents what?"

"Are they still giving you a hard time?" he asks bitingly. "About art school."

Right.

So my parents haven't talked to me in three weeks.

Ever since that weekend when I finally stood up to them like I should've a long time ago, they haven't made any contact with me. Usually they have their assistants call me at the school to keep me updated of any events that I need to attend during visitation weekends. But I've heard nothing in the last three weeks.

I'm not sure how I feel about that.

On the one hand I'm relieved that it's all out there now, but I'm also sad that finally owning up to my feelings has made them even more distant.

Shrugging, I tell him, "They're the same. I think. I haven't spoken to them since... you know."

The party.

I can't say it.

Because so many things happened at that party.

So many things ended and so many things began. And I just... I can't handle it.

I can't handle him being so close to me, looking at me like this.

Asking questions, showing concern, looking angry and agitated on my behalf like we're still together. Like there's still something between us when I know there isn't.

"Can I..." I clear my throat. "Can I go? I —"

"Ledge is a good guy," he says abruptly.

"I'm sorry?" I ask, pressing myself into the edge of the sink.

He doesn't answer right away.

I don't think he can. He's suddenly gone extremely rigid. Not only his features, which were already tight and smooth to begin with, but also his body.

I can see his biceps bulging and flexing through the sleeves of his shirt. His chest isn't faring so well either. It expands and goes all massive as he takes a breath, widening his stance.

As if preparing himself to say his next words, which come out more or less as a thick growl. "He's my brother. The youngest brother. I've watched him grow up. I brought him up basically. And as I said, he's a good kid. A little impulsive, but that's to be expected. He's the baby of the family. Well, after Callie."

"Ledger is a good kid," I repeat, unable to say anything else.

A muscle starts ticking on his cheek as he goes on, "Yes. And he's young. A lot younger than me. He just got drafted, Ledge. And even though he's just starting his career, I know that he'll go far. He's talented. A good player. Needs to think things through sometimes. But I'll be there, helping him. And he lives in New York."

"New York," I parrot his words again.

A short nod. "Yes. Where you're going. For college. So yeah."

I've gone sort of numb right now, watching him, *hearing* him, that even when I try to say something of my own, all I can come up with is, "Yeah what?"

My question makes him go even more rigid.

He already was when he started talking.

And through it all, his stillness has only grown. His posture has only grown tighter, more brittle.

Like he's repelling something.

Repelling his own words.

"Yeah, you should say yes," he clips, his biceps flexing again. "To him."

And my heart drops.

It falls right through my chest and goes down on the floor.

Like he reached inside of me, from all the way over there, plucked it right out of my rib cage as if it were a flower and threw it carelessly on the ground.

So this is what it is.

He's come to tell me that it's okay to date his brother.

But then…

But then I can't shake the feeling, this *other* feeling that I have, right at the center of my belly. That makes me dig my nails into the first aid kit and say, "You mean about the date."

"Yes."

"Because he's young," I continue, watching him, watching the effect my words have on him. "A lot younger than you."

He breathes through his nose. "Yes. Twelve years."

"And because he just got drafted."

"Correct," he confirms, something rippling through his features. "He's going places. He's going to be one of the best players. He might even go to the European League. So he has a bright future."

I stare at him for a few beats.

I stare and stare at him.

At his still form. *Lifeless* form.

At the fact that he can barely get any breaths in or out.

Before I say, "Unlike you."

I think I've slapped him.

That's what it looks like at least.

He draws back slightly.

Not a lot, but since I'm watching like I always do, with all my heart and soul, I notice it.

I notice a vein appearing on his forehead as I keep going, "I mean, you clearly have no future. You're not going places. You're staying here. You won't even go to New York. Where he lives. And where I'm going to be." When he doesn't answer, I prod him, "Right?"

Still he takes a few moments to answer, "Yes."

"So you think going out with your brother is the right move for me."

Looking into my eyes, he says, "Yes. It's the right thing to do."

Right thing to do.

That's what he said when he called me into his office and told me that we were over.

That's *exactly* what he said.

Along with a bunch of other things. Things that I kept focusing on for the last three weeks.

Idiotically, stupidly.

So fucking stupidly.

Not anymore though. Not anymore.

Now I'm going to focus on the real thing.

The truth.

Of what happened that day in his office.

I smile then, big and bright and fake. "Of course, I'm all for doing the right thing. So I think I'll say yes. I have to admit that I did think it would be a little weird, going out with your brother, given our history. But I think I was wrong. I think he could be the guy for me. The right guy. Besides, you're with the right girl of your own, aren't you? You're with your dream girl and I think it's time I got a dream man of my own."

# CHAPTER THIRTY-FOUR

I'm wearing my yellow ball gown.

The one I wore the night I met him.

I've kept it close to me ever since that night. I brought it to St. Mary's with me even.

I think tonight is a good night for it.

To wear the dress he first saw me in.

I'm also wearing my favorite lipstick, his favorite too: Pinky Winky Promises. Along with a ton of jewelry, because he likes me in jewelry, and that belly chain he gave me, which I have to admit I did keep on despite everything.

Despite what he did.

But anyway, I've made myself up just the way he likes it.

Just the way he dreams about.

Because now I know what he dreams about.

I *know*.

And I'm going to tell him that.

I'm going to tell him what I know when I see him.

Because that's where I'm going.

I'm sneaking out of St. Mary's and going to his house in the middle of the night. I'm sure he'll have plenty of things to say about that, about me roaming the streets in my pretty ball gown at midnight, but the thing is that I'm none of his concern now.

He gave me up himself.

So I don't care.

Anyway.

When I do reach his house, I don't go for the door.

Even though I know he's awake; he doesn't sleep much and I'm sure he's definitely not sleeping tonight. Because only hours before he told me to go date his brother.

So he must be restless.

He must be in pain.

I'm not though.

For the first time in days, I'm not in pain. I'm not dead.

I'm angry.

I'm furious.

So I go to his truck that's parked out front, on the empty, sleepy street. I set down my messenger bag I brought with me from school and, bending down, I root around for my favorite spray paint: pink. Also purple. Along with other colors.

And then I get to work.

On his truck.

I wave my arms around as I go. I make circles and lines as I fill his truck with colors. With flowers and stars. With clouds and rainbows. I even go so far as to make unicorns on his black masculine fucking vehicle.

*Take that, Conrad Thorne.*

*Take it.*

Because I'm going to shove magical horses and pink glitter down his throat even if it's the last thing I do. I'm going to fill his dark life with bright sunshine and he can't stop me.

He can't stop me from giving him his dream in Technicolor.

And then I'm going to knock at his door so he can see what I made for him.

So he can look at it and weep, all alone in his house.

Only I don't have to knock at his door.

He opens it all by himself as I reach the end of the graffiti.

He emerges out of his house, all sweaty and panting — probably from kicking the ball all alone in his backyard like he usually does — his overgrown hair messy and hanging in his eyes, looking like the man of my dreams.

Although for a second, something about him gives me pause.

The fact that there are... streaks of paint. On his bare forearms and also his white t-shirt.

There's one on the side of his jaw and I...

"Bronwyn," he says like he can't believe I'm here, standing in front of his house. "What... What the..."

At his deep but bewildered voice, I decide to not care.

I don't care why he's got paint on him.

It's none of my business.

He made it so.

So he can go to hell right now.

"Hi," I say, waving at him while still holding my spray paint, which I then throw away in his yard.

Wiping his parted mouth with the back of his hand, he walks further out, getting to the edge of his porch, squinting at me, at the can that I just threw away, before focusing on his truck.

"I thought I'd make you something," I tell him in a false, cheery voice. "Since I never got to finish that wall in your bedroom. Plus I think you definitely deserve a gift after how you helped me earlier today. You keep doing that, don't you? Helping me. Helping me see things. You helped me see your brother, which I never would've done if not for you."

That gets him moving.

My dig about his brother.

Now instead of simply staring at what I've drawn on his truck, his eyes snap back to mine. His eyes clear out as well. The slight look of confusion goes away and they become alert, flashing before he moves.

Before he bounds down the stairs of his house, strides across the driveway and comes for me.

And I'm ready for him.

I'm so totally ready with a wide stance and a lifted chin.

Reaching me, he growls, running his eyes up and down my dress that's now covered in pink and purple and red and yellow splotches. "What the fuck do you think you're doing?"

"I told you. Making you a special gift for helping me out with Ledger today."

He clenches his jaw at 'Ledger.'

"How'd you get here?" Before I can joyfully inform him how, he takes the right guess. "You take the bus?"

"Yes," I tell him enthusiastically. "Although I will say that if it wasn't my only choice, I wouldn't have taken it. People kinda stared at me a lot in my outfit." His eyes become slits at this but I don't care, I keep going, "Which I specifically wore for you. Because I know you like me in this. My ball gown, my lipstick. All my jewelry. My hair."

Then, widening my eyes, I add in, "But *please*, don't tell Ledger, okay? I don't want to start off our relationship with him knowing that I'm dressing up for another man. For his brother no less. I mean how tacky and —"

"Stop," he booms, his hands fisted at his sides, "saying his name."

I clench my own fists then, at his anger, his jealousy.

He's *jealous*, isn't he?

Of his own brother.

He's jealous even though he ended things.

He gave me up three weeks ago.

"Why?" I ask, staring into his angry blue eyes. "Why shouldn't I say his name? He's the right guy for me. He's young. He's got a bright future. He's going places. He lives in New York. You said so yourself."

"I'm not —"

"As opposed to you," I cut him off, leaning toward him. "A liar."

"What?"

I shake my head then. I clench my teeth. I somehow clench every single part of my body as I say, "That's what you are, aren't you? A fucking liar."

"Bronwyn," he warns.

I chuckle harshly at his stern voice. Angrily, bitterly, as I say, "I should've known. I should've fucking known that you'd do something like this. You've done it before, right? You've lied to me before. Not once. But *twice*. You lied about not remembering me. Back when you started at St. Mary's. And then you lied about not wanting me when in fact you were obsessed with me. And I forgave you. I forgave you both times. But not anymore. I'm not going to forgive you this third time. Because I know. I know you're lying again."

He's seething. I can see that.

He's burning up and I want to tell him to pace himself.

Because I haven't even gotten to the good part yet.

We're only covering the basics right now.

"Aren't you, Conrad?" I prod him. "You're lying about being with her." I raise my hand then before he can say something, "Oh, not exactly. Not in those words. You never said to me that you were going with her. You never said those exact words but you *implied* it. That day in your office. When I kept asking you and asking you. When I kept poking and prodding as to why. Why, Conrad? Why did we have to end? You used her as an excuse. You used the excuse you *knew* I'd accept. You used the excuse you *knew* would make me stop asking questions. Because you didn't want me to ask questions. Because if I had, then you'd have to admit the truth. Then you'd have to face it. And you didn't want to. And I'll also tell you why. It's because you, Conrad Thorne, are afraid."

He flinches at my words.

And it's not a small flinch, it's a big one.

It's more of a spasm running through his body. As if I've jolted him.

And like the idiot I am, I want to wrap my arms around him. I want to give him comfort.

But no.

I'm not his wallflower anymore. I can't give him my softness.

All I can give him now is the truth.

The things that I didn't see before but now I do. After the party.

"You know, all this time, I kept thinking about it and thinking about it," I say, my heart pounding and pulsing and thrashing in my chest. "I kept thinking, why don't you want that new job in New York? Why do you keep turning it down? Why do you want to stay here if you hate it? If you hate this house. If you think it's a dump. If you hate this town. Why don't you want to *see* that you love coaching? That's why you do it all the time. You do it during the week. You do it on weekends. You do it because you have such a passion for it. But you don't want to admit that.

"And I kept thinking, why? I kept thinking, how can I convince you to see it? To see that even though what you dreamed for yourself didn't pan out, doesn't mean that what you have now is any less worthy, is any less joyful. It doesn't mean that you can't want new things, that you can't build a new life, a life that *you* have made for yourself despite everything. That's what you always tell people, don't you? That you should make your own life. So I kept wondering why. Why won't you do the same for yourself? Why won't you dream new dreams? And the reason is that you're afraid. You're afraid to *dream*."

At this I can't stop it.

I can't stop the tear that rolls down my cheek despite everything.

Despite telling myself to be strong and aloof and distant like he usually is.

At the sight of my tears, his flinch is even bigger and he takes a step toward me but I step back.

I don't want him to touch me.

I don't want him to touch me ever.

And I'm glad that he doesn't push. That he can see it on my face, my determination.

So he stands there, his chest moving up and down in waves, his fists clenched, his eyes studying me so closely, so minutely.

So torturously.

"You're afraid to wish for things," I say, when I've finally managed to get that lump of emotion down my throat. "Because if you *don't*, then you won't have to go through the pain if they don't come true. If you don't dream then you won't have to go through the pain if those dreams break. Because you went through it once. Years and years ago. You went through the pain back when you were a teenager. You wanted to go pro. You wanted to get out of this town. You wanted a rich beautiful girl. You shot for the stars and fell short. You told me that. And it hurt. It hurt so badly that you shut yourself out. You closed all your doors. You stopped focusing on yourself and made others the center of your world. Because it's easier that way. It's easier to be angry and alone and to stand still because if you walk, you could stumble. You could fall. You could get *hurt*. And you don't want to."

And then I pause because I don't know if I should say it.

I don't know if I should let him in on this secret.

A secret that I've only now discovered.

But I'm done with this.

I'm done with him. I'll tell him and I'll leave him to ponder over it. And I'll go back to my dorm and I'll do what I've been doing all evening, ever since the get-together ended: cry and sob for my stupid love story.

For this stupid man that I can't stop loving.

Taking a hiccupping breath, I continue, "It's easier, isn't it, Conrad, to end things with a girl than to actually admit that you've fallen in love with her."

I thought it would make him flinch again. It's the biggest blow I've dealt him yet.

The blow I specifically came to his house to deal him.

But it doesn't.

My words don't make him flinch.

They only make him stare at me, my tears that are still falling, with more agony, more torment.

"You love me," I continue, hoping to finish soon so I can leave. "Don't you? Not her. Me. I'm your d-dream girl. You told me that. That I could be someone's dream girl and you meant yourself. That night at my dad's party before… she came. Maybe you loved her in the beginning, when things s-started between us, but you love me now. You love me and —"

I stop talking because I think he's reached his limit.

I think he's done all he can to hold himself still and away from me, because he comes for me then.

He comes for my waist that he puts his hands on, gripping the flesh tightly, so tightly and gloriously, and pulling me off the ground. He plasters my front to his and with me wrapped around him — because my thighs and my arms can't help but wind themselves around his heated and familiar body, despite the fact that touching him wasn't my plan — he walks a few steps and settles me against his truck.

He grabs my tear-streaked face with both his hands and rasps, "Stop crying, Bronwyn. Please. Just stop crying, baby."

"D-don't call me that."

Pressing his hands on my cheeks, he leans closer and I squeeze my thighs around his hips, feeling his weight, his heat, his body that I haven't felt in weeks.

That I never thought I'd feel again in this lifetime.

"I'm sorry," he tells me, looking me in the eyes. "I'm so fucking sorry."

I push at his shoulders. "No, you don't get to say sorry to me anymore. You don't get to… I loved you and you lied. You –"

He goes still at my declaration.

Still and frozen.

His face is even more stunned and stricken than it was back when he witnessed Ledger asking me out on a date. And I think that maybe I can break free of him, now that I've shocked him with my truth.

A truth I wasn't planning on telling him.

But you know what, fuck it.

Fuck him.

I don't care. I just want to get away from him.

But when I go to push him again, he doesn't budge.

He doesn't go anywhere.

His body is like a mountain and his hold feels like forever.

"You love me," he repeats, his eyes fierce, hair grazing the side of his cheeks.

I punch his chest again. "Yes." Another punch and a push. "You fucking asshole."

He digs his fingers in my hair. "Since when?"

"Since always," I snap, staring into his beautiful, shocked face.

"Always."

"Yes," I bite out. "Since I met you that night and you stopped to help me. Since you inspired me. Since you came to St. Mary's. I've loved you since forever. And you lied to me. You let me believe that you wanted someone else. For three whole weeks. *For three whole weeks*, you let me believe that my love was destined to suffer. That my love was doomed because the man I'm in love with wants to be with someone else. You —"

"Your love is doomed anyway," he thunders then, finally coming out of his shock.

"What?"

His hands, which had moved down to my waist and the back of my neck in order to keep me safe when I was struggling, wake up now as well.

His fingers dig into my flesh tightly, like hooks, like thorns as he says, "You think I'm afraid to dream, yeah? To want things for myself. To wish for things. To walk into the fucking unknown. Yeah I was. At one time. I was afraid of the pain, the agony, the hurt of broken dreams. I didn't want new goals. New ambitions. I didn't want any of that. And yes I lied to you because of that. I pushed you away. I used the one thing that I knew you'd believe. Even though I haven't wanted Helen for a long time now. I thought I did but... no. Not since you. But the reason I *stayed* away, for three whole weeks, despite every cell in my body screaming at me to confess the truth, is because I'm afraid for you.

"I'm afraid that I can't give you the things that you deserve. I'm afraid that I don't *have* anything to give you. And I don't. This here, this is my life. This is all I've known, whether by choice or circumstance. This town, this job. And yes, I tried to shoot for the stars once and it didn't pan out and it fucking hurt and I closed myself off, but that doesn't even matter anymore. Fuck that. Fuck soccer. Fuck her. Fuck every single thing that I've ever wanted before you and failed to get. What *matters* is that I can't afford to fail now, do you understand? I can't afford to *not* have things pan out now. Because the stakes are too high. The stakes are you and I'd be damned if I failed you. I'd be damned if I dragged you down with me. I'd be damned if I kept you for my own selfish reasons when you're meant to be out there, making art, living your life, living your dream. I'd be damned, Bronwyn, all right? I won't do it. I can't."

He swallows, his eyes roving over my face frantically, urgently as he rasps, "You're too important. You're too fucking precious. You're my... You're my soft, fragile, velvet wallflower and I'd be damned if I crushed you with my rough hands and my thorn life when I have nothing to give you."

When he finishes, I'm a wreck.

I'm a mess.

Of tears and breaths.

And love.

I'm a mess made of love for this man.

God.

*God.*

What is wrong with me?

What is wrong with *him*?

Why can't he see that he's already given me so much? He's already given me everything.

My hands, which were pushing him away only a few seconds earlier, latch onto him now. My thighs tighten around his hips and my fingers fist whatever they can find on his body, his t-shirt, his hair and pull him closer as I whisper, "But you already have. You already have given me so much, Conrad, don't you see? You've given me everything. Without even asking. Without even saying a word. You've set me free. You've made me see myself, embrace myself not once but twice.

"And you did it because that's who you are. Inspiring and wonderful and protective and strong. So you can't fail. You can't. Not with me. Because I love you for who you are. I've *loved* you for who you are. I've loved you even when I thought you loved someone else and I love you now when I *know* you love me back. I choose you for who you are. You're the center of my universe. You're my gravity. And all I want is you. Just you. The way you are. My thorn. My dream man."

As soon as I finish, he comes for me again. This time for my mouth, and he kisses me.

And even though I know I shouldn't kiss him — he lied to me; he's been torturing me, torturing himself for the past three weeks — I do.

I kiss him back.

I kiss him back to show him that I love him and the only thing I want from him is *him*.

Something I didn't even think was possible.

Something that even *I* didn't dare dream about.

A dream about us.

Together.

So I kiss him back and tell him that now I will. I will dream of us and he needs to dream about us too.

But then a voice comes and splinters the moment. The same voice that made everything fall apart on the night of my dad's birthday party.

"Con?"

We break apart then, our mouths coming off of each other.

And just like that night, I don't know what to do. I'm frozen. I'm useless.

Not him though.

He presses the back of my head and tucks me in his chest, hiding my face, as Helen takes in the scene.

A girl wrapped around Conrad and an explosion of colors and paints.

Graffiti on his truck.

And when she makes out what the graffiti is — a girl in a yellow ball gown with tons of jewelry — and that's the girl who's wrapped around Conrad, her voice is even higher than before. "Bronwyn?"

And just like that, I think, everything ends before it has even had the chance to begin.

## CHAPTER THIRTY-FIVE

I'm panicking.

And this time there *is* a reason to panic.

This time a tragedy has definitely struck. The sky has absolutely fallen.

Because someone saw us.

Someone being Helen. The worst person who could've seen us.

And it was out in the open.

On a dark and sleepy street with nowhere to hide. Not a door or a wall to take cover behind like we did at my dad's party.

And once I got out of my frozen mode, I wanted to say something to Helen.

I wanted to tell her that it wasn't what it looked like. But then that would've been completely ridiculous because we were *wrapped around* each other. We were kissing each other. I was kissing him and he was kissing me and we were so engrossed in it that we never noticed the world.

We never noticed someone walking up to us.

Someone who got there in a car.

Which I know now.

Because as soon as she saw us, she recognized who it was in his arms, she *understood* what was happening, she spun around and strode over to her car. She opened the door, got in and slammed it shut, driving away. And all of that was so loud, so booming that it's a wonder that we never heard her. That we never paid attention.

But we were paying attention then.

As soon as she drove away, I told Conrad that we needed to go after her. That we needed to stop her and explain things to her. I told him that I'd tell her that it was me and that I was the one who snuck out of school in the middle of the night. So I was the one breaking all the rules and so I should be the one punished.

But he put a stop to it.

He put a stop to all that.

And he said, "Trust me."

That's all.

The exact words he told me on the night of the party, and then he kissed me on the forehead and drove me back to St. Mary's. And while dropping me off when I still wouldn't let it go, he said, with all the confidence and assurances in his voice, "I'll see you tomorrow."

And now it's tomorrow.

It's Monday morning and school is on.

I'm in the cafeteria, pretending to eat, to appease my friends so they don't get too worried about me — I haven't shared with them what happened last night — when all I want to do is throw up. When all I want to do is run out of here and go up to his office. And if he's not there yet, then look for him around campus.

But I'm afraid.

I'm afraid that I might make things worse. By going to him now.

By being close to him and being *seen* together with him.

Because what if Helen has already told everyone, the teachers, the principal? What if she's already reported us and what she saw? And if so, then me trying to talk to Conrad would be a disaster.

Even more of a disaster.

Isn't it?

They could all point fingers at us and say, *look how close they are. How she looks at him and how he looks at her. It must be true.*

So if that's the case, if Helen has already reported us, then maybe instead of looking for Conrad, I should look for Principal Carlisle. Maybe I should go to her directly and tell her that it was my fault and take all the blame on myself. I could tell her that I tried to seduce him. *Me*. I forced him to kiss me and that I wouldn't leave him alone.

Which for the most part is correct. On the surface.

But then, what if Helen *hasn't* said anything?

What if Conrad managed to stop her?

He said to trust him, right?

So maybe he talked to her before school and got it all sorted out. And me going to Principal Carlisle would be the biggest disaster of all.

So maybe I should stay here in the cafeteria, eat my breakfast like nothing has happened and wait for him to find me first.

To tell me exactly what is happening so I can react accordingly, because things look normal so far.

Until they don't.

Until the door of the cafeteria is flooded with all the people that I've been thinking about, Principal Carlisle and teachers. Well, only a few teachers, but also the vice principal, the principal's assistant and the vice-principal's assistant.

And a man.

A dark man. Threatening and severe.

Or at least that's what he looks like to me because of what my state of mind is.

He has slightly curly hair, or rather wavy, dark in color, chocolate brown if I have to pick a shade. His eyes are dark as well. Maybe chocolate brown again; I can't tell from this far. And his jaw is the kind that you think is forever clenched because the muscles on it, the slant of it is so severe and taut.

That's what makes him look like a threat, I decide.

Or someone you shouldn't mess with.

That and his shoulders.

His chest.

Massive and broad under the dark gray shirt that he has on, and a jacket. A dark gray tweed jacket.

I'm not sure who he is and what he's doing here and why he's regarding us all with a grave expression, but I don't have a good feeling about this.

Not a good feeling at all.

I'm already starting to stand up, with the intention of approaching their group that has come to stand up front by the food bar, and taking whatever it is they're here to dole out to us. Because they're here for us, aren't they? For Conrad and me. Only I don't understand the purpose of their coming here like this.

But then all my intentions vanish when I hear a fist thumping on the table.

It's Poe.

And she's glaring.

At that threatening, severe man.

Why would she be...

And then I get it.

We all get it, Callie and Salem and me.

It finally clicks: *tweed jacket.*

We're all about to say something to Poe, opening our mouths, when Principal Carlisle speaks. "Good morning, everyone. I apologize for interrupting your breakfast like this. I understand that it's highly unusual and you all might be confused, but there's nothing to worry about. There's something I would like to share with you and I thought that it would be better doing it in person rather than sending out a mass email or announcing it in the school newsletter. And since we don't have assemblies at St. Mary's, this seemed like a good time."

She throws us all a small smile. "I'm both pleased and saddened to announce that I will be leaving my position as the principal of St. Mary's at the end of this year."

The room that had gone silent at their abrupt and strange arrival erupts in murmurs. But one look from Principal Carlisle and everyone shuts up. "I've been extremely lucky to be a part of this institution for as long as I have. I've cherished every moment that I've spent here. I've cherished every student and I've tried to help them as best as I could. This school has been a big part of my life for years, sometimes my whole life, but now it's time to move on."

With that she turns to the man beside her, who hasn't shown any emotion throughout this little speech. "And as bittersweet as this moment is, I'm very glad to be leaving it in extremely capable hands. This is Mr. Marshall. He has been on the board for a long time now and when I expressed my desire to leave, he was more than happy to step in. Which means, starting next term, he's going to be your new principal. Principal Marshall."

She goes on to say something more and then hands clap in welcome and excited conversations resume. But I don't care about any of that. I'm more concerned about Poe. We all are.

Who's still glaring at him.

Callie is the first to speak. "Is that... your..."

Poe narrows her eyes behind her glasses.

And that's our answer.

It's her guardian who wears tweed jackets with elbow patches. And who up until now we all thought was super old because Poe kept lying about his age. He's definitely not old, that's for sure.

"But he's like, very..." Salem trails off when Poe snaps her eyes over to her.

"Don't say it," she says, all deadly calm.

"Sorry," Salem mumbles.

I know what she was going to say though.

Something that didn't occur to me right when I first saw him.

Maybe because he has such a dark, threatening aura about him. And because my life is basically a mess right now.

And Callie knows it too, what Salem was going to say, because she asks, "Is that why you never showed us any photos even when you admitted you were lying about his age? Because he's so..."

Poe glares at her too. "Don't."

Callie raises her hands in surrender and then mimes zipping up her lips. Which Poe finds satisfactory before turning her attention to me. "You. Do you have something to add as well?"

I look at both Salem and Callie before shaking my head and saying, "Not really."

"Good. Because I don't want to hear it." She pins all of us with her stern gray-blue bespectacled gaze. "Yes, he's not old as we all knew already. And he's fucking... good looking, okay? There, I said it. He's good looking."

"He's not just good looking, he's fucking glorious," Salem says.

"He's like... wow," Callie goes then. "And maybe I'm exaggerating things because I'm pregnant and hormonal. But I don't think I am. I think *everyone* here thinks that."

Poe bangs her fist on the table again. "I knew it. I knew you'd say that. I knew that as soon as you took a look at his *glorious face*" – she eyes Salem – "you'd forget what he did to me. And —"

Callie reaches out for her fist then. "Hey, of course not. We'll never forget what he did to you. He's our sworn enemy. Till the end of time."

Salem chimes in, "Yes, exactly. Glorious or not, he's the man who sent you here. And even though if you hadn't come here, we never would've met and that would've made me sad, I still hate him. We'll always hate him for that."

This gives Poe a little relief.

"And we know you're freaking out at seeing him like this," I decide to reason a little with her. "But didn't you hear what Principal Carlisle said? He's not going to be the principal until next term. And we're all graduating in a few weeks. So maybe it's not as bad as we're all thinking."

Poe's face becomes even more grave at my observation and I don't understand how.

None of us do.

But when Callie goes to ask her about it, Poe snaps her hand back and stands up abruptly.

And leaves.

She strides out of the cafeteria that's still buzzing with excitement and loud chatter. In fact it feels even more crowded now than it was before Principal Carlisle arrived with her news.

And in the midst of all that chatter and enthusiasm, I see him.

I finally see the man I've been looking for.

The man I'm in love with.

He's standing at the threshold of the cafeteria, tall and so visible, so mine.

And everything comes in swinging, the worry, the fear, the feeling of impending doom and I can't sit here any longer. I have to go to him. But I'm worried about Poe as well and Callie's here and...

"Hey, me and Callie are gonna go look for Poe, okay?" Salem says, coming to my rescue as she has done so many times in the past. "Can you grab me a muffin, Wyn? Before the bell."

I shoot her a look full of gratitude as I nod. "Yeah."

She smiles. "Thanks."

Then she helps Callie up from her chair and they're off, looking for Poe. And when they're out of sight, I head in his direction. I have very little time before the bell and I need to talk to him.

I need to make sure that everything's okay, and if not, then how I can help.

I just hope that me going to him like this won't make things worse.

When he sees me approaching him, which he basically did the moment I stood up because his eyes were on me, his gaze becomes liquid.

It becomes shiny and full of warmth and... love.

God, he loves me.

He *loves* me.

I know he hasn't said it yet, not in those exact words, but I can see it in his eyes.

It makes me happy. And it makes me angry.

It makes me want to kiss him and punch him and hug him and rage at him.

For doing what he did.

For putting me through everything.

For loving me the way he does.

When I reach him, I ask the question I asked him three weeks ago. "Is everything..."

He thrusts his hands down into his pockets, dipping his chin and saying, "Everything is fine."

"Is she..." I look around, completely in tune with our surroundings, with people and if they're throwing us looks; no one is so far, thankfully. "Is she going to say something? Because if she is, I'm ready. I'll tell them that —"

"You don't need to worry about her," he says calmly with a slight smile. "Or anyone. I've taken care of it. She's not going to bother you or say anything. You just focus on your finals, all right?"

"I don't care about finals. Tell me what happened. Tell me how."

His eyes rove over my features, still calm and unhurried but intense, as if he's trying to memorize my features. "It's four weeks. Less than four weeks even. I want you to hold on until then, yeah? I want you to hold on and I want you to know that I'll come for you."

"What?"

His jaw moves back and forth as he stares and stares down at me. "I'll come for you, Bronwyn. I'll be there when you're done with your finals, with St. Mary's. I promise you that."

"What does that —"

This time my words are swallowed up by the shrill sound of the bell, which is followed by loud and booming noises of dragging chairs and conversations and people thumping their food trays at the assigned spots.

"Go to class," he says, dragging my attention back to him, to his denim blue eyes. "I'll see you soon."

I take a step toward him, hoping to stop him.

Grab onto him and ask what the hell is he saying. What does he mean he'll come for me? Why is he promising me that?

But I can't.

Not here.

Not where everyone can see.

So I stand rooted to my spot as he leaves. As people move around me, go to classes, to their lockers, collect their books. At some point, someone comes to collect me as well. It's Salem and with her, I go to my class. I sit through lectures and lessons until the lunch period.

When Poe grabs my hand – who after her earlier display of rage has calmed down and looks sassy and bubbly as usual – as I'm standing up from my desk and without a word, drags me out of the class. She takes me to a quiet spot at the end of the hallway, by a classroom and a glass window and says, "Wyn, listen, my sources picked up something."

My heart starts to pound in my chest. "W-what?"

She looks around. "There probably won't be any more soccer practices for the rest of the term. And..." She grimaces. "And a few people saw Coach Thorne leave with a bunch of scary-looking dudes just about an hour ago."

"What does that mean? What scary looking dudes?"

"I don't know. But it looked like they were cops."

# CHAPTER THIRTY-SIX

The Original Thorn

Fourteen years ago, I stopped dreaming.

My mother died. The woman who raised me, who loved me and who chose the wrong man to spend her life with. She deserved better.

So much better than what she got.

But she passed away before I could give that to her.

And along with my mother, I lost everything else as well.

I lost soccer. I lost the love of my life at the time. I lost all my dreams.

It was a natural reaction to stop. To never open that door again. To never go through that pain when I was already hurting over losing my mom.

So it was easy.

To stop dreaming I mean.

It hasn't been so easy now.

I dream now.

I dream every night. I dream all day.

I dream when I close my eyes. I dream when my eyes are open.

And it all started three weeks ago.

It all started the day I lied to her and let her go.

And it sent me into a panic, the fact that I couldn't stop myself from dreaming, from wanting. It scared me. I was petrified. So fucking petrified.

And then I was angry.

I was angry at myself for not learning my lesson. For not getting it through my head that I wasn't supposed to dream. I wasn't supposed to want things, crave things, long for things.

It only brings me pain.

It only makes me miserable.

So I turned my house upside down. My empty, dump of a house that she was trying to make new. For me.

I broke things. I punched things. I raged at things.

Until I realized something.

As I sat in my bedroom, by that unfinished colorful wall that mocked me and taunted me with her absence, I realized that I no longer care about the pain. I no longer care if my dreams come true or not. I no longer care if I'm afraid.

I no longer *care*.

About anything other than her.

I never thought that *anything* could be worth going through that pain again. That I wouldn't go through that misery, that desolation for anything or anyone.

But I was wrong.

I would do it for her.

It's her.

She is worth it.

She is worth all the pain, all the agony. She is worth letting go of my stupid fucking self-preservation and jumping off the cliff for. She is worth walking and falling down for. She is worth stepping into the unknown for.

Her absence – which was and *is* much more painful and agonizing than any pain my broken dreams have caused me – made me realize that for her, I'd do it all.

So yeah, I have been dreaming about her for the past three weeks.

I've been dreaming and dreaming, knowing that I'd already let her go, and that I could never get her back. Knowing that every single dream I weaved would be broken, would be unfulfilled.

But it was okay.

I only cared about her.

The girl who sees me like no one else has.

And for whom I spent the afternoon, holed up in a jail cell.

Which is where I'm coming out of right now.

I thought everything was fine though. That I'd taken care of everything last night.

But apparently not.

As soon as I dropped Bronwyn off at St. Mary's, I called Principal Carlisle.

I told her what happened and what Helen saw. And then I told her the truth. I told her what had been going on for the past few months. What my intentions were moving forward.

And so I was quitting.

I couldn't stay in a position that could jeopardize my goals, Bronwyn's reputation. Even for the next four weeks.

I also told her that I would submit to an investigation if need be. I would cooperate and sit through whatever internal reviews she thinks might be necessary.

But my only condition was that it be kept quiet and strictly confidential. Which was in their favor as well; no one wants a student/teacher scandal especially at a reform school. And because I wanted them to keep *her* out of it. And if in order to do that I had to take the blame on myself or if they had to put this on my permanent record, I was okay with that.

I'm not sure why but at the end of my story, Leah — Principal Carlisle — looked extremely tired.

Maybe because it was the middle of the night or the fact that earlier that year, she'd already gone through a couple of such situations. One I'm familiar with — my own sister getting pregnant and Leah still keeping her on. And the other involving one of my sister's friends, Salem, and her own son, Arrow.

Whatever the case may be, she said, "The news won't come from me. But if Helen chooses to share it and involve the board, then I'm not going to stop her. This is a serious situation, Conrad, I hope you know that. There will be questions about authority and consent and code of conduct. The only reason I'm not taking any action by myself is because I know you. I've known your reputation for years. It's beyond reproach and because you chose to come to me and you're willing to quit and sit in for a formal investigation if need be. And the fact that she's eighteen. Maybe that makes me an irresponsible adult and a teacher. But again, if others want to ask questions, I'm not going to stop them."

So then the only thing left to do was talk to Helen.

I knew it wouldn't be easy. To convince her to let this go. Given that again she was at my house for the very things I've denied her and refused to give. She's not really good with giving up on what she wants.

So I didn't even try.

All I said was that the truth was out in the open and that I was quitting. So if she wanted revenge, she had it. But if she wanted more, she was welcome to do whatever she wanted to me but not to *her*.

But I guess she didn't listen because she still involved *her*.

Her father.

Who had me arrested.

So far I've managed to find a solution for that as well. Temporary but effective, seeing as how I'm bounding down the stairs of the police station, having just made the bail.

With the help of the last person I wanted to call.

Reed Jackson.

He stands, leaning against his white Mustang, waiting for me as I stride across the street. When I reach him, he straightens up and jerks his chin at me. "You okay?"

"Yeah," I reply truthfully.

I *am* okay.

Usually by this time of the day, my shoulders start aching. My skull starts pounding and I have a tightness in my muscles that no amount of stretching or pills can take away. And these past three weeks the pain has been really bad.

Not today though.

Today I'm surprisingly okay.

"Appreciate you bailing me out," I continue.

He shrugs. "It was nothing." Then with a small smirk, "And I think I've got something for you."

I go alert. "Fucking finally."

He frowns at that. "These things take time, all right? He's the fucking DA. He's got his shit locked up tight. My guy had to dig and dig."

"And."

He shrugs again. "And I think we hit jackpot. He's sending over stuff later. I'll call you when he does."

Three weeks ago, at her dad's party I made a promise to her.

I promised that I'd set her free.

Even though she'd finally taken a stand, I had a feeling that her father wouldn't let her go so easily. So I knew that I had to do something. I had to permanently eliminate his threat.

And so that's the other reason I called Reed today.

Because he's already helping me out. Because he's the only person I know who can help me out. Because Reed Jackson has connections.

Or rather his father, the wealthiest man in Bardstown and four towns over, does.

And I need those connections, that influence to go up against a DA.

I need leverage.

"So what's the damage?" I ask him.

"What damage?"

"For bailing me out today. And for finally getting your hand on the jackpot. What do I owe you?"

He stares at me like I'm talking gibberish. "Nothing."

I frown. "Nothing." He nods in response and I continue, "So you're saying that you walked into the room and they let me go. And that guy of yours isn't going to charge you anything?"

He smirks again. "Well, I know this is the first time for you, seeing the dark side of Bardstown, but these guys, they're my minions. My dad's minions. They just do the things I tell them to do. And well, it usually helps that my father is filthy rich."

I study him, his arrogant face.

His attitude has always bugged me. He used to be my player when I coached Bardstown High and I always thought that he had talent. More so than a lot of kids I've coached. And I've always thought that it was thoroughly and utterly wasted on him.

"You tell Callie?" I ask.

All his cockiness and smirk and arrogance, everything that I've always hated about him, melts away at my sister's name. "Fuck no," he replies almost angrily. "And no one is going to tell her anything. She's already under a lot of stress, all right? Her back is bothering her. She can't move around a lot. She's always angry and hormonal. And she's got fucking finals on top of it. No one is going to tell Fae anything. She doesn't need that shit right now."

Fae.

She calls her by his own name, which I have to admit really bothered me in the past.

But not anymore.

Especially when he somehow has the same level of protectiveness toward her like me. Like all my brothers.

I mean he's never going to win against us, against how much *we* care for Callie, but it's good to see that he's right up there.

Not to mention, I've finally come to see that he's got more to him than what he portrays. So yeah.

"Good," I say, agreeing.

Callie doesn't need to know anything right now; that was the other reason why I wanted to keep everything with Principal Carlisle and St. Mary's quiet. I'll tell her everything myself when the time comes but not before.

I feel Reed studying me for a beat before folding his arms across his chest and asking with his typical smirk, "So who's she?"

"Who's who?"

"The girl," he says. "For who you got arrested."

I shove my hands down my pockets to hide the immediate effect at her mere mention. "Why does it have to be a girl?"

"Because when men do stupid fucking things, things they never thought they'd do in a million years, things they never even dreamed of doing, there's usually a girl involved," he answers. "A pretty one too. You're looking into the DA, the DA had you arrested and I'm pretty sure even though you made bail for now, he's coming after you. I mean, until he sees what we've got against him. So who is she? The lucky girl. Who got Coach Thorne to break all the rules and go to jail for."

Lucky girl.

Yeah, I don't know about that.

I don't know if she's lucky or if this is a cruel joke.

I've been dreaming about her, yes. But I don't know if *she* should be dreaming about someone like me.

Someone as hard and rigid and so still. Whose life is so limited and small.

For someone as old as me, I haven't seen much of the world, have I?

I haven't done anything. I haven't gone anywhere.

I haven't achieved anything of my own.

That's why I stayed away. For three whole weeks.

Despite getting over my cowardly fear of dreaming, of wanting things. I wasn't protecting myself for the past three weeks, I was protecting her.

From me.

Because her future is out there. Her future is big and bright and in New York.

How could I be selfish with her when I knew I wasn't good enough for her? When I knew I couldn't give her the things that she deserved.

That's why I pushed her toward Ledger.

Even though it killed me. Even though for the first time in my life, I felt jealous of him. Of my own brother.

So much so that I wanted to punch him and punch him until he gave up the idea of going out with her.

And not to mention, how could I go to her when I lied to her?

Like an asshole, I took advantage of her trust yet again. I told her the one thing that would get her to back off. That would get her to *move on*. To live her life. To forget about this short lived dream fever of a time we had. To forget this teenage crush on me.

I didn't think that...

She loved me.

Me.

I never thought... I never thought that she could dream of me. That she could want me like that. I never understood the depths of her feelings and I should have.

I *should* have.

Because she had shown me, hadn't she?

She'd shown me time and time again that she was different. She was more. She was *mine*.

And I hurt her again.

I fucking hurt her and put her through my bullshit again.

Coming out of my furious thoughts, I look at Reed. "Are you speaking from experience?"

A troubled look enters his eyes before he waves it off and shrugs. "I wouldn't know what to do with a pretty girl." Then, rather quietly, "Except to ruin her."

I chuckle then.

I didn't know that I had it in me right now but still.

"You know I always wondered why Callie chose you," I say. "Why after multiple warnings, numerous lectures about you, she still fell for you. I think I have my answer now."

His eyes are narrowed. "And I'm on tenterhooks, waiting to hear it."

I chuckle again. "It's because you're like me."

"What?"

"You are."

"Is that supposed to be a compliment?"

"Fuck no," I say much like he did a few minutes ago. "I'm an asshole. And her name is Bronwyn."

His eyes flare with interest, with recognition. "Fae's friend."

I'm not sure if I like the fact that he knows my Bronwyn but I'll allow it for now. "Yeah. People call her Wyn."

Amusement lines his features. "What do you call her?"

A wallflower.

*My* wallflower.

And she calls me thorn. *Her* thorn.

So again as I promised to her at St. Mary's this morning, I'm going to her.

And I'm going to give her what she wants.

If she'll still have it.

If she'll still have me.

## CHAPTER THIRTY-SEVEN

I look myself in the mirror.

I'm wearing yet another pink ball gown. This one is more off-shoulders than strapless but like the one I wore at my dad's birthday party, it hugs my body.

My chest to be specific.

Although it's not for other men or guys.

It's specifically for Robbie.

Because he's visiting from college and he's expressed a desire to meet me. To forget my bad behavior from that summer and give me another chance.

My parents are extremely ecstatic about it.

And about the fact that I can't say no now.

Despite telling them, just recently, that I would. That I would say no to the things that I didn't want to do. That I was done. I was free and that I was finally taking control of my life.

But it's okay.

I don't want it. I don't want the control. I don't want to be free.

Especially when my freedom is so expensive.

When it comes at the price of *his* freedom. His reputation. His well-being.

I don't want my freedom if it hurts him.

If it gets him... *arrested*.

I press a hand to my stomach at the thought. Because it looks like I'm going to throw up again.

Even though I haven't eaten much all day – actually I don't think I've eaten at all ever since my father told me what he did to Conrad yesterday afternoon – I'm still throwing up constantly.

After Poe told me about what she'd found out, about some men accompanying Conrad out of St. Mary's and that they looked like cops, I knew. I *knew* it had something to do with my dad.

And Helen.

And that it was worse than what I'd been thinking and dreading yesterday morning. I thought Helen would report me and Conrad to the principal but she did something worse.

She went to my dad.

So I rushed over to the principal's office where Principal Carlisle already knew why I was there. She let me call my dad and he sent a car over to bring me back home.

I expected a dire atmosphere when I reached. Like it was the night I vandalized my dad's car or even on the day I expressed my desire to go to art school. I fully expected to be screamed at. I fully expected to be condemned and called names in loud voices.

But there was pin drop silence. My mother didn't even say a word and the voice that my father used was soft and polite and so business-like.

"I want you to give up this crazy, irrational idea of going to art school," my dad said, looking me in the eyes, appearing every inch the ruthless lawyer that he is. "You will of course have no contact with him now or in the future. You will not try to see him or call him or get in touch with him in any way or form. Principal Carlisle has assured me that he's quit his job and that's the only reason I've decided to let you take your finals. But you will stay here; you're not going back to the dorms. You will stay here and you will behave. You will act like every inch the daughter we've raised you to be. If you promise me these things, I will make this go away. I will let him go free. No harm will ever come to him. There will be no rumors. It will be as if this never happened."

Of course I promised him those things.

Of course I gave my father everything he wanted. He could have *everything* as long as he let the man I'm in love with go free.

I just never thought that it would come to this. That my own father would see an opportunity and use it against me.

That's what he did, didn't he?

Helen told him and like an excellent lawyer, he used that information to get what he wanted from me.

So here I am.

Back in my house, attending another event.

This one's less lavish and elaborate since it was a last-minute idea but no less important. I think my parents want to celebrate the fact that I'm once again theirs and so they decided to throw a dinner party – Rutherfords are attending.

Breathing in deep once or rather several times, I take one last look at myself in the mirror and leave my bedroom to go downstairs and join the party. I'm not sure how much I'll be able to eat or if I'll even manage to sit through the whole thing without wanting to throw up, but I will try my best.

On trembling legs, I descend the stairs, cursing myself in the head for not taking Martha's advice about at least having some juice. I probably should have because I really think I'm going to throw up again and this time it's going to be in front of all these people who are milling about in the foyer and the living room with their champagne glasses and...

I lose my train of thought because someone strides in through the front door.

Someone tall and broad with dirty blond hair that hangs in his navy blue eyes. Someone whose sight jars me so much that I almost miss a step and grab onto the bannister with both hands so as not to fall and go tumbling down the stairs.

What is he... What is he doing here?

I knew that he was out.

I knew that; Martha told me.

Like Poe at St. Mary's, Martha has her own spies and sources in the house. I'd asked her to keep an eye on things – I told her about Conrad yesterday when she came to my room to drop off something to eat after my confrontation with my dad – and let me know as soon as she heard something. And last night, she told me that she overheard my father on the phone. He was talking about Conrad being out and he sounded extremely pissed.

I'm not sure why my father was angry but I was just happy that Conrad had his freedom.

And looking at him right now, at the proof that he's really out, I can't stop my heart from leaping in my chest, from beating like a happy bird that he seems okay. That he's fine.

Until I realize that he shouldn't be here.

Not *here*.

Not in my house.

But before I can bring myself out of my stupor and even think of doing something – like rushing down the stairs to go meet him as he stands in the wide foyer of my house, his eyes sweeping through the space, looking for something – someone else appears in my line of vision.

Someone that jars me even more and gets me moving.

My father.

He strides over to Conrad whose jaw clenches as soon as he sees my father approaching. And whose eyes have narrowed to dangerous slits as soon as my father reaches him.

I'm there as well.

Or at least I'm at the bottom of the stairs where I can hear my father say, "You've got some nerve –"

Conrad cuts him off though.

Not only by his words but also by almost slapping something on my dad's chest. A sort of a thick file that slightly shocks my dad.

"Yeah, I do," Conrad growls. "And that's why I'm here to tell you that it's in your best interests to back the fuck off."

"Excuse me?"

Conrad takes his time responding as he sweeps his cold, lethal eyes over my dad's face. "You're a piece of shit, you know that? I mean lawyers usually are. But you take the cake because you're not only a piece of shit when it comes to your work, you're also a piece of shit when it comes to her. Your daughter."

My heart jumps when Conrad mentions me and it completely flies out of my chest when he says the next part: "You didn't think I'd let her go, did you? Just because of your temper tantrum yesterday. Because if you did, then you're even stupider than I thought and what this file says." He glances down at the file for a second before continuing, "I suggest you read it. And then I suggest that you think about what will happen if others get to read it. And when you've thought it all through and come to the *right* conclusion, I want you to destroy every little thought in your head about trying to keep her here. About trying to scare her or manipulate her or stop her from achieving her dreams. Do you understand? Because if I get even a *hint* that you're thinking about touching my Bronwyn or hurting her or making her life difficult, I will personally make sure that this file gets into the hand of every media outlet in this town and in this state."

With that, Conrad lets the file go and my dad's hand snatches to catch it before it can slip and fall to the floor.

And then his eyes land on me, the man I'm in love with and who I thought I'd never get to see again.

Directly, unabashedly.

As if he knew I was standing there, by the stairs and as soon as he focuses on me, he begins to walk over, his footsteps loud and sure.

So loud that I think people have started to notice.

Well, they'd already started to notice that something was wrong when Conrad had arrived with angry eyes. And then my dad intercepted him and had a heated exchange. And now my dad looks like he's been struck, his features all tight and shocked and angry.

Not to mention, me.

I was standing by the stairs, all frozen and afraid, watching them.

So yeah, I think they know.

And I think my dad is going to do something. That any second now, he will come out of his stupor and stop Conrad from approaching me.

But he doesn't.

Nothing happens.

On the outside at least.

On the inside, my body is chaos and things explode when he reaches me and rasps, "Hey."

Even now when I think danger surrounds us in the form of my dad and so many people here, I can't help but think that this is his first – very first – greeting to me.

Usually, I'm the one who smiles and greets him but this time it's him.

He smiles or rather his lips pull up an inch or two as he stares down at me.

"What are you... You can't be here," I tell him unable to think of anything else to say.

While his jean blue eyes were all cold and dangerous when he was looking at my father, they are all warm and shiny now. "I told you I'd come for you."

"But my dad. He will... What did you give him? What's in that file?"

His jaw goes tight before he replies, "Something that will get him to back off."

"Back off how?"

His eyes sweep over my face, unafraid and confident. "I promised that you wouldn't have to do this again, remember? These parties, these events. You wouldn't have to do anything you didn't want to. And you don't."

My heart squeezes in my chest and my eyes sting.

My whole body stings with so much love for him. So much need and longing and I whisper, "I was so afraid. When they took you. Poe told me a-and I didn't know what to do. I didn't... I don't..."

He steps closer and brings his hand up to my cheek, cradling it and I grab onto it like my life depends on it. "Hey, you don't have to be afraid anymore. You never have to be afraid. Not from these people. Not from your father. It's done. It's over. Forever. I've taken care of it."

I press his hand on my cheek. "I'm not afraid for myself. I'm afraid for you."

His eyes go soft as he says, "Nothing is happening to me either."

"Forever?"

"Yeah," he whispers, his fingers digging into my cheek. "Forever."

His voice, his tone, the utter belief on his face makes my body sag in relief. Finally.

It chases my fear away.

Or at least most of it.

I guess it won't vanish totally until I'm away from this place. Away from the people who have tried to harm my Conrad.

So I whisper, "Take me."

Like always, I don't have to tell him what I mean.

Because I think we speak the same language, him and I. We speak how thorns do to roses. And how leaves speak to fall. How stars speak to the sky.

We speak with our hearts.

Our souls.

So he grabs my hand, his fingers threading with mine, and he does what I asked him.

He takes me.

Away.

# CHAPTER THIRTY-EIGHT

I'm in his house.

In his living room.

Right in the middle of it and he's by the door.

For some reason, tonight reminds me of the first time I came to his house. How nervous I was during the ride over and how all my nervousness vanished once I stepped into his space.

His life.

How safe I felt. How at home.

I still feel that way.

Safe and sound and at home.

In fact, I wasn't even nervous during the ride over.

I'm not so sure about him though. Because he looks on edge.

He looks... uncertain as he stares at me.

Even though he's standing in his usual way, leaned against the door, arms folded, there's a tightness on his frame.

A dull thrum of something agitating.

I guess it's all the things that are unsaid between us.

All the things that we didn't get to resolve that night, the night Helen saw us kissing. The night I told him that I loved him, and he told me that he didn't have anything to give me.

"How did you know I was home?" I ask.

"Leah," he replies, watching me steadily. "She called. Told me your father was keeping you home. Wouldn't let you come back to St. Mary's."

"He said that he'd let you go," I tell him. "If I agreed to his... conditions."

He scoffs, anger simmering in his eyes. "I figured that. I figured he'd pull something like that. Fucking piece of shit." Then, "So even if Leah hadn't called, I was headed to your house anyway. To see your father."

"To give him the file and tell him to back off."

"Yes."

"How did you get it?"

"Reed." When I frown, he explains, "I called him right after your dad's birthday party. I knew that even if you stood up to him, he wouldn't take it sitting down. So I wanted a way to permanently shut him down. Something to keep him in line for now and always." Breathing sharply, he adds, "I also took care of Helen."

"How?"

His jaw is rock hard for a second as if in distaste. "I told her if she opened her mouth again, I'll open mine too. And if I do, then it's going to hurt her far worse than it ever did me. Or you. Because I'm the man she's been trying to fucking sleep with for the past year."

"What?"

"She's not the only one who knows how to play dirty. Especially when the thing that she's trying to fuck with is the only thing I care about." I swallow at his words, and he continues, "So she's going to sit down and keep her mouth shut. Again, for now and always."

I fist my hands.

For so many reasons.

The fact that he gauged the danger even before I did. The fact that he protected me from it, found a solution for it.

Like a thorn.

My thorn.

But he pricked me too, didn't he?

He hurt me. He lied to me. He tortured me for three weeks.

I notice him beginning to say something, but I get there first and ask, "What is that?"

I'm not ready to hear his apologies though. I'm not ready to let him off the hook yet. So I point to the spot on the wall by the door but he doesn't even look at it as he replies, "A hole."

"Why's there a hole in your wall?"

"Because I punched it."

"Why?"

He watches me a beat, his eyes penetrating and so blue. "Because I was angry. Because I made you cry. In my office that day. Because the house felt empty when I came back after. Emptier than usual and because I knew that was how it would always feel. For the rest of my life."

Because he pushed me away.

He gave me up himself.

Something presses in my throat, something prickly but I ignore it and say, "So you missed me."

His jaw moves back and forth as he watches me for a second before answering, in a very guttural voice, "Yeah, I missed you. I really fucking missed you."

At his frank, raw words, that thing in my throat grows but I tell myself to be strong. I tell myself to hold on.

Not yet.

"It's your own fault," I say.

Something about my fierce words makes him throw a lopsided, self-effacing smile. "I know."

"Don't expect any sympathy from me," I add just to drive my point home.

"No. Not in a million years."

I clench my teeth at his easy acceptance, his eagerness to take my anger. "I…"

I'm not sure what I was going to say because something occurs to me.

I remember something from the other night, the night I made graffiti on his truck – which is still there by the way. He hasn't even washed it off yet and just like the fact that he punched a hole in the wall because he missed me, I'm not letting that graffiti thing affect me either.

Instead, I spin around and make a beeline to his bedroom, leaving him to follow me.

Which he does.

As soon as I reach his bedroom, my heart starts beating so loudly, so roaringly that I think it will never stop. That my heart will go on beating even after I'm dead.

On buzzing legs, I walk up to the wall – the bare wall I was trying to paint for him – and press my hand on it. "Did you paint it?"

"Yeah," he replies from behind me.

When I left, the wall was half gray and half powder blue. Not to mention, there was a half-made cherry blossom tree that I was in the process of making.

For him.

I picked the cherry blossom because it indicates new beginnings.

New joys. New dreams.

Now the wall is all blue. The cherry blossom is as I left it though.

And it's as if he can hear my thoughts, he explains, "I couldn't..." I spin around at his voice and he continues, "I didn't know how to do what you do. So I left the cherry blossom alone."

"What do I do?"

"Make everything rosy and colorful." His eyes bore into mine. "Like you."

God.

I hate him. I hate him so much.

Because no matter what, no matter how much he hurts me, I can't stop loving him.

I can't squelch this longing inside my chest.

"You lied to me," I say, my voice wobblier than I'd like it to be. "You *lied*."

His features bunch up as he swallows. "Yeah."

"You tortured me for three weeks."

"I did."

"I'm not –"

"I have something for you," he says roughly, standing at the door.

"What?"

He thrusts his hand down his pocket and fishes something out. A folded paper. Or rather a bunch of folded papers. All crinkled at the edges. All untidy and somehow extremely precious to me, before he even tells me what they are.

Swallowing again, he says, "For days, I made you read those letters you wrote me. In my office. Every day, you'd stand there so bravely and read me your dreams. The things you thought about and I was... I'd be in awe of you. Of your courage. Of the fact that you trusted me with the most intimate parts of yourself." He pauses to clench his jaw before continuing, "I'm not that brave. I've never been. You were right that night. When you called me a coward. Because I'm that. I'm a coward. But..."

He pauses again and this time he looks down at those papers and I swear, I swear to God, I almost go to him.

I almost tell him that he doesn't have to do this.

He doesn't have to do something that makes his hands shake.

That makes a tremor go through his body.

Because that's what's happening right now.

He's shaking.

But he speaks before I can do anything. "But I've decided to be brave. I've decided to have courage. Because I want to tell you a story."

"What story?" I whisper.

His hands tremble some more as he says, "The story of how I lost my dreams and how I found them."

Then he glances down and opens those pages.

But apparently, he doesn't need them. Because when he begins, he looks up.

At me.

Into my eyes.

As if he has all the words of his story memorized.

"Bronwyn,

I'm not very good with words. Neither spoken nor written.

Usually, I just let my gestures talk. My clenched jaw. My eyebrows. My narrowed eyes.

You were right when you said that I stare people down like I want to crush them under my boots. I think I perfected that look back when I was ten or so.

Mostly because I had twin brothers who were two at the time and extremely difficult to reason with. So I had to develop a system to get them to listen.

But anyway that's not the point.

The point is that I'm not good at expressing myself. But I'm going to try.

So I can tell that I've always seen myself as a tree.

A sturdy, solid tree with a thick trunk and dependable branches. A tree that stands tall and strong through all seasons and weathers and years. And that stands still as the world goes on around it and that everyone comes to, to take shelter from the harsh sun.

I wish I could say that this imagery is mine but it's not; it's something that I saw in a storybook that I used to read to Callie when she was little. And when my mother died and I came back to take care of things, I'd look at that tree every night when everyone went to sleep.

I was trying to not sleep during those days, see.

I was trying to keep my eyes open at all times. Because when I closed them, I'd dream. I'd dream of New York City. I'd dream of the team that I left behind, all the trophies that I'd never win, the girl that I thought I wanted to spend my life with.

I'd dream of all the things that I didn't get to do, that I *wanted* to do.

Very, very badly.

So every night, when sleep threatened to put me under, I'd bust out that book, flip to the page where that tree was drawn and stare at it for hours.

I'd stare at it and stare at it.

Until it was burned in my brain.

Until I could sleep and only see that tree behind my closed eyes.

And I saw that tree for fourteen years.

But then I met someone.

A girl.

In the middle of the night, she sat on the side of the road, wearing a yellow ball gown, drawing roses on her thighs. She had rosy skin and big silver eyes. Her hair was long and Rapunzel like. That she initially had up in a very complicated bun before she chose to take it down and reveal it to me.

I thought she was a mermaid, that girl.

But she told me later that she was a flower.

A wallflower.

I guess it makes sense though. She is soft and velvet and sweet.

And colorful.

Anyway, we talked that night. She told me about her dreams, her passion. She reminded me of myself in some ways. She reminded me of my own passion, the fire that I had in me for my own dreams.

And maybe that's why when I walked her back home and left, I looked back.

I looked back to see her one last time.

She was nowhere to be found though. She vanished as abruptly as she had appeared before my eyes like a vision.

I thought of her often after that. I wondered if she managed to keep her passion alive in her. If she managed to keep that fire burning. Something that I couldn't do. Something that I wasn't *willing* to do.

I wondered if I'd ever see her again and then I did.

Eighteen months later.

In the most unlikely of places.

She stood before me on the soccer field, just like the last time, looking like a vision. Only this time she wore a school uniform and a long, thick braid. And for the first time in fourteen years, when I went to sleep that night, after seeing her again, I saw something behind my closed eyes.

A streak of yellow. A flash of Rapunzel hair. Big, beautiful silver eyes.

I'm not going to lie, it fucking terrified me. It sent me into a panic.

So much so that I woke up. I went for a run. And I think I ran for hours that night. And many other nights after that.

In fact that's what I've been doing ever since I saw her again.

I've been running. Both literally and figuratively.

Because she scared me, this girl.

Her courage. Her bravery. Her strength.

It scared me that she fights for the things she believes in. That she never ever gives up. That she somehow softens up the rough edges of my life.

That she dreams.

But more than that, I think I've been scared of the fact that she makes *me* dream.

And she makes me dream in a way that for the first time in fourteen years, I want to move. I want to walk. I want to forget that I'm a tree, rooted to a spot, standing still.

For the first time in fourteen years, I simply want to be a man.

A man who takes chances. A man who takes risks. Who steps into the unknown. Who walks on strange roads. Who's brave enough to make a few wrong turns and strong enough to keep walking until he finds the right path.

For the first time in fourteen years, I want to be a man who dreams.

Because that's what she does.

She inspires me to dream. Not to mention, she inspires me to be the kind of man that *she* dreams about.

So this is the story of how I lost my dreams and how a girl named Bronwyn helped me find them once again.

Yours, Conrad who you call thorn and who wishes and hopes and fucking dreams to call you his wallflower."

My sniffles are the only sound when he's done.

Which is then drowned out by the loud sounds of his footsteps. As he strides over to me. Like he was waiting, just waiting, for his story to be over so he can come to me.

I was waiting for that too.

For him to come.

For him to touch me.

To cradle my face like he's doing right now. To kiss my forehead with such affection and reverence like he just did while wiping my tears off.

"Bronwyn, please," he begs, his voice all rough and thick. "Stop crying, baby. Just stop crying. I'll do anything, okay? I'll fucking do anything you tell me to. Just stop crying. Stop crying, Bronwyn."

But more than that, I think I was waiting to touch *him*.

So I *grab* onto his wrists, onto him as I say, hiccupping, "It's your fault. It's all your fault. Y-You have done this."

He presses his palms on my cheeks, tipping my face up and breathing over my wet lips. "I know. I know it's my fault. And I'm going to make it up to you. I'm –"

I dig my nails in his wrist. "No. I don't want you to. I hate you. First for hurting me and then making me hurt *for you*."

Dropping his forehead on mine, he rasps, "That was not my intention. I didn't mean –"

"You looked back?" I ask, speaking over him, my teary eyes studying his tight features. "That night. When you dropped me off at home?"

His fingers flex on my cheeks at my question. "Yeah, I did. I looked back." Then, a moment later. "I think I told myself that I was doing it to make sure that you got inside okay. But I was…"

"You were what?"

He shakes his head slightly. "I just wanted to take another look at you. To make sure that you were real."

My heart squeezes in my chest. "And I inspire you."

At this, a fierce look enters his eyes, an emphatic look. "Yes. I know you always say that I've inspired you but that's not true, Bronwyn. It's never been true. I'm not inspiring, *you* are. It's because you can do anything you want, anything that you put your mind to. It's because every time I look at you, I see colors and I smell roses. It's because before I met you, I was barely alive. I was a dead man walking. But you managed to raise me from it. You managed to bring me back to life. You cast a spell and my lungs started breathing. My heart started beating. My heart started *feeling* and at first, it was painful. I thought that I'd explode. That my heart would burst and break into a million pieces with how much you made me feel. But again, somehow, *someway*, you managed to expand my heart too. You managed to make it bigger, stronger so that I could fit you. So that I could fit all the things you made me feel after fourteen years. So it's not me, baby. It's you."

Oh God.

I'm not… I'm not strong enough for this.

I'm not strong enough for him.

For the fact that I've heard countless stories where a muse inspires the artist. But I've never heard of one where the artist ends up inspiring the muse too.

And I don't know what to do with that. I don't know what to do when he makes me feel this way.

All soft and velvet like flowers. But also fierce and passionate.

So strong that I tell him, almost angrily, "You're *not* a tree."

"No."

"I won't let you be a tree, Conrad, okay?" I insist, my eyes boring into his. "I won't. I refuse."

His lips tip up again, as if he can't believe my fierce tone, as if he can't believe someone would use it for him, on his behalf.

"And I don't want to be," he replies, his grip still as strong. "I want to move. I want to walk. I want to be wherever you are. I want to go wherever you go." A thick emotion ripples through his features as he says, "To New York."

"What?"

He stares at me a beat. "I took the job."

I freeze for a second. Before my mouth falls open and I breathe out, "You took the job."

"It starts in the fall."

"No way."

His eyes turn slightly amused at my breathy tone. "Yeah."

And I go up on my tiptoes, my heart almost bursting out of my chest. "When?"

"A couple of days later," he says. "After I... After I lied and sent you away. I..." He takes a moment to gather his thoughts. "I came home that day from St. Mary's and punched the wall, I broke some furniture, turned everything upside down. But then, I... I brought out your sketches. The ones you made at practice. The ones you'd always show me and I'd always refuse to see, to hear what you were telling me. I brought them out and I couldn't stop looking at them. I couldn't stop hearing your voice, your *belief* in me, in the fact that I could... I could love my job. Something that I've always seen as a symbol of my failures. I couldn't play myself so now I teach. So I called them. I called them the very next day and I agreed to do a tour of the facility. And when I went there, I did all the things you told me to. I talked to the players. I talked about the game, the strategy, their strengths and weaknesses and how I could help them, guide them. How I could make them... better. And I let myself enjoy that for a second. I let myself *like* the fact that I'm helping them. And I-I realized that I do. I do enjoy that. I do enjoy being around the game, around the team. I do like teaching and bringing the best in them and I... You were right."

"I was right," I repeat.

"Yeah. I think I," he licks his lips, his eyes shiny, a tiny bit excited too, "I think I like it. I think I love it. I love what I do."

My heart is so light right now. So airy and happy.

So his.

"You took the job," I say again, this time my eyes filling up with the tears of joy.

"I did," he rasps, his own eyes liquid. "But not only because I love it. But also because it's in New York. It's where you're going."

And then it clicks.

I was so happy to hear that he took the job that he's clearly going to rock with his insane coaching skills, that I neglected one thing.

"So when you..." I frown up at him. "When you cornered me at that get-together to sing praises of your brother, you knew. You *knew* you were going to be in New York too."

"I did, yeah."

"But you still pushed me toward him."

His eyes flick back and forth between mine. "Yes. Because I thought I was doing the right thing."

"What if I'd agreed to your insane idea, huh?" I squeeze his wrists. "What then? You were going to watch me date your brother. In New York."

His jaw clenches and clenches before he somehow manages to say, "Yes. If it made you happy. If he gave you what you wanted and needed."

"And what about you?" I ask, shaking my head. "What would *you* have done while watching me be happy with your brother?"

It doesn't even take him a second to reply, "Dreamed about you."

"What?"

He comes to rest his forehead over mine as he says, "I would've dreamed about being with you. About touching you and kissing you and getting to love you. I would've watched you with my brother and dreamed about a life with you. I would've dreamed that it was me you'd chosen. Not him. Because when it comes to you, Bronwyn, I'm not afraid to dream anymore. I'm not afraid to dream about you even if you dream about someone else."

I close my eyes then.

I close them, clench them.

And just breathe for a second.

I let myself breathe and absorb his words before I open my eyes and ask, "Why?"

"Because you're my dream girl."

I press my forehead against his. "You think that you'll say all these things, the most wonderful things that a girl has ever heard and you'll write me a letter, again the most wonderful letter that anyone has ever written for a girl, and I'll forgive you?"

"No." He shakes his head. "And I don't want you to either."

"What does that mean?"

"It means that I don't want you to forgive me," he says, looking me in the eyes. "Until I earn it. Until I earn your forgiveness. Until I make you *believe* that I'm going to do everything that I can to make you happy. To make you smile, to make you laugh, to give you everything that you deserve. I know you said that you only want me. And Jesus Christ, I'm yours. I'm fucking yours, Bronwyn. Every inch of me. But I won't stop until I give you every star in the sky and every flower on the ground. I'm going to lay it all down at your feet. I'm going to decorate you like you decorate yourself. I'm going to earn you, Bronwyn. And I don't want you to forgive me until I've done all that."

God, he's an idiot, isn't he?

He is.

And I'm in love with him.

Completely and irrevocably.

"You want to earn me," I say, moving away from him slightly and trying to look all serious.

He rubs his thumbs over my cheeks. "Yes."

I keep my eyes narrowed and bratty even. "Are you a hard worker?"

His own fill with tenderness at my question.

At the memory of me saying those words to him back when I was trying to seduce him. Back when I was trying to convince him that I'm a good girl and so he should let me suck his cock.

"Yes," he says, his voice all serious-like even though his eyes are all soft. "I was a straight A student and the captain of my soccer team." Then, "With a perfect strike record."

Of course.

My hardworking baby.

"A fast learner?"

"Fuck yes. I once had to cover a friend's shift at the restaurant where I worked. He was a bartender and by the end of the night, I was mixing up drinks while juggling three bottles."

"You were not," I say, all impressed.

He throws me a lopsided smile. "I was."

"That is impossible."

"Is it?"

I shake my head at him, a smile threatening to break out. "So basically, you're the good guy of Bardstown, huh?"

"Yes I am."

"Except when you distract me from my work."

"Except then, yeah."

Sighing, I let go of his wrists and bring my arms up, winding them around his neck. "Fine. You can."

"I can what?"

"Call me *your* wallflower," I say, burying my fingers in his long-ish hair, referring to the last sentence in his letter.

His own hands move then.

And in turn, come to bury themselves in my hair. "Yeah?"

"Yes." I press my body to his. "I wasn't ready to hear it before. I was too mad. But I'm thawing a little."

"So does it mean that I'm doing a good job?" he rasps, his fingers flexing in my hair. "Of earning my wallflower's forgiveness."

"Yes." I nod. "But if you ever, ever, hurt me or lie to me like that again, Conrad, I will –"

"No," he speaks over me, his voice, his eyes, even his fingers all grave and serious. "Never. Not like that."

"Promise?"

"Yeah, baby. Pinky promise."

I finally smile and something breaks loose on his face, his body. He loses his tightness, that edge that he was on ever since we'd arrived at his house and presses his body to mine in response.

"Tell me," I whisper, my heart beating and *beating* in my chest.

I don't have to explain myself to him or what I want because he understands.

Like he always does.

And tells me, "I love you."

I have to part my lips then.

At his thick, raspy words.

At the sheer, raw love on his features as he continues, "I'm in love with you. I've probably been in love with you for a long time. I just..."

"You're just an idiot," I complete his thread for him.

A lopsided smile. "Yeah, I'm a fucking idiot for taking so long to realize it."

"And to even think that I'd ever choose anyone else let alone your brother," I tell him then, with all the love in my voice and my eyes. "Because I love you too. And I choose you. Now and forever."

His nostrils flare at my words. His chest shifts with a breath. His stomach hollows.

It's like he's absorbing my words now.

My love for him.

"Forever," he repeats like I did back at my house.

"Yeah, forever."

And then we seal our promise to each other with a kiss.

A lovely, rosy, thorn kiss.

# EPILOGUE

Two months later

"I have something to tell you," I say, as soon as Callie shuts the door to her room and turns around to face me.

Her eyes narrow at my words. She also folds her arms across her chest as she asks, "Does it have anything to do with why you came here in Con's truck?"

Shit.

"You saw that?"

"Yes." She raises her eyebrows. "I also noticed that his very black and very masculine truck has splotches of pink paint on it. *Pink*," she pauses to let it take effect, "being your favorite color."

Yikes.

The remnants of my graffiti that I made for Conrad two months ago. I keep telling him that he needs to take care of it and get it out completely but he doesn't listen.

But whatever.

Right now I'm more concerned about the fact that this isn't going as I planned.

And I swear I planned.

That's why as soon as I got here, to her house that she's lived in since she got pregnant, I told her that I wanted to talk to her. And that I wanted to do it in private. Hence we're in her room.

I clear my throat before saying, "I wouldn't say that pink is my favorite color per se. I like it but I also think that –"

"Wyn," she cuts me off.

Which is just as well because I don't know why I was saying that. Pink *is* my favorite color and I'm so done hiding things from her.

So fucking done.

School's been over for a month, and I've been waiting and waiting to share all my secrets with her.

And finally the time is here but I'm a little freaked out. And it doesn't help that with her blue eyes pinned on me like that, she totally looks like her brother.

Her oldest brother.

The one I'm in love with, albeit secretly.

Although I do have to say that it's only a secret from Callie. The rest of the world, all my St. Mary's friends, her other brothers, Reed even, know.

So taking a deep breath, I blurt out, "I'm in love."

"What?"

Damn it.

I should've said the whole thing. That I'm in love with one of her brothers.

I take another deep breath and walk up to her. She watches me with suspicion. Especially when I put my hands on her shoulders and tell her, "Can we please sit down?"

I don't wait for her answer. I simply direct her to the bed and give her a gentle nudge so she takes a seat.

"Okay, I'm sitting now," Callie says, her hands in her lap. "Are you going to tell me?"

Choosing to stand, I wring my hands and nod. "Yes." Then, "So do you remember the man that we used to talk about? The one I met the summer before I was sent to St. Mary's. The one who told me to follow my dreams and later I drew, you know, graffiti on my dad's car. Because I was feeling inspired."

"Yes. Your dream man."

I swallow when she says that. "Right. So that man, I met him again."

Her blue eyes go wide. "Shut up. You did?!"

"Yeah."

"And?"

Okay, the moment is here – actually, literally right here – and I just jump into it. "He's your brother. Conrad. And I'm in love with him."

I thought her eyes would go wider at this. Or she'd flinch or blink or squeal at the information I've given her. But all she does is stare at me silently, her eyes unwavering before she says, "Tell me everything. Right now."

And I do.

I tell her everything. Every *single* thing that I have been keeping from her. From the fact that when I saw him for the first time on the soccer field, I started an argument with him to get him to notice me and he took away my privileges the next day, to the fact that he was still in love with his old girlfriend who happened to be one of the teachers. Or rather he thought that he still was. I also tell her about the days when I thought he didn't love me and that I'd forever be without him. And then I end with the fact that he got arrested because of me and how Reed came to the rescue.

In more ways than one actually.

Because Reed not only got that file on my dad – I asked Conrad specifically to tell me what was in there and after multiple attempts he divulged that there was evidence against my dad regarding evidence tampering, witness tampering, bribery and whatnot – but he was also the one who bailed Conrad out.

Which finally solved the mystery of why my father was so angry that day when he was talking on the phone. Something that Martha shared with me while sharing the news of Conrad's release. Not to mention, it makes me think that maybe my dad was lying to me about letting Conrad go. Maybe he had no intention of doing so and that's why he got so furious when Conrad was bailed out anyway.

When I'm done, Callie simply breathes, her hands tight in her lap, her frown thick.

And I let her.

I let her absorb all this information, the months' worth of secrets. But when seconds and minutes pass without a word from her, I get anxious.

So much so that I can't stay silent myself. "I know this is a lot. I know that. And I swear I wanted to tell you. So many times. I swear, Callie. I just…" I shake my head, my eyes stinging. "At first I thought he didn't remember me and so I thought it didn't matter. And when I found out that he did, I just… I'd hid so many things from you by then and I didn't know how to tell you. The more time passed, the more scared I got and I'm sorry. I'm so *so* sorry, Callie. And I ..." I sigh, clasping my hands in front of me. "I just love him. I love Conrad so much."

She finally looks at me, her eyes grave. "Is that why you were so sad? All those months."

I bite my lip. "Yes."

"Because he thought he loved... Miss Halsey. And all that other crap."

"Sort of, yeah."

Her lips purse. "So he made you cry."

"What?"

She shakes her head, her fingers fisted now. "My brother, the brother I always thought was so good and amazing and wonderful, made you cry. He made my best friend cry. Because of his stupid stuff. I can't... I can't believe it."

I finally take a seat beside her. "Callie, no. It's not his fault. Well, some of it is. Like at the end. But he's not –"

"My brother is an asshole, isn't he?" she breathes, still shaking her head. "He's *exactly* like my other brothers. He's exactly like Reed. Oh my God, that's why he hates Reed so much. Because Con is an asshole himself. Oh my *God*."

"Callie, no, listen –"

"You know what, I'm going to go talk to him," she says, ready to get up. "I'm going to give him a piece of my mind."

But I stop her.

I grab her hands in her lap and say, "Callie, listen to me. Listen, okay? You're not going to talk to him. Because everything is fine now. It's all in the past. Whatever happened. And all the stuff that he did, pushing me away and whatnot, he did it not because he's a bad guy. He did it because he thought he was doing the right thing. And it made me angry, yes. But it's over now. It's over. He won't hurt me. Not like that. In fact, he takes care of me. And I'm really happy, Callie. He makes me happy. And I think... I think I make him happy too. I think I give your brother joy and I really wanted to do that. I really wanted to make him happy and smile and laugh and just make him live his life, you know? And he makes me live mine. He accepts me and supports me and *believes* in me. He loves me." I squeeze her hands. "So yeah, everything is fine. I'm just... I just don't want you to be mad about this. I don't want to lose you. You're my best friend and –"

That's when Callie hugs me.

She hugs me tightly and I do the same.

"You're not going to lose me," she says, moving away, her eyes wet. "You're never going to lose me, Wyn. You're my best friend too. I love you. I'm just so sad that you never told me. That you even doubted for a second that I'd leave you or be mad at you."

I swallow, blinking away my own tears. "I guess... I never had a lot of friends before St. Mary's. I never had people who understood me or who supported me. And I was so afraid that I'd lose it. That I'd go back to being all alone like I was in my town and..."

This time her anger is for my town as she says, "Your parents are assholes."

The subject of my parents is still painful.

It still twists my heart and makes me cry.

It's been two months since I walked out of that party with Conrad. And since then, I haven't heard a word from them. Not during that last month at St. Mary's. Not even when my finals were done, and the school was over.

I thought my parents would at least contact me then. After the finals I mean. Not to welcome me back home from the dorms – I already knew that they wouldn't; not after how I left the party with Conrad in front of everyone – but to at least, talk to me or say something about graduating high school.

But they didn't.

And they haven't yet.

It's like I'm dead to them.

I take another deep breath to will the pain away. The utter sadness that my parents would probably never talk to me again. Not to mention, I try to ignore the fact that after everything they've done to me and to Conrad specifically, I'm still such an idiot that I miss them.

"I'm just..." I begin, sighing and this time, Callie grabs my hands to give me the strength that I need. "It's still hard for me to believe that my dad got him arrested. It's just so surreal to me."

And the fact that my father has been involved in such illegal things.

God.

It's like I never knew my dad. Or maybe I did. I just didn't want to see it.

"Oh and Miss Halsey," Callie goes. "I can't believe she *told* on you guys. And to your dad. I mean wow. That obnoxious freaking *rat*. If I'd known. I would've taken her down. I swear to God."

It's not a surprise that Callie, my best friend, would say this. Because my other best friends, Poe and Salem, have said similar things when they found out what Helen had done.

In fact, I had to actively stop Poe – *multiple times* – from pranking Helen at school.

First, because Poe was already – *is* already – in a lot of trouble. Gosh, I feel so bad about her and her situation right now. And second because according to Conrad, he'd already taken care of it, of Helen.

Even though it was a little hard for me to believe in the beginning. That Helen would stay quiet and not try to go after us again.

She didn't though.

Which is a good thing for many, many reasons.

One of them being that the last month at St. Mary's was... tough.

I got to go back to St. Mary's, yes – all thanks to Conrad – and I'm so grateful for that because I know I would've missed my best friends. But as I always knew would happen, there were rumors.

People had already seen Conrad being taken away. And then *I* was taken away later that day in my dad's car, and I didn't come back until a couple of days later.

So yeah there were rumors and questions.

It's actually a wonder that Callie hadn't figured it all out before I told her. But I guess her pregnancy has been difficult on and off and that kept her occupied those last few weeks.

But I have to say that as difficult as those last weeks were, there were some silver linings.

Like for example, Principal Carlisle took over my counseling so I didn't have to see Helen. Which worked out great because even though I had stopped my friends from taking any sort of drastic action against Helen, I don't know what I would've done if I had come in direct contact with her.

I'm not a violent person but just the thought that she tried to hurt Conrad makes me boil with rage.

So much rage.

But anyway like I stopped my friends, I stopped myself as well.

Especially because I didn't want to create another scandal when we'd barely managed to come out unscathed from the previous one.

*Especially* because not only did I get to go back to St. Mary's, but Conrad also got to stay on the faculty for those last weeks.

This was not an easy feat at all though.

I first had to convince him to come back. Which he wasn't ready to do because of our relationship. But when I explained and re-explained how his absence might affect Callie – whom we were still keeping in the dark because of her pregnancy and stuff – he agreed.

And then there was Principal Carlisle.

She wasn't in favor of this at all. In fact she even involved the new principal in this decision, Principal Marshall.

When I heard of that, I lost hope. After so many stories about Mr. Marshall from Poe, I thought he'd never agree to this in a million years.

But somehow, he did.

He agreed to bring Conrad on for the last few weeks. As long as Conrad promised to not have any interaction with me during school hours and my grades were handled by Coach TJ.

"I know," I say, squeezing Callie's hands. "I'm just glad that it's over. I'm glad Helen didn't do anything. Conrad got to keep his job. And that my dad seems to have backed off as well."

Along with not contacting me, my parents – my dad specifically – haven't contacted or gotten in touch with Conrad either. They haven't done anything to harm Conrad or hurt his reputation.

Sort of like Helen.

"All thanks to your Reed," I continue.

Which makes her blush and whisper, "He's pretty amazing, isn't he?"

I smile. "He totally is. I always told you."

Oh, Callie and Reed are totally back together now. In fact, they're married; they got married a couple of days ago.

Something that I really, *really* wished for. Because not only Reed is amazing, but he's also perfect for my best friend. He makes her happy like Conrad makes me happy. And I'm just so ecstatic that they were able to put their differences aside and come together.

Oh and another happy news: they have a baby!

A baby girl named Halo.

She's five weeks old and she's the most precious baby ever. With the most loving parents in the world. Both Callie and Reed are super crazy for her. As I knew they would be. I knew they would make the best parents and they do.

So now they're a happy family of three.

Suddenly Callie beams, squeezing my hands. "My brother is your dream man."

I chuckle at her excitement like it's only now hitting her. "I know."

"This is incredible," she breathes out, shaking her head in disbelief. "Oh my God. This is like a fairy tale. This is like... magic. All this time. I mean we talked and talked about him and turns out, it's my brother. It's Con."

"Yeah." I shake my head too. "It's crazy. It's perfect. *He's* perfect."

Callie giggles. "This is the best thing ever. You're dating my brother."

I laugh. "I so am."

Then she gets serious. "Is that why he's been so happy? It is, isn't it?" She swallows. "He smiles more. I've noticed that. And he has this lightness about him. Like he's not so uptight and angry all the time. It's you, isn't it?"

I bite my lip. "I'd like to think so."

"God, Wyn." She hugs me again. "Thank you. Thank you so, so much for doing that for my brother. If anyone needed it, it was Con." Then, moving away, she swats my arm. "I can't believe you didn't tell me. I could've known all this time. I could've helped you even."

"I promise to tell you all the things from now on," I say, chuckling.

"You better."

With one last hug, we both get up and leave to rejoin the others in the living room. And as soon as we get there, my heartbeats jack up.

My skin breaks out in goosebumps. My thighs buzz and sting, especially where I decorated them last night. Under his heavy, intense, *heated* scrutiny.

Because there he is.

The man whose name is written on my skin.

And it's not just the fact that he's mine now – completely and utterly mine – that makes my heart go crazy. It's also the fact that he has something in his arms.

Or rather someone.

Baby Halo.

Who's sleeping on him, on his chest.

So Conrad has this magic touch. Whenever Halo is crying or fussing and Conrad is around, he takes her in his arms, sits down on the couch, all sprawled and lazy, and rubs her back in circles.

Five circles in, her big blue eyes start to droop. Her cute little mouth falls open and her fists go slack. And then she goes out like a champ and looking at her like that, all sleepy and flushed and so quiet, you wouldn't even know that she was fussing minutes before.

Now as well, Conrad is on the couch and Halo is peacefully sleeping on his big chest, her small, chubby arms spread wide and sort of hugging her uncle. And her uncle has his gorgeous face dipped, his dirty blond hair hanging over his forehead and his cheek resting on Halo's dark-haired head as he simply breathes.

But when he senses me there, at the threshold, he looks up.

I smile as soon as his jean blue eyes hit me.

Only so I can assure him that everything went fine.

Because he was worried on the way over. Not of Callie's reaction but because I was going to be the one talking to her instead of him. Which is what he wanted to do initially. But I insisted that she was my friend and I wanted it to be me so he gave in.

Now he slowly stands, with Halo in his arms, who is then taken away from him by Reed. Actually, Reed jumps to take Halo away like he was looking for an opportunity to hold his daughter himself.

See? Totally gone for his baby girl.

As soon as Halo is out of Conrad's arms, Callie says in a low voice so as to not disturb Halo, "You and me, we're going to talk." Pointing her finger at her oldest brother, she continues, "You're a jerk, Con. Seriously. I never expected these things from you."

Which makes Reed chuckle as he takes over the duty of rubbing Halo's back. And also, Ledger who's sitting on the other end of the couch, playing with his phone; he's visiting from New York.

Callie glares at Reed. "You're no better." Then addressing Ledger, "You're actually the worst, Ledge. At least these two had the guts to accept their feelings in the end. But not you. You can't handle the fact that you've got *feelings*. For a girl."

At this Reed covers Halo's ears as he says, sort of in disbelief, "This asshole has feelings. For a girl. What girl?"

Callie shakes her head at Reed. "You're clueless, aren't you?"

Because Reed totally is.

The girl Callie is talking about is his own sister, Tempest.

While Ledger snaps, albeit on a lower voice too, "Shut the fuck up, Callie."

And so ensues their argument but I don't pay attention to them.

Because Conrad has started to move.

He's started to approach me, and my smile starts to grow.

By the time he reaches me, I'm grinning. Which sort of eases his tension; I can see that. But he still asks, his eyes roving over my face, "You okay?"

I put my hands on his chest. "Yeah. It's over."

"It is, huh," he murmurs.

Because it truly *is* over.

There are no more secrets now.

None.

And I'm so glad about that. *So* glad. Because Conrad – after a lot of poking and prodding –shared everything about his relationship with Helen and how they had to hide way back when, and how he used to hate that.

It broke my heart. That he had to hide.

That *we* had to hide as well.

But now everyone knows about us.

Even the boys on his team. The Bardstown High team that he's been coaching as a favor this summer. Even they know who I am and why I sit on the bleachers and watch the practice with a sketchpad in my lap.

Not that he needs it now.

For me to show him how utterly magnificent he looks while coaching soccer, guiding his students.

And playing with them.

Because he did last week. He played with his students and it was amazing. The boys were happy; they'd never had the opportunity to play with or just have fun with their coach. And I was happy too. Not only because I'd been trying to convince him to do that for ages but also because God, the way he moved.

The way he dominated and owned that field, all powerful and graceful like.

It really turned me on.

So much so that I jumped his bones as soon as we got back home.

"Now everyone knows." I beam. "And my best friend doesn't hate me."

He puts his hands on my waist. "Of course she doesn't."

Frowning, I tell him, "She kinda hates you a little though."

His features tighten up as he replies gravely, "As she should."

I fist his white shirt. "No, she shouldn't. I told her."

His fingers flex on my waist. "Told her what?"

Taking a step closer to him, I crane my neck up. "That you make me happy. And that you take care of me."

"I always will," he says like he always says these words: as a promise.

He does.

I mean he's always been super protective. But I didn't know the extent of his protectiveness until I graduated from St. Mary's and actually moved in with him.

While my parents chose to abandon me, Conrad chose to wait for me. Outside of those black metal gates the day I got out of St. Mary's.

So he could take me away. So he could bring me home.

To his old house.

That we have since painted and made new.

Even though we wouldn't be staying there for long. Since we're both moving to New York in a couple of months, me for my art school and him for his new job. But Conrad wanted to update the house since it's always been theirs and he wants himself and his siblings to have a home in Bardstown if we or they ever choose to return.

Anyway, I didn't know how sweet he could be. How caring. How gentle and wonderful.

Until I started living with him.

Especially when I cry about my parents. When I get sad that they would never accept me for who I am. That they would never accept him.

He holds me then, on those days and nights.

Even though it makes him angry, my sadness, my tears. It makes him want to rage and go to my parents and shake some sense into them. Because that's how he is, all protective and loyal, my thorn.

But he lets go of his own anger and gives me what I need.

He hugs me, whispers sweet nothings in my ears. He even draws baths for me, scatters rose petals in the water, lights up candles to soothe me. He promises me that one day I'll stop crying for them. He'll make it so. He'll fill my life with so much happiness that I won't even feel the pain.

Which makes me cry even more.

Because he's so clueless, isn't he?

My life is already so happy.

Because he's already made it so.

"I also told her that I make you happy," I whisper then.

At this, his eyes turn soft. "Yeah, you do."

"She thinks these days you smile more."

"Yeah?"

"Uh-huh. I totally agree. You look very handsome when you smile." I step even closer to him so I can whisper, "And I'm not going to lie. It totally turns me on."

He smirks, his fingers going tight on my waist as he drags me even closer, bringing our bodies flush together. "Maybe that's the reason then. That's why I smile. To turn you on."

"So I jump your bones?"

"Fuck yeah."

I chuckle and press a soft kiss on his smooth, hard jaw. "Also you really need to get rid of that lingering pink paint from your truck. Even Callie thinks that it looks weird on your manly black truck."

He dips his face toward me, his lips ever so closer. "Well then you should tell her that I'm not too manly for pink. And neither am I too manly for flowers. Either loving them. Or drawing them."

I clench my thighs then.

Because he's right.

He's so totally not too manly for either pink or flowers.

Because he drew one – a pink flower – on my body last night. Before he loved the one that's in between my thighs.

Actually he's drawn several of them over the past few weeks.

Now along with writing his name on my skin, he draws on it as well. On my thighs, my belly, my breasts, my collar bones, the back of my knee, the back of my neck. And then once he's done, he loves me and fucks me all gently like I'm really a flower.

And when *that* is done, it's my turn.

To draw on him.

To paint him with colors.

In fact, I made a pretty little rose on his right shoulder blade last night and colored it pink.

"You do know though that you suck at drawing, don't you?" I ask, raising my eyebrows.

Oh, he totally does.

He's the worst with drawing. Or anything artistic.

He squeezes my waist. "You mean like you suck at soccer."

I chuckle. "Yes. You're as good at art as I'm at soccer." Then, "But I love it. When you draw on my body."

"I know," he rasps.

I go to say something but a voice cuts through the moment. Ledger's.

"Get a room, you two."

Oh shit.

I'd completely forgotten that we weren't alone.

I mean that's nothing new. I always forget the world when I'm in his arms. But now as I look around, Callie and Reed are gone but Ledger is still on the couch, and I blush.

Conrad notices my red cheeks and without taking his eyes off me, he addresses Ledger, "Go away."

Which Ledger does a second later, grumbling.

Gosh I love how dominating Conrad is. And how all his siblings jump to do his bidding at his one word.

My thorn.

I throw him a mock frown then, tightening my fists in his shirt. "Oh no, not Ledger. I liked when he was here."

That gets me the reaction I was looking for.

Growly and jealous.

Which is so ridiculous. Especially when I've already explained it to him the reason why Ledger asked me out in the first place.

Just after he took me away from my parents' party and we got together, the topic of Ledger came up – Conrad wanted to talk to him – and I told him that there was no need for that. Because there was no way Ledger had any interest in me. He likes Tempest. Who apparently likes him back as well. Only Ledger hasn't gotten his shit together yet as Callie said.

But anyway, since then Conrad *has* had a talk with Ledger – despite my protestations – and Ledger *has* explained to Conrad as well that he didn't mean anything by it and that Ledger was happy for the both of us.

But still my thorn gets prickly when Ledger's around. And since I'm his flower, a slightly naughty flower, I try to take advantage of it.

His hand moves up and makes a fist in my hair, pulling my head back. "Stop talking."

Clenching my thighs again, I smile slowly. "You're so easy."

His eyes narrow. "I don't like the way he looks at you."

I chuckle because he's crazy.

And so adorable.

So I give him another soft kiss. "He doesn't look at me at all. He likes someone else, remember? I told you. Even Callie talked about it just now."

His eyes remain narrowed and his grip in my hair tightens even more. "Yeah, no. I don't think I believe that. I haven't noticed anything."

"That's because you never notice anything other than me," I tell him.

At this, he loses his frown and hums. "Yeah, that may be the case."

"And because you're fucking clueless."

At the F word, his body goes all tight, his eyes turning bright and dominating. "Language."

Oh God.

He should seriously stop being so sexy. We're at his sister's house.

"What about it?" I ask, twisting my fists in his shirt.

"Watch it."

I bite my lip to control my smile. "Why, because you've got a sister my age?"

He bends down slightly, as if to intimidate me. "No because I said so."

I widen my eyes. "Yes, sir."

A shudder runs through him then, his fingers flexing in my hair, my waist where he's still holding me all possessively. "You remember what I told you? About you calling me sir."

Peering at him through my eyelashes, I nod. "You said that if I ever called you sir again, you'd make sure that that's what I call you forever."

"Yeah."

Suddenly something occurs to me.

Something naughty.

And it's not my fault that it did.

It's him.

It's because he's just so... fucking sexy and authoritative and dominating.

Going up on my tiptoes, I bring my lips up to his and whisper, "But what if I call you something else?"

"What?"

I bite my lip, pondering if I should.

A second later, I go for it. "Something that starts with a D."

He frowns in confusion, and I swear I burst out laughing then and there. But I need to hold on. I need to shock him a little. If I didn't, then I wouldn't be trouble.

For him.

Now, would I?

So I stretch myself up further and bring my lips to his ear. And then I tell him what I'll call him. The word that starts with a D and ends with a Y.

And he goes still.

Like completely and utterly still.

Moving back, I look at his face. It's blank, his eyes cool. Except for a clenched jaw – really clenched jaw – there is no movement on his face.

Yikes.

I think I crossed a line here, didn't I?

Fuck.

"Conrad, I was kidding, okay?" I tell him. "I totally was. I was just trying to shock you. You don't have to freak out. I swear. I –"

He cuts me off by letting go of me and moving away.

I open my mouth to calm him down again. But he grabs my hand, rather tightly, before calling out, "We're leaving."

And then he pulls on my arm and starts walking, jogging almost, dragging me behind him and that's when I burst out laughing. He brings me to his truck and opens the door. Putting his hands on my waist, he picks me up and almost dumps me on the seat but before he can get away, I grab his collar and keep him.

"You liked that, huh?" I whisper, smiling.

The blue in his eyes is all gone now, replaced by black. "We're going home."

Home.

Yeah, where we live together, him and I.

All cozy and comfy.

I move his long-ish hair out of those pretty, lusty eyes. "I love you."

They do go tender at my soft declaration for a second and he picks up the necklace with pink stones that he gave me a few days ago and pulls on it, bringing me in for a long, wet kiss. At the end of which, he rasps, "I love you too, baby."

I smile at his endearment before I order, "Okay, take me home. And get your game face on. Be all angry and growly. Be my thorn."

He kisses me again before he asks in an amused voice, "Yeah? Why?"

"So you can teach your wallflower all the lessons," I whisper against his lips.

At this, his kiss turns shaky.

Because *he* turns shaky.

Because he's laughing.

I can't believe he's *laughing* while kissing me. This is supposed to be romantic and sexy.

But it's okay.

I love when he laughs. I love when he kisses me.

I love him.

The Original Thorn

Once upon a time, I was afraid to dream.

Because I thought the pain wasn't worth it. The pain wasn't worth the euphoria of dreaming. The agony wasn't worth the ecstasy of hope.

But then I met this girl. On the side of the road at midnight. Or rather 11:15 PM.

She looked like a dream and I was on a quest to punish myself for dreaming.

It's quite poetic.

As she would say.

She'd probably even draw something in her sketchpad to depict the moment. Because that's who she is.

She's an artist.

She's colorful and imaginative. She's made of roses and pink glitter. She clinks when she walks and her skin is like gossamer.

She's art itself.

The girl who makes me laugh. Who makes me dream.

The girl I'm in love with.

My wallflower. My Bronwyn.

THE END
(For Conrad and Bronwyn)

# POE

*When: Mr. Marshall's first appearance in the cafeteria*
*Where: St. Mary's School for Troubled Teenagers*

I'm going to kill him.

I am.

I know people think I'm joking. But I'm not.

I'm serious.

I'm super fucking serious.

Now more so than ever.

I just have to find him first. The asshole, the fucking devil, who sent me here, to St. Mary's.

I'm standing at the threshold of the cafeteria, where Principal Carlisle just announced that she'll be leaving at the end of the term and the devil himself will be replacing her as the new principal.

New principal.

Him.

The nerve of him.

The fucking nerve.

I run my eyes around, trying to find him – it shouldn't be hard. The man is as tall as a freaking building. A boring, vintage... *stupid* building.

And I'm right. About being easily able to find him I mean.

Because there he is, standing in front of the principal's office, wearing his boring tweed jacket with elbow patches, talking to Principal Carlisle.

Fisting my hands, I stride over to him, practically bulldozing through people in my hurry to get to him.

To get to his very sculpted and broad jaw that seems perpetually clenched.

So I can punch him there.

As soon as I get close enough, Principal Carlisle glances over to me and a sigh escapes her. That's her go to reaction when it comes to me: Poe Austen Blyton, the troublemaker of St. Mary's.

Well that's everyone's go to reaction when they see me.

Except for my girls here.

I don't let it bother me too much right now though; I'm here on a mission.

"Good morning, Principal Carlisle," I say cheerfully. "May I have a word with Mr. Marshall here?"

I can sense his eyes on me, dark and beady and yes, stupid.

But I'm not looking at him until I'm good and ready. Let him wait on tenterhooks.

She sighs again and looks at the devil for a second before coming back to me. "All right. But Poe, I want you to behave."

I keep my smile on as I reach up and draw an imaginary halo over my head. "Of course. Consider me the angel of peace and serenity for the rest of the day."

Another sigh. Then she glances over at the man beside me and nods. "I'll leave you to it."

With that, she walks away and then there are two of us. I mean if you don't count the rest of the student body population coming and going in the hallway.

Taking a deep breath, I finally, *finally* turn to him.

And tighten my fists even more.

Because I was lying before, okay?

I was lying.

His eyes aren't beady or stupid.

His eyes are... pretty.

His eyes are dark and shiny and beautiful. Soulful.

You know the kind of eyes that tell you that they've seen things and done things and felt things? His eyes are like that.

They're also dark brown like chocolate and I used to love chocolate.

Until him.

Now I hate it because I hate him.

I hate how pretty his eyes are.

"Hey, Mr. Marshall," I say. "Long time, no see."

I want him to sigh like Principal Carlisle just did. I really do.

Or at least shake in his brown leather boots from fear.

But he doesn't.

He doesn't sigh or shake or show any kind of reaction at my presence or my overly cheerful greeting. Except, "Poe."

Again something I hate.

That he is so unshakable.

So calm and cool.

In the face of trouble aka me.

"Can we talk?" I ask him with raised eyebrows.

He runs his eyes over my face for a second or two before nodding and reaching over to open the door to the principal's office. "After you."

I take a deep breath again and step into the room. When I hear him come in and close the door, I spin around. "What are you doing here?"

Standing at the door, he runs his eyes over my face again, all cool-like. "Talking to Principal Carlisle." Then, "Or rather was talking to Principal Carlisle."

"Cut the bullshit, okay? What the fuck are you doing here? At St. Mary's."

It looks like he was expecting this question because he leans against the door and folds his arms across his chest as if settling in for a long debate with me before saying, "I know you think this is a part of my diabolical plan of ruining your life but –"

"Diabolical?" I scoff before running my eyes over him, his body.

From the top of his rich dark hair that has a tendency to curl to his dark eyes. Before going to his massive shoulders and that dark gray tweed jacket that should look boring and it does.

But for some reason, it also makes me curious.

It has always made me curious.

About things like are his shoulders really that broad and what about his chest? Is it really that muscular or is that padding underneath that old-fashioned suit jacket?

And every time I think that I want the lightning to strike me down

The fact that I'm *wondering* about the enemy.

"You don't have the panache or the personality for that," I tell him, injecting as much venom in my voice and my features as possible. "You need a certain flair to pull something diabolical off."

My words don't affect him at all as he murmurs, "Something that you clearly have."

I shrug. "Clearly."

He hums, staring at me. "Well not everyone can be as diabolical and stylish as you are, Poe."

I narrow my eyes at him. While he keeps them all calm and composed with a very slight hint of amusement.

"Why are you here?" I ask again.

"Leah is a friend," he says. "She told me she was planning to quit as soon as possible and I offered to fill in the position. Until they can find someone permanent. Which should be by the fall I think."

I know Leah is his friend.

That's the whole reason he sent me here almost three years ago. When he realized that he couldn't handle being the guardian of an unruly fifteen-year-old girl.

"Are you the reason then?" I ask, clenching my teeth. "For my graduation being... stopped."

He is, isn't he?

I've been wondering and wondering since I found out a couple of days ago. That I won't be graduating with the rest of my classmates.

That I'm the victim of The Unspeakable.

Something that never happens at St. Mary's. Or rather it happens extremely rarely.

I mean it's so rare that even my guidance counselor – the woman who absolutely hates me – was shocked when she informed me of this yesterday. She said that I needed to talk to Principal Carlisle about this. And that she'd help me if she could.

Which moved me, I'm not going to lie.

It brought tears to my eyes but since I don't cry in front of people, I simply sprung up from my seat and left.

I was planning on talking to Principal Carlisle this morning but before I could do that, came *this* hellish announcement that Mr. Marshall, my fucking evil guardian, is going to be the new principal.

"Your graduation isn't stopped," he informs me. "It's merely being delayed."

"And you're responsible for it, right?"

"No. Your grades are."

I growl. "Are you... Are you fucking serious right now?"

He simply blinks. "There's a minimum requirement to be able to graduate. And you're falling short of it. As long as you attend summer classes, maintain the grades and retake the tests at the end, you should be fine."

"What is wrong with you?" I burst out. "No one and I mean, *no one* in the last decade has attended summer school at St. Mary's. Do you understand what that means? Are you saying that every single one of those girls had the minimum grades?" I shake my head. "People graduate on time at this school. Because this isn't a normal school. This is a fucking prison. And you want me to stay here for another three months. I mean, seriously. What the hell is wrong with you?"

At this he does sigh.

But I'm not happy.

Because I don't think it's the sign that he's tired of me. It's more of an indication that he's patient. Like he can do this all day long, fight with me and argue with me and I'm the one wasting my time because I won't come out as a winner.

"I understand that this is unusual," he begins. "But it's for your own good. Your grades and your performance have been abysmal. It would be a disservice to you if we sent you to college without helping you improve."

I want to stomp my foot at how serious and concerned he sounds.

Like he *cares* what happens to me.

If he did, he wouldn't have sent me here. He wouldn't have taken everything from me.

He wouldn't have taken *him* from me.

The boy I loved.

"Principal Carlisle would have," I say then. "As much as she hates me, she never would have let this happen. She never would've *forced* me to stay here at St. Mary's."

At this, he moves away from the door and thrusts his hands down his pockets. "Well, Principal Carlisle isn't your principal anymore. I am and I'm not going to overlook the protocol. As I said, your graduation has merely been delayed. You want to graduate, then show up for classes, do your homework, be on your best behavior and pass the tests. If you've done all that, you're free to leave this place at the end of the summer."

With that, he walks further into the room and rounds the desk. He's going for a bunch of files when someone knocks at the door and he calls for them to come in. They tell him that his stuff is here and he nods. "I'll be there in a second. Thank you."

I was still reeling from his whole 'you want to graduate, then do these things,' but now I've got something else to worry about.

Frowning at him, I ask, "What's happening? What stuff?"

He keeps me in suspense for a second or two before leveling me with his dark gaze and replying, "I'm moving."

"Moving where?"

"On campus."

"What?"

Another sigh and again it's not because he's tired of me. But because he's patient. "I'm moving into one of those cottages. I'll be staying on campus for the summer. It's convenient."

"I –"

"If there's nothing else, I'd like to get back to work and go see how my stuff is faring. There's a lot that I need catching up on."

I stare at his jaw.

His hard, masculine, clenched jaw.

And imagine punching it.

Repeatedly.

So not only he's forcing me to stay here during the summer, but he's staying here too.

With me.

Where I'll have to see him every day.

That was the one silver lining in all of this mess: the fact that while at St. Mary's, I didn't have to look at him or be near him every second of every day.

But of course that's not the case anymore, is it?

"So you're staying here this summer. At St. Mary's," I say, staring at him. "Where I am."

He stares back, still as calm and composed. "I realize what a risk it is. To stay close to someone who so desperately wants to kill me. But I think I'm willing to take my chances."

He is, is he?

Well, we shall see.

We. Shall. See.

I'm nothing if not adaptable.

I adapted when he became my guardian. I adapted when he sent me here and I'm going to adapt now as well.

I mean once I get over this anger inside of me.

Nodding, I say, "Well, welcome to St. Mary's." A pause. "Mr. Marshall. Oops, Principal Marshall. I think it's going to be a fun summer."

"Yeah?"

"Totally. I'm going to make it so."

His features that have been all cool and blank so far, ripple with something. A mix of both amusement and challenge before he throws me a short nod. "I look forward to it."

Me too.

I look forward to making his life hell.

Because that's exactly what I'm going to do.

Just wait and watch, Alaric fucking Marshall.

To be continued in
Hey, Mister Marshall
(St. Mary's Rebels Book 4)
Poe Blyton's life is in shambles and the reason is Alaric Marshall.

After her mom's death, he appeared out of nowhere and became Poe's controlling guardian. When she protested his tyranny, he had the audacity to send her away to an all-girls reform school. A school full of iron clad rules and regulations.

But at least she's graduating soon.

Until Alaric himself arrives at the school as the new principal and takes that away from her as well.

That devil.

He's really asking for it, isn't he?

And Poe is going to give it to him.

It doesn't matter that her sworn enemy has the prettiest dark eyes she's ever seen. Or that he looks really, *really* good in his boring tweed jackets. So much so that she wants to rip them off his body and see what's underneath.

Because scorching hot or not, her new principal or not, Poe Blyton is going to ruin Alaric Marshall's life.

Buy Now

# DELETED SCENE

If you enjoyed Conrad and Bronwyn's love story, I'd be eternally grateful if you considered leaving a review.

Want more Conrad & Bronwyn? Click here to get deleted scenes.

Would you like to be notified when Saffron releases another book or if there's a sale happening? Sign up for her mailing list here!

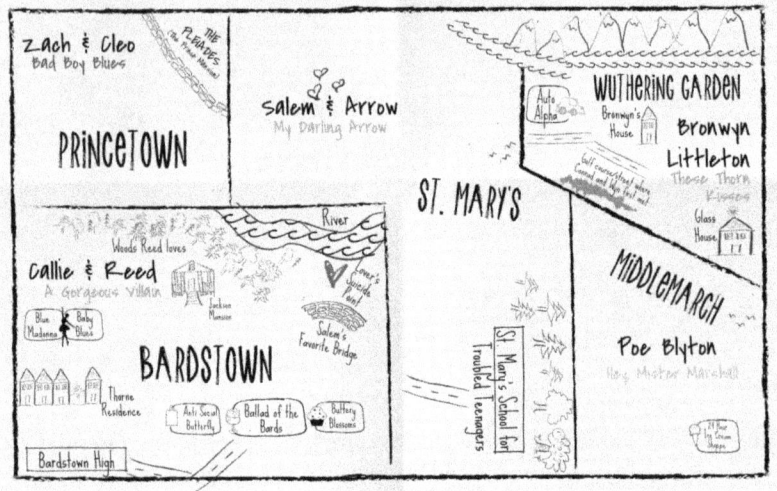

## BAD BOYS OF BARDSTOWN

St. Mary's Rebels Spinoff series
Coming soon!

You Beautiful Thing, You (Bad Boys of Bardstown 1)
Releasing June 6$^{th}$, 2023
Pre-order now!

Nineteen-year-old Tempest Jackson wants a baby.

No, her biological clock isn't ticking, but she's desperate for unconditional love. Rejected by all except her brother and soon to be married off by her father for financial gain, she aches for someone to hold close and call hers.

Enter Ledger Thorne. Soccer god, devastatingly handsome and her brother's rival.

Once upon a time they had a thing. A beautiful thing. But while Tempest thought she was madly in love, Ledger was only using her for petty revenge.

So Tempest has a plan: seduce the sexy jerk who broke her heart, use him to get pregnant and then leave him in the dust like he left her, to marry a stranger.

Only the problem with making babies is that it doesn't feel like revenge. It feels a lot like that thing they used to have: Hot and stormy, and intense and intimate.

But Tempest isn't a fool. She'll stick to the plan.

Because wasn't it Ledger who turned their beautiful thing into something ugly?

Now it's her turn...

**NOTE: This is a STANDALONE set in the world of Bardstown, a St. Mary's Rebels spin-off.**

Oh, You're So Cold (Bad Boys of Bardstown 2)
Stellan Thorne's story!
Releasing December 12th, 2023
Pre-order now!

A Wreck, You Make Me
(Bad Boys of Bardstown 3)
Shepard Thorne's story

Bad Kind of Butterflies
(Bad Boys of Bardstown 4)
Ark Reinhardt's story

For you, I fall to Pieces
(Bad Boys of Bardstown 5)

I'm Hopeless, You're Heartless
(Bad Boys of Bardstown 6)

Add the series to your TBR

# ACKNOWLEDGMENTS

1. Dani Sanchez of Wildfire Marketing Solutions, thank you for always having my back and for always giving me awesome advice.
2. Leanne Rabesa, my editor and fact checker, thank you for checking and rechecking my timelines. Also for constantly telling me that hair's singular. Sorry I always forget!
3. Olivia Kalb, for reading and re-reading my story and for giving me such great advice about how to make it stronger. My writing is better because of you.
4. Najla Qamber, my cover designer, thank you for not ditching me when I kept changing my vision of the cover on you. Thank you for putting those gorgeous lips on the cover. If anyone could do it and portray the sexiness and angst of the book, it was you.
5. Virginia Tesi Carey, my proofreader, thank you so much for being so flexible about dates and for reading this long, long, looooong story.
6. Melissa Panio-Peterson, my fearless PA. What can I say about you that I haven't already said. You're a constant source of happiness and encouragement to me in this industry.
7. Some old and new friends I made this year: Bella Love, Monty Jay and Ayesha. Thank you for sticking by me and for being on my team. Thank you for allll the amazing song recs that made writing this book such a fun thing.

# ABOUT THE AUTHOR

*Writer of bad romances. Aspiring Lana Del Rey of the Book World.*

Saffron A. Kent is a USA Today Bestselling Author of Contemporary and New Adult romance.

She has an MFA in Creative Writing and she lives in New York City with her nerdy and supportive husband, along with a million and one books.

She also blogs. Her musings related to life, writing, books and everything in between can be found in her JOURNAL on her website (www.thesaffronkent.com)

Printed in the USA
CPSIA information can be obtained
at www.ICGtesting.com
CBHW020049250624
10613CB00003B/46